ALSO BY JONATHON BURGESS

CHASING THE LANTERN, Book One of the Dawnhawk Trilogy

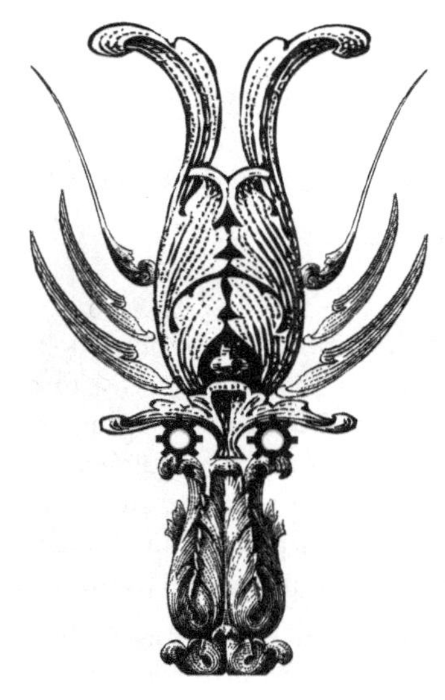

ON DISCORD ISLE

BOOK TWO OF THE DAWNHAWK TRILOGY

BY

JONATHON BURGESS

Cover Painting © 2015 Ksenia Mamaeva

Map illustration & Dragon Glyph © 2015 Vladimir Verano

Book & Cover Design by Vladimir Verano, Third Place Press

Edited by Susan Defreitas, Indigo Editing & Publications

ISBN: 978-0-9909604-1-6

SECOND EDITION

BRASS HORSE BOOKS

JBURGESS@BRASSHORSEBOOKS.COM
WWW.BRASSHORSEBOOKS.COM

For Mom & Dad

To Copper Isles
To Edrus
To Yulan and Breachtown
N
Salmalin
H.M.S. Goliath
Almhazlik Isle

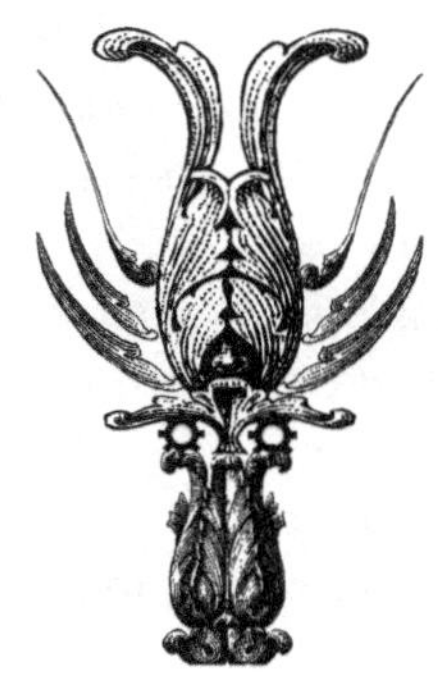

CHAPTER ONE

Things were not going according to the plan.

"That was great!" said the first mate. "You came out of the clouds and had us before we even noticed. Just like in a penny-play! My boys are going to love this." He shared a lascivious smile. "And it won't hurt my chances with the wharf-lasses either."

Captain Fengel blinked, nonplussed. He did agree with the man, if only about the first part. They'd dropped down from the noonday sky right above the merchant vessel, snaring its sails and descending to the deck before the crew had any time at all to react. The few who'd thought to resist had been quickly disarmed. Captain Fengel and his airship pirates had successfully captured their prey.

It was just that no one seemed to *care*.

The first mate appeared harmless. Still, Fengel kept the man in the corner of his eye as he glanced about, checking on the progress of the raid. They stood on the middle deck of the *Minnow*, a wooden barkentine hailing from the Perinese colony of Breachtown. The hull was a long rectangle tapering up to a bowsprit that jutted out over the clear, cerulean sea. Three thick masts thrust up from the deck, a foundation for the forest of rigging, ratlines, and sails that completed the vessel. Those last should have been billowing, full and taut against the wind. Now, however, they hung limp. Their cloth was tangled by heavy grappling hooks whose ropes led even higher, to the long, clean lines of the airship *Dawnhawk* hanging against the bright sky above.

"Now that's a thing," said the first mate, following Fengel's gaze. "Fixing our sails is going to be a pain. But it's worth it, just to see yer ship."

Fengel peered back at the man. *Don't these people realize what's going on?* At least he was properly awed by the vessel above them. Fengel felt the glow of pride beneath his suspicion.

The *Dawnhawk* was a long pumpkin seed hanging from a spindle. Thick chains and hawsers connected the rounded hull to the rigid gas bag above, a great attenuated egg of ridged cloth. Propellers hung from the stern end of the vessel, as well as exhaust pipes for the steam engines that powered them. Large triangles of shimmering fabric lay folded against the hull, the arcane skysails used to ride aetherial currents.

"Yep," continued the first mate. "Quite a thing. I've never seen the like. Everyone talks about 'em. How d'you get it to stay up like that?"

"It's a secret," Fengel muttered.

Both ships were furious with activity. Those up on the *Dawnhawk* tossed down rope and netting for the soon-to-be pilfered cargo. Fengel's own first mate, the dashing Lucian Thorne, stood upon the port-side gunwales as he supervised the crew on deck. Usually Lucian would lead the raid, but there were *considerations* now, and Fengel's presence was required.

More of his crew occupied the rigging of the *Minnow*, reefing the sails and keeping an eye on the captives from up above. He recognized Lina Stone, a diminutive city-born prostitute and recent addition to his crew. Fengel smiled. Letting her on had been a gamble, but it had paid off handsomely. Lina was competent, quick, and had saved his skin more than once. Though he did not care for that thing she called her pet, now whipping through the air to land on her shoulders. Runt was one of the scryn, a vile cross between flying snake and manta ray that all sensible sailors rightly hated.

"Scryn, eh?" said the captive mate of the *Minnow*. "I didn't think anyone could train those nasty little monsters. You pirates are just full of surprises." He chortled and shook his head.

Fengel considered having the man sent to join his crew; he was growing irksome. But no. Fengel needed to keep an eye on him. *And besides, a gentleman possesses self-control.* He turned his attention away.

The merchant vessel had a few dozen hands, all of whom stood along the railing. They were scruffy from their long voyage and nursed a few small, recent wounds. Weirdly, though, they looked more relieved than worried. A small handful of Fengel's crew watched them, led by his huge gunnery mistress, Sarah Lome.

On the opposite side of the ship stood a gaggle of civilian passengers, similarly watched by the silent Geoffrey Lords, Fengel's terrifying cook. The passengers didn't seem much phased, merely watching their captors at work and quietly conversing amongst themselves. The other members of his crew moved up and down the ship, hunting for anyone still trying to hide. Fengel himself stood near the main cargo hatchway while Henry Smalls worked to open it with a few other pirates. Rastalak, of the reptilian Draykin, assisted him.

"You'll want to watch the upper-right corner on that hatch," said the *Minnow's* first mate. "She sticks something fierce, and our carpenter is a lazy bastard who hasn't gotten round to fixin' it yet."

Henry Smalls glanced at the man. "Thanks?" he replied, throwing an uncertain look at Fengel.

Fengel shrugged helplessly. *What is wrong with these people?* Not that he was complaining, overmuch. Willing victims were far better than the alternative.

Rastalak gave a grunt and stooped to lift the hatch. Fengel still wasn't entirely sure what to make of the tiny lizard-man; he hadn't even known the fellow's gender until an awkward incident in the privy last week. Though less than half Fengel's own height, the lizard-man was strong; he raised the heavy hatch single-handedly, and apparently without any undue effort.

"Oh, good show," called one of the passengers, a matronly woman at the front of the group. She was dressed in the conservative Perinese style, a peacock feather jutting from her wide-brimmed hat.

She began to clap demurely, pausing for just a moment to glare around her. The rest of the passengers joined her, giving polite applause. Geoffrey Lords gave a worried look back to his captain. Fengel felt for the man. Of all the things expected on a pirate raid, this was not one of them.

Still, loot is loot and no one's dead.

"Here's the dog!"

Fengel winced. Only one person in the world had such a piercing, peace-shattering roar.

His wife.

He closed his eyes and took a breath, counting to three. Then he turned to face her.

Natasha Blackheart strode up from the aft-castle cabin where she'd been rummaging. Even still, his breath caught in his chest at the sight of her. Long, lustrous dark hair spilled down from the kerchief wrapped around her head to her shoulders, framing a heartbreakingly lovely face. Her eyes were golden and almond-shaped, her lips full and twisted in a cruel smile. She wore tight breeches and a distractingly low-cut blouse. There was nothing soft in the heavy cutlass at her hip, though, and the Wiley twins at her back were her loyal brutes. One carried a lit oil lantern. The other chivied along a portly man with a grey beard and captain's jacket.

"Ha!" barked Natasha. "Found this slug hiding in a smuggler's hole under his bed. Or trying to, anyway. He couldn't fit his fat arse all the way in!"

She gestured, and the twins threw the *Minnow's* captain to the deck. Fengel tried to remember their individual names, and failed, which was bothersome. He brushed the thought aside and looked to the figure at their feet.

The man sat upright with a grunt. "That was uncalled for," he said. "Got to make a show of at least *trying*. If only so's we can say such to the shipping agent." He stuck a hand out. "Now that we have observed the proprieties, let me offer our full cooperation with your piratical endeavor, so that we can get this business over quickly. I would like to be on our way before *too* much time has passed."

Natasha snorted. "Be on your way? You fat sack of suet! You're assuming you're going to live through the day." She kicked him in the side. "You'll *cooperate* in cutting yer own stones off, should I desire it. Your ship is *mine* now, you—"

"Your cooperation is most welcome," interrupted Fengel. He gave a brittle smile to Natasha. "And there's no need to be discourteous…my dear." He sheathed his saber and faced the merchant captain, offering a hand. "Let me assure you, sir, that we mean your crew no harm, and are only interested in your hold."

The captain took it, and Fengel helped him to his feet. "Thank you m'boy, thank you. At least *some* of you young people today still possess common decency. Captain Mortimer Pyke, of the *Minnow*."

"Captain Fengel, of the pirate vessel *Dawnhawk*." He thought for a moment. "And this is my absolutely *darling* wife," he added venomously. "Captain Natasha Blackheart."

The first mate gave a low whistle. "Buyer's remorse, eh?"

Fengel rolled his eyes. "She even refused my name, when we were wed."

"Enough of this!" snarled Natasha. She glared at Fengel, then faced the crew. "For all my fool husband says, you're our *captives*. We're taking your hold, your jewelry, all of it, and you seem to be forgetting that."

Ah, there we go. Courtesy was courtesy, but in her dim, roundabout way Natasha had recognized that something was amiss with these people.

"Well now," said Captain Pyke. "You've got us, that's plain as day. No need to get worked up about it. We're not even Merchant Navy, with Bluecoat marines aboard or any such. You can have our holds, and gladly."

Natasha blinked in confusion. Fengel glanced at Henry Smalls and nodded to the gaping hold. The steward clambered down inside along with Rastalak.

"We're just glad you're not the *Salmalin*," said the first mate. "I mean, you want our cargo, right? It could be a lot worse."

"Oh yes," called the woman with the massive hat. "Those people are just the worst sort of *savages*. I mean, you hear all sorts of awful things about them."

"Too true," said a man beside her.

Aha. There is *something else going on.* "What's this now?" asked Fengel.

"Frigate," said Captain Pyke. "Hailing from some barbarous city in the Sheikdom of Salomca. We heard reports back in Breachtown of her; she's been hunting Kingdom ships this last season, avoiding direct engagement with anything capable of fighting her off, coming for us defenseless merchants instead. We were worried stiff when we spied her a few days ago. She's been shadowing us ever since." He paled at the memory.

Fengel did the math in his head. *The Minnow only has three sails, plus mizzenmasts. A Salomcani frigate could easily catch up. If it was only shadowing, there had to be a reason.* Fengel cursed under his breath as the answer came to him.

"I'd rather be press-ganged by the Navy than let those jackals get ahold of me," said a captive sailor. The rest of the *Minnow's* crew all took up the conversation, rousing more emotion than they'd displayed during the entire pirate raid. Geoffrey Lords and Sarah Lome both looked back to Fengel for direction.

"Enough!" barked Natasha. "I'm tired of your gabbling; it's not important. This Salomcani ship isn't here, so let's get back to the matter at hand. Namely, taking everything that isn't nailed down."

Fengel wheeled about to face her. "Actually, dearest, it *is* somewhat important," he said, voice tight. "If you'd stop to let two thoughts hammer together in that head of yours, then you might figure it out. This *Salmalin* is a Salomcani vessel. The Sheikdom of Salomca is at war with the Kingdom of Perinault. This is a Perinese merchant ship. Which means she would have had a Perinese naval escort. An escort, that if it returned, we would not be able to escape, seeing as we are currently tied up so very neatly to the *Minnow.*"

"Oh yes," said the dowager with the hat. "The *Goliath. Very* charming captain. Stout ship too. Very modern."

Natasha wheeled about. "Will you *shut up,* you daft old biddy? This is a private conversation!"

The woman's hand flew to her throat. "Well!" she said. "I never!"

Ah, dearest wife. Always making things better. Fengel considered how best to rein her in. Suddenly, he realized that he did not care to bother. No, the sooner they offloaded the cargo, the sooner they could be on their way, and the less likely all around that they would be set upon by an irritated Perinese naval frigate. He smiled at the first mate and captain of the *Minnow*, at Natasha and her goons. "By all means, continue the conversation. However, I think I shall go below."

He tipped his tricorn hat and moved away to the lip of the hold. It wasn't deep. Wooden crates were stacked right up to the edge, forming a convenient pyramid stair down into the dim spaces where the noontime sun did not penetrate. Rastalak and Henry Smalls were standing just within the dark, examining a crate. Fengel clambered down to join them.

The cargo area continued forward, stacked high with crates that Fengel knew would stretch all the way to the bow. Thin aisles had been left, dim and shadowed spaces that he couldn't see too clearly. The planks of the floor were heavy and thick. Just below them, Fengel knew, lurked the bilge of the vessel. The faint smell of stale water rose up from it, mixing with the wood of the crates and the exotic scents of cargo.

The others looked up at his approach. "Well, what have we got, then?" asked Fengel.

His steward stood with pry bar in hand. "The lot here at the opening seems to be the most valuable," he replied. "Got shipping marks from clear around the far side of the Edrus. Don't know why they'd be coming from the Yulan. The rest is mostly dried bulk goods."

"Hmm," mused Fengel. "Breachtown has a huge need for raw goods. These have probably been in transit for months."

"This seems inefficient," rasped Rastalak. "Why so long in transport?" The little Draykin peered around the cargo hold, curious. Most of human civilization was clearly still new to him.

"Merchants try to pack as much profit into one trip as possible," replied Fengel. "It's a gamble, especially when people like us get involved. Still worth it, though, if the goods are *especially* valuable." He rubbed his hands together eagerly. "Their loss, our gain. Let's crack it open."

Henry bent to the nearest crate as a racket sounded behind them. Fengel whirled to see one of the Wiley twins clambering down into the hold. The fellow was tall and thuggish, with blond hair and pretty features. He had a particularly dim look in his eyes.

The fellow stumbled to the bottom of the stack. "Captain Blackheart sent me down to help," he said.

Or to keep an eye on me. "Then come along and help," said Fengel dryly. "What was your name again?"

"Nate Wiley, sir," replied the man.

Fengel nodded. *Nate Wiley. That's it.* He hated forgetting a crewman's name.

Henry rammed the pry bar into the lid while Rastalak wrenched at it with his claws. The lid popped free to reveal tightly packed rows of folded red fabric.

"What's this?" asked Henry.

Fengel ran his fingers over the bolts. They were of a thick cut. He smiled. "Henry, I think we've hit the jackpot."

He reached in and pulled out one bolt, unrolling it and laying it across the top of the crate. The fabric was a crimson rug with fine golden patterns stitched throughout. Henry whistled in appreciation.

"These, my fine, felonious fellows, are expensive rugs from the far away land of Catai. The well-heeled back in Perinault pay handsomely for such exotic goods."

Nate Wiley gave a dissenting grunt. Fengel glanced over at the man, who met his eyes, blinked, and looked away uncomfortably.

"I'm sorry," said Fengel acidly. "Is there something you wish to say?"

Natasha's thug reluctantly met his gaze. "Sorry, sir. It's just that these ain't what yer thinking they are."

Fengel leaned back. "Really. I suppose you're an expert on exotic furnishings, then?"

Nate Wiley winced. "A little. This is Cataian, that's for sure. But it's the cheap stuff that comes out of the southern provinces. Supposed to look like the better stuff from the famous places of the north. Look at the corner there. That small weave? It says 'made in Zhon-hei.' Because they weave 'em so quickly there, and so cheaply."

The pirate quieted as everyone stared at him. Fengel grimaced. Every pirate had a slew of oddball skills. If it was true, their loot was now significantly less valuable. "Well, they've got to be worth something, at least," said Fengel.

"Probably," said Nate Wiley. "Most people don't know, they just hear 'it's from Catai,' and call it good. I bet Mr. Grey could get some decent prices for them. You an' Captain Blackheart just need to—"

A harsh scream pierced the air, echoing down into the hold from the deck above. Fengel glanced back at Henry and Rastalak. "Stay here and get this loaded." He scrabbled back up to the deck above. He drew his saber as he clambered up over the edge of the hatch, ready to fight. Then he stopped and slid the weapon back into its sheath.

Things were much the same as before. Crew and passengers were still separated, and the pirates still watched from the airship above. Now, though, Natasha was divesting the passengers of their valuables. She stood before a small man in a shabby brown suit, who rubbed one hand as if injured. Geoffrey Lords stood beside him with a sack. The other Wiley brother shadowed Natasha, lit lantern still in hand.

"I'm sorry," said the little man. "I didn't mean to yell. You just pulled, and it stuck."

"Give us that ring," snarled Natasha, "before I cut your Goddess-damned finger off." She drew a dagger at her waist to make good on the threat.

"Sorry, sorry," said the man.

Fengel flushed with anger. "What is the meaning of this?"

Natasha, the pirates, and the passengers all looked back at him. Geoffrey Lords had the decency to look abashed.

Fengel strode over and snatched the sack from his cook. "I asked, what you think you're doing, Mr. Lords?"

Geoffrey winced. He opened his mouth to reply, but Natasha spoke up first. "We are looting and pillaging, Fengel." She glared at him, voice tight with frustration. "That should be obvious, even to you."

"That doesn't mean we need to start cutting off fingers! The people are being cooperative."

Natasha stared at him a long moment. "Good Goddess above! We are *pirates*, Fengel. Have you forgotten that? We're here to take their things!"

"Um," said the man in the suit. "I think I can get the ring off."

"That doesn't mean we can't keep a certain level of decorum! We have a reputation to maintain."

"Yes," cried Natasha. "As pirates! As plunderers! Raiders of the sea!"

"Natasha's Reavers, mayhap, but Fengel's Men have always been *gentlemen*."

"But they're not just Fengel's Men anymore, now, are they?"

"And they're not your Reavers either!"

"Really, it's coming off now," said the passenger. "It's just that I've gained some weight lately."

Fengel glared at the man. "Shut up." He paused and took a deep breath before looking back to Natasha. "Though you are incapable of seeing it, there's a perfectly logical reason behind this. Gentlemanly conduct results in more cooperative participants."

"Who cares about participation?" yelled Natasha. "If they don't participate, we just cut their heads off and take their things anyway!"

"Which guarantees that those who catch wind of that fact will fight us all that more in the future!" cried Fengel.

"Good! Then I'll know I'm alive!"

"No! It just gets more of your people killed!"

"Not if you kill everyone else first! That makes sure you've got their attention."

"Which isn't needed if they're cooperating in the first place!"

"People tend to need reminders," she said sweetly. "Let me show you."

Natasha drew a flintlock pistol with her free hand. She casually aimed it at Captain Mortimer. The man ducked aside with a yelp, and the first mate threw himself likewise aside, cursing. The gun went off with a crack like thunder, a thick plume of stinking sulfurous smoke erupting from it.

The shot was off target. It smacked into the ship's bell with a loud and echoing call before spinning off in a wild ricochet. The ball hit the iron capstan in the middle of the deck, deflected upward, and impacted the mast just inches away from where Lina Stone stood. The young woman yelped and flinched away from the shower of splinters, losing her grip on the rigging at hand.

Her pet scryn screeched in surprise and flailed its weight about. Lina yelled at it and the creature became even more upset, coiling up to push away from her as it threw itself into the air. The added motion threw Lina even more off balance as she windmilled desperately.

It did not help.

Fengel watched as she toppled from her perch. Lina reacted quickly, though, whipping out a long dagger from her belt and stabbing into the sail beside her. It tore, but slowly enough that it looked for a moment as if she would ride it all the way down to the deck safely. Then she hit the cross-stitching joining one section of sail to another. The dagger was yanked from her grip, and Lina fell, landing hard with a thud from fifteen feet up.

Fengel wheeled on his wife. "You utter madwoman! Someone might have been killed!"

Natasha looked embarrassed. "That was the *point*."

"But not one of our crew! It's a good thing that you're *such* an awful shot."

"I can hit the mark when it counts!"

"No, you can't. You never notice a damned thing either, until its too late! Just like that storm you got us caught in the other week. I *told* you to watch for it before I went below!"

"It was a sudden squall," hissed Natasha. "And you're one to talk. You're so obsessed with cleaning your coat that you missed the call on this ship three times over."

"Proper grooming is an important part of comportment," Fengel replied with dignity. "As if you don't spend an hour perfecting that 'disheveled-yet-attractive-pirate-princess appearance' each time we come back to port." He paused, turning to one of the male passengers, looking for an ally. "Women, right?"

The man nodded gravely. "Quite right, sir. I swear, every time I try to take my wife out to the opera, she wastes half the night 'prettying up.'"

The old dowager with the fancy hat raised an eyebrow. "That, sir, is a crass and unworthy generalization." She looked to Natasha. "Are you going to let that stand? How often does your husband here avoid his duties to slip off with his mates?"

"Ha!" barked Natasha. "You'd think him, Henry and Lucian were all joined at the hip. Mixed crew, my arse! Just the other night I found the three of them playing cards in an empty hardtack crate."

Fengel flushed as he realized that everyone on deck was now a part of their argument, and that it was probably his fault. *Whatever. We're done here for now.*

He pivoted on his heel and took a step back toward the hold, where their loot awaited. He paused at the lip, unable to resist. "If someone wasn't so unbearably afraid of being her father," he called back, "then maybe I would spend more time on deck."

There was a pause, and then a surprised shriek of anger. Fengel half turned, eager to catch the look of rage etched across Natasha's face. His smug amusement changed to alarm as she grabbed the oil lantern from the nearest Wiley twin and threw it straight at him. Fengel ducked, barely, and the thing sailed overhead in a beautiful parabolic arc.

Right into the cargo hold.

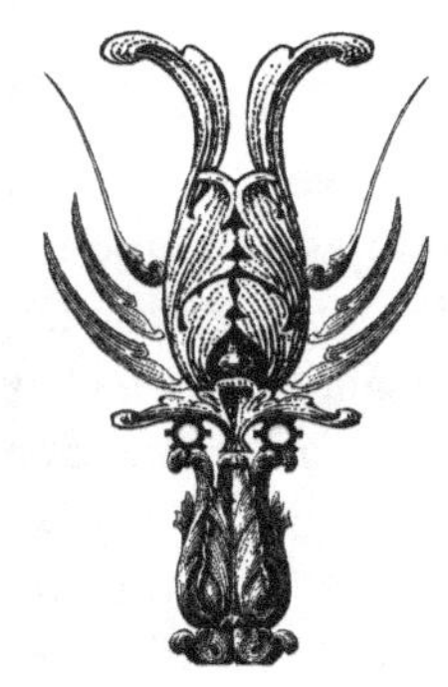

CHAPTER TWO

LINA PICKED UP ANOTHER RUG. It split as she did so, separating down a charred section she hadn't seen at first. She made a small sound of disgust and threw the pieces into a pile with the others.

"This one's ruined," she said aloud.

Her voice echoed in the almost-empty hold of the *Dawnhawk*. It bounced from the bulkhead walls, with their portholes peering out into night. It carried from the distant forward bulkhead all the way down to the stair at the stern, past the single lantern dangling overhead, through the insufficient illumination it cast on the burned and broken crates from the earlier raid on the *Minnow*. The air was thick with the smell of smoke and wet ash.

"Only in comparison to your beauty," said Allen.

For the Goddess's sake. Lina didn't want to have to deal with Allen right now. Her whole right side ached and there were still splinters in her neck from Natasha's ricochet. Also, Runt was still upset with the earlier incident and refused to leave her shoulder. He'd been overeating of late, too.

She glanced over at Ryan Gae, the only other person in the room, who smiled in quiet amusement. "I am flattered," she replied, "that I hold up well to a cheap foreign rug charred into stinking ash." She glared at Ryan. "But I wasn't asking for the comparison. Tally that one down as ruined."

Her two friends couldn't have been more different if they'd tried. Allen was short and frail where Ryan was tall and stout. Allen wore the heavy goggles and leather coat of a Mechanist, while Ryan dressed in the loose shirt and trousers of a lifelong pirate. While Ryan laughed at the world, Allen always seemed to have something in his hands to hide behind. And Allen, unlike Ryan, was nursing a massive crush on Lina.

Ever since their first meeting several months ago, the young Mechanist had followed her around like a lovesick puppy. She'd thought that the supervision of the older Mechanist they had on board would rein him in a bit, or keep him too busy to bother her. She thought wrong. He wasn't troublesome like other men could be, the ones she'd been forced to cater to for so many years. Just bumbling and annoyingly persistent. She wasn't in the mood for either anymore, and maybe not ever again.

Allen retreated behind his copy-board. Lina hauled another rug from the scorched crate before them. It was large and heavy, and unleashed a cloud of ash when she pulled it free. The particulates caught her in the face, stinging her eyes. Lina cursed and let the whole thing fall to the deck. When she blinked her eyes clean again, she saw that the rich red fabric was blackened and burnt.

"Ruined too," said Ryan.

"And the others beneath it?" asked Lina, voice raw.

Ryan peered into the crate. "Total loss," he said sadly. "We're not making a single bent sovereign from this load."

That was going to be a sore spot with the crew. Today's attack was the fourth failed raid with the integrated crew since their return from the Yulan Interior. The treasure from the *H.M.S. Albatross* had already dwindled, most of it going toward clearing Fengel's debt with the Sindicato. There hadn't been any real plunder since, and it was making everyone touchy.

Lina kicked the wooden side of the crate. She whirled away, swearing in frustration. "This is the fourth damned one!" she cried, wheeling back on her friends. "How are we going to take the Breachtown Counting House if we can't even steal a pile of cheap carpets?"

"Now, lass," said Ryan, hands up in a calming gesture. "It might not be all that bad. There might be a few we can salvage." He glanced dubiously at the remaining pile of crates.

"No. *No.* They're all trash, and this has been a complete waste of effort." She stepped up to her friend. "I almost died today, Ryan, and it wasn't a stupid accident or some enemy blade. The captain's witch of a wife almost shot me. Shot. Me."

"She didn't mean to," said Ryan weakly.

"Because I didn't catch her attention," snarled Lina. "Rastalak is still laid up, and last I saw, Henry Smalls wasn't doing too well either. Even Nate Wiley got caught in the fire, and he's one of her original crew! Today was a catastrophe, and tomorrow is only going to be worse." She closed her eyes and took a breath. Runt squirmed on her shoulders, upset by the tone of her voice. Ryan didn't say anything this time. Allen remained silent as well.

"Look," she continued. "Keep going through this mess if you want. I'm going up above before the stink makes me puke. I'll find the first mate and let him know." Lina turned on her heel and marched to the stair. Ascending it, she climbed through the narrow hatch at its top to the higher decks of the *Dawnhawk*.

She rose into a small alcove, set off to one side in a dim, narrow hall. Down the far end to her left, she knew, would be the engine room and lair of the Mechanist, a member of that peculiar secret society of machine-smiths. Lina shook her head and glanced down the hall the other way, toward the rest of the ship, where the crew bunked on the quarterdecks and another stairwell led up to the stern hatch of the deck, past the captain's cabin.

Lina had scarcely reached that stairwell when she heard the noise. Shouting, angry and strident. It echoed down to her and into the quarterdeck, only a little muffled. The captains were yelling at each other. Again.

She sighed. *Forward hatch, then.*

What she thought of Natasha hadn't changed at all. There was a time, though, not too long ago, when her opinion of Fengel had been quite different. Lina had been eager for his attention then, a swarm of butterflies taking flight in her stomach whenever she received it. He'd seemed dashing and handsome, and though she recognized the crush for what it was, she had been powerless to ignore it.

That had changed quickly enough. Though she was still fond of Fengel, he was just as mad, in his own way, as the angry bag of cats that he called his wife. He was just her captain now, nothing more. *I am* done *with that kind of thing. Romance, relationships, any of that; I'm just* done *with it.*

Lina strode past the stairwell and into the quarterdeck, going for the mess hall door at its far end. As she moved through, exhausted pirates with bloodshot eyes stared up at her from their hammocks. A few of her crewmates, old and new, tried to muffle the noise of the argument above; blond Tricia had a balled-up shirt over her head, and Geoffrey Lords stuffed pistol-shot wadding into his ears. None of them slept. Fengel and Natasha had probably been going at it for a while now.

Lina moved through the inner passages of the *Dawnhawk,* the captain's tirade fading to blissful quiet. Lina felt more comfortable here, less aggravated. She found the forward stair and climbed up through its hatch to the outside world above.

Cool night air washed over her. It smelled of salt and the sea, clean and welcome after the ashy stench of the hold. Above her floated the gas-bag envelope, a ridged canvas ovoid that held the airship aloft in the sky. Heavy chains and cables connected the deck to the gasbag, along with ratlines and rigging on the port and starboard rails. Secured oil lanterns and ambient moonlight shed soft illumination over the deck of the vessel.

The wind changed, bringing with it a myriad of irritated shouts. Runt tensed at the noise and Lina looked to the deck. The sound came from the evening watch crew, split into two distinct, arguing groups. Lina watched the nearest pair as they squabbled over a bucket and mop. Charlie Green was one of Natasha's Reavers originally, and Elly Minel had served with Fengel for years now. Past them near the port-side railing, two more pirates hung suspended from the gasbag as they checked the hawsers connecting it to the airship. Fat Thomlin and grizzled Jeremiah Frey had belonged to different captains originally as well, and they looked over each connection twice before shouting its status over each other down to where a third person waited below. But most of the noise came from a large crowd down near the helm.

Lina's irritation returned full force. *It's not enough that Fengel and Natasha squabble like a pair of children, they've got us fighting too.* Lina shook her head. *Enough.* She had to get away from this, somewhere quiet, peaceful. But that was the trouble with a ship; there were only so many places one could go.

Her eyes caught on the rigging that stretched up to the gas bag and beyond. *That'll do.* Lina adjusted Runt and moved over to the gunwales. She clambered atop the exhaust pipe onto the rigging. Her bruised limbs protested, but Lina ignored the pain. She climbed, yet as she did the voices from the squabbling near the helm rose up to her.

"Loaded, you overgrown cow!"

Lina glanced back down to see Reaver Jane, Natasha's current right-hand woman, in a heated argument with Sarah Lome, Fengel's huge red-headed gunnery mistress. The two were positioned on either side of an equipment locker, just up from the helm. Members of both sides of the crew surrounded the pair, watching intently. The locker was open and its contents had been pulled out: muskets, cutlasses and maintenance equipment for each.

"Keeping them loaded is insane!" roared Sarah Lome.

"They're going to be uncocked," replied Reaver Jane. "So what's the problem?" The piratess was of average height and weight, with dark hair cut shoulder length. Lina disliked her. The woman was shrewd and dangerous.

"Standing orders from the captain are to keep all weapons unloaded and unarmed, to prevent any misfires, wet powder, and so forth. As gunnery mistress, it's my responsibility to see that order carried out," said Sarah Lome.

"And *my* captain wants us to be ready should we need these guns. Which won't do a damned bit of good if they aren't loaded. Why do we even need a gunnery mistress when we don't have any Goddess-forsaken cannons?"

"Your captain is a drunken whore who hasn't the first idea how to run a proper ship!"

"And yours is a fop who can't give a hard order to save his life!"

The argument escalated, the crew now shouting encouragement. Even the aetherite navigators, Konrad and Maxim, called out from their shared station.

So much pointless, wasteful bickering. Lina shook her head and continued her climb. When the argument below was occluded by the curve of the gasbag, she paused to rest. With her good hand and leg mooring her to the rigging, Lina looked out onto the world.

Night enclosed the airship in a single sheet of velvet that stretched across the sky. The brilliant coin of the moon and the pinprick light of the stars starkly illuminated the *Dawnhawk*, high above the twisting chop of the Atalian Sea. For a moment nothing seemed to exist but the sea, the airship, and the cold light of the sky. Then the faint shouting from the deck below rose up to her.

It's like we're the only ones in the world, and yet we still can't stop fighting. All of Lina's anger drained, leaving only frustration and melancholy. *What am I going to do? I can't leave. This is my home.* If only there were some simple way to fix things, to restore order, to get people working together....Lina shook her head and continued her climb.

She reached the pinnacle of the gas bag, where the rigging swept up and over the top before falling back down the other side. Her first time up here had been a terrifying experience. Now it was simply precarious, if no less daunting. At the very apex was a thin wooden deck, running the length of the airship and sewn into the canvas, allowing slightly less risky movement. Halfway down the length of the 'bag was a shallow wooden cupola. Lina spied the tops of four heads poking up over its edge.

Curious, she moved over. The inhabitants resolved into Henry Smalls, first mate Lucian Thorne, Gabley the lookout, and a white ape. All four were playing cards.

"I call," said Lucian. "Four knaves."

He threw down his hand as the other two groaned in disgust. The white ape bared its fangs at him.

"Well, it's not my fault you ate the first hand we gave you," Lucian told it. The first mate was blond, dashing, and handsome; everything that a pirate straight out of the penny-plays was meant to be. "It was a good one, too."

The ape growled low in its throat, then bent to pick at the fleas in its fur. Lina didn't know quite where it had come from, or how it had even gotten up here. The thing subsisted on morning dew, rainwater, and the seabirds that frequently perched atop the gas bag. It had proven almost impossible to remove, far more vicious and adept at moving around the top of the gas bag than anyone else so far. Fortunately, it seemed fond of Gabley, and the nervous young man had thus been put permanently on lookout duty.

"Chirr," said Runt. Lina's pet did not get along with the ape. After consulting a disgraced animal doctor back in Haventown, she'd learned that not only was Runt male, but that fighting with other members of his sex was common among the scryn. The white-furred beast looked up at the noise and bared its teeth in unhappy surprise.

Lucian stopped gathering up the ship's biscuits they were playing for and glanced at Lina. "Miss Stone," he said in greeting. "Hallo. What brings you up here?"

"Cargo's a lost cause," said Lina, voice flat. She felt tired. "Sorry, Henry; you got burned for nothing. What are you two doing up here?"

The steward sighed. His hands were covered by bandages, with another wrapped around his head. Henry Smalls, Nate Wiley, and Rastalak had all been in the hold when the fire started. Natasha's flung lantern had come perilously close to crippling or killing them all.

"The captains," said Lucian, "are having a spat. As their second in command, I decided it was prudent to hide for awhile." Lucian shook his head, then started shuffling the cards together. "Feel free to join us for a game."

Lina stayed where she was. "Counting house raid's going to be a fiasco," she said.

Lucian paused. Then he went back to cutting the cards. "Probably so," he said with a rueful smile. "I think it just might be the end of us all."

"You don't mean that," said Henry Smalls.

The first mate stacked the deck and set it aside. The white ape promptly picked it up and put it in its mouth, letting out a happy *ook*.

Lucian frowned. "Gabley, get those back for me." He turned to the steward. "Henry, we're supposed to be working together. A divided crew can't fly an airship, and a divided crew sure as spit won't be able to make a raid on the largest Perinese colony on this side of the world."

The steward frowned. He looked down at the bandages swathing his hands, at a loss for words. The wind whistled about them. Lina did not shiver. This far south, the weather was warm even at night.

"It's Natasha's fault," said Henry after a moment. "When she shows up, Captain Fengel can't think straight, can't help but fight her."

"It's not just her, old stick," said Lucian gently. "It's the both of them. And we're all of us too much a part of their crew to walk away. It'll be the end of us, like as not."

Henry nodded slowly. Gabley gave a muffled cry for help. The white ape was gnawing distractedly on his head.

It's their *fault though, not ours.* Lina's indignation and frustration mounted again. *There has to be a way out. But what? Jump ship? No! This is my home! But what can I do? Damnation! Fengel and Natasha; if only they could work together, or even better, just weren't in the damned way anymore.*

She started as it came to her.

"I've a suggestion," Lina said aloud. "I think it'll solve all of our problems too, the counting house raid and everything else. But it's something that everyone needs to hear. Lucian, let's all go back down below, and you can stop Sarah and Jane from killing each other. Then I'll tell you what I think."

The two officers looked at her, then at each other. Lucian shrugged. "All right. I probably shouldn't be up here anyway."

They all stood and left the cupola, ignoring Gabley's terrified cries. Lina scratched the back of Runt's head, her stomach sinking. What she was about to suggest could get her strung up. *But we can't keep going on like this.* She moved to clamber down the rigging.

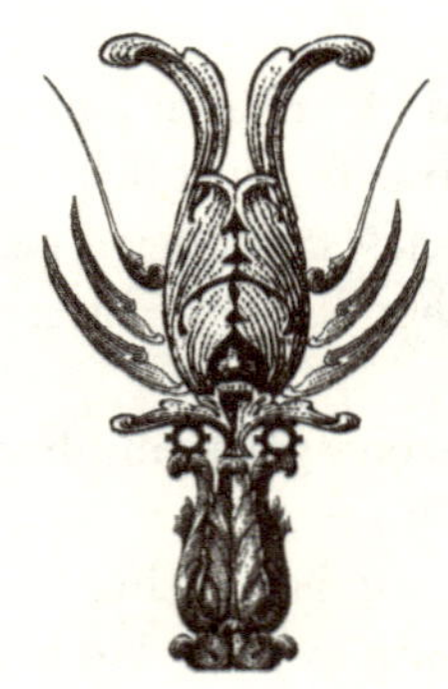

CHAPTER THREE

Natasha clawed her way back to consciousness.

The bitter details of half-remembered dreams washed against her thoughts like coastal flotsam after a storm. She pushed them aside, uninterested in the gibberingly insistent feeling that there was some sense to be had, that if she'd just focus a little harder, some fog-logic truth would be recalled. It was never worth the effort.

A fine coating of fur covered her teeth. Her tongue was thick in her mouth. Worse than either was the horrible taste filling the back of her throat and crawling up into her sinuses, the aftermath of too much rum.

She smacked her lips and grimaced, reached down for the bottle that should be just within her grasp. Her fingers brushed only the wood of the deck and the drawers built into her bunk. Natasha turned her head to look and saw nothing.

Ye Goddess. I've finally done it. I've drunk myself blind. A bitter thought crossed her mind. *Fengel always said I'd do it one day.*

The thought of her co-captain was like an iron nail across a chalkboard. She pushed his criticism away and considered her predicament. *This makes things difficult, but there's no reason I couldn't still command. Hmm. My fighting days are done, and maintaining crew discipline will be troublesome. I could just fire off a pistol now and again at random. Pretend that whoever I hit I've been displeased with. Yes. That should suffice. Now, where's that bottle?*

Belatedly she realized that she wasn't blind; her eyelids were simply closed, and would not open. Quick testing with her fingers revealed them to be glued shut by tears, fine grit, and kohl. A bit of work removed the offending debris, and Natasha opened her eyes.

She immediately regretted the act. Daylight streamed in from the windows directly above the captain's bunk. It filled the room, skull-splittingly over-bright. Natasha groaned and threw an arm over her face.

The world refused to leave her be. The taste in her mouth, the light in the room and a suddenly insistent need to use the privy all pressed in upon her. Natasha considered going back to sleep, but she could almost hear her father's voice, chiding her for rising late. Grumbling to no one in particular, Natasha narrowed her eyes and pulled herself slowly into a sitting position.

The captain's cabin of the *Dawnhawk* was sumptuously spaced for an airship. A holdover from their nautical forebears, Natasha had expanded the design of the room when she'd commissioned the vessel. A wide bunk, big enough for two, sat just beneath the stern windows. Tasteful cabinetry lined the walls, holding clothing, weapons, and other such sundries. A large table dominated the middle of the cabin, nailed in place.

There was surprisingly little clutter about the room, a sign of Fengel's influence. The man could not abide disorder, fussy old maid that he was. What was home without a little mess? Only a few things hinted that anyone lived here; her boots, sword belt, the pillows near the door where she'd apparently thrown them, and a pile of the errant rum bottles laying on their sides in a corner, where they must have rolled away from her bunk in the night.

Natasha brightened. She stalked over and grabbed up one of the latter. It was sadly empty. A quick check revealed the same for the others.

"Fengel," she croaked, "hoist yer ass from that bed and go get me a drink. Whatever time it is, I need breakfast." Her stomach rumbled. "And some food wouldn't go amiss either."

He did not respond.

Natasha whirled back to the bunk. "Didn't you hear me? I said—"

The bunk was empty. The blankets and pillows were all tangled up on his side into a mass that she'd dimly, groggily mistook for her oh-so-obnoxious husband. She glanced over at the pile of gear near the door and it came back to her, yesterday's raid and their hours-long fight afterwards. How that fight had ended was buried in a haze of rum, but it was obvious that he'd given up and gone to sleep somewhere else.

The thought was vaguely infuriating.

Her mood plunged. Snarling, Natasha grabbed up her boots, belt and a pair of pistols from a cabinet. She unlatched the door to the cabin and stalked out into the hall beyond.

Right, then. As usual, there's only one person on this damned boat that I can count upon, and that's me. Things have probably gone to the Realms Below while

I've been asleep. Time to get to work. Breakfast, then to put some order into those sots and wastrels that I let crew this vessel. First, though....

She passed three store-room doors and reached the privy. The door was shut and rattled when she tried to open it.

"Occupied," came a voice.

Natasha drew a pistol, placed its barrel against the door where the latch would be, and fired. Thunder erupted in the space, echoing up and down the corridor. Splinters flew from the wood of the door and its frame, showering her slightly, their tiny pinpricks angering her further. Natasha grabbed the wooden handle of the door and yanked it open.

One of Fengel's flunkies sat on the wooden toilet, the ratty little man, Oscar Pleasant. His trousers were down and his hands were clasped over his ears. He looked up at her, eyes wide in shock.

"Blood of the Goddess!" he yelled.

Natasha reached in and yanked him by his hair out into the corridor. The sky pirate toppled to the floor of the deck. She stepped into the privy, closed the door, and tended to her business. A few moments later, Natasha left the small closet and stalked down toward the mess in search of food, while a terrified Oscar was still sobbing on the floor.

The stern stairwell led down to the quarterdeck and the mess hall. Natasha stalked into the former, where the night-watch was sleeping in their hammocks. Or at least, should have been. She paused as she realized that the room was almost empty, with only a few people currently unconscious within. *Probably dicing when they should be resting.* She frowned and made a note to be particularly harsh today. The counting house raid was coming up soon, and there wasn't any room for slack on that job. Natasha tromped up to the door to the mess, not caring a whit for the noise she made.

The benches of the mess weren't quite empty. A lone figure sat at a table near a porthole, several large tomes open before him, along with paper and charcoal. Natasha vaguely recognized the younger of the two Mechanists, the one she'd effectively impressed into service upon the old *Copper Queen*. For the life of her she couldn't remember his name.

He'd have to do.

"You," she growled.

The youth started. He looked up at her, face covered in coal dust. "Ma'am?" he said.

"What's your name?"

"Al-Allen, ma'am."

"Well, Allen, get back in the kitchen and get me something to eat."

Allen the Mechanist looked at her, then back at the kitchens, then back to her again. "Ma'am, I think Geoffrey Lords just stepped out for a smoke. He'll be back in a minute—"

"You're here, he's not. Go cook me something."

"But ma'am, I'm just the Mechanist, and the younger one at that. I can't cook—"

Natasha leveled a gaze that shut him up. "Look," she said sweetly. "It's morning—"

"Midafternoon, ma'am."

"Midafternoon, then. I require drink. Failing that, food. Since I'm apparently out of drink, I need food. Now, since I can't be arsed to cook it myself, that means someone else has to, and today that someone is you. I've used up one pistol by going to the head. The other's still loaded. Do you understand?"

She held Allen's frightened eyes. He nodded nervously, and she twitched her head toward the kitchen. The younger Mechanist slid from his bench, stumbled, hit the deck, climbed to his feet, and then ran through the portal into the kitchen.

With nothing else to do, Natasha walked over to where he'd left his books and drawing equipment. The texts were written in Perinese, and concerned the arcane subjects of physics, construction, and aether science. Natasha paged through them, bored. The books weren't entirely beyond her, sky piracy required a certain understanding of such subjects, but they weren't exactly interesting.

Loud cursing and a clatter erupted from the kitchen. She ignored it, taking up both Allen's charcoal-stick and his copy of *The Mechanics of Aeronautical Flight,* and amused herself by writing obscene jokes in the margin of the text, complete with illustrations. Minutes passed and the activity quickly paled; she found herself taking multiple pages worth of borders to draw a particularly complex scene she'd once been part of in a Salomcan brothel. Natasha snorted at the memory and paused in fond, somewhat incredulous, remembrance.

Thick dark smoke started to flow into the mess hall. Natasha shut the book and rested her chin on one hand, drumming the fingers of the other on the table. *He's taking forever in there.* She was hungry, but now that she was awake and sober she wanted to be up, she wanted to be moving. Objects at rest tended to stay at rest, and any time she wasn't visible to the crew was time that they could slack, could forget themselves and their purpose, could even forget *her*.

I'll eat later. Natasha stood and left the mess hall, just as a flickering red-orange glow appeared in the kitchen, accompanied by soft weeping and the smell of something burning. She made her way to the stern stairwell, then up through the aft hatch and onto the outer deck of the *Dawnhawk*.

Bright afternoon sunlight greeted her, the wind a soft breeze playing with her hair. Today was sunny and warm. Around her the airship hummed, nothing seemingly amiss. The exhaust pipes puffed steam up to join the clouds while the propellers spun lazily. The current watch went about their duties.

Natasha nodded to herself. Then she stopped as one small detail of the scene caught her attention; the propellers. Last night they'd been on course for a northeastern-running aetherline. They should have reached it hours ago, negating the need for powered flight.

That's odd. There was something else as well. Something intangible. She glanced about the deck, where the current watch tended to their tasks, both halves of the crew working in harmony.

Natasha blinked. No one was fighting, even passively. The propellers were strange, but she felt pleasantly surprised at the change in the crew. *Good. Maybe Fengel's worthless lackeys are finally coming around.* Fengel's crew were competent, more or less, but slow and weak. When she had agreed to work with her husband, she'd also vowed silently that they'd do things the proper way, or not at all. It appeared that they were finally taking the hint.

Still, why are we running on the engines?

She glanced around for any obvious answer. Nothing seemed out of order, but she did spy Lucian Thorne up near the bow. He'd do. Natasha stalked up to talk to the airship's first mate.

The man irritated her. He was competent, capable, and loyal; at least to Fengel. To her he was merely polite, though he always seemed to execute the orders she gave. But Natasha was positive that he worked actively to undermine her command.

Lucian was watching something out beyond the ship while several crewmen coiled ropes and hammered a small wooden crate shut. Natasha strode up to the first mate with her mouth open, prepared to deliver a withering stream of demands. As she came up beside him, she stopped.

There was an island off the bow in the light blue waters below. The *Dawnhawk's* course would take them right past it. It wasn't terribly large, just a ring of jungle around an oddly shaped low mountain peak, further ringed by broad sands and the occasional hill.

"Where in the seas are we?" she demanded, wheeling on the first mate. "Why are we running on propellers?"

The first mate smiled. There was something, an edge to it, that Natasha didn't like. "The Atalian Sea, still," said Lucian. "Fairly close to the equator. We aren't very close to any aetherlines here." He gave a nod to the men and women working nearby.

Only one of them belonged to her old crew, though she couldn't remember his name. The others all belonged to Fengel. They looked to Natasha, then each other. Then they stood and left. She was pleased. *They're finally learning their place when I'm around. Good.*

"I'm not terribly familiar with the area," continued Lucian. "The maps call it Almhazlik, or 'Discord,' if you speak Salomcani. Isolated, but with plenty of fresh water and fruit and whatnot."

Natasha glared at him, hand resting on the pommel of her cutlass. "Of *course* I speak Salomcani, you idiot. Why in the Realms Below have you changed our course? We should be more than halfway to Breachtown by now."

Lucian sighed. He looked away, then back, eyes serious and holding her gaze. "Captain Blackheart, I've meant to talk with you about that. The crew isn't happy. We're nowhere ready for this raid yet. If we pursue that plan now, a lot of people are going to die. Don't you think it's a bit too soon?"

Natasha snorted. "Breachtown is a ruin after that uprising of theirs. That counting house will never know what hit it." She did feel a little mollified. Lucian had finally used her proper name and title, at least.

Lucian pinched the bridge of his nose. "Captain, yesterday's raid was a disaster. Four people almost died, and that was all our own doing. We're not working well together, and there are constant conflicting orders—"

"That was Fengel's fault," snarled Natasha. "If he hadn't gone all soft-hearted on everything then it would have worked out just fine. Now, answer my damned question. Why in the Realms Below are we here, of all places?"

Lucian gave her a long look. Then he glanced away. "Not certain, Captain. But I believe your *husband* gave the order to the helmsmen directly."

A bolt of irritation flashed through her. "Of course he did. Apparently he doesn't trust even you, of all people, and you've always been his dog. A proper captain goes through her first mate! That's what you are *for*." She whirled on her heel and stalked down the deck without even looking to see if he'd heard her.

The helm was back on the stern of the airship, a holdover from the sail ship template used by the Mechanists who built the thing. Natasha stalked toward it, even more irritated by having to cross the distance. Those men and women who saw her coming found reason to be elsewhere suddenly, which pleased Natasha. One of them didn't, though.

He was big and knelt upon the deck, facing away from the bow. Even from the back she recognized him as one of her thugs, the Wiley twins. He worked alone, though, his brother still recuperating from the fire yesterday. Natasha was suddenly incensed that he hadn't noticed her.

She kicked over the pile of shiny metal clips he was polishing. He started, then looked up in surprise, visage going flat once he saw her.

"Captain?" he asked.

Natasha bent, snatched up a ring, and shook it in his face. "Rust!" she snarled at him. "Look at this! You miss a spot again and I'll put you up on lookout duty for a month!" The ring was clean, but that was beside the point: yelling made her feel better.

Something in his face stopped her. The big pirate nodded slowly, never looking away from her eyes. "Duly noted. Captain." He stared at her, and she was the first one to blink. "May I return to my task?"

She nodded. The big pirate backed away. Something was off here, something amiss. But what? The twins, along with Reaver Jane, had been her most loyal servants ever since joining crews with Fengel. They obeyed her every command without complaint. Natasha could almost hear her father's approval: to him, an obedient crew was all that mattered. She thought of looking into it further, but the twin had returned to his task. *Maybe he's just sullen. I hear twins get that way.* With a shrug, she made her way back toward the helm.

The helm of the *Dawnhawk* was composed of a ship's wheel and a large wooden gearbox studded with numerous dials, gauges and levers. A speaking tube was mounted to the box, ostensibly for communication with the engine rooms below and the Mechanists who dwelled there. It had never worked properly. Linkages and gear-trains connected the helm to complex propeller assemblies hanging from the rear of the airship, and connected the skysail armatures hanging from its hull. Both of the helmsmen watched Natasha approach silently.

Maxim and his counterpart Konrad were both aetherites, which meant that they were crazy. As she understood it, the daemon familiars they carried about with them were a constant source of nagging irritation, wheedling aetherwrought Workings in exchange for small mischiefs played upon their crewmates. This did not make them generally popular with anyone. Her father in particular hated them. They were necessary, however, for only an aetherite could see the great aetherlines that ran throughout the world and so enabled efficient airship flight.

Maxim was rail thin and had originally come from Fengel's crew. Konrad was stocky and one of her own. Ever since the two crews had merged, both magicians had kept a sleepless, antagonistic vigil over each other. That was annoying, as it meant that Natasha couldn't have Konrad's powers free for her own behalf.

Fengel's aetherite glared at her. Konrad simply stared. Both looked pale and shaky from lack of rest. Konrad opened his mouth to greet her. Natasha cut him off.

"Where are we?" she demanded. "And how did we get here?" Out of the corner of her eye, she saw Lucian move up behind her and to one side.

"Near the equator," said Konrad, his heavy Greisheim accent twisting every word. "The Isle Almhazlik."

"I know that," Natasha snapped. "What are we doing here?"

Maxim smiled viciously. "Fengel—" He fell silent as Konrad glared at him.

"Captain," said the large aetherite, "we must talk. Reaver Jane, the others, we are all concerned."

A wave of irritation roiled over her. *Can't anyone around here do what they're told?* She glared at Lucian. The man was obviously slacking on discipline. "Later, Konrad," she said, wheeling around to face the helmsman. "I asked you a damned question. Now, are you going to answer it, or am I going to have to beat it out of you?"

Konrad's face settled like stone. He glanced at his counterpart, who gave him a look, almost as if to say 'I-told-you-so.' Konrad looked to Lucian. "I do not know why we are here," he said. "Your husband, the Captain, bade us take this course. He did not say why."

Her irritation transformed into white-hot anger. "Goddess strike him down!" she hissed. "You people are useless. Where is he?"

"I believe," said Lucian smoothly, "that he's currently in the cargo hold, examining the carpets from yesterday's raid."

Natasha whirled on him. "Then why didn't you tell me that?" she snarled.

He held out his hand theatrically. "You wanted to come over here and find out what these two knew."

Her hand tightened on the hilt of her cutlass. She wanted to scream at him, then run him through. *No. Wait. Hold onto that for the person who deserves it.* Natasha growled wordlessly at Lucian, then moved to the stern hatch and descended. Down she went, passing her cabin and the splintered door to the head, then the quarterdeck. She paused for a moment at the stair to the hold; the faint smell of smoke drifted up from the mess. There was also shouting. Natasha recognized the voice as the usually silent, terrifying cook, Geoffrey Lords. *What's got into him?* She gave a shrug and continued to the cargo hold below.

The space was mostly empty. A single lantern hung from the ceiling to provide a small pool of light over several rugs, leaving the rest of the great space in darkness. Her husband walked amongst the rugs, examining their damage. Fengel was bent over and did not notice her approach.

"You *worm*," she snarled. Fengel straightened in surprise and looked back to her. Natasha marched over to stand on the same rug he now examined. "How dare you hide from me down here?"

"Hide?" said Fengel, disdain dripping from his voice. "I'm the one that came looking for you. Apparently, you'd finally left the cabin. I knew that would happen eventually, if only because I intentionally limit the rum you keep there."

"That *was* you," Natasha growled. "How dare you paw through my things!"

"Because someone kept leaving the half-opened bottles in my clothing! Look, look at this." Fengel stood back and spread his arms. The fine vest beneath his waistcoat was stained across the left breast. "This was my favorite vest! And now the dye has all run because you couldn't be bothered to clean up after yourself."

Natasha pinched the bridge of her nose. "Ye Goddess. You're bitching about your clothes. Again. What are you, some prissy Perinese socialite? Never mind, I know the answer to that."

Fengel arched an eyebrow. "A gentleman has certain standards of dress to maintain—"

"A gentleman has certain standards to maintain," she mimicked, voice obnoxious.

Fengel glowered. "Very well. I was coming down here to find out what ridiculous course you've put us on, but talking with you is impossible. I'll just go and correct things, as I usually do."

He moved to walk past her, and she stuck out an arm to bar his way. "What? No. I came down here to ask *you* why *you've* put us on this ridiculous course. We should be halfway to Breachtown by now!"

"Exactly," said Fengel frostily. "The counting house raid, remember?" He made to push her arm away, then stopped. "Wait. But I didn't order a change in course."

Natasha frowned. "Well, I certainly didn't."

"Then who did?" asked Fengel.

"Now!" shouted a voice.

There was a great commotion in the darkness, and the rugs they stood upon shot upward. Natasha lost her balance and collided with Fengel, the two of them suddenly flung together into the middle of the net that appeared out from beneath their feet. It cinched tight, and they rose into the air of the hold, swinging crazily. Natasha fought to orient herself, but she'd fallen to her side, one leg out through the mesh, one arm bent painfully behind her back and up against Fengel.

"What's the meaning of this?" she cried at the whirling cargo hold. "Let me down before I cut your stones off!"

"Thankfully," said a voice, "that's not an issue for me."

A figure appeared out of the darkness. She was waiflike, with knife-hacked hair and that horrible scryn pet of hers. Natasha recognized Lina Stone, the ex-doxy on her husband's crew. Natasha opened her mouth to shout again, then fell silent as others appeared in the dark.

Reaver Jane, Henry Smalls, Sarah Lome. All the crew she hadn't seen up above or in their bunks walked out of the dark, some of them holding guidelines for the trap she had stepped into.

"Miss Stone," cried Fengel, holding his monocle in place. "What is the meaning of this?"

"She's got to go, Captain," said the waif.

Fengel nodded sharply. "Ah. A capital idea. But you seem to have caught me too by mistake."

Lina shook her head. "Sorry, Captain. You've got to go too."

From where she lay, Natasha could just see her husband's face. She enjoyed a moment of small, vicious glee as his monocle fell away in shock to dangle from its chain between them.

A rustling came from overhead, then daylight flooded the hold. Natasha twisted to see the great hatch to the main deck being levered aside. Lucian, the Wiley twins and both helmsmen were preparing to winch up the rope to the net she hung within.

"Enough of this," she yelled at the crew above and below her. "Let me down this instant, or I'll gut the lot of you, and then shoot you to boot!"

She was ignored. Natasha tried cursing them, their fathers, forefathers, and any children they may have had. Fengel repeatedly tried to speak reasonably, but her traitorous crew paid no attention. They were pulled up and dumped unceremoniously on the upper deck, surrounded by the pirates already here.

Natasha used the moment to try and get her balance. The fresh sea air blew her hair about the inside of the net, disorienting her further. *Hands and knees and space enough to draw my sword. I can cut the mesh and get free.* Fengel tried to do the same though and she toppled. Hands reached through the net to grab at her blade. Natasha fought, but others held her down while it was removed, and Fengel's saber as well. She punched and kicked and bit, but to no avail.

The two of them were dragged to the bow, the crew standing in a semicircle around them. Above, the sun hung just enough past the curve of the gas bag to illuminate them both. A sense of deja vu passed over Natasha. *Oh Goddess. Not again.* She was in the exact same spot she'd been in six months ago, when Mordecai Wright had led a mutiny on her. *First the rum, and now this. This day just keeps on getting better.* What her father would have said didn't bear thinking on.

Lucian stepped up out of the crowd. "Captains," he said. "This looks bad, and believe us, we wouldn't be doing it if you two weren't so horribly screwed up with each other. You spend all your damned time fighting, and having us wage war as well. We've had four failed raids now in preparation for this counting house heist, and it's all *your fault.* So, a Crewman's Vote has been taken." He gestured off the bow. "This is Almhazlik Isle. Should be perfectly deserted, and perfectly safe. We're going to drop you off here while we all head north and raid Breachtown. You two are going to work out your disastrous relationship issues before they're the doom of us all. Afterward, we'll swing by and pick you up. Now, do you have anything to say before we continue?"

"I'm going to chew out your throat and piss down the hole," snarled Natasha.

Lucian sighed. "I mean, do you have anything *constructive* to say?"

"I *said,* I'm going to chew out—"

Konrad, her aetherite, stepped forward. "I try to warn you!" he complained, accent thick with emotion. "I try to tell you limits of my magic, how it works. But you never listen! You *waste* it!"

Natasha stared at him in confusion. Why would she ever want to know *that?*

"Even you, Henry?" asked Fengel. Natasha glanced over at her husband. His face was pale with shock and betrayal. "Haven't I been a good captain?"

Henry Smalls looked out sadly from the crowd. "Sorry, sir," he said heavily, holding up his bandaged hands. "Not lately, no. But you'll get better, sir. This is for everyone's benefit. And we'll have you back, right as rain."

Lucian clapped his hands. "That's that, then. All right, let's send them over. Watch out for Natasha, she bites."

"You'll be sorry," Natasha growled as the crew grabbed up the net, her and Fengel in it. "You'll come crawling back, and when you do, you'll—"

The crew pitched the two of them overboard.

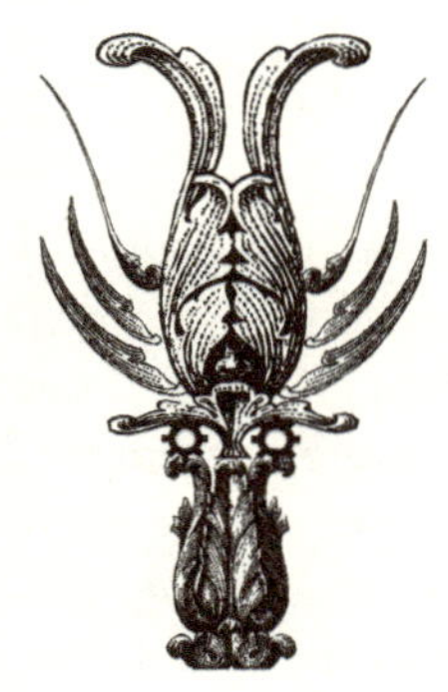

CHAPTER FOUR

But how did I stumble?

Fengel stared after the airship as it floated away without him. Natasha's struggles with the net pulled him back and forth, yet all he could do was watch the retreating *Dawnhawk*. What mistake had he made, to push them so far? *Never let them see you stumble.* That was his personal motto. So how had he stumbled? Fengel did not know.

Natasha growled as she tried to free herself. She fought with rope mesh until she found the mouth, and stretched it just wide enough to crawl through. Then Natasha pulled herself out onto the hot sand of the beach and clambered to her feet, running into the surf with both fists upraised at the airship.

"You goat-sucking bastards!" she screamed at the top of her lungs. "You yellow-bellied cowards! Thieves! You Goddess-damned *sky pirates!*" She waded out until the water was waist-high, each wave pushing her back toward the island. Natasha floundered and fought against them, trying in vain to chase after the *Dawnhawk*.

Fengel pulled the rope mesh over his head and freed himself. He did not stand, however. Instead, he hugged his legs up to his chest and rested his chin on his knees. His hat lay beside him in the net. He did not put it back on. *Why did they get rid of me? I was a good captain, wasn't I? And I was straight with them, respectable, even when I didn't feel it. I tried to be fair, to project that image. Image is everything. Never let them see you stumble. Where did I stumble? Where did I go wrong?*

Natasha jumped and beat at the waves, now too far out to stand. She screamed and yelled incoherently. Fengel glanced at his wife, annoyed at the distraction from his train of thought. Then it hit him like a sledge.

"You," he whispered. "You're the one they meant to get rid of."

Natasha tired quickly. Though mighty, her rage was no match for the ocean. She lashed out once more, sending a light spray of sun-dappled seawater after the retreating airship. Then she collapsed. The waves picked her up and pushed her back to the shoreline. There she lay a moment, gasping and exhausted. Fengel glared as she rolled over onto hands and knees, the surf surging over her.

He leaned forward and jabbed an accusatory finger at her. "You're the reason they did this."

Natasha glanced up at him in confusion. "Go drown yourself," she said reflexively. She staggered to her feet and stretched, puffy blouse now limp and clingy. Natasha ruined the effect by loudly hawking a great gob of mucus and seawater down onto the sand. Then she stalked up the beach towards him.

Fengel climbed to his feet to confront her. Natasha ignored him however, walking past to a small wooden crate that had landed behind them, presumably also left by their mutinous crew. She sat down cross-legged beside it, working at the nailed-down lid with her fingers.

How dare you ignore me? He opened his mouth to give voice to his thoughts and stopped as he took in the panorama past her. The white, sandy beach ended a dozen yards farther inland, stopping at a dense jungle of palms and thick underbrush. Tropical birds flew through the branches and made raucous, high-pitched cries as they went. A mile or so deeper into the isle, the jungle rose to meet the slopes of a great steaming mountain dominating the center of Almhazlik. A ridge descended from both sides of the volcano, running all the way back down to the ocean and encompassing this part of the island shore in a pie-shaped partition maybe half a mile at its widest.

The mountain struck him most of all. Its slope rose up from the jungle to a dimly glowing crag that puffed white clouds off into the bright blue sky, like the boiler steamstacks of his own rogue airship. Weird monoliths dotted the outer skin of it, sharply triangular pillars of rock. One was larger than all the rest. It rose up several hundred feet above the western tree line in a form that could only have been carved by human hands: the shoulders, neck, and reptilian maw of a dragon, all weathered and covered in jungle foliage.

Almhazlik Isle was not as deserted as his crew had believed.

A loud crack brought him back from this discovery. Natasha lay back upon the sand, and was ramming her boot heel down atop the crate. The lid took two blows before breaking inward. Natasha chortled at her success and sat upright to pry aside the broken planks of wood still nailed to the crate.

Fengel refocused on what was important. "It's true," he said to her. "It has to be."

Natasha ignored him. She pulled objects forth from inside the crate; a tinderbox, some rope, foodstuffs. These she tossed aside. Heavy packets of hardtack and rolls of rock-hard, razor-thin salted jerky landed in the sand between them.

"They meant to get you with the net, but I got caught as well," he insisted. "They couldn't let me out without freeing you, so that's why I'm here. They've just flown off to the other side of the island, waiting for me to find them."

The mound of supplies between them ceased growing as Natasha hit the bottom of the crate. There wasn't much, enough for maybe a week or more of rough living. His wife gave a cry and sat back happily, holding a dark bottle of rum with both hands.

"What I'm hearing," she said wickedly, "is denial." She placed the cork between her perfect teeth and bit with a pressure than Fengel knew could sever fingers. With a hollow noise, Natasha pulled the cork from the bottle and spat it to the sand. "A gentleman has certain standards to maintain," she mimicked mockingly, "if he doesn't want his crew to toss him overboard. Oh, I have to look nice and talk like a stodgy Perinese jackass if I don't want my crew of brigands to find a manlier captain." She tittered to herself and took a long pull off the bottle.

Fengel felt himself flush. "I am *not* in denial. You're the one whose been so Goddess-damned obnoxious that you've been pitched by a crew. This is the second time this has happened this year!"

"That was Mordecai," Natasha growled.

"Oh," said Fengel with a false lightness. "You're right. It was the fault of your nasty first mate. You were perfectly innocent." He hardened his voice. "Probably because you were drunk on a raging four-day bender that left half the men back in port crazed or blind from the pox."

Natasha glared at him. "You pompous, insufferable bag of wind."

"Floozy."

"Jackass."

"Slattern."

Natasha smiled suddenly.

"Mock me all you want," she said. "Use that creatively bankrupt brain of yours to come up with all the high-sounding insults you can. Do whatever you have to in order to keep looking away from the truth; that Lucian, Henry, and all the rest *didn't want you anymore.*"

Fengel froze. He found it hard to breathe. His vision narrowed to a pinpoint tunnel, with Natasha's mocking smile at the center. She was infuriating. Obnoxious. Dreadful.

And right.

Past the excuses, past his irritation with her, he knew what she said was true. *They've turned on me. She's right. And after all that I've done for them.* His stomach seemed to drop into an abyss. The sky threatened to smother him. He should have known better. They were pirates, after all.

Fengel's irritation ignited into a burning ball of anger. His face flushed. His monocle fell free. Calmly, he wedged it back into place, deciding to set rationality aside and give an output to this growing rage. It was the only sensible thing to do, after all. He reached out and snatched the bottle of rum from his wife. Flipping it, he caught it by the neck and whipped it down hard at the crate. The glass shattered into dozens of pieces, soaking the wooden box and the pale white sands with rum.

Natasha stared at him in unbelieving startlement. "What'd you do that for?" she cried.

"Because I didn't want you to have it anymore," he said smugly.

Natasha screamed and threw herself at him.

Her fingers, and nails, were aimed for his eyes. Fengel threw up his hands to grab her wrists, succeeding only in being hit with her whole weight in a full-body tackle. They went rolling off the net and onto the sand of the beach, sending her bandana flying free and his monocle to dangle from its chain. Coming to a stop, Fengel found himself on his back, Natasha astride him. She yanked one wrist free, balled up her hand, and lashed out. The blow connected across his cheekbone, jarring and painful. He swept his free hand out and slapped her, not a stinging tap, but a full open-handed blow. Natasha grunted and rolled with it, climbing off of him.

Fengel looked for a weapon. Something, anything that he could use to get the upper hand. The crate was too large and mostly still in one piece. His eyes alighted on the packet of hardtack, shaped like a brick wrapped in cheap paper. He grabbed it up in both hands, shifting back just in time to see Natasha with a sheaf of dried beef jerky held like a dagger. She lashed out and caught him just under the eye. The thinly sliced meat was as hard and sharp as a wooden blade. Fengel felt pain, and then something hot and wet as he threw himself back out of her reach.

He staggered quickly to his feet, the packet held out before him like a shield. Natasha did as well, weaving the beef back and forth like the experienced knife fighter she was. She leapt out in a feint, but Fengel spied the trick and pulled aside. He thrust out a leg as she overextended. Natasha tripped and rolled down the beach. Fengel made to follow.

Natasha came to a stop at the shoreline and leapt back up to one leg. She looked for him, just in time for the packet to come crashing down on her forehead. The bundle of hardtack split, exploding out in rock-hard crumbles that splashed down into the ocean spray. Natasha groaned, her eyes crossed, and she collapsed backwards. As she went, some instinct, some trained killer skill made her lash out at him. The jerky jabbed deeply into his thigh. Fengel gave a cry and fell to the damp sand.

Accursed witch! He looked down at his leg, at the hunk of beef sticking out at a right angle from his trousers. Fengel pulled it free and tossed it away, blood staining the tip. The wound and the salt from the meat worked together, turning a dull ache into sharp agony.

Her shadow gave him half a moment's warning. He wheeled on the sand as Natasha fell at him, fists clasped together in a blow that missed and sent sand spraying. Fengel reacted, grabbing at her throat and wrapping his hands around it. She corrected, grabbed his.

They struggled, rolling back down into the waves. His vision blurred, from lack of air and from the chop of the water. The tide sucked at him and tried to pull him out to sea, but the weight of his wife kept him pinned against damp sand and tidal water. All he could see was her face, beautiful even now, grimacing and wide-eyed with her own efforts.

Black spots sprung out through his vision. His strength failed him. In moments it was gone, his hands now like that of a puppet without its strings. They slacked and fell with a splash onto the sand and foamy water swirling around him. Amazingly, Natasha slackened her grip as well. She fell away to one side. Breath returned, painfully. Fengel reflexively sucked in a great chestful of air, not caring how much it hurt. Dimly he heard Natasha do the same.

He recovered slowly, too weak to do her further harm, but knowing that she was spent as well. As soon as he could, Fengel flopped over and crawled up from the surf, then unsteadily up onto his knees. Fengel glanced back to where Natasha was feebly laying, glaring hatefully up at him.

His anger was dulled. He stared down at his wife and grimaced. "I'll show you," he said, "and I'll show them too." In his ears his own voice was small and tinny.

Natasha raised one hand, made a fist, and extended a single finger.

Fengel staggered away and up the beach. The provisions that his crew had left were ruined, stamped into the sand and scattered. The tinderbox was missing, as were the other packets of hardtack. A few larger pieces looked mostly unbroken. He retrieved two, as well as his hat. Then he stalked down the beach without looking back, sun overhead, the jungle to his right, and the traitor ocean on his left.

The commentary of that surf was unrelenting. It mocked his outrage, overshadowing the call of the jungle birds and the sighing passage of the breeze. Beginning slowly, quietly, it swelled to a muted roar as it toppled forward onto the sand, only to pull back into the ocean with a hiss, starting the process all over again. It was consistent, yet irregular. Fengel could not find a rhythm with which to match his steps. Before long the divisions between one moment and the next seemed to slide away.

Fengel could not maintain his anger. He paused after awhile to take stock of his surroundings. Glancing around, he realized that his steps had taken him significantly closer to the ridge of rough cliffs near this end of the beach. Looking back, he couldn't even see Natasha anymore, or where they had landed. The curve of the island hid it completely. Out over the ocean, the sky was a clear blue that seemed to go on forever, only the clouds and the almost-gone speck of the *Dawnhawk* marring it.

Wild desperation took him. Fengel dashed out from the sand and into the water, chasing his wayward crew.

"Fellows!" he cried. "Come back! I'm sure you had a perfectly good reason for what you did, I just can't think of it!" He pushed against the surf, now thigh-high, his boots completely soaked. "Please, now, lads," he called. "I'm sure we can come to an accord. D'you want more grog? I can do that! More time ashore? Done!"

Fengel waded until the water was at his chest. "All right, you were right, I can see that now. Whatever it was we, I mean I, did, I can change that. Just come back, lads. Please? Don't leave me here. Lucian? Henry? Lina?"

His voice echoed across the waves. The ocean laughed at him, smothering it with the incessant pounding of the surf around him. The distant speck of his airship, his command, disappeared, winking away as if it had never been. All the energy and drive in Fengel drained away, replaced with a hollowness in his stomach. He gave up struggling and floated on his back, letting the ocean carry him ashore. When it could push him no farther inland, he sat up and stared at his trouser legs and the water lapping about him. They were covered with wet sand.

They left me here. They really meant it. Fengel reached up to cover his face with a hand. *What's the point? Why go on? I'm stuck here. They really and truly meant to leave me here.* He kicked at the sand petulantly. *I guess I'll just have to make a go of it, then. Exile on a deserted island. Things could be worse, I suppose.*

Fengel felt very tired, but this exile made certain things necessary. The first was shelter. He glanced around at the beach, the jungle, and the cliff wall. The beach offered nothing to protect him from the wind and the rain. Likewise, the ridgeline was without cave or cranny. The jungle, though....

Jutting out from the foliage and onto the sand was an enormous banyan tree. Its central trunk was massive and sprawling, spreading branches like a many-fingered hand outward, where they bent again to put down thick root-columns of their own. The upper branches were covered in thick banks of green leaves that gave shade and shelter to everything below them.

That could work. Fengel could almost see it now, a cozy cottage situated up above, rooms on each trunk connected by whimsical rope bridges. He rolled the image over in his mind, and was pleased by it. It wouldn't be *that* hard to implement. *If my crew ever come back, won't they be sorry to see what a splendid life I've made for myself here.*

Fengel nodded to himself and walked up to the trunk of the banyan. First things first: he needed to get atop the structure in order to properly survey it. Fengel removed his coat and set it aside, then tried to climb up the tree. The task was easier said than done, however. His boots were suited to walking the deck of a ship, not clambering up a surprisingly slick tree trunk. Also, his wounded leg protested every time he bent it too far. He fell. Then tried again, with similar results. After the fifth collapse back down to the ground, Fengel gathered his coat and glared at the tree.

Fine, then. More moderate means of shelter will have to suffice. At least for now.

An image came to mind of a simpler dwelling at the base of the tree. A cottage formed of branches and carved lumber. Fengel nodded to himself and started gathering deadfall.

There was surprisingly little free wood, however. After a span of minutes he only had three small branches in hand. And there was another setback, one he hadn't counted upon; he needed something sharp with which to shape the wood. His crew had taken his sword, dagger and emergency knife. There might have been one in the supply crate, but either Natasha had it, or it was buried now somewhere under the sand. Which came to the same thing in the end.

Fengel sighed deeply. *Well. If I can't have a house just yet, I can at least have a fire.* He returned to the tree line with his branches and knelt before the sand. Lucian Thorne, traitor though he was, was an accomplished survivalist.

He'd tried to show Fengel the trick of fire more than once. Thinking back, it seemed easy enough.

Place one branch upon the ground like so. Then, sharpen the end of the other branch, stick it on the first, and spin. Hmm. He hadn't any knife to cut the branch with, but it was just friction between the two sticks. How hard could that be?

A few minutes later Fengel threw the two branches away in frustration. They landed in the sand, one sailing so far as to land at the tide line. The surf pulled it into the waves, then deposited it back up higher than it had landed, mocking him.

Fengel closed his eyes. He ran a hand through his hair.

His "loyal" crew had stuck him here. He and Natasha. But they'd said it was only temporary. Perhaps in his shock he'd forgotten that. *How long is the trip to Breachtown from here? This place is near the equator, so likely three days by aetherline and steam. Then the same for the trip back.* He just had to last that long.

He moved to sit cross-legged where the tree line cast shade over the beach and pulled a piece of the rock-like biscuit from jacket. "What am I worried about?" he said aloud to no one in particular. "Things are probably falling apart without me there."

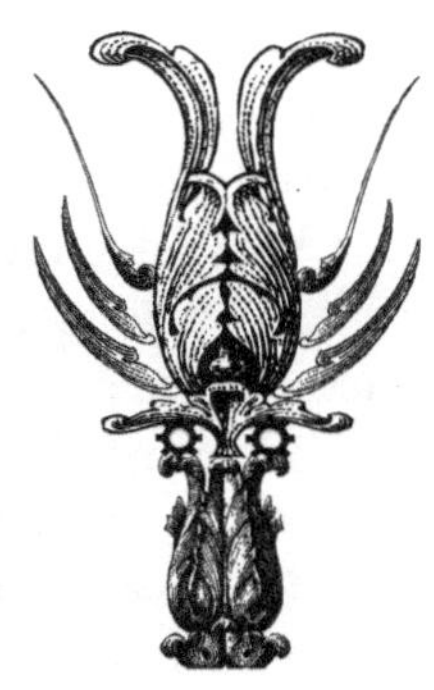

CHAPTER FIVE

THINGS WERE GOING SURPRISINGLY WELL.

Lina shifted in her crouch over the canister while Rastalak adjusted his rubber hose. She scanned the interior of the gas-bag envelope. It always made her nervous, coming up here. Seen from the outside, the balloon keeping the *Dawnhawk* aloft was a great ridged spindle. Once inside, though, things were altogether different. Diffuse daylight revealed a hollow yet cluttered space, with a long central strut running down the middle of the envelope. Wires and armatures branched out along its length, stretching to the metal poles that kept the canvas skin rigid, so that the whole arrangement put Lina in mind of a winter-deadened tree lying on its side.

Between the wires and struts hung the gas cells, small oblong sacks of treated cloth. The contents of the cells were an open secret, a light-air gas capable of lifting the heavy wooden hull of an airship off into the sky. The precise nature of the gas was guarded jealously by the Mechanist Brotherhood, but working around it every day, Lina and the other sky pirates knew just enough to be afraid. The stuff was both poisonous to breath and insanely flammable. Outside, she could forget these details. Stuck within the gas bag, that became rather more difficult.

Lina shifted again in her crouch and adjusted her gas mask. The catwalk she hunched upon led from the gas bag entrance behind her to the larger walkway balanced upon the central strut. The old Mechanist stood farther along it, shrouded in his heavy leather greatcoat and gas mask. He held a long metal wand in one hand and swept it back and forth, checking for gas leaks.

The older Mechanist was clearly everything Allen aspired to be. Responsible for maintenance aboard the airship, he focused on his duties with a kind of cold fanaticism. Where Allen was nervous and annoying, the Mechanist was stoic and secretive. Lina didn't even know his name.

Lina had been lounging near the stern deck with Rastalak when the Mechanist had appeared to dragoon them both. This wasn't uncommon. Tradition held that the work of a ship's Mechanist was more important than almost anything else. Right now that meant hunting down a gas leak. Thankfully, it had only been the one cell, and quickly tended by the two of them. At the old man's direction, they'd ripped out the leaky cell, put in the new, and were now charging it up.

Lina turned back to her friend. "He's finished looking over the stern," she said, voice muffled by the mask. "Is that done yet? I want to get this over with."

Rastalak blinked up at her, his nictitating membrane slightly slower to clear away. Shorter even than she was, Rastalak wore only a pair of trousers with a hole cut in them for his tail. He prodded the bag carefully with the back of one talon, then nodded and closed the locking valve on the gas cell. Rastalak worked slowly and deliberately. The bandages swathing his hands obviously made the movements difficult.

"Full," he said. His voice was raspy still from the smoke he'd inhaled aboard the *Minnow*.

"Let's pack up then," said Lina. She bent to help him seal up the canister and unplug the hose.

"You are twitchy," he said when they were done. "Nervous."

"These cells are just waiting for a stray spark," she grunted.

The reptilian pirate shook his head. "It is just as dangerous, when we are down below."

Lina frowned. "Yes, but it's different, standing here and *looking* at the things."

He hissed in amusement.

Lina stood and stretched, ignoring him. She walked over to the Mechanist, boots clanging on the catwalk. He looked down at her approach.

"Is the task complete?" he demanded.

"Yes, sir," said Lina. "Topped up and good to go."

"We shall see," said the Mechanist. He stalked over to wave his wand around the replacement cell. The Mechanist examined a small box on his belt and then nodded. Bending past Rastalak, he then prodded the cell with a finger and checked its seal. "Sufficient, for now," he said. "I shall finish up here myself. You are free to return to your duties below."

And not even a thank you. "Yes, sir," she said, trying to sound chipper.

When she'd been new to this life, the Mechanist had been as much a mystery to her as everything else. He'd been one of the few people to treat her decently back then, ignoring her past in favor of her natural proficiency with the airship's machinery. Fengel had consistently sent her to assist the man because of this, hoping to have someone on his crew who knew how the *Dawnhawk* really worked. Familiarity had ended up breeding contempt though, and in the end she realized that the Brother of the Cog saw her the way he did everyone else; as tools of lesser or greater quality. He was all right in the end, and it was never wise to cross him, but now she found him largely overbearing and tedious.

Lina ducked past the Mechanist for the hatch back outside. She unlocked it and pushed it wide, letting bright daylight and fresh air flood the gas bag interior. Lina scurried through, putting hands and feet to the now-familiar rigging. Outside, the canvas skin of the gas bag was a dun wall stretching in every direction, a net-wrapped counterpoint to the vast expanse of the sky. Grey-winged seagulls wheeled up near the top of the airship. Down below lay the ocean, waves churning the warm blue-green water into foam. The sun hung stark and brilliant just above the horizon and set the skysails along the hull to shining.

A cold wind pushed at her clothing and played with the tufts of her hair not pinned down by the gas mask straps. She descended until the deck of the airship came into view beneath the curve of the envelope and paused there, looking back up for her friend. Rastalak peered out from the doorway down at her. Climbing was a slow and tedious process with his burned hands.

Lina hooked one arm through the rigging. She pulled the gas mask down around her neck and instantly felt better. The air was fresh and tinged by the sea, a welcome change from the recycled leather stink of the mask.

"Come on!" she called. "I'll stay here in case you need help."

Rastalak nodded. He slowly made his way outside, shut the door, then began his descent.

Lina relaxed while she waited. She glanced down at the ocean, hundreds of feet below. *I guess it doesn't make much sense,* she conceded. She could just as likely die from some stupid accident, a slip and a fall, as get blown up by a stray spark in the gas bag.

Beneath her, the day crew went about their business. Lucian stood up on the bow, peering through a spyglass. Tricia worked with Ryan Gae on oiling the skysail armatures in preparation for an upcoming ride on an aetherline. Runt lay curled up on the starboard exhaust pipe, out of the way. Everywhere she looked her crewmates worked quietly and efficiently. Things were…remarkably peaceful. Even the crazy aetherite helmsmen, Konrad and Maxim, weren't fighting, though each still kept an untrusting hand on the ship's wheel.

It had been a full day since they'd left Natasha and Fengel on Almhazlik Isle, and things were going well. Astonishingly so. When she'd first told the crew her plan, she'd half-expected to get tossed overboard herself. Yet everyone had gone along with it, and so far they hadn't managed to crash the airship or burst into flames.

She gazed out at the ocean, bemused. *I wonder if every pirate ship could do this. Realms Below, go even further. Maybe we don't need leaders. Maybe all those kingdoms back on Edrus and all sea-going ships could just pitch their captains, kings, and sheiks, get along like we are.*

A speck of color down on the water below caught her eye. Lina blinked in surprise. It was a ship. Not quite beneath them, but close enough, obviously trying to stay hidden in the *Dawnhawk's* shadow. It was only dumb luck that the vessel hadn't been noticed before now. *That, or Gabley is slacking again.* She'd have to have a word with the white ape.

Lina scrabbled a little lower, peering down at the vessel. Months as a pirate had taught her what to look for. The ship's hull was low in the water, meaning she sailed with a full hold. She also lacked paddlewheels and the exhaust stacks of the new naval steam-frigates. Her home port could have been anywhere on the continent of Edrus; Salomca, Perinault, or Greisheim. Lina didn't know and didn't really care. She wasn't a navy ship and she had cargo, and that meant there was only one other thing she could be.

Prey.

Lina descended the rigging until she hung halfway between the deck and the gasbag. "Ship ahoy!" she cried. "Off the port-side bow!"

Heads popped up from various tasks as the crew all looked about in surprise. Almost as one they moved to the gunwales. She pointed out the ship and they bent low to look at it, exclaiming in surprise. Lucian Thorne and Sarah Lome pushed through to stand beside Reaver Jane. The first mate pulled out a spyglass and peered downward. Everyone fell quiet.

"That's a ship, all right," he said after a moment. "Perinese, I think. Barkentine. Too small to be Merchant Navy. They've seen us, obviously. Odd that they're not running full out; it's a miracle that we haven't noticed them until now. Someone remind me to have a bit of a chat with Gabley's ape soon."

He trailed off as he continued his inspection. Lina glanced back at the crew. Everyone was looking at each other, the same unspoken question obvious on each face. They were all feeling poor at the moment. Twice now they'd been back to port since the Yulan adventure six months ago, with nothing to show for it, thanks to Fengel and Natasha's constant fighting.

Lucian still hadn't spoken up. *Sod it.* Lina cleared her throat. "Well?" she asked. "Aren't we going to get them?"

The crew spoke up all at once.

"Can we?" asked Jonas Wiley.

"Why in the Realms Below wouldn't we?" asked his brother Nate, hands still swathed in bandages.

"They're running already," said Sarah Lome. "We'd have to fight the wind."

"That just means burning fuel, which we're doing already," replied Reaver Jane.

"We haven't taken a real prize in months," lamented Henry Smalls.

"But can we?" asked Elly Minel.

Lina glared down at them. "Well, why not?" she demanded, raising her gaze to the others. "I know what we're all thinking; the captains are gone. But that was the point. We got rid of them. It's not like we need to ask *permission,* for Her sake."

"But who's gonna lead us?" whined Oscar Pleasant.

"The Breachtown heist is one thing," said Andrea Holt. "We already know what we're about there. Someone's got to make the big moment-to-moment decisions, though. Do we...elect someone else captain?"

Uneasiness washed across the faces of everyone present. Lina knew how they felt. They didn't hate Fengel and Natasha. It was just impossible to get anything done with the two of them around. Kicking them off the ship hadn't been undertaken lightly.

The weird thought from a moment ago still had a hold of her, though. *No kings, no sheiks.* An idea came to her. "We don't have to," replied Lina. "Look, Lucian's normally in charge anyway, right? So when we need ordering, he takes the lead, and nothing's changed there. For the big stuff—"

"Yes," said Ryan. "That's the trick. Big stuff, like course changes and fuel and whatnot."

Lina glared at him. "Let's do it by committee," she continued. "The officers who run things normally. Lucian, Reaver Jane, Sarah Lome."

The crew looked to those named. Lucian collapsed his spyglass and shared a glance with the other officers. Then he gave a shrug.

"Could work," he said. "I'm mighty tired of an empty purse, and we've got to try this sometime."

"I guess it couldn't hurt," said Sarah Lome.

"We'll take a Crewman's Vote on it," said Reaver Jane. She frowned and folded her arms. "Committee's going to need one more on it, though."

"Who?" asked Lucian. "Three's a good number."

"I want Lina Stone," said Jane.

Lina started. The crew stared at her. Her heart fell into her stomach. "What?" she asked. "Why me?"

"Because you keep coming up with these ideas. And if everything goes tits up, you're going to be the one we blame for it. Official scapegoat. Now, let's have that vote. All in favor?"

"Hold on," called a voice. Lina, along with everyone else, glanced back to Oscar Pleasant. "I'm sorry, but this doesn't seem like a bad idea to anyone? I mean, really, a committee?" The pirate was ratlike, disheveled. No one really liked him much. Even his one-time friends avoided him of late.

Lucian gave him a frank stare. "Do you have a better idea, Mr. Pleasant?"

Oscar looked away and then shrugged. "Well, I mean...no. Not really."

"Right then," said Reaver Jane. "Now, all in favor?"

Most every hand shot up. The remainder went along once they saw which way things were going.

"That's that, then," said Lucian. "Ship's Committee, to the helm. Everyone else to your stations." He grinned. "There's a fat merchant below who needs to have his holds lightened."

Everyone roared their approval.

Lina followed the officers back to the helm. Maxim and Konrad worked together to twist the ship about, Konrad on the wheel and Maxim shouting orders down to the Mechanist in the engine room. Lucian waved Lina over.

Reaver Jane eyed her warily. "You've an awful lot to say of late," she snapped.

"She hasn't been wrong, though," said Lucian. He clapped a hand on Lina's shoulder like a proud older brother. "Lina's relatively new to the life. She hasn't got the baggage we do, and can see a little more clearly."

"Maybe," said Sarah Lome. "Four's a bad number for a committee. Could mean a tied decision."

"Well, that's why her position here is honorary, right, Lina?" He smiled down at her, and it wasn't altogether jovial. "Lass, Sarah is right. Four's a bad number for decision-making. You don't get any say more than the rest of the crew. But we'll want you here for input, all right?"

Lina thought of something sharp to say, but gave a nod instead.

Jane sighed. "All right. Enough. How do we do this?" She gestured at the deck, toward where the merchant ship would be.

"Same as before," said Sarah Lome. "We go in fast and hit their sails, drop to the deck and pacify them all. Quick and clean. It's not a military ship. I don't see no reason to change things up."

Jane nodded. "Good."

She went to leave but Lucian raised a hand. "Hold up. We offer quarter, and avoid unnecessary bloodshed."

Reaver Jane stopped. "What? Fengel's gone. Don't tell me you've gone all soft in his place."

"It's a good policy," replied Lucian. "People who think they've nothing to lose fight all the harder. There might be a few hired guards down there, but we've found that as long as it's not full of soldiers, which is fairly unlikely, people tend to see sense after a bit of knockin' about." He gave her a level look. "Remember, we're here for the *treasure*. That's the important thing."

Reaver Jane returned his gaze. "All right. So long as you remember that's what we're after."

She stalked down the deck. Sarah Lome turned to do the same. Lucian gave Lina a look and gestured for the gunwales.

That went surprisingly smoothly, she thought as she left to prepare for the attack. Natasha's crew were a bloodthirsty lot, and Reaver Jane was no exception. That Lucian got his way was surprising, though sensible. *Maybe this is going to work even better than I'd hoped.*

Lina went amidships where the equipment lockers were mounted. They'd been opened up, and gunnery mistress Lome was passing out muskets, shot, and powder. Lina took a pistol and checked it, loading as she made her way to the port side of the airship just below the bow. Aside from the flintlock, she had her pair of knives and one other thing as well. She stuffed the barrel of the gun into her waistband and blew a sharp whistle with two fingers. Runt perked up from his doze on the exhaust pipe and gave an answering screech. He rose, stretched, and launched himself to soar across the deck to her shoulder, eliciting yells from startled pirates. Lina caught the scryn and scratched behind his head while he chirruped in pleasure.

The *Dawnhawk* came into line on a direct heading for the vessel below. From the stern Lucian called out commands, and Lina felt a deep vibration in the deck below her feet as their engine kicked into higher gear.

She peered over the side as the merchant ship burst into activity. There were dozens of antlike movements amongst the rigging; sailors furling their sails in a desperate attempt to get away. All pretense was gone. They knew they'd been spotted.

Lina smiled as the airship bore down. Growing up in the slums of Triskelion, she'd learned to defend herself, but until recently she hadn't gone *looking* for any fights. Life as a pirate had changed that. She wasn't particularly bloodthirsty and did appreciate Fengel's gentlemanly code. There *was* an undeniable thrill to the chase, however, and the prospect of actually having real money again almost left her breathless.

The distance shrank between the two vessels. Now that they were close enough, Lina saw that the ship was a big three-master, with the word *Kingfisher* emblazoned in gold letters across its stern. It disappeared beneath their hull as the *Dawnhawk* overtook it, only to reappear as they veered to starboard. The captain of the merchant ship stood on the sterncastle shouting commands. The sailors scurried for the gunwales and forecastle, for weapons and belaying pins.

"Prepare the grapples!" shouted Lucian from the stern. Fat Thomlin and the other pirates assigned to the task took up the great boarding tethers, those long coiled ropes anchored to the deck, their other ends tied to thick chains and iron hooks. "Now!"

The pirates roared out. Grapnels sailed out through the air, dropping into the tangle of sailcloth and rigging below. The *Dawnhawk* shuddered as the ropes caught and pulled taut. The *Kingfisher* jerked. A sailor in the rigging tried desperately to dislodge the hooks or cut them free. Lina's crewmates threw the rope ladders and drop-lines over the side of the airship, then started clambering down before they'd even had time to fully unroll. The raid was underway.

Reaver Jane, Sarah Lome, and the other more skilled and vicious pirates dropped down to the deck. The sailors tried to fight back, but the captain and first mate gave contradicting orders that Lina's crewmates were only too happy to exploit. Lina followed shortly thereafter, stopping halfway to clamber over into the *Kingfisher's* rigging. A burly sailor was waiting for her. He was an ugly man who stank of garlic and reminded her of the obnoxious Oscar Pleasant. Lina lifted her arm and let Runt deal with him.

Lina's task was to make sure that the boarding tethers weren't cut away during the raid. They needn't have really bothered. The lookout was either down below or hiding in his crow's nest while the sailor behind her was scurrying down the ratlines as fast as he could to escape her hissing, spitting pet. Otherwise, the rigging was empty.

Things were progressing quickly on the deck. Lina moved over to the mainmast, where Lucian and a few of her crewmates fought the *Kingfisher's* captain and first mate. Lucian performed a wild flourish that sent the captain's sword flying off down the deck, then pointed the tip of his own in warning.

"Stand down now," said Lucian with a smile. "Your men are beaten. There's no need for further bloodshed."

"We'll not give in to filthy pirates," snarled the first mate, brandishing his blade. "We throw down our weapons and we're as good as dead." The man had a nasty gash across his brow, and it bled profusely.

Lucian rolled his eyes. "Please. We're here for your holds, not your lives." He gestured with his blade at the airship above them. "We are the crew of the airship *Dawnhawk*, and we have a reputation to maintain. I swear that no harm will come to you if you lay down your arms."

The captain reached out a hand and pulled down his mate's arm. "That's not what he means. You're with the *Dawnhawk*? I've heard of you. That's Captain Fengel's ship." He peered at Lucian. "D'you mean that?"

"Sir!" cried the mate. He shot a strange, intense look at his master, then jerked his head oddly toward the low sterncastle.

"They've not been a damned help since we agreed to take them back to Edrus," growled the captain of the *Kingfisher.* "We could have been a hundred leagues away by now if it wasn't for his stupid ambition. Everyone knows you can't take an airship! I'll not risk anymore of the crew on this harebrained scheme."

Lucian frowned. "What are you two on about?" He glanced at the first mate, and then at the captain again.

Lina knelt to listen. Runt landed suddenly on her shoulders, shifting her off-balance and chirping happily through a bloody maw.

"We're out of Breachtown," said the captain. "And the pacification there—"

"Marines forward!" cried a voice.

The recessed door to the sterncastle cabin banged open. Men in blue coats and tricorn hats boiled out with muskets held at the ready. They fired as they came, sending a hail of lead balls down the ship. Pirates and sailors both yelled in alarm. The Bluecoats shot indiscriminately; the first mate and captain of the *Kingfisher* both went down.

A ball smacked into the yardarm Lina perched upon, sending a spray of slivers up at her. She cursed and scrabbled back behind the bulk of the mast for cover. Below, she heard Lucian calling the rest of their crew to face the threat.

Lina waited a moment to peek around the mast. The Bluecoats had finished their first volley and threw themselves at the pirates with bayonets and sabers. Her crewmates fell back a bit at the charge, but with nowhere else to go, they rallied quickly. The two sides met and broke apart into individual struggles that spread out across the deck.

A figure appeared from the captain's cabin. He was a tall man in an officer's uniform with a long wig of powdered curls. The epaulets on his shoulder denoted him a colonel. He drew a ridiculously ornate saber and casually climbed the stair up to the poop deck. Two marines framed him as guards, swords drawn and at the ready.

The colonel gazed out at the melee below him. "Kill them all and take the airship," he cried. "Admiral Wintermourn'll make us rich as princes if we do. No quarter for pirate dogs!"

Oh Goddess on high. This whole thing was a trap. No wonder the *Kingfisher* hadn't run. The Bluecoats aboard had made her play honeypot for the *Dawnhawk*. Every kingdom back on Edrus offered a ludicrous bounty for an intact airship. Whoever this man was, he obviously thought he could claim it. Lina felt a surge of anger; they'd walked right into it. *No. No way in the Realms Below they're taking our ship from us.*

The marine colonel said something quietly to one of his men, who nodded and sheathed his blade. The Bluecoat walked over to the sternside railing, where a fat steel tube was attached to a pivot.

A swivel gun.

Lina stared. A swivel gun was a small cannon, usually used in boarding actions. No sane commander would use one against his own ship. But the Bluecoats had already shown a willingness to gun down their own sailors. Loaded with shot, it would devastate those fighting on the deck, including the Bluecoats there. Somehow Lina didn't think that the stodgy Perinese colonel would care overmuch.

The marine tilted the gun upright and knelt for a small powder keg and bag of shot stored under the gunwales beneath it. Thankfully, they still had to load the thing.

I don't have a lot of time. Lina glanced down and around. No one else on her side seemed to have noticed the danger. There *was* one ally close at hand, though. Reaver Jane stood with her back against the sternmost mast, fending off two marines at once with a cutlass and a long knife.

I've got to get down there. But how? Lina glanced around for another way, and her gaze caught on a loose rope laying on the yardarm at her feet. The far end was part of the topsail rigging for the stern mast. Likely it had been torn free by the grapnels thrown earlier.

A pistol-shot rang out below her. The ball whipped past her head, agitating Runt into a screech. Lina started in surprise as well. Acting on reflex she grabbed the rope and kicked away from the yardarm.

"Chirr!" screamed her pet.

Lina sailed through the air, over the melee, dead-on for the mast and Reaver Jane's struggle. She collided with a Bluecoat feet-to-back in a blow that stunned her and dropped them both in a heap.

Runt writhed away off her, taking flight in indignation for the relative safety of the topsail rigging. Something slammed into the deck near her head and she scrambled to her feet. It was the other Bluecoat.

Reaver Jane flicked the blood from her cutlass and raised an eye at Lina. "You keep trying these things, you're going to get hurt."

"I didn't have much choice!" she replied. Lina glanced down at the marine she'd hit. The man wasn't moving. "Anyway, we've got bigger problems to worry about. Look!"

She pointed out the colonel and his men up on the sterncastle deck. The colonel himself still called out imperiously, ordering his men like pieces on a chessboard. The Bluecoat with the swivel gun was almost finished loading it, running a rammer down the barrel and priming the guncock mechanism at the same time.

Reaver Jane understood immediately. She snatched a pistol from her belt, took aim, and fired.

The ball went wide. It sparked off the barrel of the swivel gun and ricocheted back into the face of the Bluecoat priming it. The man fell back without even a cry and dropped lifelessly to the deck.

Lina raised an eyebrow. "Good shot."

"I was aiming for that colonel," said Jane. "Here, I'll clear us a path. You go overboard and scurry up channels on the side. Take that gun. I'll go the direct route. Bluecoaties can't think a single thought on their own. If we can take care of that powder-covered popinjay up there, we can end this."

Lina opened her mouth to object, but the piratess was already away. She charged with a wild cry at the port-side sterncastle stair, lashing out at any marines she could along the way. They reacted, opening a small hole in the fighting between Lina and the starboard side of the ship.

Lina swallowed and darted for the railing. She slipped on blood and bodies and collided with the rail. Ducking a wild slash, she rolled over it and threw a prayer to the Goddess that she didn't fly off into the ocean.

Her feet caught on the channel boards anchoring the rigging from the deck up to the mast. They were barely wide enough to stand on, a ledge stretching back sternward that jutted out over the churning ocean just a dozen feet below. She crept along it with both hands gripping the ship's railing from the wrong side.

A pistol ball hit the railing above her head. Lina ducked as splinters rained down onto her shoulders. She moved a few more feet and froze as two struggling men slammed into the rail. Both of their swords went flying, missing the top of her head by inches and clattering across the channel board before dropping into the sea. They cursed and lashed at each other, a Bluecoat marine and one of her own crewmates, Jonas Wiley. The Bluecoat threw a punch that folded Wiley over, then drew a dagger from his belt. But a fume enveloped him as he went for the killing blow, like heat-haze on a hot summer's day. He fell to the deck, screaming.

Lina blanched and glanced back up at the *Dawnhawk*. Just as she'd suspected, Maxim and Konrad both were hanging over the gunwales, casting aetherite spells where they could to assist. Lina didn't know, and didn't want to know, the specifics of their power, though Maxim had told her that each Working was bartered at dear cost from their daemon familiars. Their efforts might help buy time, though it wouldn't change the outcome in the end. Lina still had to reach the sterncastle.

Somehow she made it. The sterncastle deck appeared on her right just as the channel came to an end and a long window into the captain's cabin appeared. Another gunshot rang out nearby and she heard Jane's wild battle cry, followed by the clatter of swordplay.

The sterncastle railing was only a few feet above her. As well, the swivel gun. Lina took a breath and placed the tip of her boots on the bare lip of the window frame. She grabbed the base of the railing and strained to lift herself. Slowly she rose up, once again able to see and hear the battle. Lina expected a stray bullet or blow from a sword to take her head off at any moment. Amazingly, none did.

The colonel and his man stood at the port-side stair down to the deck. Reaver Jane was only a few feet below, making up for her lack of advantage with sheer ferocity and bloody-mindedness. The third man was on his back, a bloody hole in his forehead where Jane's ricochet had taken him.

Lina got her leg up to the sterncastle and scrabbled upright. She grabbed the broom-handle haft of the swivel gun and pulled it around to face the colonel. The cocking mechanism was already primed, and the flint-headed hammer was up.

"Hey arseholes!" she cried. "Leave off if you don't want to be chumming the waters with yer innards!"

The colonel glanced over his shoulder. He stared at her, the tip of his blade dropping in surprise. The man at his side gave a yell and collapsed as Jane slipped in a blow at his shins. She quickly moved up the ladder and held her blade to the colonel's throat. He started in surprise, then threw his weapon down in disgust.

"I surrender," he said sourly.

"Lucky for you, you son of a bitch, we're actually taking it today." Reaver Jane narrowed her eyes. "Call off your men." The Perinese soldier frowned, but raised his voice to comply. One by one, the small struggles died down on the deck below them.

No one threatens my ship, Lina thought savagely.

Overhead, Runt screeched their victory.

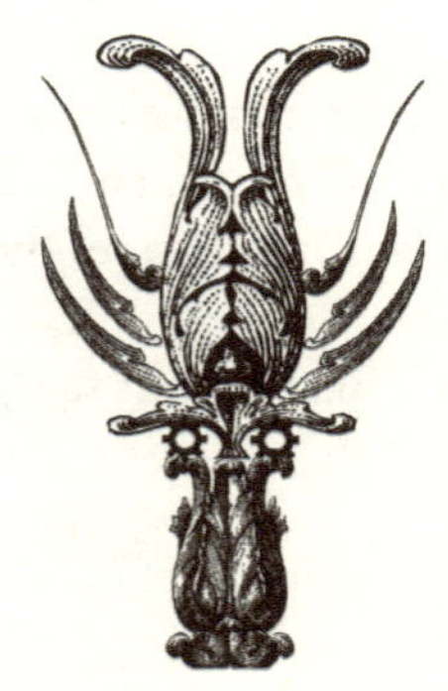

CHAPTER SIX

The parrot was screaming again.

Natasha rolled over to glare at it. The motion made her shirt bunch uncomfortably between her body and the dusty earth. A root now stabbed at her ribs. She ignored these to focus her hate on the obnoxious avian above her.

Die, damn you.

The creature was colorful. Its stumpy legs were a bright orange. The great oversized beak was a soft, butter-yellow. Whenever it stretched, brilliant plumage stood out in a vibrant explosion made all the more intense by the soft green backdrop of the foliage.

But the bird was also loud.

It had a raucous, piercing cry that shattered any sense of peace in the jungle about her. Since just before dawn when she'd finally fallen asleep, it had sat in the canopy above Natasha's head. Periodically it broke out into a harsh, ear-splitting racket, no doubt attempting to attract some tone-deaf mate.

Natasha fumbled for something to throw at the bird, fingers searching across the ash-dusted earth and finding nothing that she could use. Irritated, she rolled back over and glanced around her encampment. It was small and mean, positioned under the spreading branches of an ancient baobab. The tree had outfought all competitors, leaving the ground beneath it a bare clearing covered with deadfall and surrounded by the thick green jungle. Directly above, the branches were burned and bare of leaves. A slant of early morning light filtered in through this hole to brighten the space.

She grimaced as she took in the damage. Trying to make a fire had *seemed* like a good idea last night, in the dark and in the cold. How was she supposed to know that a bigger pile of wood would burn hotter, not longer?

Her unused tent lay against the base of the tree trunk. It had collapsed again, an ugly and misshapen thing she'd gotten fed up with trying to fix sometime after midnight. Seeing it in the daylight just stoked her anger. A tent shouldn't have been *that* hard to throw together, not with the cloth and twine left behind by her rebellious crew. Just before the cobbled-together thing lay her ill-conceived fire pit, an ash-covered scar she'd failed to dig nearly deep enough. Amazingly, when things had spiraled out of control, the tent had not caught fire.

Other bits scavenged from the beach lay about the clearing. Most were garbage now, trod into the ashy dirt and broken, burned or inedible. After putting out the blaze, she'd not bothered to reclaim them before collapsing to the dirt in exhaustion.

Her eye landed on a piece of hardtack biscuit only a few feet away. Natasha grabbed it up and looked back to the parrot, invoking a prayer of pain and spite as she threw.

She missed. She could almost hear the voice of old Euron, her father, berating her for it. The parrot ignored her missile and puffed itself up into a riotous ball of color. Then it shrieked in indignation. Natasha winced at the sound. A small lizard fell from some upper branch to land in the dirt, stunned.

Goddess on high, I need a drink. Natasha cursed the bird silently, then pulled herself up to sit cross-legged. Her tongue felt swollen. It tasted like something had crawled down her throat and died. Her neck was still sore from yesterday's argument with Fengel. Every inch of her back ached from sleeping on the ground. The leaves and dirt in her hair made it a tangled mass.

Sitting up hadn't helped. A dull throbbing began at her temples and it grew with every passing moment. Natasha pulled up a hand to rub the headache away, then stopped. Her whole arm shook with a slight tremor.

Natasha closed her eyes. *I just need a drink.*

The parrot screamed again.

"Would you just shut up and die?" she snarled.

It stopped and looked around. Then it squawked and flew off. Natasha blinked in surprise, then sighed in relief. Now maybe she could get some peace.

Another sound broke the silence. Something crashed through the jungle underbrush. It was large and getting closer, no mere parrot. Natasha looked about for a stray branch to use as a weapon. She found nothing; all of the deadfall had been burned last night in that bonfire. Instead, she took a breath and scrabbled to her feet. Whatever it was, it wouldn't find her unawares. Her father always said to meet trouble standing. She hated to admit it, but he had a point.

Fengel pushed out into the clearing. He stumbled a bit at the sudden lack of foliage and staggered to a halt. Regaining his balance, he glanced up and around. His eyes landed on Natasha.

He gave a disappointed sigh.

"I was afraid that was you," he said tartly. "Even on a deserted jungle island, your screech could wake the dead."

They'd only had their...*discussion*...on the beach yesterday afternoon, but Fengel looked far worse for wear than he should have. His clothing was torn in places, and there was a scratch on his monocle.

Of course. This is all I need today. Their most recent argument had not been the worst they'd ever had, or the most violent. She still did not want to have to deal with him right now, though. "That was a bird," she hissed. The pounding at her temples grew stronger. What was he even doing here?

"Yes, yes," Fengel replied with disinterest. He glanced around the clearing. "Goddess above. What happened here?"

Embarrassment encroached on her irritation. *I'm a pirate captain, not a damned woodsman.* "I don't know what you're talking about." She folded her arms.

Fengel gave her a vicious, mocking smile. "What I'm talking about is the utter devastation of this patch of woodlands. Almost like someone started a bonfire underneath a tree and didn't think it through."

"Like you could have done any better," she replied through gritted teeth.

"I did just fine last night," said Fengel. "Thank you very much." Her husband straightened a little, tilting his head back.

She recognized the mannerism. He was lying. "Horseshit," she said, breaking out into a wicked smile of her own. "You never could rub two sticks together to save your life, no matter how many times Lucian showed you." Folding her arms, she rocked back on one heel. "Tell me, when did you slink back to the beach for the supplies you thought I'd have missed?"

Fengel flushed and looked away. "I was only going to watch you go through rum withdrawals, but it turns out you'd left. Along with pretty much everything that wasn't ruined." He looked pointedly around the clearing. "The tinderbox, at the very least, you found." Fengel stared abruptly at something behind her. "Oh my goodness. What is *that*?"

He strode farther into the clearing. Natasha glanced over her shoulder. The only thing behind her was her tent.

"Is that...some sort of barbaric lean-to?" He grinned viciously back at her. "It must be. It's got the blanket and twine from the crate."

"It's a tent," she said flatly.

"Of course, of course," he replied. "Only, it appears to have died of something. Some tropical disease, perhaps." He rubbed his beard. It was scruffy and unkempt. "No, I revise my earlier statement. Its demise appears to be due to an acute case of incompetence."

Natasha glared at him. "What are you even doing here?" she growled. "I thought you were going to 'show them all.' Shouldn't you be dashing into the waves after our loving crew?" He looked back at her, startled embarrassment plain upon his face. "Oh, that's right. It's funny, how far the wind can carry things. 'Lads, lads, come back.'"

Fengel flinched. He pretended to ignore her. "It just so happens," he said after a moment, "that discovering you here is merely an unpleasant surprise, as any right-thinking person would expect. I have decided to explore the rest of the island. And the only pass through the ridge I can see is a hill in this direction."

She raised an eyebrow. "You're going to explore the island?"

"Yes. And thank you for reminding me of that. Cheerio." He gave her a mock salute and crossed to the far side of the clearing. Without a backward glance, Fengel pushed into the greenery and was gone.

Natasha frowned. Something wasn't right. Her barb hit home, that was obvious. Their abandonment had affected him deeply. *So why isn't he sulking on the beach for another two days? Why this sudden urge to search the island? It's not even noon yet, for Goddess's sake.*

That had been her own plan, after he'd strode off down the beach yesterday. Establish a camp and find something other than rocklike hardtack or murderous salted jerky to eat. There had to be fruit, or something here. But there wasn't any reason, at least so far, to cover half the island for that.

Maybe he just can't stand being stuck so close to me. The thought was strangely angering. Well, fine, then. The farther away he was, the better. She'd do just fine on her own—

It came to her in a flash. *He's thought of another way off the island!*

Natasha dashed across the clearing and into the underbrush after her husband. Dense vines and thick ferns pushed her back. She fought them aside only to find more in her way. "Fengel!" she cried. "Get back here!"

His only reply was a hurried thrashing through the jungle.

She cursed and pushed on after him. Natasha ducked low branches, plowed through ferns, and jumped low roots. With every step forward, the jungle seemed to fight her back. She growled and redoubled her efforts, only to trip on a root and lose her balance. Hands out, she clutched at a low-hanging vine for support. It pulled free and writhed in her grip. Surprised, she glanced down. She was holding a thick green snake. It hissed angrily. Natasha windmilled to get her footing back, then whipped the disoriented snake with a flick of her wrist and sent it sailing off into the greenery.

Fengel continued to press forward while she paused for breath and balance. The air here was thick and heavy. Rich earth smells filled her nose, and sweat was already beading across her forehead.

Not rid of me that easily. Natasha narrowed her eyes, took a breath, and began the chase again. His wild clamber through the underbrush grew louder. She was gaining on him, she realized. Then she found out why. The earth beneath her feet was curved up into a slight incline; the hill he sought. Faintly Natasha remembered the ridge Fengel mentioned, how it descended from the volcano in the middle of the isle. This hill had to be just below it.

The incline became steeper. Natasha grabbed at the foliage and used it to pull herself along. The exertion and her long night were taking their toll. She grit her teeth and climbed. All around her, the jungle brightened as the foliage thinned. She could see him now, maybe two dozen paces ahead and almost crawling up the slope. Up a little higher loomed the top of the hill, an open space and brightly lit.

Natasha pulled herself to the trunk of a tree. She put her back to it, facing uphill. "Fengel!" she called out in between breaths. "I know you're up to something! What is it?"

He glanced back at her. "Nothing," he said, likewise panting. "Go light another fire. And this time, stand in it!"

She threw herself back at the hill as Fengel redoubled his efforts. A dozen feet became ten, then five. As he crested the hilltop, Natasha leapt, catching his boot around the ankle. He toppled and fell. She scrabbled into the sunlight atop him, rolling him over to grab the front of his shirt.

"You," she panted, "only get away when I *let* you. Now. What are you—"

His open palms clapped over both her ears. The world swam, and dark spots appeared in her vision. It felt like a mule had just kicked her in the head. Fengel rolled away as she toppled. Natasha crawled to hands and knees reflexively. When she looked up, Fengel was kneeling with his back against a rock, on guard.

Past him spread the hilltop, a flat plateau nestled in the crook between the black ridgeline and the rocky slope of the volcano. Basalt stones covered the springy grass that grew here, some of them just like the weird rock monoliths jutting up at irregular intervals from the steaming mountain. At the far end of the hill, a wide crack appeared in the ridgeline, allowing passage through. Behind them, the jungle spread in a verdant panorama all the way back down to the beach. She could even see the small black hole she had burned through the canopy last night.

Natasha ignored the view. It wasn't what was important. "Fess up now, you sly bastard. You found a way off the island, didn't you?"

"No," he said with a glower. "I have not."

"Liar. You've found another way off the island. But it's past the ridgeline. That's why you came up here."

Fengel shook his head. "You're mad. I've found nothing! Now go away and leave me alone, you lunatic."

She had him again. "You're *lying* Fengel. I can tell. I can always tell."

He glared at her. Then he stood and deliberately turned his back on her, before stalking across the hill for the pass through the ridge.

Natasha rose and followed. *Trying to ignore me now? Typical. Well, it's not going to work.* Her husband was clever, when he wanted to be. But he was never able to fool her for long. And he wasn't nearly as determined as she was.

They crossed to the rocky cliff that separated this portion of the island from the rest. Up close it looked strange—oddly smooth in some places, hard and brittle in others. *Lava flow,* she realized.

The crack in the ridgeline was easily wide enough for a man to pass through. Fengel entered with only a single backward glance, frowning as she followed him. Inside the passage, the bright midmorning sunlight faded to a dank gloom. Natasha kept an eye out for whatever it was he was looking for, determined to outwait him.

It didn't take long. Halfway through he whirled to confront her. "Goddess's teats! Will you leave me alone? Even marooned on an island, I can't get away from you."

"Tell me what you found," she said.

"Nothing!"

"Tell me what you found."

Fengel yelled in frustration. He stomped the earth and lashed at the air in frustration before facing her. "If I tell you," he said between pants, "will you go away?"

Natasha cocked her head to one side, considering. "Maybe," she said. The two of them were more-or-less evenly matched at the moment. But it seemed that the more passive avenues of aggression were still open to her. She was enjoying herself, she realized.

Fengel pointed up.

Natasha blinked at him. *Oh no you don't.*

He sighed. "Look up."

She shook her head. "I'm not falling for that."

"No, it's up there. Look up."

Warily, Natasha looked up to the volcano. On this face the slope was rocky and malformed. Though the crack in the ridge was tall, she could clearly see one of the large rock formations that dotted the side of the steaming mountain. It was different than the others, now that she bothered to look more closely, covered in vines and at least a hundred feet tall, wider across than the *Dawnhawk's* hull. There was something peculiar about it too....

Natasha blinked as she realized she was looking at a statue. It was ancient, of strange workmanship. Someone had carved a massive stone statue in the shape of an upright dragon. Over the years the foliage had grown to cover the thing. *How did I miss that from the beach?* Natasha pondered for a moment. She had to admit that she'd been *very* angry yesterday, though justifiably so.

"I don't get it," said Natasha, returning to the matter at hand. "How is that going to help you get off the island?"

Fengel grit his teeth and closed his eyes. "I was telling you the truth, you daft bint. I *haven't* found a way off the island. But I saw this yesterday, and thought about it some more. If it's not some ancient Voornish relic, then someone else had to carve it, which means that this island may not be deserted."

She blinked at him in confusion. "So?"

"So...maybe they have a boat, or at the least, food, fire and shelter."

Natasha blinked again. Then she started forward. She walked past Fengel toward the far end of the gap. Sunlight there revealed a similar grassy hill on this end.

"Hey!" shouted Fengel as he chased after her. "Where are you going?"

"I'm going to meet them first," she called over her shoulder.

"What? No, get back here. It's my plan!"

"Nope," she laughed.

"You horrible madwoman! Get back here! I thought of it first!"

The crack widened to reveal the opposite side of the ridge. Natasha heard him scrabbling after her and dashed out onto a grassy ledge that sloped its way down to more jungle. The island stretched before her in a similar panorama to the one behind her, thick jungle rolling all the way down to a beach. Past the beach the waters were blue and green, fringed by a rolling white surf that crashed onto the sands. Beyond them floated a wide wooden structure with three tall masts, the latter covered in the telltale white canvas of sails.

A ship.

Fengel crashed into her. "It's my idea, damn you. And you'll just screw everything up. You always do, you're too aggressive! But if we're going to get help, it'll take tact. It'll take subtlety."

She shoved him aside without looking, and he fell to the dirt. Fengel sprang back up with one hand formed into a fist, ready for another argument. Natasha pointed out at the ship. "Look," she said.

Her husband narrowed his eyes. "I'm not falling for that."

"No, out there. Look."

Fengel glared at her suspiciously, then slowly looked out at the ocean. Spying the ship, his hand fell back to his side, unclenched. "That's a ship," he said wonderingly.

"Huh," said Natasha. She raised an eyebrow at Fengel. "You're actually right for once. The island isn't deserted."

She whirled about and punched him in the ribs. He folded, eyes bugging wide and mouth comically open. Natasha leapt away and ran for the edge of the hill. Her husband made a high-pitched keening noise as she ran down and into the jungle.

The foliage was just as thick down here as it was on the other side. Vines, ferns, snakes and underbrush all hampered her movement. The gloom made her footing difficult, and until now she hadn't appreciated that Fengel had blazed a trail for her to follow during her earlier chase. Still, as long as she ran in a straight line, she'd reach the beach before he did.

A riot of color appeared, landing on a low branch just ahead of her. It was the parrot from this morning, or one close enough to it. The bird lifted its butter-colored beak in surprise at the racket she made. A gleeful cackle worked its way up her throat. Natasha made a fist and swung, putting all of her weight and momentum behind it.

The parrot squawked just as she hit it. Her knuckles hammered into its brightly-plumaged breast, connecting squarely and sending the obnoxious thing flying from its perch in a haze of rainbow feathers. Natasha laughed in glee and forged on ahead.

A noise reached her from behind, a crashing through the jungle only a short distance behind her. Apparently Fengel had recovered from her sucker-punch.

"Too late, hubby dearest," she called over her shoulder. "I'm going to be first!"

"So what?" he called up to her. "You don't even know who that is!"

Euron Blackheart would have warned her against being so hasty. Natasha didn't care. "It doesn't matter," she replied. "Sailors are sailors! I think I'll do the 'poor damsel' bit. Say you kidnapped and ravished me, oh woe. That always pulls the heartstrings." She laughed. "Just like that time off the coast of Capricanto! Remember that you *are* moderately infamous, Fengel dearest. A notorious criminal! Who wouldn't want to save me from you, and claim a fat bounty to boot? Then it's homeward bound, and *revenge.*"

"You're daft."

"Daft like a fox!"

"That's not how that goes!"

She laughed, refining her plan as she went. It was solid enough, one she'd used before in a pinch. Deception wasn't her favorite tactic, finding brute force and intimidation preferable. But Natasha had learned the lesson of practicality a long time ago. Ruthlessness only worked from a position of strength. Unfortunately, she didn't have that position at the moment, or any way to get it.

The jungle thinned. Beyond the crash and clatter of her movement through the underbrush, she heard something else: the faint roar of the sea. She was almost there. Natasha practiced her lines in her head. Fengel was right. She didn't know who the sailors were. But fortunately, she spoke several languages fluently.

The underbrush parted suddenly. The bare earth beneath her dropped away into a faint incline, sloping down a dozen feet to a wide patch of sand only intermittently broken by small tufts of yellow grass. The jungle spread out around it, stretching a little farther toward the surf.

There was a camp here.

It was not a small one, either. Out near the farthest edges of the jungle it started, a line of grey pup tents arranged with military precision into several orderly rows. Several campfires smoldered between them and a number of long trestle tables were covered with tools, plates, and muskets. The camp stretched all the way back down the beach to the tide line, where three longboats sat beached in the sand. Only a short distance away, too close to be anything but beached, sat the ship.

It was big, a warship. Either a ship-of-the-line or a very large frigate. She was new as well, with a steam stack in the stern and both port and starboard paddlewheels amidships. A triple-row of cannon nosed out of her ports to face the island, black barrels shiny in the morning sun. Faint golden lettering stood out just below the bowsprit, though she couldn't quite make out the name.

The camp was not empty. Men moved about without any sense of urgency, though there was a strange, almost mechanical pattern to the way they moved. She couldn't see their clothing too clearly from where she stood. That didn't mean much, though. Most navies were somewhat ragged in appearance.

A ship was a ship. So long as it sailed, and she got to it before Fengel, Natasha didn't care who was on it. She tore a sleeve and adjusted the neckline of her blouse lower. Then Natasha pinched the inside of her wrist until it hurt, and willed the tears to come. Mussing her hair, she ran forward.

Or started to. Fengel crashed out of the jungle and grabbed her wrist. *Oh, for the love of....*Natasha opened her mouth to snarl at him, then stopped. This could be good for her, actually. If someone saw them struggle, it would make her story all the more convincing.

"You horrible harpy," he growled. "You—"

Her husband cut short as he glanced up and took in the scene before them. Then he paled. Natasha drew in a breath to scream, trying not to smile.

Fengel promptly clapped a hand over her mouth and yanked her back into the jungle. She fought him, biting and swatting with her free hand.

"Good Goddess, stop!" he cried. "You haven't any idea what we're running into. That's a Perinese warship!"

Natasha bit his hand and slammed her heel down on Fengel's toes. He fell away with a yelp.

"Help!" she cried.

Fengel cursed and grabbed her around the waist. She made to plant her knee in his jaw, then checked herself. *Wait. Weak and helpless, remember.* Natasha flailed ineffectively at his back.

"Oh, help me!" she cried again.

"Confound it, woman!" growled Fengel. "Stop!"

The bushes off to one side parted. Five men in the blue uniforms of Perinese Bluecoat marines appeared, muskets at the ready. Natasha noted that they were likely a watch picket; they hadn't come from the beach.

Perfect.

"Get him off me!" she implored the men.

Fengel looked around and swore. He released her and tried to run the way they'd come, but it was too late. Two of the Bluecoats stepped in and clubbed him in the back with the stocks of their weapons. Already half-bent, he collapsed to the jungle floor.

Natasha let herself fall to her knees. Shouts came from the direction of the beach. The commotion had been noticed.

One of the Bluecoats stepped forward and held out a hand, bowing low. He was tall and fit, with a long nose and oily curls bound into a ponytail beneath his tricorn hat.

"Are you all right, good lady?" he asked.

Natasha sniffed and tried not to smile. "I am now," she replied.

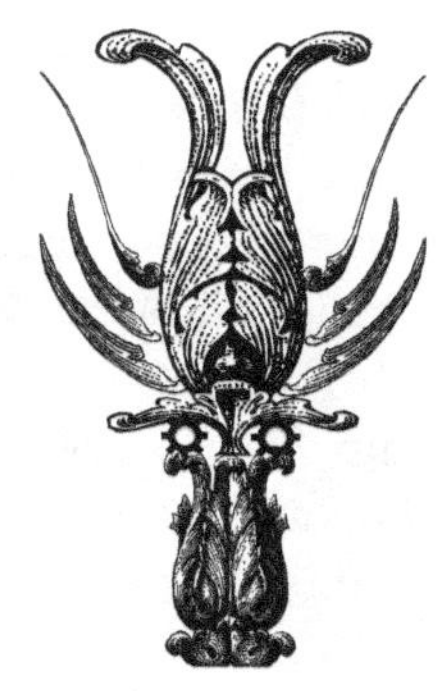

CHAPTER SEVEN

Captain Fengel wondered what he had done to deserve this fate.

That meat pie I stole from Matron Shrieveport? No, I was only seven. And besides, she'd gone round the bend and was making pasties out of all those husbands she'd axed. Hmm. I did drop Black Robin adrift in the ocean with nothing but an empty pickle barrel. Though, in my defense, the fellow did try to murder me.

A thought occurred to him.

Could it be all the piracy? Surely not. There was that missionary ship with all those nuns. We did *stay on and patch things up for them again, though. And my apology was very eloquent.*

The sharp tip of a bayonet poked him in the back. Fengel glared back at the man, but picked up his pace. There wasn't any point in antagonizing the Bluecoats further.

Five of the blue-coated soldiers marched him down the beach toward their camp. All were simple privates, fresh-faced youths conscripted from the inner counties back in the Kingdom of Perinault. The sixth and last was a naval officer, a sub-lieutenant by the braid below his shoulder. He stood a little taller than Fengel, with a long nose and oily curls bound into a ponytail. The sub-lieutenant walked at the head of the group, leading the way back while Natasha simpered at his side.

She glanced back over her shoulder to wink at him. Incoherent rage boiled up inside Fengel. Natasha had done it to him again, had won out against the odds, clawing her way up over him to grasp victory. They weren't even fighting over anything this time. Goddess knows he'd meant to avoid her as long as he could. He'd only left the beach to find out who had carved the dragon up on the mountain. Who they were, or if they were even human didn't matter. They'd at least have fire and food, a significant improvement over the last night's miserably rugged experience.

And now here they were, captured by the Royal Navy of the Kingdom of Perinault.

They descended to the camp. It was very recent. The tents were set out in traditional military formation, a long, orderly line of cloth with a latrine dug off behind it. Several fire pits ranged down its length. Crates, sacks, and other supplies were stacked neatly in large piles to one side, the sheer volume surprising. These had to be most of the supplies from their ship, including several large barrels of black powder. Behind those hunkered a portable ship's forge—poorly placed, in his opinion.

Nostalgia washed over him. The camp was set with a mindless order-for-order's-sake mentality that he remembered from his navy days. The fire pits were directly in the way of the wind, not sheltered at all by the jungle or the ship, as common sense would dictate. The latrines were also dug slightly uphill from the tents; a rather foolish thing if one stopped to think about it, yet perfectly in accordance with the Military Code of Instruction.

Past the camp was the ship itself. Three things struck Fengel about it. First was its anchorage. The vessel was far too close to shore, and thus surely grounded. The second was its unfamiliar make. She was a ship-of-the-line, though small and built for speed, with modern paddlewheels amidships. Lastly was the gold lettering across her bow. This was the *H.M.S. Goliath.*

That's the missing escort for the Minnow. Now, what is she doing here?

The sailors and Bluecoat marines of the camp crowded around as Fengel and his captors approached. One of the marines stepped out from the press. Fengel blinked at him. The bars on his shoulder denoted him a sergeant, but the man was a hunk of jerky in uniform. Beady eyes stared out from beneath a slanting brow and a lumpy, repeatedly broken nose. Cauliflower ears adorned the sides of his head.

"What you got there, Hayes?" he asked

"I'm not entirely certain, Sergeant," said the sub-lieutenant. "They stumbled over our picket—"

"Oh," cried Natasha. She clung to Hayes's arm and pressed herself against the man. "They *saved* me. Just as I was about to be ravaged by that brute of a pirate."

Fengel grit his teeth. His wife was in fine form at the moment.

"A pirate?" said the sergeant. "Here?" he frowned, then peered at Fengel and Natasha more closely.

"Well, they're not from the *Salmalin,*" replied Hayes.

"He's not. But with skin like that, she could be, and the golden eyes to boot. She speaks the King's tongue without an accent, though. That says Copper Isles pirate to me."

It seemed to Fengel that his own status was a foregone conclusion. Cheerfully, though, everyone now stared anew at Natasha, and not in befuddled admiration. A surprised frown flashed across her face, so quick only Fengel recognized it. He smiled and reappraised the battered Bluecoat. The man was a brute, but a clever one.

"That's ridiculous," snarled Natasha. She caught herself and fell against Hayes's chest. "However could you think such a thing?" She gazed imploringly up at the sub-lieutenant with glistening eyes.

Fengel rolled his eyes. *Oh, for the love of the Goddess.* His wife preferred brutality and ruthlessness, which was why she only had a few simple tricks up her sleeve. Unfortunately, this one seemed to be working. It usually did, when she bothered. The sub-lieutenant had that slack-jawed, glazed-over look that Fengel had seen far too often on other men.

"Nonsense," said Hayes. He smiled slightly. "The poor lass has obviously suffered very dearly at the hands of this man. I'm taking them both to the Commander, and we'll whistle the truth out of him then. Your business, *Sergeant* Cumbers, is to tighten the perimeter against any of this fellow's associates."

Hayes glared for a moment before resuming his pace back towards the ship, gently supporting Natasha. The sergeant narrowed his eyes at the sub-lieutenant, then turned back to the other Bluecoats.

"Oily peacock," he muttered. "You heard 'im, lads. Get back to your pickets. Smith, fall out and join the others. I'll help escort this prisoner off to the Commander. That smarmy fool doesn't tell *me* what to do." Then Sergeant Cumbers took the lead of the marines and prodded Fengel down to the beach.

Hmm, mused Fengel. *Discontent among the ranks? What's the story here?*

The party reached the shore, where Hayes was helping Natasha into one of the longboats resting on the sand. Fengel got in at musket-point, then sat quietly as the Bluecoats heaved the vessel into the water and climbed aboard. Two grabbed oars and pushed them out toward the *Goliath.*

While Natasha whispered thankful nothings to Sub-Lieutenant Hayes up in the bow, Fengel focused on the approaching warship. She was definitely beached, sitting only a few hundred feet from the shore and ever-so-slightly atilt, so that her starboard broadside presented itself almost to the camp. The rigging was tattered, and signs of new woodwork were apparent along the deck. This ship had seen battle, and recently.

The longboat pulled up aside the warship, just behind the large steam-driven paddlewheel. Hayes called out, and a rope ladder was dropped down from above. He led the way, followed by Natasha, and then Fengel. Cumbers and the other marines still down in the boat watched his wife climb with small smiles, occasionally elbowing each other. Fengel, they followed with muskets.

Never let them see you stumble. Fengel maintained his composure on the way up, but his irritation at Natasha paled before the reality of stepping aboard a Navy warship again for the first time in a decade. Tyranny, poverty, and risking life and limb for a commanding officer who didn't even know your name. That was what he'd left behind. No, more than left behind. He'd stolen the horse and burned the bridge, changing himself into something completely antithetical to these people. And the Royal Navy weren't the forgiving sort.

Maybe it wouldn't be so bad. Something was bound to come up. All he needed was an opportunity. Several potential possibilities, such as the split between the sergeant and Hayes, had presented themselves already. Fengel gritted his teeth and climbed onto the deck.

The *H.M.S. Goliath* was a warship, with every bit reflecting that fact. Her lines were straight, efficient. Cannons ran in orderly rows down either side of the deck like stubby iron teeth. She even bore two pair of chase guns up at the bow, heavy Long Nines. The poop deck atop the stern was low, with two swivel guns for the helm crew, mounted for use in boarding actions.

Strangely though, the ship was almost abandoned. Aside from an older man who might have been the carpenter and his assistants, there were no sailors, no more Bluecoats. Unless they were all below, the *Goliath* had lost a fair share of crew. Those back down on the beach didn't nearly account for the complement he would expect aboard.

Cumbers and three of the Bluecoat marines ascended from the longboat below. A mad thought bloomed in Fengel's mind. Kick the first one off the ladder as he climbed aboard, then a right hook to Hayes, subdue him just long enough to take his sword…but no. He was too far down the mouth of the dragon at this point. Where would he go? Perhaps he could dive off the starboard side of the ship, swim around to another part of the island. More likely Hayes would run him through, or a musket ball would catch him as he swam.

"Riley Gordon," called Hayes. "Run along to the commander and let him know we've caught a prize."

Fengel looked over to see one of the carpenter's assistants approaching from up the deck. Riley was a young man, small and thin, who moved with the furtive air of someone hoping not to be seen. He balanced a heavy timber across one shoulder and seemed to be having trouble with it.

"I'm busy," said Riley. "Gotta get this down to the poop deck."

Fengel blinked at the disrespect. On a Perinese ship that kind of attitude would be punished with the lash. Something odd was going on, or Hayes was not very well-liked. He studied the sub-lieutenant. *Probably both.*

"You're right you're busy," said Hayes. Color rose in his cheeks. "You're going to drop that timber and run along to the commander before I jam it so far up your arse you'll be spitting splinters."

Riley flinched. He ducked his head and set the board on the deck with difficulty. When he straightened, he gave a sloppy, defiant salute to Hayes, then jogged down toward the sterncastle cabin.

Hayes said something under his breath and jerked his head in the same direction. Cumbers grinned openly, then signaled the Bluecoats to prod Fengel forward. As he went, Natasha caught his eye. She smiled—a small, satisfied thing meant only for him. Fengel ignored her and stood a little straighter, made sure his hat was aligned and his monocle was clamped tightly into place. The scratch over its lens gave the stern of the ship a marred appearance.

Hayes stopped before the sterncastle door. Riley Gordon had shut it after entering a few moments ago, another insult to the sub-lieutenant. Hayes rapped lightly with a knuckle.

"Enter," croaked an imperious voice.

Hayes opened the door and stepped inside. Natasha followed, and a Bluecoat prodded Fengel again with his bayonet. He glared at the man before following his wife. *I am going to need a new coat after all this.*

The tang of whiskey and the sweet-sour smell of corruption filled the air, undercutting the faint aroma of stale sweat. Fengel took a moment to let his eyes adjust to the gloom before going any further.

The cabin wasn't spacious. Unlike his own, sumptuous lodgings aboard the *Dawnhawk*, the space was barely large enough for the six other people in the room. Hayes and Natasha stood just before him, framed against little Riley Gordon. The center of the room was dominated by a large captain's table, a multipurpose piece of furniture that could host dinners and hold charts. Atop it sat a heavyset older man in officer's clothing. His breaths rasped overloud in the space, and it was obvious that there was something wrong with him. Even though his shirt was open to the belly and his graying curls were damp with sweat, he exuded a presence of dignity and control. *This must be the commander,* Fengel realized.

Another figure stood behind the commander, a gaunt fellow with a shock of white hair. Both his hands were spread above the shoulders of the man before him, a bright, electric light dancing between his fingertips in time with the commander's labored breathing. Fengel blinked in surprise. Perinese ships didn't often have an aetherite aboard.

The last person in the room was a young boy in midshipman's clothing. He stood beside the commander with a damp rag and a bucket. Periodically he dabbed sweat from the commander's cheeks and brow.

"You had better have a damned good reason for interrupting," said the commander. His voice was imperious, rich and cultured, the very sound Fengel had always aspired to. "Mr. Dawkins's Workings are in short supply these days, and they're the only thing keeping me upright."

"Of course, Commander Coppertree," said the sub-lieutenant. Hayes's earlier pomposity was gone, replaced by oily obsequiousness. "My picket happened across this poor lass out in the jungle. We barely saved her from being ravished by this brute of a pirate here."

Damnation! He was actually repeating Natasha's spiel. This was a poor way to be introduced to the leadership here. Possibly the poorest. "That is a ridiculous and base assertion—"

The butt of a musket hammered into the backs of his knees. Fengel toppled mid-sentence to the floor of the cabin.

"Shut it, you," growled Sergeant Cumbers.

Fengel pursed his lips. Carefully, he climbed back to his feet.

"Pirates?" scoffed the Commander. "Out here? Well now, that seems moderately unlikely." He glanced at Natasha. "What is your story, madam?"

Fengel looked the man over again carefully. There was something odd about his voice. He spoke with difficulty, as if he wasn't getting enough air. His throat was slightly distended and his veins stood out against his pale skin. The whole scene struck Fengel as oddly familiar, somehow. Where had he heard of an illness like this?

Natasha touched a hand to the small of her throat. When she spoke up, her voice was choked, anguished. "It was horrible. Just…just horrible. I—"

"They're both pirates," said the boy with the rag.

Commander Coppertree peered over at him. "Eh? What's this now, young Paine?"

The boy nodded. "I studied the postings like you told me to, sir. They're air pirates, the both of them." He gestured. "That one's Captain Fengel of the *Flittergrasp*. And she's Natasha Blackheart. There's a big prize for the both of them."

"Oh really now," said Coppertree. He glanced back to the assemblage before him. "And what do you have to say to this?"

"The boy is mistaken," growled Natasha, her irritation shredding any hint of helplessness.

Fengel straightened. He might not be able to save himself, but he would be damned to the Realms Below if he wasn't taking Natasha with him. "My apologies for the ruse," he said. "Mrs. Blackheart simply doesn't know when she's lost. You have us both dead to rights. But you have, however, missed out on one important fact."

"Oh?"

"Yes. Unlike her, I am a *gentleman*."

Silence filled the room, but for the hissing pop of the aetherite's spell, and the faint sound of Natasha grinding her teeth.

"I see," said Coppertree. His eyes were sunken, and his breaths more shallow. "Sergeant Cumbers, is that you I spy in the doorway?"

The Bluecoat sergeant touched his forehead in obeisance. "Aye, sir."

"How did *Hayes* find these two, and not your pickets?"

Cumbers blanched. "Dumbest luck sir. The men are arrayed—"

"Insufficiently," interrupted the Commander. "Toss these two into the brig. And you can help guard them yourself for the moment. Once we deal with the Salomcani and get ourselves righted again, we can haul them back to the admiralty and have a big show of hanging them."

"Sir!" protested Cumbers.

"No!" hissed Natasha. "Wait, this is a mistake—"

"Come now, dearest," said Fengel with a savage glee. "These men are professionals. They've surely got our number."

"Shut up!" she snarled at him. Natasha glared at Midshipman Paine. "You little shit. I'm going to cut out that tongue of yours and wear it as a necklace. I'm going to turn your feet into—"

Paine recoiled. The Bluecoats intervened, led by a now-angered Sergeant Cumbers. They wrestled Fengel and Natasha back outside and then down below. The lower decks of the *Goliath* swept by at a blur, yet it was still everything that Fengel expected from the interior of a warship, oiled wood and military efficiency. They were brought to a padlocked cell on the berth deck near the stern, three walls of stout iron bars built up against the starboard-side hull.

Fengel went first, offering no resistance. Suspecting what was coming next, he stepped aside just in time to hear a cry of pain from one of the marines, and to see Natasha thrown to the cell floor. The door slammed shut and the Bluecoats glared at the two of them, one shaking his hand where Natasha had bit him, the other locking the padlock closed again.

Most of the men left. One young marine stayed behind along with Sergeant Cumbers. They sat at a table a short distance away, glaring at the prisoners and muttering to each other. Fengel glanced down the rest of the deck. It was wide and open, hammocks hanging from the bulkheads below the portholes, sea-chests positioned beneath these in turn. Spears of daylight were the only illumination.

He smiled cheerfully at Natasha as she stood. "That certainly went well."

"Shut up," she snarled.

"It was *such* a devious, cunning plan. 'Make sultry noises at the nearest officer in charge.' Inspiring. It almost worked too. Except that you apparently attached yourself to the most hated man in the crew. Pity that Bluecoat sergeant, the commander, and even his cabin boy had the good sense the Goddess gave most things that can walk to ask who in the Realms Below you were."

Natasha glared at him, one eyelid twitching. "I didn't see you enacting any clever plan."

"No!" shouted Fengel. "Once I saw that it was a *Perinese warship,* I was going to run away. But you had to run your damned fool self right at it, just for the chance to screw me over!"

"You want an apology?" she spat. "You're not getting one. I saw a chance and took it. You're the one who's content to spend the rest of your days trapped on this island. Me? I've got blood in my veins, not milk. I want revenge. I'm going to get off this rock and get my ship back, and those pissant crewmen of yours are going to regret ever even thinking of mutiny."

Fengel rolled his eyes. "Who do you think you're fooling? Me? Listen to yourself." He affected a high-pitched falsetto. "'Oh, my incredibly foolish plan to sleep my way home aboard a *Navy warship* didn't work out. I think I'll rant for awhile about how mean and vengeful I am.'" He shook his head. "Please. And don't talk to me as if this were all my people's fault. This is the *second time* you've had a mutiny led against you. Or do you keep forgetting that? You're a terrible captain."

"Terrible?" she stepped up to him, her chest almost touching his. "At least I *am* one. Lucian, Henry, and that giantess of yours do all your real work."

Fengel ignored the jibe. "You're only a pirate because men won't pay to sleep with you," he growled. "And you're only a 'captain' because of your father."

Natasha blanched as if he'd shot her. Then her features hardened into an ugly, angry mask. "You dare?" she hissed, voice tight with sudden rage.

"Oh yes," he said with relish. Fengel felt weirdly buoyant, excited. Years of resentment and frustration boiled up. He couldn't stop. He didn't want to stop. Fengel bulled on before she could recover from her shock. "You don't know the first damned thing about leading a crew of men. You mistake brutality for coercion and think attractiveness leads to admiration in others. You're a cruel, greedy woman, who shirks any responsibility to drown herself in drink and bedplay with utter strangers. Mordecai Wright covered for your flaws with his strengths. He was a bastard, but an efficient bastard, and efficiency is something that's absolutely alien to you. Old Euron Blackheart gave you your first ship, it was his reputation that made your crew sign on as well. And look how you've cocked up all three of those things. Admit it: you haven't got a damned thing of worth going for you on your own."

He glanced over at Sergeant Cumbers and the other guard. Both watched in bemusement. Fengel winked at them.

Natasha sucker-punched him in the gut. His air whooshed out of him and he folded down to the deck.

"You smarmy sack of scryn-leavings," she snarled. "You're in love with the sound of yer own voice more than you ever were with me. You've got an awful lot of answers for a glorified figurehead. The monocle, the hat, the stiff upper lip, they're all just bits and props for you, an attempt at legitimacy. A real man wouldn't need them, he wouldn't even think of them!" She put a foot on his shoulder and kicked him over. "You're a fat sack of hot air, and you weren't ever anything else. Without your crew you're *nothing*, and you never were."

A red haze covered his vision. He tried to marshal a rebuttal, but the words didn't come. Her jibes shouldn't have touched him, they were small and he'd heard it all before. But somehow, something was different now.

He reached out and grabbed her standing leg with both hands, yanking her knee toward him. She toppled with a surprised cry and hit the deck. Natasha was quick, back up and on her knees before he could move. But he was ready. His open-handed slap cracked across her face.

Words finally came. "The *Flittergrasp* was mine!" he roared. "The *Dawnhawk* is mine! My crew listens to me because I lead them. *I'm* the one who decides and directs them. I clawed my way up from slavery on a stinking Perinese frigate to be a better, fitter captain than you could ever hope to be!"

She recovered from his blow to lash out with her hands, viper quick. They closed on his throat. He raised his own to free himself, but moved too slowly. Natasha wasn't intending to choke him. Her forehead rammed into his face, right between his eyes. The world shifted and brilliant stars bloomed across it.

"I'll kill you," she snarled. "You puffed-up piece of trash. I've pillaged more, plundered more, than you could ever hope. I'm a *real* pirate: what you only pretend to be. You were busy throwing away your airship in Triskelion while I was reaping my own weight in gold. When men talk about the airship pirates of the Copper Isles, they're talking about *me*. You'll never amount to anything. I'll come back from this and be more terrible, feared, and successful than you could ever dream of being!"

He bent his head and bit at her knuckles. Natasha yelled in pain. All his words were gone now, and there was only the rage he held for the woman in front of him.

Distantly, he heard the click of the padlock and the metallic squeal of the cell door opening, followed by the tromping boots of the Bluecoats. Natasha grunted as they rapped her with their musket-butts. He smiled. Then they laid into him as well.

The guards hauled her out of the cell and off across the deck. She screamed and swore at him. He replied, shocked on a dim level by how incoherent he was. When she disappeared above-decks, he crawled back to sit against the bulkhead, panting.

Something wet was all over his face. Stunned, he realized his nose was bleeding, spilling down to stain his shirt. He pinched it shut and breathed through his mouth. Weirdly, Natasha's yelling grew somehow louder. The staccato rap of boot heels on the ceiling deck above helped him understand. They grew until he heard the clink of chains, and her awful epithets echoing as if she was only a room away.

Fengel glanced up until he found it, a small empty knothole in the wood of the deck above him, little bigger around than his thumb.

He listened to his wife rant and rage until it palled. Occasionally, the urge to yell back at her, to continue letting her know what he thought of her, took hold. But everything tasted of copper, and he didn't trust himself not to sound too nasal. Instead, he watched as Sergeant Cumbers and his other guard returned.

Both sat at a nearby table and ignored him. Cumbers dabbed gently at a newly bloodied lip. The other fellow was the same from a moment ago, a young, freckled man with a thin, sandy mustache, obviously still on his first tour of duty.

"As if we didn't have enough to deal with," muttered Cumbers. He shook his head. "Pirates."

"Don't know why the commander didn't just have us shoot 'em," replied the other.

"Well, if these two are semi-famous"—he thrust a thumb toward Fengel—"then there's a fat bit of prize money once we deal with the Salomcani and make it back home, and they'll still be just as dead then as now."

The sandy-haired fellow nodded. He produced a deck of cards. Cumbers took them and dealt out hands for a game. They proceeded to play before the younger one looked up again. "Sergeant...you think we're going to be able to fight off the Salomcani? That we'll get home?"

Sergeant Cumbers made a dismissive gesture. "Pshaw. Course we are. You saw how they ran from us after that last action. *Goliath* is a trim ship. If we hadn't run aground on...whatever that is down there, we'd have chased the *Salmalin* down and finished her off by now. She was taking on water last we saw: she's somewhere else on the island. No, Simon, me lad, once Commander Coppertree is better, we'll track down that floating barge of theirs and clean it of their backward kind, get what we need to patch up, and be steaming on home."

The younger Bluecoat, Simon, licked his lips nervously. "Commander's gonna be okay, though, right? Only, he don't look so good. And next down the chain is Hayes."

Cumbers grunted. He paused in dealing out the next hand of cards. "That, the commander does not. Hadn't seen him since we landed here, actually. He's definitely looking the worse for wear. But he's made of iron, our commander. And he's got Mr. Dawkins with him; aetherite'll keep him going." The soldier pointed a finger at his friend. "And let me tell you, don't be worrying about Hayes. Ain't a true Kingdom marine going to follow that oily bastard should it come to it. No matter if he's next in line. I watch after you boys, and I aim to see you get proper treatment."

Fengel cocked his head. *So that's it. There's a hole gaping in the chain of command.* He glanced back at the knothole, narrowed his eyes, then scooted closer to his guards, up against the front bars to the cell.

"Excuse me," Fengel said. "I couldn't help but overhear. What's wrong with your commander?"

Both guards looked back at him. "Shut it, you," said Simon. "Yer bound for a noose and that's that."

Fengel raised an eyebrow. "My word. I was simply curious. There's no need for rudeness."

The men stared at him. Then Sergeant Cumbers barked out a laugh. "Listen to you. Not a quarter-glass ago, you an' yer girl were fit to tear each other apart. No need for rudeness. Ha!"

The mention of Natasha made his gorge rise. "Alas," he said with deepest loathing, "I have the unfortunate luck to be married to that abominable creature."

"Huh," grunted Cumbers. "She's easy on the eyes, at least."

"Let me assure you, good fellow, that it is not worth the price I've paid. I would be much obliged if you would put a bullet in her heart. Preferably silver, and blessed by a priest."

The guards stared at him. Then Cumbers chuckled. Simon joined in, and Fengel smiled. "Heh," replied the scarred Bluecoat after a moment. "I think I said just the same thing about my own fourth wife, that harpy." He sobered. "But don't think that'll get you any closer to freedom."

Fengel waved a dismissive hand. "Perish the thought. I was simply curious. You appear to have had a rather rough time of it, was all."

Cumbers nodded. "Aye. Had a three-day running fight with those Salomcani raiders. Took our fair share of knocking about, but drove them down to this little spit o' land. Before we can track them to the far side of the island, though, we run aground. Damnedest thing too, from what the ship's craftsmen tells me. Salomcani trap or something weirder."

"Oh yeah," said the other guard. "Big hunk of brass poking through our hold. I saw it, the other day. Hayes sent me down there to help out. Huge bloody hole in the hull. I think it's Voornish!"

"Voornish?" mused Sergeant Cumbers. "Now there's a thought. Anyway, just as we're about to set out, Commander comes down with something awful. S'keeping him laid up, like you saw. Aetherite's keeping him steady so he can recover. If you trust that witchery."

"What's wrong with him?" asked Fengel.

"Oh, all sorts. Bleeding from the ears, nose, mouth, other places what don't bear thinking on. Can't breath easy either, or get enough water from what I hear. That's sore going: we haven't found a spring on this island yet." The soldier looked away, hiding the uncertainty in his face.

It came to Fengel in a flash. "Gimbal's Flux," he said. No wonder the Commander's symptoms had seemed familiar. During his first trip to the equator years ago he'd contracted it. It was an obnoxious and awful disease that he'd never heard of before that point. *And there we have our final opportunity*, he thought.

"What?" asked the guard. "What're you on about?"

"It sounds like Gimbal's Flux," repeated Fengel. "I had it several years ago. A lot like the scurvy, really. It's lethal if not treated right. A fairly simple thing to do, though."

The guards looks at each other. "This ain't some joke," said Cumbers. Any nascent friendliness evaporated.

Fengel raised his hands innocently. "Dear fellow, I wasn't pretending it was one. But all your commander needs is a strong dose of lemon juice, as much as he can take, for the next three days. That, fresh air, clean, boiled water and fish liver squeezings will put him right as rain. A perfectly harmless treatment for a sick man or a healthy one." He waited a moment and cocked his head. "Haven't you a surgeon on board?"

The men digested this. Cumbers stood abruptly. "No. Fellow took a scimitar to the gut during the last boarding action." He looked to his fellow. "Mr. Dawkins needs to hear about this." He turned back to Fengel. "And if you're lying, we'll string you up ourselves, bounty be damned."

Fengel spread his hands again. "Believe me, sir, I've nothing to gain at all. But, as I said before, I am a *gentleman*."

The guards stared at him a long moment. Fengel held their gazes. Cumbers nodded, then took his fellow away to the upper decks. Fengel watched them go, then stood and checked the bars of the cage.

It was locked tight and without weakness, as he'd expected. *Ah well.* He looked around the deck, peering outside through the porthole, then up at the knothole.

Fengel grabbed the ribbing of the bulkhead wall of the brig. He lifted himself up until he could place his head reasonably near the hole.

"I know you heard all of that," he said harshly. "So, hear this too. You thought that if you moved quickly enough, forcefully enough, that you would succeed with only a simple trick. Well, you failed, because you are not clever, you are not patient. Now watch and learn, you horrible bitch. I'll show you how a real leader reverses his circumstances. I did it once before, and I can do it here too. And when I'm on top, the only things you'll get will be what I give you. I'll say yes and let you have whatever you want. But only when you *ask* me. And you'll know each and every time that what you have is only what I choose to bestow you."

Her answering stomp sent dust through the hole. Fengel jerked his head to one side. He lowered himself back down to the floor and sat. Then he waited for his guards to return.

Fengel smiled.

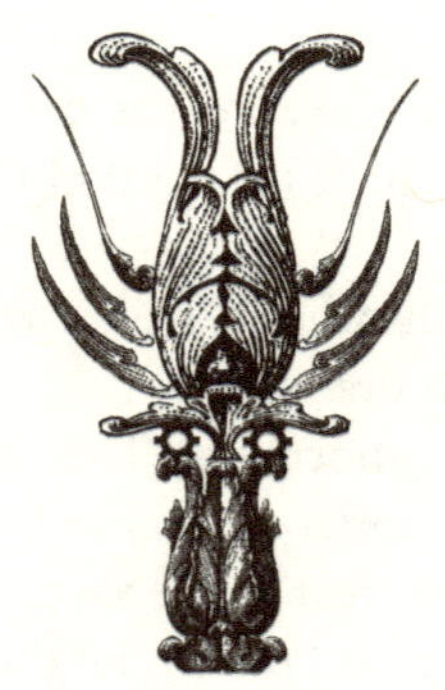

CHAPTER EIGHT

"I'm gonna buy a man," said Andrea Holt

Lina stared at her friend.

"Now, what's that look for?" Andrea shook a piece of rope at her. "Don't you be judging me, 'Miss I-left-the-cathouse-to-be-a-pirate.'"

"No, not that." Lina shook her head. "I just always thought you and Ryan were a couple."

Both of them sat on the upper deck of the *Dawnhawk,* where the starboard exhaust pipe emerged. It ran down along the gunwales and out past the stern, puffing steam in a thick white contrail, the impermanent footprint of the airship upon the sky. Lina preferred this spot when she had nothing pressing to do, as it was always warm and gave cover against the weather if she sat down behind it. On a clear night like tonight, it was the perfect place to finish simple tasks.

"On and off," agreed Andrea. "But you've got me to thinking, lately. Why should I let myself get tied down? Besides, I've got to spend my share of the loot on *something.* Three raids in as many days! If we keep getting this lucky, we won't have to hit Breachtown at all."

Lina rolled her eyes. "It's not luck."

And it wasn't. At least, not entirely. They'd taken surprisingly few casualties during the *Kingfisher* raid, along with a nice bit of loot for the hold. But the Royal Marines had been a nasty surprise, one that had made the crew more cautious. The pair of stray merchant freighters they'd found afterward had been hit quickly and efficiently along their way to Breachtown.

Andrea waved the subject away. "Anyway. I told you what I'm gonna get. What about you?"

"Oh, I don't know." Lina dropped the old rope they were working on unraveling, still mostly in one piece. She reached up and scratched Runt where he coiled atop the exhaust pipe. The scryn made a soft chirrup, contented. "Clothes and whatnot, a bit of drink for Runt. Maybe a new knife. It's nice just to *have* it, y'know? I like coming back to port and having Mr. Grey show me my account. And this next time, it's gonna be fat."

Andrea blinked at her. "You leave your stash with Grey?"

"Sure. Safer than a bank. He's with the Sindicato, right? Who's going to cross them?"

Her friend touched Lina's forearm gently. "Lina, dearest. The Sindicato are thieves."

"Well, yeah, sure. But they're all about *business*," she replied. "You know, profitability. Taking a cut of what I deposit makes more money over the long run than just taking what I give them. I'd never come back again if they nicked it all once, right?"

Her friend looked out over the deck. The Wiley twins were fooling around on the rigging opposite, illuminated by moonlight. Nate, the injured one, laughed at something his brother did. "I suppose that makes sense." she said after a moment.

Lina bulled on. "Look. Where are you keeping your sovereigns? The rings I see, that's a classic, but let me guess, the rest is in your kit bag, right? In the bottom rolled up in a kerchief or a stocking?"

Andrea started. "How did you know that?"

Lina gave her a dry look. "Please. It's the same thing I did at first. It's what all the sailors I used to know did, back in Triskelion. A ship's a ship. None of us have any private space. We don't even keep the same hammocks. What's to stop someone like Oscar Pleasant from taking my stash when I'm not looking?" She shook her head. "No, deposit with the Sindicato has worked well, when I've actually got something for them to hold. You should give it some thought."

Andrea rubbed her chin. "I dunno. At least I know where my money is, and anyone that touches it is going to suffer...but I suppose it's worth thinking about."

They went back to unraveling the rope. Lina kept her face still, hoping her argument had been convincing. She'd practiced the pitch quietly to herself often enough, but this was her first attempt on another person. *Need to tighten it before I talk to the others*, she thought. *At least, if I want that finder's fee from Grey. Hmm. Who next? Maxim? Or would an aetherite just trust to his spells to keep his things safe?*

Tromping footsteps interrupted her thoughts. Lina looked up to see Allen stalking up the deck. In his goggles and buttoned greatcoat, he *almost* looked like the Mechanist that he strived to be. But only almost. The coat was a little too large for him, and he fought constantly with the goggles.

Allen stopped in front of them. He bowed low with one hand behind his back. "Fairest Lina," he said, voice muffled through the collar of his greatcoat. "Your radiance shines brighter than the jewels for which your forebears were named."

Lina stared at him silently. Andrea covered her mouth and tried not to laugh. She failed.

"'Stone' is a common name in Triskelion," Lina replied flatly. "Like 'Smith' in Perinault. As for my parents, my mother left me on the poorhouse step when I was a babe. The matron there sold me off to a bordello as soon as I had my first blood. How does *that* reflect on my forebears?"

Allen stared at her through his goggles, uncertain. "Um," he mumbled.

Lina rolled her eyes. "Was there something you needed to tell me?"

He started. "Oh. Oh yes. Committee-Member Thorne sent me up to get you, said he wanted you present for a meeting in the ship's galley."

So that's where Sarah Lome disappeared to. Lina groaned. She was starting to regret ever suggesting the idea of the committee. The crew were working well together when Lucian was in charge and there was plunder to be had. But otherwise, everyone just kind of...dithered. Nothing ever got done in the committee meetings.

She dropped the rope and climbed to her feet. "All right then." She turned to Andrea. "I might not be back for a while."

Her friend shrugged, still amused over Allen's flattery.

Lina held out an arm toward the exhaust pipe. "Runt? You coming?"

The scryn opened one sleepy eyelid. The secondary membrane slid back more slowly. "Chirr," he said in disinterest.

"Suit yourself," she replied, feeling just a little betrayed. Not even her pet wanted to be involved in the meetings anymore. Lina looked back to Allen. "I assume you've some excuse for walking me belowdecks? Supplies that need checking or some such?"

Allen looked away and shuffled his feet. "Need to grease the lift from the coal stores to the engine room."

Lina nodded. "I thought so. Let's be off then."

She led the way down the mostly empty deck. It struck her then how strange that was. Quiet nights were just that. When there weren't any pressing duties, Gunnery Mistress Lome usually gave out busy work, though sometimes she let them slack. Yet even when she did, the *Dawnhawk* was still occupied, the crew all near their stations and waiting until the change of watch at dawn. Now it was just…empty. Fat Thomlin and Tricia lounged up near the bow, playing dice. Andrea and Runt crouched against the starboard exhaust pipe. At the helm stood Maxim, lazily keeping their course true by himself.

That was an even stranger thing to see. The aetherite and his counterpart had been like two male cats ever since the merging of the crews. Both refused to give up their place at the helm. They spent their Workings and spells either harassing each other or keeping themselves awake for days at a time. Ever since dropping off the captains, however, they'd simply stopped. Neither had spoken about it to anyone else, or acted like anything was out of the ordinary. Now Konrad usually took the day-watch and Maxim the evening, with Henry Smalls taking over in between, as an aetherite was only needed for course correction along the curved aetherlines and to guide them through junctions where the pathways met. Lina, like everyone else, didn't quite know what to make of the situation.

As she watched, Elly Minel passed by the helm, and Maxim waved cheerily at her, motioning the pirate woman over for a chat. Lina grimaced. Talking with Maxim was frustrating, and by the look on Elly's face, she knew it; if he wasn't about to pull some mean-spirited practical joke on you, then he would try to bore you with the mechanical details of his magic. The aetherite didn't seem to realize that none of them wanted to know.

A hooting cry echoed across the airship. Lina looked over to the Wiley twins, clowning around in the starboard rigging. Nate Wiley, the injured one, stood atop the exhaust pipe there, his burned hands still wrapped in gauze. Jonas Wiley dangled out over the ocean, hanging upside-down from the rigging, facing inward at the deck.

What are those idiots on about now? she wondered.

Lina considered just ignoring them. Then she glanced around the deck. *No. I'd better go see what they're up to.* Lina tried to share an exasperated look with Allen, but for once he wasn't staring at her. She followed his gaze and then moved away from the hatch, walking over to the starboard side of the airship.

As she approached, Jonas took a deep breath and let go the rigging. He dropped several feet before catching himself in a rough handstand that set the rigging to stretching and shaking with the movement. His brother gave a laugh and clapped his burned hands together. Then he grimaced in pain.

Lina sighed. "What in the Realms Below are you two on about?" The Wiley twins weren't her favorites. They were thuggish, crude, and violent. When Natasha wasn't around, though, they seemed all right.

Nate Wiley turned around. "Heyo, Lina."

"Miss Stone!" said Jonas. "Come on up here and give us a kiss, eh?" The big pirate's face was flushed with all the blood running to his head.

"Not if you were the last man in the sky," she replied.

"Jonas," warned his brother. "She's on the committee."

"So? What's that matter?"

Lina felt uncomfortable. She technically was, which had her feeling a lot more responsible of late. Unreasonably so, in her opinion. *That's probably why I'm over here right now.* She shook her head. "Never mind that. What in the Realms Below are you doing?"

"Oh, just showing my brother here something he can't do," said Jonas. "Watch."

He pushed up and let go, performing another handstand before dropping a few feet more down the rigging. Jonas caught himself again, but the rigging bounced violently with his movements.

"Eh?" he said. "How's that?"

Lina stared. "That's really, really stupid Jonas. You want to go for a midnight swim?"

"Oh, come off it, Lina. I know what I'm on about."

He pushed up again as a gust of wind whipped past them all. Jonas flailed for the rigging, and missed. Lina watched in surprise as her crewmate plummeted out of sight.

"Jonas!" cried his brother.

Lina leapt up the exhaust pipe and to the gunwales. She pushed past Nate Wiley and grabbed the rigging, leaning out over the ship. Jonas Wiley wasn't lost, just quite yet. The thuggish twin dangled from the airship, gripping one of the brass skysails folded up against the hull. The winglike armature stretched and bent as she watched. Far below churned the Atalian Sea, moonlight reflecting unsteadily from its waters.

Lina swallowed. Once, Andrea had told her that a fall from this high up into the ocean would be like hitting cobblestones.

"Help!" howled Jonas Wiley. "I'm slipping!"

Nate stared at Lina in a panic. "My hands! I can't get him, my hands still don't work right!"

Allen peered past her shoulder, blanched, then pulled back. Lina ignored him, focusing her attention on the problem. *All right. Think. He's got to weigh eighteen stone or more.* The Wiley twins were big boys. She certainly wasn't. If Sarah Lome were here she would have just pulled the idiot back aboard. Yet she had disappeared shortly after the watch change belowdecks, probably for the stupid committee meeting. By the time Lina ran and brought help, Jonas Wiley would be lost.

The skysail bent again with a metallic wail. A spring somewhere close to the hull of the airship snapped with a twang. Lina stepped back from the gunwales. "Okay. We need a rope. Allen, give me—"

The young Mechanist was on the rigging up above her. He dropped the coiled end of a rope to Lina, a boarding grapnel tied to one end. Then he ascended to where the gas bag met the rigging and started threading the rope through a stanchion moored to the underside of the gasbag. "Make sure he grabs this," the young Mechanist called down. "Then help me pull."

Lina left him to it. She crawled back over the gunwales, one hand on the rigging. Jonas let loose a loud cry as the skysail bent again. "Jonas!" she called. "Here, grab this with your free hand." She lowered the hook until it was right next to his shoulder.

"I'm gonna fall!" he cried.

"Not if you grab the hook," Lina replied.

The big pirate looked at the bobbing grapnel next to him with wild eyes. Tentatively he reached out to it. Then the armature snapped. Jonas flailed, just grabbing on with his free hand as the skysail cloth tore loudly. The rope went taut, his weight yanking it from Lina's hands. Allen gave a cry from up above and she glanced up to see him dangling from the other end of the rope. The stanchion was acting as a pulley, with the heavier pirate on one end, and the young Mechanist on the other, his weight and grip the only thing keeping Jonas Wiley from falling into the sea below.

Andrea appeared suddenly, along with Maxim in tow. They grabbed for the rope below Allen. Maxim wrapped its length around his arm while Andrea hollered up the deck to where Tricia and the others were dicing. "Get over here!" she shouted. "We've got a man overboard!"

Lina leapt back to help. She took ahold of the rope as her crewmates hauled it down. Bit by bit it came, until Allen could finally reach the deck. Back over the gunwales, Nate Wiley stood ready. When his brother rose into view, he wrapped his arms around the man in a bear hug and pulled him back aboard. The two twins toppled back off the gunwales and the exhaust-pipe to land upon the deck. Lina, Andrea, and Maxim all ran over to check him over as the others arrived.

"Oh Goddess," sobbed Jonas Wiley.

Nate looked up at them, holding his brother in his lap. "He's all right," he said.

"What were you thinking?" yelled Lina, throwing her arms wide. "That was the dumbest thing I've ever seen!"

Allen scrabbled past her. He climbed up the steam pipe and peered over the gunwales, then gave a low groan. Lina blinked and shared a glance with Andrea. She pushed past the idiot twins and moved up to Allen's side.

"Look," said the young Mechanist. Lina followed his arm out to the skysail armature. It was a bent and ruined wreck. The shimmering gold cloth fluttered in the wind, torn. "That's going to take forever to fix," he said.

Lina's heart leapt into her throat. She gave a groan of her own. *Oh good Goddess in the Realms Above.* A ruined skysail. The Mechanist was going to have kittens.

Right. Jonas Wiley was safe, there weren't any immediate dangers. She'd been called down to the committee, who really needed to know what had just happened anyway. If she moved fast enough, she could escape before the Mechanist arrived. The man almost seemed to have a sixth sense about the machines aboard the airship. She did *not* want to be around when he saw this.

Lina hopped back down to the deck. "I've got to go let the committee know about this," she said to no one in particular. She pushed through the small crowd and made a beeline for the hatch. Just as she reached the stair going belowdecks, something occurred to her. Lina sighed, stopped, and turned back. "Hey, Allen," she called. "Good job."

The young Mechanist glanced at her from his perch atop the gunwales. She winked at him, then descended through the hatch before he could say anything that would embarrass them both.

The hatchway stair led down past the captain's cabin to the quarterdeck. At the far end of the hammock-filled room lay the ship's galley. Lina paused at the foot of the stair before crossing through the hall. The space was dark, only illuminated by pale spears of moonlight shining through the portholes in the hull. It was far from empty, however. Each hammock was filled with sleeping crewmen, with a few of the crew drinking or playing dice in the corners.

Lina frowned. She recognized more than a few faces that should have been up above on deck. *So that's where all you lazy bastards got to.* None of them seemed to have heard the commotion up above.

She shook her head and moved through the door into the galley. Unlike the berth hall, several oil lanterns lit this space, an extravagance for the four people occupying the room. The three members of the Ship's Committee sat together at one of the big benches in the center of the galley. Henry Smalls was here as well, sitting off to one side by himself, busily wiping down several knickknacks with a rag and a jar of polish. Everyone looked up as she entered.

Lucian Thorne looked tired. "Miss Stone," he said. "How goes the watch?"

She took a breath. *Best be out with it.* "Jonas Wiley almost went overboard. He and his brother were clowning around. Caught him back up, but one of the skysail armatures is bent, and the cloth torn. It's pretty badly damaged."

Sarah Lome cursed and started to stand. The big piratess wore tiny spectacles and her huge fingers were stained with ink.

Lucian put out a hand. "Wait, Sarah." He looked back at Lina. "Is anyone still in danger?"

She shook her head. "Only once the Mechanist finds out. That's going to be ugly. Worse than when he caught Oscar Pleasant using the propeller assembly to sharpen his knives. Allen's seeing to it as best he can. And Andrea's got the crew in line. Those that are up on deck, at least."

Sarah Lome colored an ugly shade of red and started to move again. Lucian grabbed her wrist. "Wait, Sarah. Let it lie a moment. We've *got* to go over these matters before tomorrow. Nothing's on fire, it'll all keep."

"Those sod's are slacking off again!" she snarled. "I'll tan their hides! Not to mention the damned Wiley twins. The Mechanist is going to throw a fit."

"It can wait." Lucian's voice took on a hard edge.

The huge piratess frowned mightily, but sat back down a little farther away from the papers spread before her. The first mate gestured Lina to a spot beside Reaver Jane. Lina moved over and sat down. The woman glanced at her dismissively. Lina was still uncomfortable around her, but since their fight on the *Kingfisher,* things had been a little easier between them.

Lina frowned. There was a tension in the air, something other than the news she'd brought. Papers were scattered over the table, along with ink and quills. A few plates of food lay about, along with half-empty mugs. Lucian looked focused, Jane bored, and Sarah Lome confused and irritated. Lina glanced over at Henry Smalls. The older pirate had a hip flask and a set of monocles out on a cloth before him.

"Henry," she asked. "What are you doing?"

He flushed in embarrassment. "Oh, nothing, nothing. Just...keeping busy. Thought I'd get things ready for the captains, when we're ready to go pick them up." He bent down over the hip flask, avoiding her eyes.

"More like he don't know what to do with himself," said Reaver Jane dryly. "Now that His Lordship is gnawing on coconuts."

"Enough," said Lucian. "Let's get back to business." He took up one of the papers before them. "We've got to get through this list. Now...ah. Here.

I think we should promote the white ape to Head Lookout. It spotted that last freighter before Gabley did, and we should reward that."

"Seems reasonable," said Reaver Jane, almost instantly.

"Sure," said Sarah Lome. "Whatever." The huge woman glanced at Jane, Lucian, and Lina in turn, glowering.

Lucian made a mark on a piece of paper. "All right, that's that. Next item. Sarah, have you gone over those light-air reports from the Mechanist?"

The usually fearless gunnery mistress flinched. She glanced guiltily at the papers before her and picked up a quill. "Uh. Let's come back to that."

Reaver Jane rolled her eyes. "Still? You *can* do arithmetic, can't you?"

Sarah Lome ground her teeth. "You want to do this then?" she asked. "Eh? You want to do this?"

The other woman held up her hands in mock submission. Sarah Lome glared at her a moment before looking again to her paperwork. Her posture changed, become hunched, almost intimidated. Lina blinked when the huge woman chewed nervously on the nib of her quill.

"Right," sighed Lucian. "I'll put that on the list of things to come back to. Next thing though...ah. Oscar Pleasant is missing. Only noticed it this evening. Looks like we might have left him down on one of the freighters we pillaged. Or he might have gotten gutted."

He's gone? Lina perked up. Oscar was easily the most obnoxious member of the crew. He'd made her first few days aboard the *Dawnhawk* a miserable experience. They'd eventually come to an accord, violently, avoiding each other ever since. If he was really gone, she wouldn't shed any tears.

"Should we go back?" asked Sarah Lome.

Lucian mused. "Hmm. I've never been particularly fond of the fellow. You, Jane?"

"Who?" The dark-haired woman was picking at her fingernails with a dagger.

"Right, then. Let's put that off for later. Next task is something far more important." He sketched some numbers on the sheet of paper before him. "Now, the original plan was to ride the aetherlines up to Breachtown, hit it hard, then burn coal to get away. But we've used up a lot of fuel going off after those last two merchants. With the added weight as well, I don't know that we have enough coal to rely on for the return trip to Almhazlik and then back to Haventown."

"That's easy," said Jane. "We burn coal to get to Breachtown, then ride the aetherlines out of the colony."

"What?" replied Sarah Lome. Jane's suggestion seemed to cut through her unease. "No. We should use as little as possible to reach the nearest aetherline, then ride that to Breachtown. After, we burn coal to get away. That'll be a more reliable route out, and faster. People are going to be after us if we pull this off."

"Hmm," mused Lucian. "I think we should take a mixed approach, myself. Get back on course, ride the 'lines, and do the same after we hit the colony."

Reaver Jane stopped picking at her fingernails to raise an eyebrow at him. "Every day we float up here is another day we're down provisions. And the crew is ready. Get us to Breachtown fast, I say."

"We need to be cautious," said Sarah Lome. "We can't afford to botch this up."

"To the Realms Below with caution."

Lina listened to them argue. *Why am I even here?* It was obvious that they didn't want her opinion. She glanced at the scattered papers, the ink and quills, the old, cold food. It hit her then that the three ship's officers had been at this for *hours*. She sighed. *This is pointless. Someone should just make a decision. What about the skysail?*

"Well, the two of you just think about it," said Lucian. "I'll put it back on the list, though we're almost out of new things that need discussion. Jane, what's the status of our powder stores?"

Lina glanced away from the discussion. Henry Smalls caught her eye. He gave a small, sad smile, then went back to polishing one of Fengel's monocles.

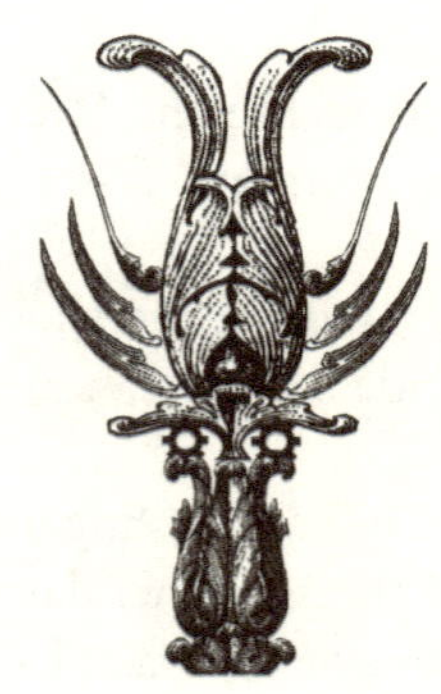

CHAPTER NINE

They were laughing again.

Her husband's obnoxious voice echoed up through the knothole at her feet. Natasha stamped on it. Their noise stilled for a moment. Then Fengel said something and his new cronies were back to snickering again.

Natasha kicked out, this time in general frustration. The chains around her ankles clattered. She wasn't held in a proper brig, or even a cell like the one below. Instead, she stood shackled to a ring hammered into the gun deck. Fat black cannons to her left pointed their noses out the starboard-side gun ports at her back, and the wall of the stern powder magazine framed her to the right. The scents of iron and sawdust filled the air. A shaft of early afternoon sunlight warmed the back of her shirt.

After two days of capture, no one stood direct guard over her anymore. At first word had spread quickly, bringing plenty of the *Goliath's* crew to visit their attractive captive. The tactic of appealing to her captors having failed rather miserably, she didn't bother even trying anymore. Instead, she glared in sullen silence, unleashing a torrent of verbal abuse when their leering faces had grown to be too much. Her father had been right, of course: never make allies when you can make victims.

Most of the Perinese crew went away eventually, though late that first night a portly sailor had paid the guards to look the other way for a bit. But the fools left her hands free. After the man had been hauled away screaming and without his nose, her guard was changed, and no more visitors were allowed to see her save the commander's boy when he came by to dole out her gruel. Midshipman Paine said little and slid her food over with a ten-foot pole.

Fengel made another joke in the deck below. There was silence, and then at least five people laughing. Natasha grit her teeth. His guard normally was just two men.

I'm going to make him sorry, she fumed. *Going to teach him a lesson he'll carry in his bones, the pompous, smarmy bastard. That windbag blowhard. Arse-headed jabbering idiot. Fool. Clown.*

She'd run out of insults for Fengel a day or so ago. Now she struggled to come up with anything really original. Natasha didn't care. All she could think about were his last words to her. They haunted her, as did their last argument. Fengel had told her what he really thought. He mocked her accomplishments, all that she'd ever done and been. Just thinking of it made her breath come short and her heart hammer in her chest. No one talked to her like that and lived. No one.

But it was worse than that. He'd taunted her, told her what she'd done wrong and how he wouldn't have made the same mistakes, how he would succeed where she had failed. Fengel promised that he would claw his way back up on top, and bring her too, but only if she begged it of him. And he was making good on his promise. He was winning. He had company all hours of the day now. Commander Coppertree had even sent him tea.

Natasha glowered. She would not beg. Instead, she would find another way out. Somehow.

And then he'll pay, she vowed again. *And these fools here. And those traitors on my ship. They'll all pay. Every last one. In pride and gold and blood.*

But first she had to escape.

Natasha sat down roughly with her back against the bulkhead. The manacles around her ankles hung a little loosely, but not quite so much that she could slip from them. The chain running between the two cuffs was thick and heavy. Even if she'd had a file, it would have taken a day of constant unsupervised work to cut through. Conceivably, she might just pull up the ring, but then she'd still be shackled and the guard at the other end of the deck would hear her.

She kicked out and the chain checked her leg, stopped her short. The rattle of the links sounded like mocking laughter. Natasha imagined it as the voice of her mutinous crew, of Fengel, of the fools aboard the *Goliath*. She stoked her anger with the injustice of it all and let it drive her further in her desire for escape, but she didn't rage. She tamped it down and hunted the deck about her for something, anything, anything at all that she could use.

The tools for the heavy cannon at her left might have been of use, but they were all racked up near the ceiling, just out of her reach. The weapon itself offered no purchase, though if she could have turned it around and fired it down toward the ring, her shackles, and Fengel's head, she would have.

Natasha rolled around to face the wall behind her. Though the chain at her feet twisted, it allowed the movement without too much awkwardness. She grabbed at the lip of the gun port opening and peered out at the island of Almhazlik, framed like some penny-playwright's dream. The Atalian Sea rolled past the *Goliath* into a surf that curled up onto the beach with a crash. Just beyond lay the encampment, the crew of sailors and Bluecoat marines working like busy ants at innumerable tasks that she didn't care to contemplate. Past them rose the jungle, lush and green, filled with strange flora and fauna. And at the center of the isle rose the volcano, studded with its weird formations and the massive draconic statue. White smoke puffed lazily from the summit.

Movement down in the camp caught her eye. A trio of men dressed in officer's clothing walked with steady purpose throughout the bivouac. She recognized the useless Sub-Lieutenant Hayes, the ship's aetherite Dawkins, and Commander Coppertree himself, the leader of her not-quite-floating gaol.

Natasha ground her teeth at the sight. Last time she'd seen the man, he had been on death's door. Now he inspected the camp in full uniform, if using a cane and not walking quite as quickly as he probably could. Just like Fengel had intended, she'd heard every single conversation with his guard about the commander's illness. Apparently, his suggestions were being followed with a regretful effectiveness.

Her husband was proving more successful in his plotting than she had thought.

The master of the *Goliath* stopped at the makeshift armory of the encampment. His two men halted behind, trying not to bump into him. The "armory" was simple, a stack of powder barrels and cloth bags full of shot, with muskets heaped around a trestle table wrestled down from the ship. A small ship's forge stood dangerously close by and served both the armory as well as the carpenter's "workshop," a similar arrangement consisting of a nearby table heaped high with a mishmash of broken tools in need of mending. Commander Coppertree made a show of inspecting the arrangement, then gave a number of orders to the carpenter working there. The aetherite looked bored. Hayes nodded emphatically at everything the Commander said, like a small dog trying to please its master.

Natasha glared at the scene. Her frustration and anger grew by the moment, all the little insults and failures stacking until she could barely see through her rage. Natasha sputtered and choked, trying to find the words to express everything she felt.

She took a breath and yelled out at the beach, "You scurvy-ridden, donkey-loving, scryn-sucking arseholes! When I get out of here, you'll pay! You'll all pay! I'm going to gut you and wear your intestines for a belt! I'm going to burn your homes and loved ones alive and then dance in the ashes! You're all going to pay! You're all going to pay for what you've done to me!"

Natasha screamed at them until her breath gave out, and then a little more. She screamed until she collapsed, panting, against the bulkhead. It smelled of oiled wood and sulfur from the guns. The tropical sun warmed her hair through the opening of the gun port.

They're going to pay, she vowed for the hundredth time. Natasha caught her breath. She pulled herself up again, hands on the lip of the port. Screaming at everyone felt good, but it didn't get her any closer to her freedom. No, she needed to get back to examining her surroundings. As she stood, however, Natasha noticed something odd out on the beach.

A small ridge of rock jutted out from the jungle, just west of the camp. No more than ten feet high, it didn't even stretch all the way down to the shore. She'd noted it before; the *Goliath's* marines simply avoided it when the their patrols took them down the beach in that direction. Now, however, Natasha spied a figure laying low across the top of the ridge; someone furtive was watching the camp.

They were too far away to make out clearly, but she thought she spied a fringe of red beard below a dusky face. He wore a brown leather vest and clutched an unsheathed scimitar in one hand. Whatever he was, he certainly wasn't Perinese.

"Hello," Natasha muttered aloud. "What's this now?"

Two more figures appeared atop the rise, heads bobbing as they crawled up into view. One was large, with long dark hair, while the other was short and stout. They appeared much the same as their fellow. It came to her then: these were the Salomcani that the *Goliath's* crew were so concerned about.

Natasha tapped her chin. Was this just a scouting party? Or a raid? And how could she use it to her best advantage? A distraction would give her time to work at her fetters, maybe slip free. But without any tools she wasn't going to break her chains.

She scrabbled to her feet and looked down at the other end of the deck. Her guard sat on the stairwell there, half dozing. If she could get him to come over she might have a chance. But she had to hurry. If an attack was imminent, he'd leave the gun deck as soon as the noise started.

"Hey!" she hollered. "Hey, you blue-breasted arsehole! Get over here!"

The man started awake, looked around until he identified her as the source of the noise, then shuffled slightly out of sight.

Damn you to the Realms Below, she cursed. She could swear at him some more, try and taunt him over. That would take time, though, a luxury she did not have. Seduction was out of the question, too.

Natasha looked up above the nearest cannon. The tools used by the cannon crew hung from a rack attached to the ceiling for easy reach: a swab on a long pole, a staff-like rammer, and the linstock. The last was the her best option, a short polearm with a long blade at the end and a complex jaw arrangement along the crosspiece for holding a match. If she could get her hands on that, maybe she could pry up the ring in the floor, or break the links on her chain. The idea had crossed her mind before, but she'd thought herself too far away from the tools to reach them. Maybe she simply hadn't tried hard enough.

The chain rattled as she pulled it to its length. Natasha reached, stretching herself toward the wooden pole of the linstock. Her fingers almost brushed it, tantalizingly close. She put one hand on the iron cannon to brace herself and tried again. Then she fell against the weapon with a clatter.

Natasha cursed and flung herself upward. The wooden pole brushed against her fingertips. *Why didn't I keep one of those bowls of gruel?* she wondered. *Or a spoon?* That might have given her the reach to get the linstock down. Instead, she had wasted them, using them as ammunition against the young midshipman assigned to feed her.

Her chains rattled as she struggled. When she fell again, her elbow struck the side of the cannon painfully before she collided with the deck. "Hogspit!" she cried in anger and frustration. Natasha slammed a fist on the deck and kicked out, sending her chains rattling. "Poxied gut-leavings of a diseased whore!"

Heavy boots tromped up the deck. Her guard rounded the rear of the cannon into view. He held his musket up, armed and ready. This one, at least, took her seriously.

"Here now! What are you on about this time?"

Oh sure, now you show up, she thought. "Oh sure," she said aloud. "Now you show up."

The man glared at her. He was shaped roughly like a potato, and sweated in the tropical heat. "What? Get away from that cannon. Hayes has had them all kept loaded and primed. I'm not to let you muck about with them."

Natasha stared at him. Then she looked at the cannon. *Loaded? What kind of ass keeps a whole gun deck primed?* What were they even going to fire upon? The tilt of the ship aimed the broadside at the beach.

She pushed that detail away. Her fish had been hooked. She just needed to pull him alongside. *Carefully now, carefully. This is going to take subtlety. I can't threaten him. Got to convince him to come close. Demure. I've got to be demure. Wait. What does that mean?*

"Oh," she said. "I just need—"

A great battle cry from outside the ship interrupted her. Shouts of alarm and surprise echoed from the Perinese in reply, accompanied by a great clatter of swords and the crack of musket and pistol shots. Her guard started.

"What in the Realms Above is that?" he cried. The Bluecoat stepped over Natasha to peer out her gun port. "Goddess above! The Salomcani are attacking!"

All right, thought Natasha. *Or he could just step over here on his own.* She didn't stop to consider her luck. Instead she coiled her legs and prepared to trip him. He was too close to use the musket. That meant he was hers.

A thunderous explosion roared on the island outside. Natasha instinctively ducked, covering her head. Half a second later, the bulkhead wall of the ship resounded with dozens of sharp thumps as a scattering of debris rapped it from outside. She peered up, hoping the marine hadn't fallen back.

The man stood still before the gun port. Then he toppled back to the deck in a slow arc, dead. A half-repaired hatchet stood embedded in his face.

What in the world? Natasha peered outside. Battle raged up and down the Perinese encampment. The armory, however, was a blackened crater. Someone had knocked a powder barrel against the ill-placed forge.

Natasha didn't stop to question her luck. She crawled over to the Bluecoat and grabbed the haft of the hatchet. The man twitched distressingly; it seemed that he wasn't quite dead yet. Tugging and pulling, she eased the tool out an inch at a time, eventually coming free with a spray of blood that drenched her face and shirt. Natasha spat, but the coppery taste still remained.

She ignored the corpse and focused again on her freedom. Sitting, she stretched both legs until the chain between them was taut. Then she hacked down with the hatchet as close as she dared on either side. The blood on the blade ran down the haft, making it slick against her palms. Natasha held tight: this wasn't the first time she'd had to perform tricky work covered in someone else's ichors.

The chain bent and jumped with each blow. Sparks and slivers of iron flew across the deck. At last it broke, only a few links away from her right ankle. She did the same to her other leg, impatiently hacking until her fetter there separated as well. Then Natasha stood and threw the hatchet at the rear bulkhead, sinking it deep into the wood as she howled a wordless cry.

I'm free!

A cascade of all the vows and promises she'd made flooded back through her mind. But not yet, not yet. First she had to make good her escape.

Natasha crawled over to her dead guard. She took his musket and swordbelt, strapping the latter around her own waist. He carried a smallsword, much lighter than her preferred cutlass, but it would do. His boots she took as well. Pleasingly, they were just the right size.

Now prepared, she glanced back outside. The Salomcani still pressed their attack even after the explosion. Many looked injured on both sides. She couldn't have asked for a better distraction. Now was the time to get away.

She left her prison and strode up the deck toward the stair at the bow. As she went she slapped the rear of each of the fat iron cannons, feeling almost jovial. Halfway up the deck, she stopped and paused to look at the heavy weapons. One had to keep one's promises, after all.

A quick inspection of the cannons confirmed that what the dead guard had said was true. Madly, each was primed, powdered, and ready to fire. All that was needed was for the guncocks to be pulled back and then triggered.

She worked quickly. Leaving her musket up by the stair, she moved to each cannon and pulled back the tiny hammer-arm positioned above the touch-hole. They locked into place with a click, thundering devastation held at bay by a bit of clockwork. Dangling from the back of each mechanism was a long leather lanyard. A quick jerk and the guncock would hammer a piece of flint down at a steel striking pan, inciting the weapon to fire. When the last of the heavy guns was ready, Natasha took up the leather lanyard and peered out beyond the ship.

Both crews had recovered a bit from the explosion moments ago. Burning bits of wood peppered the beach, and some of the tents in their row were on fire. Bodies lay scattered about, more dead from the forge explosion than from the fighting. The Perinese struggled to regroup into a formation, but the Salomcani were fast and skilled. She spotted Commander Coppertree at one edge of the fighting, up near the jungle's edge, protected by Hayes and his pet aetherite. Whenever one of the raiders moved too close, the ship's magician sprayed caustic light their way. Hayes waved his sword, but failed to attack anyone.

Natasha glowered. She stepped back clear of the gun port and took a firm grip on the lanyard. "Retribution is at hand!" she yelled. Then she pulled the lanyard.

The clockwork mechanism leapt forward. Sparks erupted and the cannon fired, sending a great deafening gout of flame and smoke belching out beyond the ship. The weapon recoiled, checked only by the heavy tackles that bound it to the bulkhead wall on either side of the gun port. The sound of its thunder echoed throughout the deck.

Natasha didn't wait to check the results. She cackled and moved to the next cannon, taking up the lanyard there. It fired with a similar thunderous eruption. Then she moved down the line, laughing as she fired upon the beach and the bloody struggle taking place upon the sands.

Her ears rang by the time she reached the stairwell and her new musket. The whole deck stank of sulphur and was filled with smoke. Though her lungs burned for clean air, she felt almost light, buoyed up by joy. Unfortunately, she couldn't wait to see the results. Freedom still beckoned. Cocking the hammer back on her musket, she carefully climbed the stair.

Natasha ignored the other decks she passed through. They were unoccupied. It seemed that everyone aboard the ship had joined in to fight off the raid, at least so far. No one appeared to bar her ascent. The dank gloom of the stairwell lightened as she climbed, until at last she stepped out from the hatch and onto the main deck of the ship.

The sun was bright overhead. Too bright, after three days belowdecks. It joined with the ringing in her ears to obscure her senses. Natasha held up her musket while the world slowly slipped into focus.

She was not alone on the deck, she saw. The carpenter and two assistants stood at the gunwales with their backs to her, exclaiming in horror at the beach encampment below. None of them seemed to have noticed her yet.

Even with the cannon smoke rising up past the hull she could see the devastation she had wrought. All fighting was ended. Bodies littered the sandy beach, scattered and stark against the black scorches left by her cannons. The Salomcani were in full retreat. Those who could grabbed sacks, tools, and whatever spoils they found as they fled. The Perinese were simply trying to regroup. Even through the ringing in her ears she heard the shrillness of confused orders, the cries of the wounded and desperate yelling. Nothing had ever been sweeter.

"You!" cried a voice. "You did this!"

Natasha looked back. The carpenter had seen her. He was old and grizzled, with muscles on his arms like thick cords of jerky. The man ran at her, a hammer raised in his hands.

Reflexively, she took aim with the musket and fired. The weapon gave a sharp crack and ejected a plume of smoke. She tossed it aside and drew the smallsword, taking up a stance.

She felt, more than heard, his hammer hit the deck. As the smoke cleared, she watched him crumple to his knees. The ball had taken him square in the chest. He shook and gave a long gasp as blood pooled on the planks around him. Natasha grinned up at the remaining two men. She recognized them. One was the commander's boy, Paine. The other had been aboard when she'd first been captured, two days ago.

"All right, then," she said. "Who's next?"

They fled up the deck, hollering wordless warnings at the top of their lungs. Natasha moved to where they'd stood, calmly stepping over the dying carpenter, and surveyed the battle again. She tried to pick out Coppertree, Hayes, or anyone else who had personally wronged her, but there was too much smoke and devastation. One thing did stand out, though: a large group of the Perinese were pointing at the ship, and her in particular.

Hmm, she mused. *Time to go.*

Natasha sheathed her blade and stalked up the deck toward the port-side bow. It occurred to her that she hadn't given thought to what to do next for her escape. Her father would have chided her for that. Fortunately, no one else on the ship was opposing her. Unfortunately, there wasn't a ready longboat or launch anywhere in sight.

She reached the quarterdeck and peered over the side of the *Goliath.* Beyond, the surf rolled in toward the isle, a soft blue-green, clear enough that she could see sand a few fathoms below the surface. There wasn't any ready boat over here, either. She was going to have to swim.

Nothing for it, then. Natasha kicked off her new boots, made sure her sword was sheathed, and dove overboard.

The water was a cool shock after the smoke and stinking air of the ship. Her momentum from the dive carried her down and through it until she touched the sandy floor of the ocean. It was deep enough, just barely. Natasha kicked off from it and swam.

She swam underwater as long as she could, until her lungs burned and her limbs ached. When she surfaced for air, she was pleased to see the *Goliath* a goodly distance behind her. Natasha corrected her course and swam away with broad over-arm strokes in parallel with the beach, heading west around the island. East would take her back to the isolated part of the isle the treacherous *Dawnhawk* had dropped her upon, and there was little point in that.

Natasha swam until the steamship disappeared around the corner of the isle. The surf pushed her constantly inland. She fought it only a little. When her limbs felt like wood and she couldn't swim any farther, she floated, letting the tide deliver her back onto a short, rocky shore just beneath the jungle canopy. She lay there, panting, getting her strength back and enjoying the shade.

A figure appeared overhead. Natasha blinked up at a rough, dusky face with a heavy red beard and twin mustachios set below golden eyes. His clothing was finely made, if tattered. A scimitar hung from his hip. Other raiders appeared around him, carrying weapons, stolen goods, and a fair share of fresh wounds.

"Well," said the man in perfect Salomcan. "What have we here?"

Oh, by the Goddess's teats, Natasha swore silently. *I just did this!*

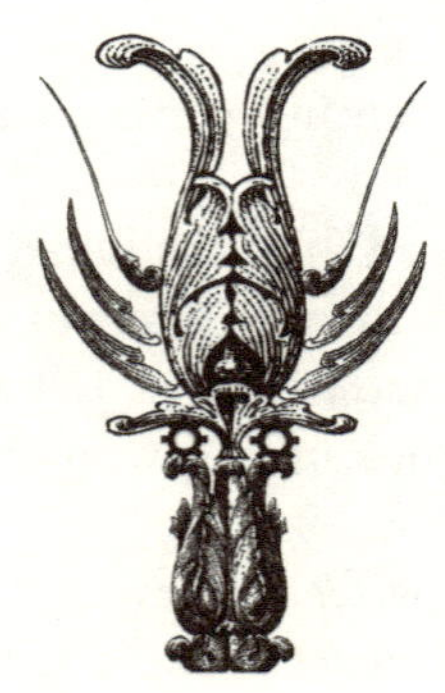

CHAPTER TEN

Fengel shifted in his crouch. He tried for a better angle through the bars of his cell at the padlock holding it closed. The hot metal gaff-hook slipped in his hand. He fumbled for a tighter grip on the makeshift lock pick, ignoring the stink of smoldering cloth and the growing pain in his fingertips. The bent piece of metal was his best chance of escape right now. Dropping it didn't bear thinking upon.

Slowly, carefully, Fengel adjusted his grip. He teased again at the padlock. From outside the ship came the cries of the wounded and dying, punctuated occasionally by the pop of musket fire. Both the Salomcani and the Perinese sounded as if they were reeling after the mad firing of the ship's broadside at the beach. Fengel pushed the noise out of his mind to focus on his freedom.

His hook found the inner latch. Fengel took a breath. The Perinese navy had far harsher methods of discipline available aboard a ship, and so rarely spent excessively on security. This padlock was a simple thing. But it had been a long time since he'd had to tease open a chest or slip past a door without the key.

If I can just.... He twisted the hook to the right and a loud click sounded. The padlock snapped open. Fengel dropped his makeshift pick and removed the lock. Retrieving his hat, he swung the door open wide, rose from his crouch, and stepped out of the brig cell to freedom.

The berth deck was still empty. At the first cries of battle, both of his guards, Sergeant Cumbers and Private Simon, had run off to join the fighting. Aside from Commander Coppertree and the ship's carpenter, he was likely alone aboard the *Goliath*. And Cumbers had let slip that the Commander was well enough to inspect the camp today. Fengel knew he needed to move quickly. This chance wouldn't last. Especially with the recent action of the ship's guns.

That had been Natasha, he knew. It was just the kind of vindictive, ruthless action she would take. It also meant that she was on the loose. She wouldn't have done such a crazy thing unless she was already making good her own escape, somehow.

Well, he admitted. *Probably.*

Fengel moved up from the stern toward the stair at the head of the deck. He kept an eye out for a weapon as he went. Nothing availed itself. Regretfully, he started climbing. When he reached the base—and at each new landing—he stopped to peer up the deck. His hands itched for a sword. If he'd been properly armed, he never would have been captured by the Perinese in the first place. If he ran into anyone now, he'd be forced to surrender.

The interior of the ship was weirdly silent after the clamor outside its hull. The air was dusty and scented with the smells of tar, rum, and just-fired guns. Unwelcome nostalgia washed over him. Fengel hurried his ascent until the hatch that opened onto the deck appeared above, sunlight flooding the stair. He moved to its lip and peered out.

The day crashed into him. High above hung the early-afternoon sun, obscured by billowing columns of smoke that rose from the beach to cast weird shadows upon the deck of the *Goliath*. A soft wind blew in from the ocean, setting loose sails to flapping overhead. The cries of the wounded mixed with the screams of gulls and the roar of the surf below.

Three figures huddled against the starboard gunwales. Fengel recognized the young midshipman, Paine, a boy of twelve with sandy hair. The second was the shifty sailor Riley Gordon. Both had passed through the berth deck on occasion, saying little, lingering just long enough to listen to the tales and jokes that he spun for Cumbers and others among the crew. Beneath both of them lay a third figure, an older sailor curled up and groaning in a pool of his own blood. This must be Harvey, the ship's carpenter.

"He needs water," said Riley Gordon, eyes wide. The young seaman had his shirt off, pressed against the carpenter's chest. Blood covered his hands up to his wrists.

"Don't be daft!" cried Paine. His shrill voice threatened to crack. "He's not pregnant. That pirate woman shot him before she scarpered. We need to get Dawkins an' his spells."

Ah, mused Fengel. *Natasha's gone then.* He relaxed a little. Neither of the two had seen him yet. Also, he didn't have to worry about meeting the psychotic hyena he called a wife while unarmed.

A quick glance told him that he was otherwise alone. He could easily make a run for the port side of the ship, either dive off and swim for a distant bit of shore or commandeer a dinghy. His escape would be complete. *A hop, a skip, a swim and I'm free again.*

Except...that wasn't good enough anymore.

He'd been making progress. He'd been *winning*, just like he'd sworn he would. A little bit of polite commiseration had worn down the reservations of his guards. After, they'd been a great source of information, even bringing others in the crew aboard for nightly card games, which Fengel was always careful to lose gracefully. As well, Coppertree seemed on the mend thanks to his advice, putting the hated Sub-Lieutenant Hayes that much farther from any real chance at command. The commander had sent him tea yesterday. Carefully, Fengel had worked the opportunities that came to him, gaining a little ground with every passing hour. He'd been confident that eventual freedom and a mutiny, real or engineered, would give him what he wanted. Then Natasha would learn, once and for all, that he was every bit what he claimed to be.

Ideally, he should have stayed put in his cell. The attack had changed things, though, or so he'd thought. Certainly, he had his chance at freedom now, but wasn't that just running away? Just another form of giving up? Yet if he did stay, what could he do? How would he succeed now?

By never letting them see you stumble. Fengel squared his monocle, adjusted his hat and climbed up onto the deck. He strode with purpose for the starboard gunwales and the two crewmen hunched there. Focusing on Riley Gordon, he tilted his head to look down his nose at the man.

"You're both wrong," he said. "What your fellow needs is a *surgeon.*"

Both sailors peered up at him. Paine blanched. "It's the other one!" he cried. "He got out!"

Fengel ignored him. "Fortunately for you," he continued, "I am a scholar, as well as a gentleman. Now, I know you've no physician aboard, but you've his tools still, yes?"

"Help!" cried Riley Gordon. The small man scrabbled backward for a belaying pin hanging from the gunwales.

Fengel hardened his voice. "Enough tomfoolery, Riley Gordon. You will get me catgut, needles, carbolic acid, and something to pull the ball out, or this man will die. If he expires for lack of your willing cooperation, I will surely discipline you and it will go hard. Do you want that?"

The sailor stared at him. Fengel narrowed his eyes. A long moment later, Riley Gordon shook his head ever so slightly.

"Capital," said Fengel, relaxing. He made a dismissive gesture. "Now. Catgut, needles, carbolic acid, and a spoon if need be. Go find some."

Riley Gordon nodded, eyes downcast. He stood and fled back into the sterncastle. Fengel ignored the silent midshipman and knelt beside the dying carpenter. He rolled up his sleeves and pulled back the shirt covering his hapless new patient. The man groaned senselessly and blood poured afresh from a bullet hole just over his midsection. Fengel frowned as he prodded the wound. Doctoring had never been a talent of his, but he'd watched the resurrectionists back in Haventown on occasion, and anatomy *was* a part of swordplay. He was certainly willing to give it a go. Besides, the ball hadn't gone too deeply; he could feel it maybe an inch below the skin. If it hadn't perforated something vital, the man might even live.

"What happened?" he asked brusquely.

"The o-other pirate," stammered Paine. "I, ah, I mean your wife, sir. She appeared on the deck while we were watching the battle. Shot old Harvey as soon as we noticed. Then she slipped off the ship somehow."

"Where's your aetherite? The man Dawkins."

"He was with the commander. Them and Hayes were down in the camp when those Salomcani bastards attacked."

Fengel frowned. For all his bluster and show, a Working would go a long way toward keeping the carpenter alive. Still, he was too far along to back out now.

Paine returned with a bag and a steaming bowl. Breathless, he set them both down next to Fengel. "I brought the old surgeon's kit. Oh, and hot water."

"Good," said Fengel. "Now hold him down."

He stretched out the groaning carpenter and positioned both young men to either side. Then, with a prayer to the Goddess, he set to work. Thankfully, the task proved less difficult than he feared, though quite messy. Either the carpenter was preternaturally tough or Natasha hadn't loaded enough powder into her musket. He pulled the lead ball free of the wound with a pair of tweezers and patched up the hole as best he could. When finished, Fengel sat back and regarded his handiwork with not a little pride.

"There," he said, reaching over to fastidiously wash his hands. "That should keep him from gushing out all over the deck anymore."

Midshipman Paine stared at him. "What? You can't be done! He's still leaking, and the stitching's all crazy."

Fengel glared at the youth. "I'm sorry, are you a surgeon? Are you? No? I didn't think so, *midshipman*." He glanced back at the patient. Thankfully, the man was still unconscious. "Still, he might not make it. Someone had best go retrieve your aetherite."

Paine and Riley looked at each other.

"But, there's still all that fighting down there," said the younger man.

"We've got to watch over Harvey," said the other.

From the sounds echoing up from the beach, Fengel doubted that any real fighting was occurring anymore. "Indeed," he replied. "You watch your fellow. *I* will go and retrieve Mr. Dawkins." He stood without looking at either sailor. Fengel grabbed up the surgeon's kit and moved over to the gunwales.

Beyond, the Perinese encampment was a ruin. The wounded and dead were everywhere, separated by bomb-blasted craters in the sand gouged out by the *Goliath's* cannons and the firing of the powder store. Smoke billowed from burning tents. Marines and sailors stood shell-shocked, yelling at each other and milling about in general. Some fired musket shots into the jungle at the now-gone Salomcani raiders. Fengel did not see the blue coat of Commander Coppertree.

A rope ladder hung from the deck down to the water. Thankfully, one of the longboats was still tied there. Fengel descended quickly and took up the oars, facing the ship as he rowed for the beach. Trepidation mounted and he thought again of just fleeing for some remote part of the isle. What if someone saw him? Recognized him? His back itched at the thought of a bullet fired his way. He was a prisoner, technically, and still an enemy to these people. One that they ultimately wanted dead at the end of a rope.

I can do this, he vowed. *Never let them see you stumble.*

The bow of the boat scraped onto sand. Fengel took a breath and rolled out of the little ship with as much aplomb as he could muster. He strode up onto the shore, the water crashing at the backs of his legs, trying to knock him off balance.

A Bluecoat marine knelt at the edge of the beach. He was young, with red hair and freckles, a Perinese Northman. The Bluecoat had a cracked-open powder barrel before him, along with several empty horns. He tried to fill them with shaking hands that scattered black powder everywhere.

"Private," barked Fengel, guessing. "What are you doing down there?"

A half-filled powder horn flew up into the air as the young Bluecoat started. "Sir!" he cried, blinking up at Fengel. "I'm refilling for those on the front line! Sir."

Fengel made a dismissive gesture. "The battle is done for now. Fall in and follow me."

The Bluecoat clambered up to his feet and made a salute. Fengel tried not to smile, instead frowning as if displeased. He strode ahead into the rest of the camp.

A crater in the sand came into view just ahead. Water geysered from it, an unexpected natural fountain. Fengel peered over the lip. Within was a shallow depression, only a few feet deeper than the surface of the beach. At the bottom lay several large horizontal pipes, half-buried and brassy in the afternoon sun. One was cracked, the source of the spray.

What's this? he wondered. The *Goliath* had run aground on something strange just off-shore as well. *Could this be Voornish work? Are there ruins buried under this shoreline?*

Fengel glanced up at the draconic monolith upon the mountain. The carving was even older than he'd thought, then. His earlier search for natives would have proven futile. The Voorn were long, long dead.

None of that changed his immediate plans, however. The nameless private staggered to a stop beside him, the powder horns he had filled clutched tightly to his chest.

"Private!" barked Fengel. "Climb down there and see if that water is fresh."

The Bluecoat hurried to obey. He tried to set the horns down and clumsily dropped them all. Flushing, he slid down into the depression. There he cupped his hands and knelt down low to drink. Then he yelped and staggered back to fall back against the side of the crater.

"S'fresh sir," said the private, glancing back up. "But hot."

"Of course," replied Fengel, as if he hadn't expected to find it any other way. "Good that it's fresh, though. Now quit playing around down there and fall back in line."

He strode past the crater to where a Perinese sailor lay on his back next to a Salomcani corpse. Blood covered the man's face and he hugged his arm gingerly. Fengel knelt beside him.

"Sailor," he said, pulling out the surgeon's kit. "Let's see that arm."

"Feel weak," said the man. "Head hurts."

"Then we'll take a look at that too," replied Fengel calmly.

He snapped his fingers and the nameless private appeared. At Fengel's direction, they looked the man over. He had an obviously broken arm and a deep gash across his brow. Fengel applied more impromptu first aid, arranging a splint and washing the head wound. Before long the sailor was standing, with the private supporting him. The man didn't offer a name and Fengel didn't ask. So far, at least, both appeared to think of him as one of their officers, though more likely they were just responding to someone who appeared to have authority. Which, for now at least, was part of the plan.

Fengel led them through the ruined encampment. Speed was of the essence. The Perinese were divided, confused. But before too much longer they'd organize, and his window of opportunity would vanish. Where he could, he repeated the trick, tending to any wounded Perinese survivors and taking imperious command of any of those milling about. Before long a small knot of ten people followed him around the beach. A few of them he recognized from his time in the brig. Thankfully, his luck still held; no one seemed to realize who he really was yet.

"Hey!" called a voice. "That's the prisoner! He's escaped!"

Fengel's stomach lurched. He looked to the sound of the voice. Two marines clambered over a pile of charred rubble at him. They were his missing gaolers, Sergeant Cumbers and Private Simon. Both men were unkempt and bloodied. Both held smallswords. Fengel suddenly felt his acute lack of armament, and the presence of all the enemy sailors and Bluecoat marines he'd gathered at his back.

Never let them see you stumble.

"Ah," he said, forcing himself to sound pleased. "Sergeant Cumbers! Glad to see you alive, and perfect timing indeed." Fengel unshouldered the surgeon's kit and flung it at Simon. The young marine dropped his sword and grabbed it up awkwardly. "We're running low on bandages, so you might have to run back to the ship for clean linen, if there's any to be had."

Cumbers stared at him, and the crowd at his back. "What? No one's going anywhere. Except you, I mean. Back to the brig." The Bluecoat marine recovered by yelling at the nameless private Fengel had first dragooned. "What are you even doing, you lot? We've been under attack!"

"I-I thought he was an officer," stuttered the man.

The rest of the naval crew looked at Fengel anew. He ignored them, raising an eyebrow at the sergeant. "Cumbers, if you haven't noticed, the Salomcani raid is over. Your worry should be for the brave men who have been wounded in the conflict. If we act quickly and efficiently, we should be able to save many of their lives."

The man frowned. "But you're a prisoner! Was probably you who fired the damned cannons at us all." He faced the assembled crewmen. "Haven't you lot even thought of that?"

Ugly mutters spread among the crew. Fengel turned to face them as well. "That was a cowardly, dastardly action of which I had no part. Besides, it would have been impossible for me to load all those cannons by myself."

"They was kept primed," said Simon. The private looked bewildered at the discussion before him. He held the surgeon's kit like a shield. When Fengel raised an incredulous eyebrow at him, he looked away. "Sub-Lieutenant Hayes ordered it while the Commander was still caught up sick. In case we all had to fall back to the ship."

Fengel shook his head. Every single crewmember he had chatted with over these last few days had let him know how little-loved the sub-lieutenant was. Now was a perfect time to remind them of that. "Idiotic. The man is not fit to command a set of tableware." He let sorrow creep into his voice. "No, lads, we all know who was responsible for that tragedy. It was that hateful harpy of a woman, Natasha Blackheart. I heard her break free of her own bonds during the struggle. Honor demanded that I free myself to go after her in order to prevent whatever tragedy she would brew up. Alas, she must have fired the broadside and shot the poor carpenter before I released myself."

"Harvey's been shot?" came a voice from the crowd.

"That he has," replied Fengel gravely. The crew seemed to quiet a little at this revelation. "I've seen to him for the moment, pulled out the ball and patched him up. But he could use more aid." He straightened and clapped his hands together. "Now. There isn't much time to lose." He gestured at a trio of the more able-bodied sailors. "You three, find something in which to fetch potable water. I've discovered a small fountain of fresh water back near the shore. This private can lead you to it. Simon, Sergeant Cumbers, attend me as we see to others who are injured. The rest of you, clear a place here for the injured. There must be order to this chaos."

"But you're a prisoner," Sergeant Cumbers insisted.

Fengel hardened his voice. "Cumbers. Your people are *dying*. I am here to *help*. If you insist on focusing on things of minor importance, then you can accompany me to keep me under guard while we save lives. Is that clear?"

The man held his gaze for a moment, then looked away. "Yes. Yes, sir."

"Capital." Fengel folded his hands behind his back. "Well then, let's be about it."

Well, thought Fengel as he led the organization of the Perinese crew. *That could have gone a lot worse.* The sergeant had dashed his initial control of the shell-shocked crewmen. Still, he'd known it couldn't last. And amazingly, he was leading them. Not one of the *Goliath's* mates seemed to be used to any kind of command at all aside from Cumbers, and even he looked a little lost. Those he'd already rescued looked at Fengel differently now, but the mutters he overheard named Natasha and Hayes just as much. Excellently, more than a few remarked on how she'd attached herself to the sub-lieutenant during their initial capture.

Good, Fengel thought. *I can use that.*

They gathered up more of the wounded and brought them back to the spring where Fengel had designated the makeshift infirmary. He did what he could, and before long couldn't say that things were going poorly. The vast majority of those still living, about twenty in all, were gathered together, with only about a third seriously injured. Sergeant Cumbers followed him, ostensibly "guarding," but proving an efficient assistant all the same.

Private Simon stalked up to them. "Mr. Fengel, Sergeant Cumbers, sirs," he said. "That's all the crew we could account for, save for those out at the tree line."

It was time to push things a little more. "Call me 'Captain,' if you don't mind," said Fengel. "I am still master of my own ship, even if it's not here." He shoved the thought of the *Dawnhawk* away. This move could go poorly. The more the crew of the *Goliath* used his title, the more used to it they would become. Yet it might be an unwelcome reminder of his status as a pirate. He frowned at the marine. "And what do you mean, those at the tree line?"

Simon looked uncomfortable. "I found Hayes. Sub-Lieutenant ordered some men to set a perimeter to watch for the enemy. Dawkins is with him. They're arguing. Ah, you'd best come see...Captain."

Fengel nodded. "Take me to him. Sergeant Cumbers, you and a few others should come along as well. Ah, after all, until we find the Commander, Hayes is next down the chain of command, yes? Best keep him safe."

Unhappy looks flashed across the faces of every man within hearing distance. *Perfect.*

The young private led the company up the beach toward the tree-line ridge where Fengel and Natasha had first been captured. Sub-Lieutenant Hayes stood there, arguing angrily with the aetherite, Mr. Dawkins. Five Bluecoats stood nearby, facing the jungle and looking awkward. At their feet was one of the heavy work tables. It had been blown farther up the beach by one of the explosions during the fight. Now it lay upside down, and oddly, as if it were laying atop something.

"We're going after the damned Salomcani, and you're going to assist us," shouted Hayes as they approached. "I am ranking commander and you will do what I say, *Mr.* Dawkins!"

"I'm not part of your little pony show," hissed Dawkins. "I'm a civilian, thank you very much."

"A civilian in a time of war, Mr. Dawkins!" Hayes jabbed a finger into the other man's chest. "I could have you flogged, you know! I'm sure that the bite of the cat would make you more willing."

"I should like to see you try it," replied the aetherite. He made a fist of one hand, and the light around it dimmed. The stink of burned milk filled the air.

The group of Bluecoats and sailors with Fengel took a step back. Hayes' eyes widened and his mouth gaped in outrage. Fengel stepped smartly forward and held up both hands.

"Hold now, hold. What's all this fuss then?" He gestured past the picket at the jungle. "The enemy is out there, yes? There's no need for rancor amongst the ranks."

Both men glanced at him.

"Who the devil are you?" asked Dawkins.

"That's the damned pirate!" snarled Hayes. "That Captain Fengel. What is he doing out here? Cumbers, you idiot, you were supposed to watch him. Couldn't you do that right, at least?"

Beside Fengel, the marine sergeant stiffened. "Don't you talk to me like that, you greasy peacock. Who died and made you ruler o' the roost?"

"He did!" Hayes pointed at the table.

Fengel glanced down along with everyone else. Up close now, he saw an arm, clad in the blue sleeve of an officer's coat, sticking out from under one edge. The hand was curled into a claw, thrust up at the sky.

"Is that the commander?" asked one sailor quietly.

"When the cannons aboard the ship went off," said Hayes, "this landed on him. He's crushed flat, Goddess rest his soul." He glared at the rest of the crew. "Which puts *me* in charge, and I'll discipline any man who dares say otherwise!"

Ugly muttering spread amongst the crew. Fengel glanced back to see that the few people behind him had grown to a crowd. Everyone who could stand had made their way over, once they'd heard the shouting.

"He *is* the only officer we've got left," said one sailor at the back.

"Bollocks to that," said another. "I'm not following him."

"But that's treason!"

"To the Realms Below with it!" snarled Sergeant Cumbers. He stepped forward and shook his fist at Hayes. "I don't care if it *is* mutiny, I'm not taking orders from you!"

Fengel glanced at the chaos. He couldn't have planned it any better himself. *Here we go, then.*

He stepped forward so that everyone could see him. "Gentleman," he said, raising up his hands. "Gentleman. It appears you are in a crisis. As a completely neutral observer, let me be the first to offer up a solution." He paused for effect. "What if *I* were to take a temporary stewardship of the *Goliath*, until your enemies are removed and the ship is sufficiently repaired to get us all home?"

Dead silence met his statement.

"What," asked one sailor. "You want to take the captaincy?"

Fengel blinked. "Temporarily, yes."

"That's outrageous!" shouted Hayes.

"He's a pirate!" cried one sailor.

"He saved my life, though," said a Bluecoat. "Or at least bandaged me up."

"He could have run when he broke free," mused Dawkins. He peered at Fengel. "Why didn't you?"

Fengel raised an eyebrow at the aetherite. "Because I am a patriot," he lied. "And because I could not stand idly by while good Perinese men bled out their lives onto the sand. I would never propose to replace your commander, but as I am familiar with command, and as you seem to be in a bit of a pickle, I would consider it my duty to help steer you all out of the difficulties in which you find yourselves. To help you heal your hurts, repair the ship, and to take bloody vengeance upon those Salomcani cowards who ambushed you all so."

"No!" screamed Hayes. "Absolutely not! He's a pirate! And all of you who can stand and hold a gun are coming with me to avenge ourselves upon the *Salmalin!*"

Fengel could have kissed the man. Even those who were uncomfortable with the idea of mutiny muttered angrily at the sub-lieutenant now.

Sergeant Cumbers nodded. "Y'know what? I like it." He glared once at Hayes and then faced the rest of his crewmen. "I think the captain here has a good idea. *He* obviously knows what he's about, and cares a good deal more about us than this arsehole." He jammed a thumb towards Hayes. "Besides, what kind of damned fool orders powder kegs placed next to a forge?"

The rest of the crew muttered to themselves. Hayes stared at them, stunned and apoplectic.

Fengel whispered an aside to the sub-lieutenant. "Don't be foolish," he said. "Continue on like this and they'll lynch you." Hayes glared daggers at him. Fengel ignored the man and looked to the crew. "There's a simple tradition where I come from, that we use to resolve questions like this. The

Crewman's Vote. Everyone who thinks it a good idea to allow me to captain the crew of the *Goliath*, albeit in a *temporary* fashion, raise a hand."

A smattering of hands, those who most hated Hayes, sprung up. After a moment, a majority could be counted among the crowd.

"And those who are willing to submit to the *rule* of *Sub-Lieutenant* Hayes, raise a hand."

Hayes's hand shot up. No one else's did.

Fengel clapped his hands. "Capital. Well, no time to waste. Sergeant Cumbers, Mr. Dawkins, if you could attend me, I could use your skills. Lads, come away from the tree line. Those Salomcani devils are long gone by now. Now, you three, see if you can find any food among the wreckage, and salvageable cloth...."

He continued to give commands, providing order to the chaos. Hayes glared at him, then stalked off toward the jungle. Fengel let him go. When the men were sufficiently organized, and his two new officers were appropriately distracted by their tasks, he looked to the jungle and the burning mountain.

"Let's see you do *that*, you horrible witch."

The volcano rumbled in response.

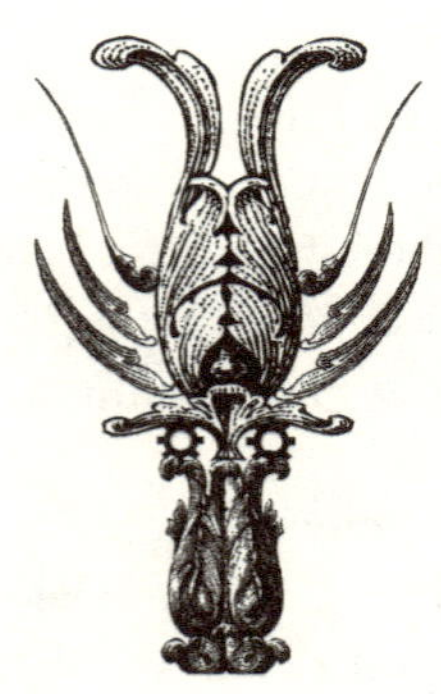

CHAPTER ELEVEN

"Oh, by the Goddess's *teats*," swore Lina Stone.

"That's an appropriate sentiment," muttered Ryan Gae.

They stood at the bow rails of the *Dawnhawk*, along with every other member of the crew. Below the airship spread Breachtown harbor, ships filling its inky water from one end to the other. Lina spied schooners, frigates, and ships-of-the-line. Most were of older construction, incorporating three masts and thick hulls dotted with gun ports for the cannon broadsides hidden within. A few were newer, with tall paddlewheels built to either side of the hull. All were made for war. There were so many of the ships that the lanterns glowing on their decks made the fleet seem a second city, one burning brighter in the moonless night than the colony did itself. This could only be the Perinese Royal Navy, the most powerful fleet in the world.

Behind the harbor lay Breachtown itself. Along the rest of the coastline, the Stormwall raged, a nigh-impenetrable barrier of shifting clouds, crackling lightning, and tempestuous winds. Above the colony, however, the Stormwall failed, as if some giant had carved a wedge from the perpetual storm, leaving the skies above clear and open to the pinprick light of the stars.

Breachtown colony sat on a curved swath of land that protruded out into the harbor. On its northern-most side rose a small hill, ideally placed to overlook the harbor and the rest of the colony. A large and stately building sprawled there, likely the governor's manor. From the hill the colony spread out, filling the safe space between the walls of the storm with homes, warehouses, and shops built in the Perinese style, wood and brick with shingled roofs of slate or tile. Aside from the governor's house, only three other buildings stood out from above; the turreted armory, the domed counting house, and a keep-like partial construction of heavy stone situated at the near end of the wharf, where it could watch both the harbor and the colony proper.

A surprised hiss sounded to her left. Lina glanced up to see Rastalak peering over the gunwales with widened eyes. She looked at his unbandaged hands. The skin there was soft and green, without scales. Rastalak had healed from his burns remarkably quickly over the last few days.

"So many vessels," said the little Draykin.

"Look there," said Reaver Jane. She pointed at the half-finished edifice. "Are they building a fort?"

Sarah Lome grunted. "It can't be anything else," she said sourly. The big woman's face was stained with ink, especially around her forehead and eyes.

A wet noise sounded behind Lina. Allen stood there with a rockfruit clutched in both hands. He gnawed at it in frustration, trying to crack the thing with his teeth. The fruit's red shell glistened wetly.

Allen froze at her gaze. He held out the rockfruit shyly. "I thought we could share," he said.

Lina narrowed her eyes at him. "I do not want any of your slobbery fruit," she replied. Allen's unexpected competence the other night hadn't changed anything, ultimately. He still mooned after her like a lonely puppy.

Lina forced Runt to lay down and looked back at the colony and the assembled ships of the navy floating before it. Of all the problems she'd considered for the raid, this had not been one of them. *Now what do we do?* she wondered. *We can't pull this off with half the Perinese military in town. Can we? It's a miracle we haven't been seen already.*

"This," said Lucian, "presents a quandary." He drummed his fingers against the gunwales. The committee-member was looking a little more ragged around the edges these days. His clothing wasn't as fastidious as usual, and dark circles hung beneath his eyes. "Original plan was to hang out at sea until nightfall, then swoop in atop the counting house and dispatch half the crew down to send up the loot just like any merchant frigate we've taken. The night covers us for now, but we're sure to be seen if we dally off the coast during the day. We won't be able to stay near the counting house for nearly long enough if that happens."

"We are not turning back?" asked Konrad. Both he and Maxim stood shoulder to shoulder.

Lina half hoped that they would. The crew had not gotten any more disciplined these last few days, even after Jonas Wiley almost fell to his death. The Mechanist and Lucian had argued loudly last night, and now the older man was in reclusion in his engine room warrens, sending Allen out for anything needed on deck. The committee spent more and more time down in the mess, arguing over minutiae.

She glanced around at the faces of her crewmembers. Half muttered and griped, angry at the very suggestion of leaving now. But a few others appeared almost relieved that someone had brought up the subject.

Lucian started. "What? No, of course not. We'll just have to make it up as we go along."

Lina frowned. Her stomach knotted. That wasn't what she wanted to hear.

"Dawn's almost here," said Sarah Lome. "We need anchorage, or somewhere high so we won't get sucked into the Stormwall. Where can we go without being seen?"

"Let me think." Lucian rubbed his forehead for a long moment before snapping his fingers. "Ah! I've got it." He raised his hands over his head for attention. "Everyone to your stations. You, Mechanist. Allen, right? Go tell that old goat to get the boilers stoked. Sarah, take the deck, please. Douse any lights and be quiet about things. Konrad and Maxim, can you whistle up a cloud? Something to obfuscate us? Like we did after punching through the Stormwall in the *Copper Queen*?"

The crowd around them dispersed. Maxim frowned sourly as Konrad shot him a questioning glance.

"That was how we got the drop on you near the Silverpenny six months ago," said Maxim. He gave a shrug.

"Madness," replied Konrad. The big aetherite looked impressed.

"It was not fun," agreed Maxim. He faced Lucian again. "That was not 'whistling up a cloud.' It was cooling of a large mass of aether. I could do it again, perhaps. It's going to stink, though, the convection ratio—"

Lucian waved him to quiet. "You just had to say 'yes,' Maxim. I've no need for the details. Work it out with Konrad. So long as we can fool a few tired lookouts, that's good enough."

The aetherites shared a look. Maxim then tried to catch Lucian's gaze. "We would have to pool everything we have. And you really should know how this would work. It will leave us largely without any remaining Workings. Amassing enough moisture via Thorp's Interroluction—"

"Yes, yes," interrupted Reaver Jane. "Enough aetherite gibberish." She gave Lucian a pointed look as Maxim lapsed into irritated silence. "Where are we going to actually go?"

Lucian pointed out at the city, past it, to the thick jungles of the Yulan Interior. "We are going to some nice, out-of-the way anchorage for the day. Some place the townies never go unless they have to."

Lina stared at the dark horizon past the Stormwall. The jungle lay there, full of strangeness and hostility. Her unease deepened. Turning, she slipped away from knot of committee-members before Lucian give some weird, arbitrary order to *her*. She moved down the deck to her normal station along the starboard gunwales, where the exhaust pipe to the steam boiler emerged. Runt lay coiled there as usual, napping. The scryn opened one black eye as he heard her bootsteps. She held out one arm and Runt unwound, springing up to land roughly on her shoulder. Lina grunted and tried to find her balance as the creature crawled his accustomed way around her scrawny frame.

Maybe we shouldn't have left them there. Lina was beginning to regret her original suggestion to strand the captains while they made this trip. Finding the whole damned Perinese Navy waiting in port should have alarmed the committee, not to mention the rest of the crew. Instead, only a few had seemed even a little put off. Lucian had barely given any thought before just ordering them ahead, preparing to dive right into the mess without even knowing what was really going on down in the colony.

But what can I do? Lina sighed aloud to herself and scratched Runt along his neck. The scryn chirped happily and wriggled, an uncomfortable, wormy sensation across her neck and shoulders that she still hadn't gotten used to.

Sarah Lome ordered the few lights on deck doused. Loose chains, or anything else that could have made noise, were tightened and secured. Lina watched in trepidation as the *Dawnhawk* prepared to pass over the city. A low, steady vibration started below the deck as the steam engine hidden there was stoked back into action. The skysails were pulled in, and a gentle whirr started as the propellers at the back of the ship began to spin.

Up at the bow of the ship, the aetherites worked their magic. Konrad and Maxim stood up at the bow with arms spread wide. Maxim exhaled, and a frosty white vapor spilled down and out over the bow, billowing as it went. Konrad did the same. Presumably, this would shroud the hull of the *Dawnhawk*. Lina didn't really trust it. She probably should have known more about aetherite magic by now, but like the rest of the crew, had little care to. She knew it was potent, knew there were 'rules,' and most importantly, knew that it tended to make the aetherite using it crazy. Though both Maxim and Konrad did seem unusually mellow of late.

Lina wrinkled her nose as the scent of the arcane mists reached her. Why did aetherite magic always have to stink so?

The harbor grew as the *Dawnhawk* approached. They lost altitude, dropping from a thousand feet above the fleet to a mere hundred. The move was unfortunate, though Lina knew why they were doing this, at least. The Stormwall could be climbed and even passed through, but it had only been Captain Fengel's quick thinking and a heaping dose of good luck that they'd survived the one time it had been tried. Even then, the airship they'd flown on had been damaged beyond repair. Down this low, the *Dawnhawk* could slip past the raging winds without any fear of getting sucked into them. Though this did put them uncomfortably within musket range to anyone on the ground. They'd be safe from that, though, so long as everyone kept their heads down.

Not that this is a great idea. Someone was bound to see them. And then the alarm would raise, and they wouldn't be able to raid the counting house successfully, and this whole trip would be a colossal waste of time.

Rastalak gave a small hiss of wonder from his post up the deck. Someone shushed him and Lina glanced over the side. Reefed topsails poked up at her, and a crow's nest went by so close that she could almost reach out and touch it. The *Dawnhawk* was passing directly over the warships in the harbor.

The assembled vessels of the navy almost seemed like a floating forest, with each mast a skeletal tree poking up at the belly of their airship. Ship after ship drifted by beneath, each one loaded with enough cannons and crewmen to sail to a far-off land, and conquer it. Thankfully, most of the sailors she saw were taking catnaps when they should have been on watch. Lina knew that would mean the lash if they were caught. Those that weren't asleep played cards with their mates, or told each other rude jokes and stories.

Past the harbor loomed the worked stone of the city wharf. More warships sat there at rest, quiet and ominous in the early gloom. Lina caught her breath at the sight of a lone watch officer striding up and down the nearest pier, directly beneath the *Dawnhawk's* path.

The officer whistled as he stalked the pier, clearly bored, not expecting anything unusual. Lina glanced at her crewmates. A few had of them had spied the soldier. Ryan Gae frowned. Tricia and Elly Minel shared a grimace. Rastalak watched with reptilian patience. There was little any of them could do. They passed overhead and the officer stopped his pacing, cocking his head. Lina was acutely aware now of the airship propeller's whirr.

He never looked up, however. The *Dawnhawk* flew past him and beyond the docks into the city. Somehow they had avoided notice. Lina sighed in relief and turned her attention to their destination, blinking in surprise as she took in the great barricades arranged to face the colony. It seemed that Breachtown was under siege, or at least considered hostile by the navy.

The scents of old smoke reached Lina's nose as they flew past the first dock buildings. Taverns, brothels, warehouses, and all those structures that were a common part of port life were burned and ruined wrecks. Some still stood after a fashion, charred timber frames jutting out of the ground like a burned matchstick forest. Most were simple piles of ash and rubble.

Lina peered into the gloom of the colony, Runt sniffing past her head at the air. *What happened here?* Six months ago they'd passed through Breachtown on their way out of the Yulan Interior. They hadn't bothered with any subterfuge then. Just flown through in the light of day as fast as they could, keeping their heads down to avoid any stray gunfire sent their way. They needn't have even worried. The colony had been a chaotic mess, still reeling from the aftermath of an aborted rebellion. Apparently, news of that event had finally reached the King back in Perinault.

The damage was less severe past the waterfront. A few houses had their windows broken and boarded up. None were ruined by fire. Though few lights burned in any of the houses she saw, they were far from empty. Lina spied a cluster of pup tents laid out in orderly rows across one lawn, campfire coals glimmering red in the dark. Other hints of occupation made themselves apparent. The Royal Marines were certainly present in Breachtown in force.

Shots rang out in some distant part of the city. Shouts followed them, and then the sound of wooden doors being battered down. Lina frowned. It was a raid, not a cry of alarm at the airship's passing. *Still.*

Lina glanced up to Ryan Gae's position near the bow. The older pirate watched the city curiously, not a hint of alarm on his rustic features. She glanced about the rest of the deck. Rastalak had climbed the rigging to peer at the human city. Near the equipment locker, Andrea Holt pinched her nose, more concerned about the stink of the aetherite's spell than anything else. On the port side of the ship, the Wiley twins were seeing who could spit the farthest. No one seemed wary.

Lina tried to relax. *Is it just me?* There was little that might happen if they were spotted, at least immediately. The navies of the world had yet to develop an effective countermeasure against the Haventown airships. Cannons were built to fire at other ocean-going vessels. Muskets did too little damage, though every pirate was wary of the stray ball. But the counting house raid hinged on surprise and remaining undiscovered. If the force occupying the town knew the *Dawnhawk* was here, they'd increase security on the streets to the point that breaking into the counting house would be impossible. And they had come so far....

Movement up near the bow caught her attention. Maxim slumped and grabbed at the gunwales, coughing. Konrad shortly followed suit. Their arcane mist evaporated. Sarah Lome, pacing in her usual place, noticed. She walked over to them and bent over, asking short, sharp questions that Lina was too far away to hear. All she saw was Konrad, shaking his head.

Lucian and Reaver Jane had noticed as well. They moved up to meet with the gunnery mistress as she stalked back to them, happily now within earshot of Lina's post.

"They say they're spent," said Sarah Lome.

"Tell them that's not an option," replied Reaver Jane. "We need that mist."

"That won't work," said Lucian. He tapped his chin in thought, then shrugged. "It's still dark out. We should be fine. Let's push on through."

"Are you crazed?" asked Sarah Lome. She slashed a hand out at the night. "We've no cover, and the city is infested with Bluecoats."

"But what can they do?" asked Reaver Jane. "Point and us and shout?"

"Yes," said Sarah Lome. "Precisely. If we're noticed then this whole plan fails. We won't be able to sneak in over the counting house long enough to hoist the loot. You *know* that."

Reaver Jane snorted. "Perinese. Please. Let 'em try to stop us."

Sarah Lome made a fist. "Don't be stupid."

"Sarah," interrupted Lucian. "We're already this far in. What else can we do?"

She stared at him, then shook her head. "This whole mess has been a bad idea from the start. We never should have gotten rid of the captains." Sarah Lome stalked away back up the deck. As she went, she shot a glare at Lina, holding it until Jonas Wiley let out a hoot of laughter; apparently Nate Wiley had spit exceptionally far.

Lucian watched her go with a shrug, then returned to where Henry Smalls held the helm steady. Reaver Jane kept her place, narrowing her eyes after the huge gunnery mistress.

Lina took a breath and looked again to the city. Runt chirped and rubbed his face against her cheek. *Great,* she mused. *Just great.*

The *Dawnhawk* kept its course for the jungles of the Yulan. They flew over cobblestone streets and narrow, tightly spaced houses. Nate Wiley gave a whispered cry on the far side of the deck and the crew gathered together to peer past his outstretched arm. From the excited, over-loud whispers, Lina discerned that they could see Breachtown Counting House up relatively close now, the goal of this whole trip. Lina realized that she didn't care.

A tall, three-story building appeared ahead on the starboard side of the airship. It was square with a bell tower atop the low, almost flat roof. From each of the four corners rose a turret, connected to each other by long battlements. The battlement walkways converged on the bell tower, forming a cross when seen up above. What windows the structure did have were thin and positioned high on the third floor. This could only be the Breachtown Armory.

Lina peered at the building. The turrets were obvious watch posts, but she didn't see anyone moving about upon them. At the same time, the Bluecoats didn't exactly stand out in the pre-dawn dark that shrouded the city.

Allen tromped up beside her, his boot steps louder than the whirring of the ship's propellers. The young Mechanist still held the rockfruit in one hand. In his other he had a heavy wrench.

"So," said Allen, voice forcibly light. "I was wondering...."

"Not now," Lina hissed.

He blinked. "What?"

Lina glared at him. "We're passing by the armory. Keep quiet, we can't afford to be seen."

"Oh," he said. He peered around into the night. "Aren't we through the city yet?"

She glared at him. "What? Look!" Lina gestured out off the edge of the airship.

Allen leaned over and started. "Oh," he replied. "I guess we are, then. I was down below helping with the boiler. Then I had to find a wrench for this fruit. Hello there."

Lina frowned, then she realized that Allen's last words hadn't been directed at her. He was waggling the spanner back and forth in a wave down at someone down below. Lina felt her heart leap in her throat. She leaned over the gunwales to look.

The *Dawnhawk* was just now passing the Armory. They were so close that she could see into the nearest parapet turret. As she'd expected, a watch-post was setup within. And in it was a Bluecoat, staring up at them.

He was middle-aged and a little portly. Lina hadn't seen him on the approach because he was laying down, napping with a small pony-keg breached next to him. He was awake now, though, and he stared back at the airship above him, giving a small, puzzled wave back to the young Mechanist. Then he scrambled to his feet.

Lina yelled back at the helm. "We're made!"

Those who weren't staring at the counting house on the far side of the deck ran over. Andrea, Rastalak, Sarah Lome, Tricia, Fat Thomlin, and Reaver Jane all appeared. Reaver Jane drew a pistol after a glance at the Bluecoat.

"Put that away!" ordered Sarah Lome. "He's not given the alarm yet. A shot from you and we're sure to be noticed."

Reaver Jane glared furiously at her. "You daft bint, he's about to sound that damned bell. Do you have some better idea?"

Sarah pursed her lips. "That doesn't matter. It's not like you could even hit him at this distance."

Jane bared her teeth. "I'm a better shot than you are, you homely ogre."

The gunnery mistress stepped up to Jane, forcing the other committee-member back. "Say that again," said Sarah Lome.

"Officers," said Ryan, voice taut and face wary at the conflict brewing before them. "He's getting away."

Lina glanced back. The Bluecoat was dashing up the parapet walkway for the bell tower at the center of the Armory roof. He wasn't yelling, but soon the whole city would know they were there.

"Well, do something, then!" snarled Reaver Jane.

Lina grabbed for the wrench in Allen's hands. She missed, snagging the still uncracked rockfruit instead. It felt like a chunk of red stone. *Why not?* she wondered. Lina reared back, took aim, and let fly at the Bluecoat.

The rockfruit sailed through the air in a long parabolic arc. *Please make it,* she prayed. The fruit flew farther than she would have thought, given its heft. Just before the marine could reach the bell tower, it connected with his head in a thump that echoed up to the airship. The marine crumpled to the rooftop battlement.

Her crewmates all fell silent. Runt chirped in surprise. "I would have bet anything that you would have missed that throw," said Tricia in an awed voice.

Everyone watched to see if the Bluecoat would get back up. Lina winced, hoping that she hadn't killed the man.

"All right," said Reaver Jane and Sarah Lome, both at the same time. "Everyone back to your posts," they said again in tandem. Each glared at the other, then they turned away. The crowd dispersed, sensing the off mood of the committee-members. Lina and Allen watched them go.

"Huh," said the Mechanist after a moment. He shook his head and then looked back to Lina slyly. "You know, I've got some more of those down below," he said. "And a half a bottle of wine I saved from dinner last night."

Lina rolled her eyes. Runt chirped and wriggled on her shoulder.

The rest of the flight through the city was tense, but quiet. Lina didn't hear any more Bluecoat raids, and by the grace of the Goddess no other watchmen seemed to notice them. She relaxed a little once they'd reached the edge of the colony. Sarah Lome and Reaver Jane were still ignoring each other. And they *were* in the Yulan now.

Things were more rural at this end of the city. The carefully constructed Perinese architecture gave way to more practical considerations. Also, the buildings were built farther apart, with much more greenery between them. It was hard to tell in the pre-dawn gloom, but Lina thought she saw fields of sugarcane and ordered orchards of tropical fruit. To either side, north and south, climbed the Stormwall.

The perpetual storm roiled. Lightning flashed in its depths and high up near its summit. For all its rage, though, the Stormwall was tamed here in the Breach. A gentle breeze played about the deck of the airship, and did little else.

She peered south, marveling at its size. It seemed deeper now, thicker, than the last time they'd passed through. Too deep, in fact. It was taking much longer to pass through than it should. Lina frowned and looked over the gunwales to the plantations below. *Hang on, we're stopping. What's going on?*

Allen coughed. Lina looked up just in time to see a sack flying through the air at her head. She caught it at the last second, falling back a bit at its weight. Runt chirruped in irritation. When she wrestled the thing away from her face, she saw Lucian smiling down at her.

"What was that for?" she asked.

"Clothes," Lucian replied. "Part two of my new Plan. Found them down below a bit ago, in the silks we'd taken from that last merchant."

"All right?" Lina didn't like where this was heading.

The committee-member gestured at the stern, and the colony at their back. "I've decided that some of us need to go into the city, make sure things are quiet, and check out the counting house before we strike it tomorrow night."

His plan came to her in an instant. Lina looked at him sideways. "You want me to dress like the locals, sneak into the city, and spend all day watching over the counting house? By myself?"

Lucian shook his head. "Of course not. You'll have Runt." He looked at the expression on her face. "Oh, don't be like that. I'll send a few more folks in to help you this afternoon. Meet them at that big statue we saw in the park. They'll have further orders, once I've thought up what we need to do next."

"What park?" asked Lina, eyebrow raised.

"The big one we flew over," he replied. "Right in front of the counting house. Can't miss it." Lucian moved past her to the gunwales. He picked up a rope ladder and tossed it over the side. "There you go," he said. "Time to be off. Now remember, you need to blend in. There's a disguise in the satchel. Rather clever of me, if I do say so myself." He abruptly walked away, preventing any rebuttal.

Lina watched him go. She tried to think of something to say, to voice one of the many complaints she had. But her chance had passed; Lucian was already gone. She glanced at the crew. None of them were even looking at her, aside from Allen. The other committee-members were ignoring each other, and pretty much everything else now. Lina glanced down at the satchel in her hands, and felt her tension return.

"I could help, if you like," said Allen, too helpfully, too quickly. "You know, with changing." He winked.

Lina stared at him. Then she sighed and moved to the rope ladder dangling off the ship.

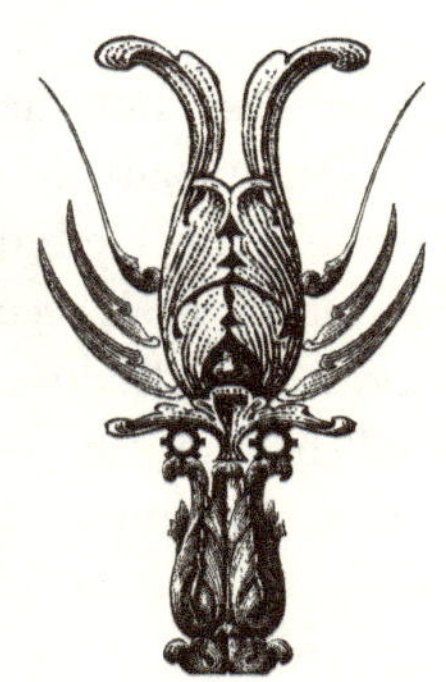

CHAPTER TWELVE

Natasha pushed the frond of a thick green fern away from her face. She clambered over the plant, hurrying to keep up. Kalyon Mahmoud had few qualms about yanking the rope around her neck if he thought she wasn't moving fast enough.

Her noose tightened as he did just that. She coughed and moved faster, tugging at the rope to keep from choking. *Soon enough,* she vowed at his back. *Soon enough. Just get us all back to your ship. Then I'll show you whom you've crossed. Oh yes.*

The Salomcani travelled through the morning jungle in a long column, aiming for the opposite side of the isle from the *Goliath,* likely where their own ship waited. These raiders were a ragged bunch. So far, she had counted twenty in all. They weren't proper navy, though; the Sheikdom's fleet was an undisciplined mob only one step up from the pirates and cutthroats of her own home port. Whether real sailors or merely licensed privateers, they were desperate, hurt, and afraid. Natasha read it in the way they clutched their stolen building supplies, in the glances they made over their shoulders back at the Perinese side of the isle.

To her great irritation, she'd been too exhausted from her swim to fight them off yesterday. Her father would have berated her for that. She should have been ready for them, should have met them on her feet. The raiders had quickly subdued her, though, bringing her along as they fled from the site of their raid. Eventually they stopped to rest for the night and their Kalyon, called Mahmoud, made all the usual intimidating noises at her. Natasha was their captive now, their prize. She would warm their beds for them and be glad for it. Etcetera.

Killing him would have been easy, but she restrained herself. Natasha decided to play along while the Salomcani slunk back through the jungle. There was weakness in the Kalyon. Fear. He blustered too hard and crowed too loudly to the dispirited crew about their recent victory over the Perinese. His grip on his men was tenuous, and he knew it. As soon as he showed Natasha his ship, she would kill him and bully those she could into place beneath her. It wouldn't be hard. Mahmoud had left her hands free. He didn't even watch her. As for the sailors, they'd be happy just to be led by someone with a spine. She was sure of it.

That would show her idiot husband. She'd strand him here, then sail back home to teach the mutineers on the *Dawnhawk* what it meant to cross her.

The jungle they moved through was much like the rest of the island. Thick mangrove trees rose up overhead, their draping branches impeding her path while wide leaves filled the spaces in between. Already the air was muggy and thick, unpleasant after the clean ocean breeze of the beach. Sweat beaded her forehead, collected on her face, and ran down her neck in rivulets. Her blouse was soaked.

A faint tremor shook the earth. It sent the trees to shivering and the vines draping their branches to swaying between the shafts of morning sunlight. Natasha caught her balance on a young mangrove trunk to her left. The earthquakes had started late last night, but the tremors were still small and far apart, at least so far. They made the Salomcani uneasy, though so long as everything wasn't falling on her head she didn't care. She had more important things to worry about.

Like revenge.

Mahmoud cursed. Natasha looked at him just as the rope leash around her neck went taut, jerking her forward. She stumbled over a log hidden beneath the foliage and windmilled just to keep from falling, as he had. A small mangrove bole rose to her left. Natasha grabbed at it, just managing to avoid joining her captor face-down on the loamy earth.

"Eyes of the Goddess!" cursed Mahmoud aloud in his native tongue. Natasha spoke fluent Salomcani, yet hid that fact for now. She watched him clamber back up to his feet and face her. "Move faster, wench," he said in broken Perinese.

Wench? Natasha glared at him. "Watch your damned footing." She was rapidly losing patience. It wasn't that big an island. She could just kill him now and find the *Salmalin* herself.

"Idiot woman," growled Mahmoud, red beard quavering. He shook a fist in her face. "You dare speak to me so? I am Kalyon of the *Salmalin*!"

Natasha gave a shrug. "I don't give half a damn for the Perinese, but at least they don't use brain-dead harem boys to run their ships. I'll talk however I—"

Something wet splattered on her forehead. Natasha blinked, pulling back in surprise. She wiped her sleeve against her face. What came away was white, sticky and rank.

"Is this...*pfaugh!* Is this bird shit?"

A flash of color blurred past. It landed on a high branch of the mangrove to her left. The parrot was garish, with a butter-yellow beak, stumpy orange legs, and brilliant rainbow feathers. It was missing a few feathers from its coat, as if someone had struck it. The parrot glared down at her with smug malevolence.

Natasha stared at the thing. "*You!*" she hissed in horror and rage. "You obnoxious piece of filth. You dare stick that ugly beak before me again? Come down here! I'm going to wring your neck and *eat* you this time!"

"Ha!" laughed Mahmoud. "There is some perfume for you." he shook his head and chuckled. "Be thankful this amuses me."

"Shut up," she snarled at him. "I'll finish you after I'm done with *that.*"

Mahmoud blinked. "What, the parrot?"

It screamed mockingly at them both. Natasha flinched at the noise. Mahmoud staggered back a step.

"Yes, the damned parrot!"

Natasha knelt, grabbing for a fallen branch. *I'm going to knock you into next week,* she vowed. Then the rope around her neck closed like a noose. Her feet flew out as she was yanked forward. Natasha collapsed to the ground, choking, clutching at her leash.

The parrot screamed repeatedly at her. It almost seemed to be laughing.

Mahmoud shook his head. "Enough games, woman." He held her leash with both hands, smiling faintly. When she caught his eye though, the smile faded and he looked away first.

Natasha pulled the noose loose enough that she could breath. *Enough. I was going to wait, but enough and more than enough. It is time for you to die, Mahmoud.* Movement up above caught her eye. Blinking slowly, the parrot almost seemed to wink at her. *And you. You go next, bird.*

Natasha grabbed up a rock and leapt at the Kalyon. Mahmoud saw too late. He cursed, falling back while awkwardly trying to draw the blade at his side.

She tripped over the log.

Natasha crashed onto the loamy earth. The taste of dirt and mulched leaves filled her mouth. Dimly she heard the ring of drawn steel and the shouts of Mahmoud and his Salomcani.

Two pairs of hands grabbed her arms, hauling her upright. Natasha spat dirt and tried to swing the rock out blindly. It missed.

Another tremor shook the earth. This one was bigger, uglier. It threatened to pitch Natasha and her captors over. Leaves, branches and coconuts fell all around them. She froze, fighting for her balance. In a moment it passed, though she had dropped her rock.

Mahmoud rose from his crouch, eyes wild and worried. "Enough of this," he said, switching back to Salomcani. He pointed at Natasha with a quivery, worried finger. "Farouk, Etarin, keep ahold of this madwoman. I will, I will discipline her when we get back to the *Salmalin*. Yes." He straightened, brushing off his pant legs. "I dislike these temblors. We must head back on the move, all of you!"

The Kalyon tossed her makeshift leash at one of the men restraining her, then stalked off ahead into the jungle. Natasha glanced at the pair of them. The one at her left was tall and broad, though he seemed to hunch a little, with a well-groomed black beard. He had deep-brown eyes and small nose. The other was short and stout, older, with a lighter beard and green eyes. Both of them were shirtless, revealing saggy skin and numerous bandages, many of which were older than yesterday's raid.

"Go," said the one to her right in atrocious Perinese. He prodded her forward, gently.

Natasha thought about trying to kill them as well. *No. Them, I need.* The realization galled her. She frowned, vented a frustrated sigh, and started to step forward. Then she knelt, grabbed up the rock, and turned to pitch it at the ugly parrot. Her captors wrestled it from her, barely, as the bird screamed mockingly.

Before long, they were moving again through the morning jungle. Farouk and Etarin kept close to her, but they were tired and occasionally fell behind. Still, they had left her hands free. Natasha shook her head at that. *How foolish can you be?* She didn't press her luck, though. Mahmoud's death was a certainty. But her rage cooled after a few moment's reflection. Somewhat. The original plan was still the best one. Find the ship, *then* kill the Kalyon and bully his crew into submission.

The bird followed the Salomcani. Sometimes it landed ahead of her, sometimes behind. Each time it screamed at her, until someone threw a stick at it or she'd travelled too far away. Natasha focused on how many ways she could cook fowl. Frustratingly, she realized that she didn't really know any.

Bright blue skies appeared overhead as the jungle thinned out into a clearing. At the far end stood a low ridge maybe fifteen feet in height. A weathered crack through its center allowed passage through. Past the ridge called the roar of the ocean, the pounding hiss of surf crashing upon the shore. Natasha gave a small sigh of relief. They were almost to the end of this trek. And she *was* tired. Physically, but more than that, she was tired of waiting.

They were halfway across the clearing when the earthquake hit.

The ground shook violently. Natasha reached out reflexively for the nearest thing at hand, the tall sailor on her right. Farouk, maybe. She thought it just another tremor at first, yet the shaking didn't abate. Instead, it worsened.

Natasha fought to stay upright while the Salomcani cried out in fear and surprise. Mahmoud fell to the ground. Farouk and Etarin dropped to their knees. Behind her cried those still within the jungle, their alarmed shouts changing to yells of fear as trees crashed to the ground. The horrible parrot gave an alarmed squawk and took to the air, a fear-puffed blur of color against the morning sky.

The earthquake worsened with every passing moment. Great tearing noises surrounded her as the foliage of the jungle ripped and tore itself apart. Rocks on the nearby ridge spilled down to crash into each other with a clatter.

Natasha kept standing out of sheer obstinance while Farouk and Etarin kneeled. She grabbed at their heads for balance. *Not gonna fall,* she vowed. *Everything else may have gone to shit, but I'll be damned to the Realms Below before I let this place beat me.*

The island, it seemed, heard her challenge. The quaking increased. Great rents split the ground across the clearing, running in crazy jagged lines that zigged and zagged as they went. The crack in the ridge collapsed, sending a shower of dirt and rubble flying. The jungle bushes all around her shook and wavered like they were waves on the ocean itself.

Then it stopped. The island gave one last great shudder, and stilled. An explosion sounded, a massive eruption that issued forth from the volcano at the center of the isle. Past the now-flattened tree line Natasha could see its shadowed bulk rising high above. A great gout of fire and ash belched forth from the peak, casting a lurid orange glow that seemed to set the whole world alight.

No magma flowed forth from the peak, however, and the falling embers, while dramatic, weren't that threatening. They were safe for the moment. The quake had passed.

She relaxed, a little. Ahead, Mahmoud knelt upon the ground with his hands over his head. Etarin and Farouk knelt next to her, grabbing at her legs for support, as if she were the only stable thing in the world. Behind her lay the rest of the Salomcani sailors in varying stages of repose. A few nursed wounds. Many cried out prayers to the Goddess. None remained standing.

One by one the sailors looked up and saw her. They stared when they did.

Natasha realized how she must have looked. Still standing strong while even the Kalyon had fallen. Beautiful and radiant as ashes fell about them.

This is exactly what I need, she thought in relief. She ignored Mahmoud, and looked out at the crew, making it a point to meet every pair of eyes. They were a pathetic bunch, she realized again. Beaten, starved, hauling pillaged lumber and nails through the jungle. It occurred to her to wonder why that was.

I can figure it out later. For now, just keep strong. And get ready to slap Mahmoud into the dirt right before their eyes. They had to be almost to the ship. A mob like this would respect strength more than anything else at the moment.

Slowly, the Salomcani crept back to their feet. Mahmoud stood warily, freezing as he looked her way, a frown curling his mustache and beard. *Are you ready, Mahmoud?* Natasha smiled and raised a contemptuous eyebrow. Here was her opening.

"Are you finished groveling like a heathen savage, Kalyon Mahmoud?" Natasha called out in clear, perfect Salomcan. "I thought we were in a hurry to get back to your ship." Her voice carried in the silence that followed the earthquake.

Mahmoud blinked in surprise. "Woman, I swear before the eyes of the Goddess that I will discipline you—"

"Kalyon!" she interrupted. "I am Kalyon Blackheart of the reaver *Dawnhawk*. I am no dockside bed-warmer, you worm, and you couldn't hope to discipline me on your best day." She undid the leash around her neck and tossed it aside. At her side, the shorter man, Etarin, voiced a complaint. She ignored him to focus on Mahmoud.

Natasha put her hands on her hips and held his gaze. This was the test. Not between her and him, she knew. Farouk and Etarin knelt, watching, heedless of the blades at their sides. If Mahmoud were to actually threaten her, it would be simple enough to draw one of those blades and run him through. No, this was for the rest of the crew, and the way to them was through their Kalyon. Fengel wasn't completely wrong, unfortunately. A good show was important sometimes. She just had to make sure that hers had teeth.

The silence stretched as their contest went on. Kalyon Mahmoud was the first to look away.

"Enough," he growled. "I will...I will deal with you later, woman. Jahmal! Get your shifty carcass up here and look for another pass over this ridge. The old one has collapsed, it appears."

Natasha smiled. She glanced down at the two sailors kneeling beside her. They watched their leader, surprise etched upon their ugly features. Tall Farouk climbed to his feet. He shook his head at Mahmoud glumly, then looked to her.

"You speak the tongue of Salomca?" he asked, almost shy.

"Of course," replied Natasha. "I am a Copper Islander. We are one people."

"Farouk!" cried Etarin. He clambered to his feet. "She is a prisoner!"

Natasha smirked at him. "I don't bite," she lied.

"That is not the point," said the shorter man.

"Oh? Then what else could you possibly be afraid of?" Natasha placed her hands on her hips. "You're starved, injured, and your Kalyon is a weak man. The worst has already happened to you."

Etarin frowned. "He is not weak."

Natasha smirked. "No? Then why are you slinking back through the jungle?"

Etarin glowered at her. It made him look like a cranky toad. "We are heading back to the ship. She is damaged, our *Salmalin*, from our fight with those Perinese dogs. The mast needs repairs, as does the rudder. Her hull needs patching in places, it is true, but even now she floats in the calm water off the shore."

"That sounds like a lot of work," she said with sudden heat. "Why didn't you just take the *Goliath* instead?"

Awkward silence followed her statement. The two sailors stared at her as if she were speaking madness. Natasha ignored them for the moment. Others had crept up into the clearing, and now listened to their exchange.

"You said that you are a Kalyon," said Farouk. "But how?"

Etarin grunted. "She is a Copper Isles pirate, Farouk. Anything is possible."

The sailor scratched his head. "But you are a woman. Women are too weak to serve aboard a ship."

Natasha gave him a contemptuous glare. "We do things differently in the Isles." She jabbed a finger into his chest, painfully. "And be certain of this. I am tougher, and certainly meaner, than your own Kalyon Mahmoud."

Etarin frowned. "Watch your tongue. Kalyon Mahmoud led us in the raid—"

"Against the Perinese?" she laughed. "You barely survived that mess. If someone hadn't fired that broadside, they'd have formed up and slaughtered you all." She met his eyes. "You want off this island? You should have fought harder, been cleverer, and taken their damned ship from them. It's what I would have done."

"Mahmoud has kept us alive," Etarin insisted.

Natasha raised an eyebrow. "And who got you stuck here in the first place?"

A call came from the other end of the clearing. Natasha glanced that way, where Mahmoud and the other sailor stood by the ridge. The place they stood was a little lower, maybe only ten feet or so. Debris from the earthquake had collapsed all along the ridge, but there it formed a steep slope. It wouldn't be an easy climb, but looked to be the best path over to the beach. The Kalyon was shouting, gesturing the rest of his crew forward. A wiry, agile man sat on a rock nearby, with a short, neat beard. He hid it well, but Natasha could see the distaste he had for Mahmoud in his body language. This had to be Jahmal. Natasha ignored the both of them and faced the rest of the crew.

"I'm letting you take me to the *Salmalin* because I want you to," she said to those around her. "I could have left any time I wanted." She twisted about, stalking to the ridge without waiting for their reaction.

Mahmoud stood a few feet up on the craggy slope. He glowered at her approach and opened his mouth to berate her again. Natasha met his eyes and held them before he could say anything. He looked away, past her to his gathering crew.

"You dogs of Salomca!" he called. "The Perinese have chased us, hounded us to this small isle. But they could not kill us, no! And they could not stop us from taking what we needed to repair our beloved *Salmalin*. Now, let us work well, and quickly, and leave the stinking Perinese to this shuddering and forlorn place!"

No one cheered, but a sort of ragged cry sputtered up from the crew at Natasha's back. Mahmoud went first, climbing up the hill. Jahmal went next. Natasha joined the line of crewmen as they formed up along the slope. Farouk and Etarin moved beside her.

The slope was steep. Broken rocks that had shattered in the earthquake made her ascent dangerous and uncertain. The man in front of her slipped, forcing her back down where a sharp stone tore her leggings. Those behind her cried in alarm and irritation. She snarled at the fellow before her and the man redoubled his efforts to move ahead.

Before too much longer she crested the ridge, crawled through a small crack down onto the opposite side. More rubble formed a similar slope on this end. She skipped and slid down it to a sandy dune on a wide stretch of beach. Natasha fought to keep from stumbling, her boots digging deep furrows into the already hot sand. She regained her balance and took a look at the Salomcani encampment.

Pale yellow sand spread out before her. It stretched to either side, curving around the island in the distance until the toppled tree line blocked any further sight of it. The beach itself was a mess. Rocks, driftwood, and fresh greenery lay upon the sands, pushed around by the long waves now dancing past the tide line to wash Natasha's boots. Man-made detritus wallowed about as well: a few rags, a barrel, some kitchen utensils. There was no sign of any encampment, at least not like the Perinese had made.

Down the wave-washed sands began the shoreline, only hinted at from the surf that crashed upon it, before breaking up and running to where the sailors stood. Past that rose the ocean, now stirred into a furious froth by the earthquake. There lay the *Salmalin*.

Natasha did not doubt that the frigate originated in the Sheikdom. Her lines were graceful, a bit more fanciful than the *Goliath*. The double row of gun ports would have sat higher in the water if the ship were not completely careened over onto her starboard side.

The *Salmalin* was a wreck. Either the earthquake or subsequent tidal waves had pushed the naval frigate higher up the beach and then tipped it completely over. The deck was cracked and broken, and two of the masts had been snapped clean off halfway down their lengths. The rest of the rigging was a tangled mess.

The ship would clearly never sail again.

A low moan arose from the sailors. Shouts and cries of dismay punctuated the groaning as more and more of the crew crossed the ridge to see what awaited them.

Natasha's thoughts grew black. *This is what I spent half the night crawling toward? This is what I wore a damned leash for? This is what I tried to be patient for?* She fumed. Every time. Every damned time she tried to set something in motion, to rise up with a plan, the world pushed her back down to the ground.

Kalyon Mahmoud looked to the crew, then back to the ship, then back to the crew. He swallowed nervously. Looking at the assembled crewmen for a long moment, he narrowed his eyes and nodded.

"Jahmal, Farouk, Etarin. Attend me."

The three sailors were staring in horror at their ship. Mahmoud hissed and Jahmal looked to him, startled out of his shock. "What, Kalyon?"

"I said, attend me."

"But the ship—"

"I can see what has happened to the ship," said Mahmoud. His voice was tight. "And we need to get aboard before the rest of the crew overcome their surprise."

The sailor frowned. "Kalyon, I don't understand."

Mahmoud glared at him. He muttered under his breath and turned away.

It came to Natasha in a flash. *Better and better.* Her father would have said to strike now. She agreed. "He's running," Natasha said aloud.

Etarin, Farouk, and Jahmal all looked her way. The noises of aggrieved surprise behind her stopped.

"It's obvious that this ship will never sail again." Natasha glanced back to see that several of the crew had heard her and were all listening. *Good.* "That means that you're not getting off this island," she continued. "But there's a whole shipful of enemies here too, with guns and food and medicine to patch up their hurts. So your Kalyon is going to hide somewhere safe. Likely his cabin, which I wouldn't be surprised to learn has been filled with food and weapons. And most of you aren't invited."

Mahmoud had frozen in his tracks. Silence now reigned upon the beach, broken only by the watery crash of the surf.

Jahmal stared at Mahmoud. "Is this true, Kalyon?" Until now, he had been quiet. Lean and wiry, he reminded Natasha of Reaver Jane.

The Kalyon faced her in a rage. He stepped toward her, one hand upraised. "Harlot! How dare you speak such falsehood! I will—"

Natasha stepped in to meet him. She punched Mahmoud in the throat with her left hand, and grabbed ahold of the scimitar at his belt with her right. His hands went to his throat reflexively as he choked. Natasha stepped back, drawing his blade free with a sound that rang across the sands. The she lunged.

The blade met a momentary resistance before punching out the back of Kalyon Mahmoud's shirt, red and bloody. He gave a startled cry of shock and pain, fumbling for the sword buried in his chest. Natasha withdrew, pulling the scimitar with her. Mahmoud dropped to the ground, choking.

Warm satisfaction rolled over her. *I swore that I would kill you, Mahmoud.* Natasha faced the crew. All their eyes were on her, wide and shocked. A few had reflexively reached for weapons. Natasha knew she had to talk fast if she didn't want to be torn to pieces.

"Listen, all of you!" she cried. "Your Kalyon Mahmoud was weak. He was afraid! And in the end, he thought only of himself. Go, look at his cabin. I am sure you will find the lion's share of food and weapons. He would have abandoned you to your enemies!"

A heavy sailor with a scarred chest drew his scimitar and stepped toward her. He wore a blue headscarf and striped trousers, but nothing else. Anger twisted his face beneath his dark beard and mustachios. "You whore!" he cried. "How dare you—"

Natasha attacked. He brought up his scimitar. She parried the blow, crossing their blades. When he leaned in to throw his weight into their struggle, she kicked him in the crotch. The sailor's eyes bulged. She stepped aside to let him fall, groaning, to the sand.

She met the eyes of every sailor there, ignoring the man who had tried to kill her. "Go," she repeated. "Look in his cabin."

Etarin looked aggrieved. He frowned and looked away. "The Kalyon did have us move the supplies," he said after a moment. "In case the raid went bad."

Jahmal looked at her angrily. "But he was our Kalyon." He pointed a finger at her. "You cut him down in cold blood. We needed him to survive, regardless of what we thought of him personally!"

She narrowed her gaze at him. *Go back to being quiet, Jahmal.* "I did what was necessary. For all of you. I've freed you from the incompetence of his leadership."

"But what will we do now?" asked Farouk. "Our ship, she is still wrecked! The Perinese will still come for us." He shook his head. "We are doomed."

"Doomed?" Natasha threw back her head and laughed. "Hardly." She gestured to the dying Mahmoud with her scimitar. "He had no plan. But I, I do. I told you what I would have done just a bit ago, were I leading your raid. Now it's the only option. The *Salmalin* is beached, but remember that there is still one ship on this island that can sail."

Farouk looked at her like she was mad. "You cannot mean the *Goliath*."

"I mean none other."

The crew all spoke up at once. Cries of surprise and incredulity warred for attention.

"Enough!" shouted Natasha.

"But they have cannons!" said one in the crowd, a man with bandages around both arms.

Natasha raised an eyebrow. "So?" She leaned forward, as if with a secret to share. "Let me tell you something I have learned. Those cannons? Whoever fired them wreaked as much harm on the Perinese as they did on you. And that explosion? It wiped out their powder stores. They've barely anything left."

The crewmen of the *Salmalin* all looked to each other.

"We are without a Kalyon, though," said Etarin.

Natasha was tempted to run him through. Couldn't these people take a hint? "Not true. *I* am a Kalyon. Follow me, and I'll lead you off of this rock, to victory, glory, and more plunder than you ever would have seen in the service of the Sheik."

"But you are a woman!" said Farouk.

"I am Salomcani!" she roared. "I was born on the Copper Isles, and their people are your people. Do you not see the color of my eyes? The blood in my veins is the same that runs in yours." She straightened, tapping Mahmoud's leg with the tip of her scimitar. "And I may have teats, but I've also got more backbone and brains than this fool ever had. He's the one that got you stuck on this damned island in the first place. And he would have left you here to die while he hid himself away."

She paused for breath and to gauge their reactions. The crew looked to each other, a few muttered quietly. Most of them watched Farouk, Etarin, and Jahmal, who appeared uncertain as well. A few glanced at their fellow in the striped trousers, wheezing on the sand. No one seemed hostile to the idea, at the least. *But they still need a push*, she realized.

"I can see you are uncertain," she said. "I can see that you are worried. Well, I have a solution. Where I come from, we have a tradition. A simple thing, where every man gets a say, and no one is an officer. The Crewman's Vote."

She raised the scimitar up and rested it on her shoulder. "Raise your hand if you wish to continue on as you are, leaderless, injured, and afraid. Don't be shy now, let's see who is willing to suffer a slow death on this island."

Many of the *Salmalin* crew looked to each other. No one raised their hands.

"All right. Now, raise your hand if you want to take a chance and live." She made a fist. "Raise your hand if you'll serve under me, while I save your hides, steal you a ship, and get you home alive."

A smattering of hands crept up. A few more raised as the crew saw their friends vote. Eventually about half had voted. Natasha smiled. It didn't matter, she knew. They were all listening to her, and already following her orders to vote. That was good enough, for now.

"Excellent," she said. "Farouk and Etarin, attend me. Jahmal as well. Those of you who are injured, sit down, and rest. Any who can still climb, come with me to the ship. We're going to unload it. All of you: we rest here for a time, see to our harms. Then we head back into that jungle, and repay those harms tenfold!" Natasha shouted the last, raising her scimitar high.

A ragged cheer met her words. Her three new officers looked to each other, shrugged, and approached.

A gurgle echoed up to her. Natasha glanced down. Mahmoud was on his side, eyes wide with fear and hate. She winked at him. His eyes rolled back in his head, and he stilled.

Natasha allowed herself a satisfied smile. *Well, then, Fengel. Let's see how you deal with* this.

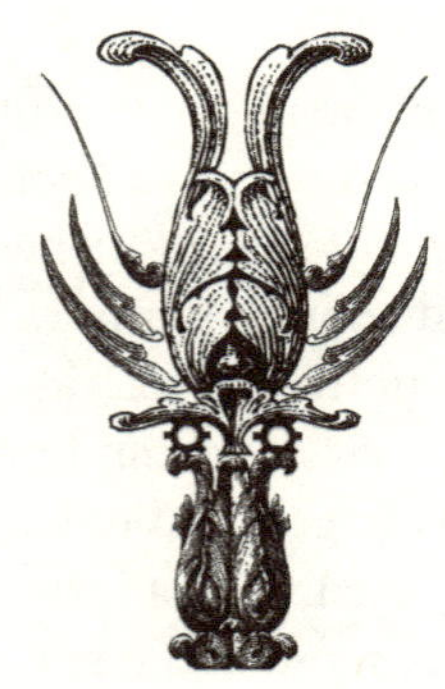

CHAPTER THIRTEEN

FENGEL PEERED INTO THE DEPTHS OF THE BILGE. Before him danced his shadow, flickering and obscuring any vision. He sighed. Reaching back, Fengel pulled Sergeant Cumbers forward so that the lantern in his hand could illuminate the *Goliath's* lowest level. Light bloomed in the dank space, revealing waist-high seawater sloshing against the ribbed hull, a low ceiling, and a few intruder hermit crabs intent on claiming the space for themselves. Something glimmered in the water a dozen feet away.

"So, as you see, sir," wheezed Harvey from the cramped stair, "hull's good an' punctured down here. It's a miracle that the quake yesterday didn't splinter even more of the frame around that weird bit o' metal. I tried cuttin' the thing away to make room for a patch, but it broke all my tools. Snapped my best hatchet right off the handle."

The shipwright held Fengel's hat and jacket for him. Amazingly, the man was alive and moving only two days after being perforated by Natasha, complaining no more than any other sailor. That was surprising. Privately, he suspected Mr. Dawkins. The aetherite said he was tapped out of Workings, but Fengel was certain he still had a few tricks up his sleeve. Still, since the crew seemed to take it as proof of Fengel's surgical skills, he didn't press the matter.

Fengel stepped down into the bilge from the hatchway stair. He gestured for Cumbers to follow and sloshed over to examine the glimmering object. The sergeant was always close at hand these days, ostensibly to better guard him. Yet he had readily performed whatever Fengel asked.

The protuberance was the color of brightly burnished brass. It rose up to just beneath the surface of the water, shaped like a perfect pyramid. Fengel nudged aside a crab and bent low to examine the thing. It did not budge when he leaned against it, and was just as hard as it looked. There wasn't a doubt in his mind what it was.

Fengel straightened. "It's no wonder you couldn't cut it with a piece of steel," he said aloud. "This, Mr. Harvey, is of Voornish make."

Cumbers gave a low whistle. "You've seen this before?"

Fengel nodded. "A few times. Six months ago, most recently. It won't budge. Likely this is a whole piece. Possibly part of those water pipes out on the beach." He shook his head. "There's no way we're freeing the ship from it without careening her over entirely."

He sloshed back up to the hatchway stair with Cumbers following. Fengel took his jacket back and donned it.

"But sir," said Harvey. "We careen her over on her side, *Goliath* would swamp. We'd never get her back over again without help from the fleet."

"Which ain't likely," added Cumbers.

"No," agreed Fengel. "Likely not."

A hurried rhythmic thumping echoed on the deck above their heads. It stopped at the open hatchway of the stair. Midshipman Paine stuck his head in through the breach.

"Sirs!" he cried. "You've got to come quick. Hayes is making trouble!"

Fengel sighed. *If it's not one thing, it's another.*

He took his hat from the shipwright and climbed up to the next deck. Paine jerked back as he emerged. Fengel donned his hat and peered down at the lad as bilge water dripped from his sodden clothing upon the deck.

"What and where, young Paine?"

The midshipman caught his breath. "Hayes has got some of the crew up on the bow deck. Tryin' to get 'em all riled up."

Fengel clasped his hands behind his back. "Very well. Let's go see what the sub-lieutenant is on about this time, then."

He led the way up through the *Goliath's* decks. The ship was in disarray. Though empty of any people, clothes, dice and other detritus lay strewn about in haphazard fashion, the signs of occupation by the surviving crewmembers. Fengel's first official act as captain had been to order everyone back aboard the warship. With their camp wrecked, no one had really complained. After yesterday's earthquake, the decision even looked somewhat prescient.

Bright tropical sun blinded Fengel as he emerged on the outer deck. He blinked it away to see the crew, playing cards or fishing as they took advantage of the liberty he had decreed for the day. At first glance, they seemed perfectly at ease. Fengel sensed a tension, though, something off in the air. Everyone had their heads bent slightly, listening to a commotion taking place up on the bow deck.

Fengel sighed. *Here we go again.* Hayes wasn't a particularly difficult opponent. In fact, quite the opposite. But as a makeshift first mate he was proving singularly untrustworthy. Fengel shifted his monocle and strode up toward the gathering.

The sub-lieutenant stood on the bow deck of the ship with a small knot of the crew before him. Hayes looked wild. His beard was tangled, and his clothes were still torn from the fight upon the beach. He hadn't dealt well with the last two days, at first laying low, sulkily trying to reason his way into command of his crewmates. Now he looked to have moved on to full-scale proselytization.

"They've killed our first mate," screeched Hayes. "They killed old Tom, our bosun. And they even killed our commander! There's not a King's man alive on this boat who hasn't lost someone to their depredations. Before that, the bastards were hunting and ravaging honest Perinese sailors!" He gestured to the far side of the island. "And they're over there!"

A mutter of assent went through the crew. Fengel watched them nod and elbow each other angrily. *Well, that's not good,* he thought. It appeared that some were genuinely angry at the Salomcani.

Which was only to be expected. The question was, how could he *use* that? Very shortly he was going to have to tell the sailors and Bluecoats that their ship was unlikely to ever sail again.

Fengel smiled as the answer came to him. *Never let them see you stumble.*

"They need payin' back," said a marine. "But we can't just run off after them. Captain's got us doing things here on the *Goliath*. Getting us shipshape again."

Hayes went apoplectic. "That man isn't our captain!" he shrieked. "He's a bloody pirate! He's just a thief!"

And that's my cue. Fengel stalked forward, putting a little extra force into each footstep so that his boots echoed out across the deck. It was a trick he'd picked up over the years, useful for drawing attention.

"Alas," he said aloud. "There's precious little to steal here on Almhazlik." Fengel frowned up at the bow deck. "Mr. Hayes. What in the world are you up to here?"

The crowd on the deck all looked his way. Some shrank back, like children caught with their hands in the cookie jar. The rest just watched, curious as to how he would react. Hayes stood defiant. Upon seeing Fengel he thrust his chin out, puffed up his chest, and squeezed his hands into fists at his sides.

"I am knocking some sense into these idiots you've bamboozled," shouted Hayes. He pointed at the island. "The Salomcani are over on the opposite shore. But rather than going after them, rather than dispensing righteous vengeance, you've got everyone bottled up here so that you can pretend to be a real sailor!" He turned back to the crowd. "Listen, all of you. You are King's Men. You took the gold sovereign and swore the oath. When we get back to the fleet there'll be glory for all. But only if we do the right thing! Only if we wipe those heathen Salomcani from the Goddess's sight and hang this damned pirate from the yardarm!"

Some of the crew appeared worried at mention of the Royal Navy. They glanced at Fengel nervously. Most, however, looked merely irritated.

Oh dear, thought Fengel. He felt for Hayes. The man wanted so badly to get his way. But he was so unsuited for the task that Fengel wondered how he'd even achieved his current rank. The sub-lieutenant managed to sound both petulant and petty at once. He buzzed like a mosquito.

Fengel rubbed his chin. "I suppose that you would lead everyone to this glory?"

Hayes stamped the deck. "Yes!"

"Really." Fengel inspected his nails. "Sergeant Cumbers?"

The burly sergeant tromped up the deck to stand just behind him. "Sir?"

"When your officers were lost and Commander Coppertree laid up, who was in charge?"

Cumbers gave a heavy shrug. "Ah, well, Commander Coppertree still gave orders. More or less."

Fengel raised an eyebrow at the man. "But who saw them out? Who made the lesser decisions? I assume that the commander wasn't bothered for every little thing."

"That would have been the sub-lieutenant, sir."

Fengel nodded. "So Coppertree ordered a camp set up, but the sub-lieutenant here was the one that ordered the provisions removed from the *Goliath*?"

"Aye, sir."

"Whyever for?" He looked at Hayes. "Were you planning on living here for such a long time? I would advise against it. There is a serious paucity of decent drink on the island."

A few of the sailors in the crowd chuckled. *Good.* They were following along.

Hayes colored. "Of course not. But we had to be prepared!"

Fengel narrowed his eyes. "Yet you ordered the powder stores to be placed on the beach right next to the forge! What kind of rank stupidity was that? It's a miracle that some stray spark didn't set the load off before it finally blew. How many of our men are dead or injured because of that lackwit decision?"

No one laughed now. Hayes sputtered, trying for a rebuttal. Fengel pushed on before he could find one.

"For that matter, was it your idea to lay the rest of the camp out like that? You dug the latrine up the slope on the beach, *above* the men's tents. What would happen when it rained?"

"Everything overflowed," groaned one sailor miserably.

Hayes blinked at him. He glanced around at the crew for support, and found none. Fengel shook his head sadly and turned his back on the man. Silence stretched out across the deck.

"The layout of the camp was in accordance with the Military Code of Instruction," said the sub-lieutenant after a moment.

Fengel rounded on him. "Oh? Did the Military Code tell you to keep the port broadsides loaded and primed? Did it tell you to leave them aimed for the camp that your mates were living in? Did it tell you to chain a madwoman up next to them?"

Hayes started. "I...that...."

"No," continued Fengel. "I thought not. Really, Mr. Hayes. The Salomcani didn't kill Commander Coppertree. You did."

The muttering rose. Everyone glared angrily at the sub-lieutenant now.

"Listen, all of you," said Fengel. "I know things are tough. And Goddess knows that I'm not the man you want. But I am what you have. This fellow"—he pointed to Hayes—"would dupe you into hunting for blood and vengeance. Yet it was his leadership that got everyone wounded and not a few people killed in the first place.

"I know some of you feel like you owe him for his rank. You're thinking about what will happen when you get back to the fleet. That's understandable. Even admirable. But listening to him is going to get you all killed." Fengel smiled. "Now, I am more than happy to listen to any of my crew with any sensible suggestions. That even includes Mr. Hayes here, should he actually have anything sensible to say."

Chuckles echoed up and down the deck. *Well,* he thought. *That's taken care of.* A glance back at Hayes told him he'd won. The sub-lieutenant stared out at the deck, hands limp at his sides. No one was even looking at him anymore, not even in anger. The man knew that he had lost.

"Now, friends," said Fengel gravely. "I didn't come up here just to chastise the sub-lieutenant. I'm afraid I've got a spot of bad news for you as well." He paused for effect. "While the *Goliath* is a good ship, a fine ship, she's in a spot o' trouble. I've been down to the bilge with Sergeant Cumbers and our shipwright and it is my sad duty to inform you all that our ship here isn't going to be sailing anytime soon."

Disbelief and dismay erupted from the crew.

"But why?" cried Riley Gordon.

Fengel held up his hands. "My friends, I don't know how much you knew beforehand, but I heard the rumors myself. And I have to tell you that they're true, sadly. We've run aground right onto some old Voorn ruin. It has punctured the hull, and isn't going to be coming out anytime soon."

Riley Gordon jumped up onto a crate and pointed at Hayes. "You rat bastard. You ordered us in too close, and you knew it!" He looked to his mates. "That son of a bitch is the reason we're stuck here."

The crew growled angrily. Hayes's eyes widened and he shrank back, shaking his head in denial. Fengel watched carefully. Letting everyone descend to a mob would be going too far. Though he felt surprisingly unmoved. Hayes had tried to have him lynched from the yardarm, after all.

Midshipman Paine sniffled. "But I don't want to grow up on a deserted island!"

"Now, Paine," said Fengel. "Dry those eyes. You don't think I'd have come up here just to disappoint you, do you?"

"No," replied Paine. "You came up because I said Hayes was planning mutiny again."

Fengel froze. "Ah, yes." He coughed. "At any rate, I do have a plan." He faced the crowd. "The *Goliath* may not be taking us away from here anytime soon. But I do know of one ship that could." He looked back to Cumbers. "Sergeant, what did you say you saw the Salomcani running away with when they fled?"

Cumbers frowned. "Wood and tools."

"Wood and tools," agreed Fengel. "For making repairs. That, my fellows, means that the *Salmalin* isn't a loss. And *that* means that we can steal it."

The men shouted a thousand questions. Fengel waved them all down. "Lads, I know what you think. You're sailors, you're Bluecoats. You'd need to be pirates to steal a ship like this. Well, fortunately for you, Mr. Hayes was actually right about one thing." He winked. "I am an excellent pirate. So let's go steal us a ship."

No one cheered. The crew quieted, however. As he belted out orders to bring up what supplies remained, to see to the wounded, and get them all ashore again, they moved to obey. He set his makeshift officers to tasks.

When everything was moving well, he made his way back to the captain's cabin.

A figure appeared in the corner of his eye as he reached the door. Hayes had followed him.

"You're using them to take the *Salmalin*," he said. "That was my idea." Tears glimmered in his eyes. "How do you do it? How do you keep winning?"

Fengel straightened. "Because you have yet to learn the difference between proper and popular," he replied without turning around. "And when each one becomes more powerful. Learn *patience*, Lucian."

Hayes cocked his head. "What? Who did you call me?"

Fengel stopped with his hand on the handle. He flushed. "Never mind. Make yourself useful and go check on the wounded. Try not to get yourself lynched by the men." Opening the door to the cabin, he fled inside.

Getting the crew ashore did not prove so onerous a task. At first, the men seemed depressed over the news about their ship. Fengel made sure to move among them, joking with and encouraging the weary, yet being stern with those who slacked. He remembered the faces of those caught listening to Hayes and pulled them aside, reminding them of the enemy across the isle and revenge. After each little speech they moved with new fire, driving their mates along with increased fervor.

His new officers proved invaluable. Cumbers was senior among the remaining Bluecoat contingent, who jumped right in whenever the grizzled sergeant yelled at them. Paine, the young midshipman, ran errands and delivered messages, also relaying Fengel's commands to the sailors themselves, whom he technically had rank over. Aetherite Dawkins had come to an understanding with Fengel, and was left alone in exchange for seeing to the wounded, with a little help from Fengel himself on occasion. Between the three of them, they assembled the few remaining armaments and what little powder was left before moving the crew ashore.

Fengel sent the Bluecoats first to reoccupy the beach. There hadn't been any sign of the Salomcani or anyone else since the raid. The action was more symbolic than practical. Cumbers's men moved warily at first, fanning out to watch the perimeter of the jungle.

The sailors came next, along with the few wounded. Fengel departed last of all. He regarded the *Goliath* with amusement as the launch rowed ashore. This was the second time he'd left a Perinese ship without its crew. *Told you I'd do it,* he thought silently to Natasha.

He snapped back to the task at hand as the little boat scraped the shore. The sailors milled about, piling their remaining supplies on the sand. Fengel examined them with a frown. Even with the Bluecoat marines, he had maybe thirty surviving men, and barely enough shot, powder, and food for half. Thankfully, though, no one was so injured that he couldn't walk or fight, barring Harvey the shipwright. Fengel climbed out of the launch and strode up through the surf. He moved up to Cumbers. Paine fell in behind him a polite distance away.

The sergeant stood beside the small pool Fengel discovered after the last battle. Steaming hot water still filled it, a jet spraying up constantly from the pipeworks in its depths. The jet seemed larger than Fengel remembered.

A deep rumble sounded throughout the isle. The ground shook and the waves shuddered into froth. The crewmen fell to their knees, shouting. Fengel fought to keep his balance. The shaking subsided a few moments later.

Fengel grimaced. Nothing like yesterday's earthquake had occurred since, but little minor temblors now occurred with increasing frequency. He glanced around to make sure no one was hurt, then continued up to the sergeant.

Cumbers turned at Fengel's approach. "Well, sir, we're all ashore, even with the shaking." He fingered his musket, glancing up at the sky. "But if we're planning to get a move on, it's almost noon now. An' we'll have to be careful. Those damned heathen raiders could be hiding anywhere in that brush."

Fengel glanced at the tree line. It was a mess. Yesterday's quake had toppled many of the tall palm and banyan trees. Branches lay everywhere. Crawling through it to the other side of the island would be difficult.

"Agreed, Sergeant Cumbers." He faced the sailors behind them. "Fellows! Attend. On the other side of this isle wait the devious Salomcani. They've hurt us, and they've stolen from us. Now it's time to pay that back." The crew muttered in a chorus of agreement. Fengel pointed to the pile of supplies. "I want every one of you armed and ready, once we lay eyes on them. Take food, water, and a weapon. Marines to the front. Those of you with injuries, stay to the back." Fengel gestured. "Now, all of you, follow me!"

He made to stride up the beach when someone grabbed his coat.

"Captain Fengel, sir," said Paine. "You're forgetting something."

The youth thrust something up at him. It was a saber in a blue enamel sheath. Gold filigree covered the basket and the grip, the latter wound with silver wire. An officer's weapon. Fengel wanted to shout with glee. Instead he took the blade with a smile. "Why, thank you, young Paine. Thank you indeed." He hadn't armed himself these last two days, lest he send the wrong message. If one of the crew gave him a blade, though, that was different.

The grip fit comfortably in his hand. Fengel closed eyes suddenly watery. He drew the saber, the hissing ring as it skittered out of its scabbard music to his ears.

He had a sword again. It felt good.

Beware, witch. I'm coming for you. With a laughing cry, he led the Perinese sailors into the jungle.

They didn't get far. The foliage was just as thick as he'd thought, with the fallen timber crushing everything together. If the trees had toppled all the way to the ground, it wouldn't have been so bad. But some of the wreckage was supported by other greenery, or had only partially fallen. The canopy was still intact, just shorter and denser now. Fengel and the men of the *Goliath* had to crawl, climb, and hack their way around as best they could.

Why didn't I just take them around by the beach? wondered Fengel as he crawled beneath two fallen palms. He dripped with sweat. Even breathing in the muggy undergrowth was difficult.

Noon came and went as he led the Perinese through the interior of the island. Thankfully their progress took them into the shadow of the volcano at the center of the isle, shading them from the hot tropical sun. The volcano stood above them, though, more ominous and defined than before. All loose dirt and rock had fallen away to reveal a more symmetrical cone. The weird protrusions were also more obvious. What he had thought at first a strange bit of geology were large metallic diamonds—yet more Voorn construction.

The draconic megalith had not fallen. More of it stood uncovered by the quake, even taller and wider than Fengel had first guessed at. It was a massive bust, with most of the torso, shoulders, neck, and head rising up from the flank of the mountain to bow out over the sea. Falling debris had knocked away some of the dirt and greenery to reveal shining metal underneath, more of the same invincible brass as the spine that had breached the hull of the *Goliath.* More fine detail could be made out on the giant icon. Its eyes were closed, as if asleep, or praying.

Fengel hacked with his new saber and pushed through a massive fern. The foliage gave way to open air and a steep, gritty embankment. Beneath him the ground suddenly shook, the plants around him shivering with another tremor. His footing crumbled, and Fengel cursed as he slid down, coming to a stop a few feet below.

The tremor stopped only a moment later. *This won't do,* thought Fengel. *We need that ship before this whole place shakes apart.* Glancing about, Fengel found himself in a small ravine. The slope back up to the jungle was only ten feet or so. Down at its base flowed a small wide stream, only a few inches deep. On the opposite side rose a similar gritty slope only a little higher, topped by yet more jungle. To the left, the creek curled out of sight. At his right Fengel spied a small, dark cave poked into the base of the volcano. The waters of the stream seemed to issue forth from here.

The foliage rustled up above. "Sir!" cried Paine. "You okay?"

Fengel glanced up to see his new officers, as well as several others, poking their heads out of the jungle. "Right as rain," said Fengel. "Just a bit of a slip. Cumbers, have the men come down here for a bit of a rest. I think this is fresh water. Move carefully, mind."

The crew of the *Goliath* descended. After Dawes tested the water and found it clean, everyone knelt to wash and have a drink. Fengel climbed back to his feet. He walked upstream toward the mouth of the cave, curious.

The opening was wide. Maybe ten feet across and just as tall. Ambient sunlight only illuminated the interior by a few feet, revealing smooth stone walls and more of the stream as it flowed outward. Something caught his eye, however. In the depths Fengel saw a glimmer.

A fluttering sounded beside him, followed by a thump. Fengel glanced over to see a parrot squatting on a rock near to the cave mouth.

It was singularly ugly. The creature had a long, butter-yellow beak, stumpy orange legs, and was shaped like a melon. Brilliant plumage covered it, a shimmering rainbow of color that would have been lovely on anything else, but here only looked garish. The bird looked tired. It panted slightly. When it noticed Fengel, it glared with over-large eyes. Then it opened its beak and squawked at him.

The noise sounded like something halfway between a honk and a scream. Fortunately, it wasn't very loud. Fengel pulled back with distaste.

A great crashing sounded through the underbrush on the far ledge above. Fengel looked up to see a woman push through the jungle atop the opposite slope. She held a scimitar in hand, wore a tattered blouse, and blinked in surprise at the sudden change in her footing.

It was his wife.

A number of Salomcani raiders pushed through the jungle to join her. Natasha stared down at the Perinese. Then she saw Fengel. "There they are!" she roared in Salomcan. "There's the Perinese bastards! Charge!"

The Sheikdom raiders raced down the slope into the crew of the *Goliath*. Most of Fengel's men were caught unawares, sitting in the stream or washing in it. They scrambled to their feet and went for their weapons.

Fengel drew his saber and ran back to join the fray. A large Salomcani with a blue headscarf and striped trousers leapt from the slope at him, scimitar raised high. Fengel stepped aside and lashed out with his blade. It met resistance as the man fell past. He collapsed into the stream screaming and clutching at now-bloodied shins.

"Rally!" Fengel cried. "Men of the *Goliath*, rally to me!"

More Salomcani charged out of the jungle. A rat-faced man appeared before Fengel, long dagger upraised. Fengel cut at the arm holding the weapon and bashed his pommel into his nose. *If I can just make it to her, I can end this quickly*. Natasha stood only a short distance away. He watched her cut down one of his crew and smiled as a Bluecoat crept up behind her with his musket held like a club. She ducked as he swung and then whirled to meet the man, lunging forward to run him through. The Bluecoat cried in surprise and pain. Natasha bent in and kissed him on the cheek, then let him crumple down to the stream.

Fengel growled in anger and charged forward. She danced back and barked out an order, sending two of her Salomcani to meet him with scimitars and daggers in hand. Fengel hacked at the one on the left, a short, stout man, eager to reach past him to Natasha. The raider parried the blow. Fengel rebounded from the block to flick a cut at the tall dark-haired man on the right, who similarly deflected his strike.

They were strong, and skilled. But Fengel knew that he was better. He fell back a step, enticing them to strike. They took the bait and he beat both blades aside, using the opening to cut at the arm of the man on the right. The raider saw the danger and pulled back, only earning a light cut across his bicep. His mate pulled his own blade back into guard and rushed Fengel, aiming for his head with the pommel of his scimitar. Fengel dodged back, drawing his saber across his assailant's thigh.

The three of them drew back with blades upraised in guarding positions. *Not bad*, Fengel thought. He could beat them, but it would take time. His wife knew what she was doing, damnably.

Time was something he didn't have. A quick glance told him that the men of the *Goliath* were sorely pressed. Cumbers fought well, clubbing a raider to the ground and firing a shot at the man who snuck up on him. Riley Gordon and Midshipman Paine worked as a team, but already sported a number of minor cuts. Aetherite Dawkins gestured at a raider and unleashed a small puff of black smoke. His assailant fell, choking, to the stream. Dawkins rabbit-punched him across the side of the head, then fled back behind his mates. Everyone else was falling back, wounded. They needed a chance to regroup, and Natasha wasn't giving it to them.

The dark-haired raider to his right lunged in. Fengel parried and bashed his assailant's face with the butt of his saber. The man fell back with a grunt and Fengel stepped in to meet his shorter fellow, knocking his blade aside and cutting at his forehead. The blow hit home and the second raider staggered back, blood seeping down into his face.

Fengel took the opportunity to lash out at a few other nearby raiders. He skewered one and cut the calves of another, taking some pressure off of his crewmen. "Fall back!" he cried. "Men of the *Goliath*, fall back to me! To the cave!"

"Ha!" shouted Natasha from somewhere in the struggle. "Run, you dogs. We'll cut you down all the same! And a fistful of golden sovereigns to the ones that bring me Fengel alive!"

Fengel's crewmen made for the opening in the base of the mountain. He gave them what cover he could, blocking and binding any pursuers, falling back foot by foot until he found himself with Cumbers in the mouth of the cave holding off five men at once. A pistol snaked in at the sergeant's chest. Fengel lopped the fingers holding it off at the wrist before it could fire.

The wounded raider screamed. He fell back. Unnerved, his mates gave pause and joined him as well. Fengel grabbed Cumbers by the shoulder and shoved him back toward the depths.

"Run!" he said. "Get the men away to somewhere we can recover!"

Cumbers panted. He nodded in the gloom and darted behind. Fengel continued to retreat, not taking his eyes from the Salomcani at the mouth of the cave until the opening was just a pinprick of light behind them.

A yell echoed down to him from the crewmen who had run ahead. Fengel closed his eyes. *Eyes of the Goddess. What now?*

He staggered back through the cave. It was uniform, a ten-foot-wide tunnel with a stream at its base. The glimmer he'd spied before was stronger now, some bright light up ahead. His crewmen fled ahead of him at top speed, shoving each other to get away from the Salomcani. The shout had come from the head of the column.

Fengel pushed his way past the others. The light ahead grew stronger until it resolved as the end of the tunnel, an opening into some great space. His crew were packed tight around something that had them swearing in surprise and panic. Fengel pushed through to see what all the fuss was about. Then he froze.

Cumbers, Hayes, Dawkins, and Paine all stood in a semicircle at the head of the column, weapons drawn and pointed at a figure standing in the stream before them. It was a metallic armature, almost a skeleton, formed of Voornish brass. Its torso, head, and forearms were like a child's suit of armor, covered in alien scrollwork. Two great glass eyes looked at them.

The construct seemed agitated. *"Variss goldeyn! Hara hailo!"* It spread both hands out at them in a warning gesture.

Fengel raised his voice. "Move aside, fellow. Or...whatever you are." He made a shooing gesture with his sword. "We're being pursued and haven't time for your babbling."

The construct cocked its head. "*Hara hailo!* You cannot be here!"

Shouts came from the tunnel behind them. Fengel heard Natasha's screech of bloodlust.

Fengel lowered his blade. *Well,* he thought. *This is all I need.* He replaced his monocle, which made the automaton looked cracked and broken. *Now what do I do?*

He glanced at the worried, angry faces of the crew around him. *Never let them see you stumble.*

"Cumbers," he said. "And you two." He pointed at the automaton. "Grab that thing."

The machine cocked its head as the crewmen stepped in to meet it.

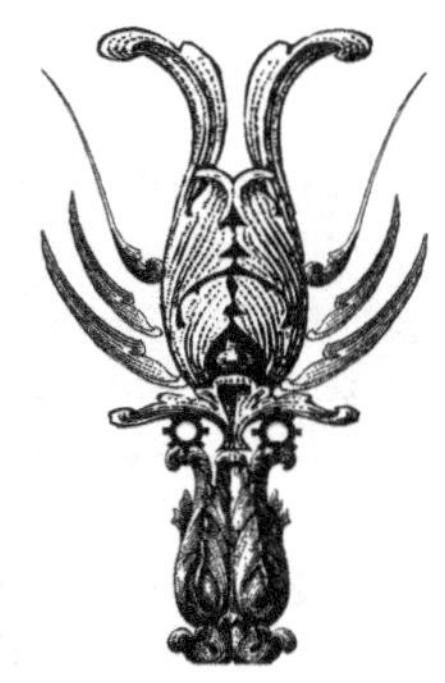

CHAPTER FOURTEEN

"I'M NOT SO SURE ABOUT THIS ANYMORE."

Lina smiled hungrily at the punter and gave Runt a caress. The scryn purred, winding over her shoulders and around her upraised arm. "Come now, sir," she replied. "Let us take you somewhere...unimaginable."

The man stared at her. He was of average height and weight, with a neat brown beard, a bowler, and now an expression of utter revulsion. "No," he said after a long moment. "I can imagine it quite clearly. I think I had better just go home."

Lina watched him walk away down the street. When he turned a corner, she shoved Runt back into place across her shoulders. Then she gave a sigh of relief and fell against the brick wall of the alley mouth.

Breachtown seen from the ground was incongruous. The original Perinese colonists had done their best to bring the Kingdom with them, resulting in a city mixed out of tedious tradition and practical compromise. Dull buildings of grey brick clustered tightly, their sharp rooftops falling down into narrow alleys, while thin windows peeked out onto small yards bounded by ornate wrought-iron fences. Yet those yards sprouted lush palms and blooming vines completely at odds with their surroundings. Tropical birds flocked to the tiny baths built at regular intervals to coax them down from navigating the turbulent rigors of the Stormwall Breach.

Lina rested in an alley between a haberdashery and a cigar shop. Across the street loomed the wide brick facade of the Breachtown Colonial Counting House, a three-story building topped with a small glass dome where all fines were paid within the colony and a portion of all the vast wealth flowing out of the Yulan was taxed. Numerous windows along the second and third floors peered down at harried locals passing by in the street below. The building was framed by an apothecary to one side and a jeweler at the other.

She'd thought the alley a great place to gather information for tonight's raid. Unfortunately, even with the city under occupation by the Perinese Royal Navy, most of the men she saw went out of their way to approach her in her disguise as a local prostitute.

I'm going to kill him for that. Lina rested against the alley mouth, and vowed vengeance upon Lucian Thorne for the hundredth time today. Climbing down from the *Dawnhawk* and slipping into town just before dawn had been easy enough. She'd been so focused on that task that she hadn't unpacked Lucian's 'disguise' until she'd found the counting house, and her alley. Only then had she discovered that the committee-member had provided her with a revealing dress, high-heeled shoes, and fishnet stockings. He'd even included rouge and a bottle of overly strong perfume.

It was insulting, irritating, and a dozen other things besides, but in the end Lina didn't have anything better at hand. At least she knew she could play the part. So, swallowing her curses and taking a nap, she'd risen around midmorning to put everything on and stash her things among some old crates at the back of the alley. So far, she'd spent most of the day observing the counting house and using Runt to scare off those that thought her disguise genuine. Hopefully Lucian would send someone to retrieve her.

Which had better be soon. The late afternoon sun hovered just above the rooftops, falling from the sky. Her reinforcements were already late, though that wasn't surprising. The park which Lucian had specified did not appear to exist. She just hoped that her crewmates weren't lost in some other part of the city.

Lina stretched and stood away from the wall. *Ah well.* Until someone did show, she had work to do. She moved again to the alley mouth and plastered on a provocative smile. Runt, torpid after devouring a toucan earlier, went back to sleep around her shoulders. Lina was eyeing a third-story window of the counting house when she noticed someone approaching out of the corner of her eye.

Goddess's hairy armpits. Were all the men in this town so desperate? Lina rolled her eyes and turned to face him.

Her smile died. The fellow was enormous. Of only average height, his girth ballooned up and out from two stubby legs, putting Lina in mind of an airship dirigible balanced on a pair of tree stumps. He wore a finely tailored Perinese suit that barely constrained his bulk, the vest and jacket on the verge of splitting with every quivering step he took. A small, pointed goatee covered his double chin, set below a thin handlebar mustache and two small, piggy eyes that peered out hungrily at the world.

Lina swallowed. Back in her previous profession she'd called men like this a "prune," due to how long she'd had to bathe to feel clean after working for one. *But it's not like that's going to happen.* She forced herself to smile wickedly and gave Runt a sensuous caress.

"What's your pleasure, sir?" she said.

The man slowed to a stop before her like a great ship coming into harbor. He stared down at her and wheezed asthmatically.

Lina waited for a response. An old woman walked past them, complaining loudly to her grown son about a lizard-monster that had stolen one of her chickens. Lina glanced after, curious. But still the fellow didn't say a thing. He only stared at her.

Lina cleared her throat. "Come now, sir. What can we do for—"

"I've got a list," he said, voice thin and high-pitched.

It dawned on Lina that this one wasn't going to be put off easily. *Time to bring out the big guns.* She gave a roll of her shoulders. Runt chirped in irritation, but obeyed the command. The scryn curled down around her waist and then tightened, pushing up on her bodice. Lina bent lower to better put herself on display.

Everyone hated scryn. No one in Breachtown had proven any different so far. Working that into a hasty routine with Runt had served her well today. The straight-laced Perinese seemed especially put off by the repulsive allure that she presented them.

Lina smiled coyly up at the man. "That's good to hear, sir. I'm just *eager* to hear what's on that list. But what's your name, sir? We should get go know each other better."

That should do it. In her experience, most men who sought a prostitute didn't like anyone knowing their names; it tended to get back to the wrong people.

"Gregory," he said, without skipping a beat.

Lina frowned. She recovered and tried again. "Well, Gregory, Runt and I want to let you know we've got something *special* on offer."

"That's good too," he replied, pausing to lick his lips. "I'm not picky."

Lina had an epiphany. There wasn't going to be anything she could do to scare this one away. *Sod it, then.* She had her limits, and she'd been out here long enough. It was time to cut her losses and run.

Lina straightened. "Actually, I've got to go."

Gregory blinked in confusion. "What?"

"Business is suddenly closed." She yanked roughly at Runt's coils. "I've... got a headache." Lina pushed past him out to the curb along the street.

"But wait," gasped Gregory, following after her. "I thought we were—"

"Nope," Lina replied over her shoulder. "Sorry. Sudden headache. You know how it is." She prodded the scryn. "Runt, I can't breathe. Loosen up."

Gregory followed after. "What if I'm really quick about it?" he asked, voice worried and plaintive. "We could just go down the alley a little ways."

Lina shuddered. *Oh Goddess.* She walked out into the street. The rustle of trouser leggings rubbing together echoed behind after her. Lina quickened her pace.

Well this is just great. Lina vowed revenge upon Lucian again for putting her in this position. Gregory wasn't taking the hint, and wasn't prepared to leave her alone, she could see. This could go badly. If she was lucky, she'd only caught the eye of someone merely socially inept, which seemed likely. But if she was unlucky, then Gregory could be so much worse. Memories came to the fore of her old brothel in Triskelion. The place had a bouncer for a reason.

Lina knew she could take care of Gregory if she had to. Her knives were stashed away, but she'd learned a few tricks, and still had Runt besides. But anything she did might call a squad of Perinese Bluecoats, break her disguise, and land her in gaol. Again she cursed Lucian. *What I need is a refuge.* She scanned the buildings on the other side of the street and her eyes fell on the apothecary. *Perfect.*

"I get these migraines," she said over her shoulder. "I should go get some medicine for them. You'll just have to catch me another time, love."

"What if I wait?" whined Gregory.

"Alas, there's no telling how long it'll last."

"You could have a lie-down first—"

A hansom rolled down the street at them. Lina jumped out past it, using the cab as cover to reach the apothecary. The front of the store was genteel, with an elegantly carved wooden sign hanging out over the street. She reached the curb, ran to the door, opened it, and slipped inside without a backward glance. Shutting the door, Lina leaned back against it with her hands on the doorknob so Gregory couldn't follow.

The knob twisted tentatively after a few moments as someone tried it from outside. Lina smiled, holding tight. After a few experimental turns, it stopped. She listened; footsteps sounded on the other side, growing fainter. Lina let out her breath and quickly glanced about her refuge.

The apothecary was cluttered but clean. Polished hardwood spread across an open floor bounded by cabinets, shelves, and racks full of strange tinctures. Herbs warred with an almost overpowering scent of alcohol for primacy, causing Runt to sniff at the air in interest. Along the right wall was a small stone hearth. The glowing embers inside dried the air and warmed the room uncomfortably. Two windows framed the front door, tightly covered with thick draperies to prevent any outside light from entering. Along the opposite wall at the back of the shop was a doorway leading deeper within the building, hung with a similar thick curtain. Before the doorway lay a marble countertop over a long wooden cabinet attached to one wall.

A man stood behind the counter, presumably the apothecary. There was something unsettling about him that raised the hairs on the back of Lina's neck. He was tall and gaunt, with pale skin like dry parchment and unblinking eyes behind heavy spectacles. His hair was white and thick, shoulder length. The clothing he wore was very Perinese: a wool waistcoat, vest, and breeches, all of which should have been sweltering in the warmth of the shop and the tropical climate. He stood stock still, staring at her.

Lina blushed. "My apologies sir, it's ah, about to rain. Just darted in here to catch my breath, if you don't mind."

The apothecary said nothing. As she watched, a fat orange tabby cat padded out from behind the counter. In its mouth was a bloody mouse, missing a hind leg and obviously dead. The cat took its prize beneath a cabinet along the left wall. Loud purring echoed out into the shop after a moment. The apothecary did not seem to notice.

Lina frowned. She ducked out from the gaze of the man. His eyes didn't follow her. *Uh, all right.* He, at least, wasn't going to be a bother. *But why am I finding the creepiest men in the colony, all of the sudden?* She ignored the apothecary for the moment and peered outside through the nearest window. Past the drapery she spied Gregory, standing in front of the shop near the street with a frustrated frown. Lina swore under her breath. Couldn't he find someone else to keep him company?

Well, she wouldn't be leaving quite yet, then. Lina whirled back and smiled at the apothecary. "I'll just be looking around a bit," she said. He did not respond.

Adjusting Runt, Lina sauntered slowly around the shop. She eyed tinctures, ointments and potions, all neatly labeled in fine script. Some of the medicines she recognized. Back in her previous occupation, it had paid to know a good apothecary, for everything from cuts and bruises to the more embarrassing afflictions endemic to the trade.

"Cubbins, you nasty little thing, don't you dare kill that mouse in here!"

The shout echoed out from behind the curtain. Lina glanced back to see it jerk aside and a woman emerge.

She was striking. Of average height with a lean frame, the woman had a presence that seemed to fill the room. Her skin was coffee colored, somewhat like the Salomcani, but far darker; the mark of a Yulani native. She wore a grey Perinese morning dress, but accented it with gold and silver rings, ebony bracelets, and a scarlet ribbon choker around her neck. Thin lips pressed firmly beneath large green eyes, combining with her sharp features to forge a harsh, no-nonsense look. Her hair was blonde, worked into a mass of frizzy dreadlocks bound tightly at the back of her head with another ribbon, their ends bouncing as she peered about the shop.

The woman froze as she noticed Lina. Her body language, previously irritated, shifted abruptly into something more welcoming. She smiled warmly and clasped her hands together, setting her bracelets to jingling. "Why, hello, dear," she said in perfect, unaccented Perinese. "I didn't hear you come in. Welcome to the Gravelin's Apothecarium. I am Omari, assistant to Mr. Gravelin." She gestured to the man behind the counter.

Lina cleared her throat. "Actually, I just stepped in to get out of the rain. I'm sure it'll pass…" her eyes were drawn again to Mr. Gravelin. She couldn't help it. There was something about him that unnerved her. *He hasn't blinked since I walked in, I'm sure of it.*

"You needn't be shy, young miss. Our Apothecarium prides itself on our discretion. Come closer, why don't you, and let's discuss your needs."

Morbidly fascinated by the apothecary, Lina approached the counter. "Is he all right? Because there is something really very odd—"

"Oh don't mind Mr. Gravelin," said Omari. "He simply has a condition, whose details I won't bore you with now—wait." The woman paused as she took in Lina's dress. Her warm demeanor vanished. "Hold on, now. You working girls know better than to show up before nightfall."

Lina blinked. "I'm sorry?"

Omari glared and folded her arms. "Look, I'm happy to help out, and at barely more than cost, I hope you realize, but *after nightfall.* I've a reputation to maintain, and having a bunch of floozies and tarts cluttering up my shop scares off the more genteel folk."

Lina flushed. "Oh. I see. No, really, I'm not here for any of that."

Omari gave her a curious look. Then she pulled back, face a mask of disgust. "By the ghosts of my fathers. Are you wearing a dead *scryn* for a *shawl?*"

Runt chose that moment to lift his head up. "Chirr?" her pet said. It eeled back and forth, mandibles spread, tongue tasting the alcohol in the air.

"No," said Lina, which was technically accurate.

The door at the front of the shop swung open. Lina winced, steeling herself for another confrontation with Gregory. Irritation at the fat man was quickly changing into anger. *If I have to, I'm siccing Runt on him this time. I don't care if it breaks my cover.*

But someone else stood in the doorway. A tall, rake-thin woman dressed in a severe black gown. Her face was pinched and her hair tightly woven into a bun, only partially hidden beneath a wide-brimmed hat covered in flowers, ribbons, and lace.

Omari smiled at the newcomer. Her demeanor shifted again to that of the pleasant shopkeep's assistant. "Why, Madam Bumquist! So nice to see you again." Omari glared at Lina, directing her out of the way with a tilt of the head.

Lina stepped aside as the newcomer moved up to the counter. The woman didn't seem to notice her.

"Why, hello, Omari, dear," said Madam Bumquist. Her voice seemed to linger, nasal and imperious. "I've just stopped in to have my prescription filled."

"I'll have it up in a moment," said Omari. "But I must mention again, good lady, that the corns will go away if you'd change your footwear—"

Madam Bumquist raised a hand to her throat. "And risk being thought out of touch? Certainly not! These boots are the very epitome of ladies fashion at the moment."

Lina peered at the woman's feet. She wore extremely high stiletto heels, balanced on the toes. They looked painful.

Omari gave a small shrug. "Well, let me get that ready for you, then." She turned to a shelf along the back wall and began pulling down bottles.

Madam Bumquist looked to Mr. Gravelin. The apothecary still hadn't moved. "Hello there, Mortimer," she said, overloud, as if talking to a deaf man. "And how are you today?"

"Not much improved, I'm afraid," said Omari back over her shoulder. She placed the collection of bottles and tinctures upon the countertop and went to work sorting them.

"Oh, such a shame," said Bumquist.

A deep, rattling groan escaped from the apothecary. He moved for what Lina swore was the first time, eyes rolling down to the bottles at his side.

"Oh, that's excellent!" exclaimed Madam Bumquist. "He's responding to me, Omari." She shook her hand in front of the apothecary. "Hello, Mr. Gravelin!"

Omari froze momentarily. Then she smiled warmly at her customer. "It's no wonder, of course. You brighten up the room wherever you go, Madam Bumquist. You'll simply *have* to come by more often."

Lina stared as it came to her. The apothecary had taken a breath before groaning. It was the only one she'd seen since walking in here. That and his glassy eyes, the horrible waxy pallor of his skin, the strong embalming-fluid stink in the room....She was certain that Mr. Gravelin was dead.

Worse than that, he was a Revenant.

A gasp left her lips unbidden. Bumquist frowned at the noise. She peered down her nose at Lina, noticing her for the first time. Then she gave a gasp of her own.

"Oh my word," said Madam Bumquist. "*Well*. I thought this was a *respectable* establishment, Omari." The woman's pinched face looked incredibly affronted.

"What?" The apothecary's assistant looked up from her work in confusion.

"Really," said Bumquist to Lina. "It's guttertrash floozies like you, young woman, that corrode the moral fiber of the good people of this city. Perhaps if you wore more clothing, we wouldn't be suffering from this accursed, mistaken occupation."

"Maybe if you wore a little less," replied Lina automatically, "the men might not hunt so hard for somewhere else to stick their nethers."

Madam Bumquist colored. Her nostrils flared, and she quivered with suppressed anger. Then she turned up her nose and strode past for the door. Lina watched her go with indifference. Her response had been reflexive; she had bigger things to worry about.

Omari gave a curse and came around the counter after Bumquist. "Wait," she said, shaking a dark bottle. "Madam, don't go. This girl isn't a customer here. She just came in to get out of the rain. I've filled your order—"

The front door slammed shut. Omari fell silent. When she looked back to Lina her face was tight with anger. "See! Why did you say that? That's exactly the kind of thing that I'm talking about. Now, get out!"

Lina certainly had no desire to stay here any longer. In all the stories she'd heard, Revenants hated the living, and craved their flesh. Though Mr. Gravelin didn't seem particularly threatening at the moment, merely playing with the bottles Omari had brought out. Still, it wasn't a risk she wanted to take. *But if I leave now, there's still Gregory to deal with.* For the hundredth time, she cursed Lucian.

"Omari," Lina said. "Believe me, I am absolutely happy to leave. But if I could just use the back door?"

Something moved on the floor between them. It was the mouse, scurrying out from under the table the cat had crawled beneath earlier. The creature tottered on its three legs without much aim or purpose. It wasn't bleeding, even though the missing leg showed dark meat and bone.

Cubbins, the orange tabby cat, leapt out from the shadows at the undead rodent. It landed with a pounce, then batted its prize around. It pulled back to let it totter back and forth before leaping again.

Omari reached down, lightning-quick, and grabbed up the cat by the scruff of its neck. Then she stomped on the corpse of the mouse, kicked it across the room into the fireplace, and pointed sharply at the door. "Out!" she yelled at Lina.

Lina stared. "Right," she said. "Right. That's…that's probably wise." Holding tightly onto Runt, she fled the Apothecarium.

Outside, the street was clad in shadow as day fell into twilight. People locked their shops and hurried homeward as the lamplighters moved about their task. Lina barely noticed. She stared back at the building over her shoulder, one hand on Runt for comfort. *What in all the Realms Above was going on in there?*

"So, is your headache better?"

Lina looked back to see Gregory. She gave a smile as brittle as she felt. *I could just sic Runt on him. No one would convict me.* Lina opened her mouth to tell Gregory exactly what she thought of him, then paused as a squad of five blue-coated Perinese marines trooped past, marching in perfect lockstep formation, their eyes cold and hard.

No. Drawing any attention to herself right now was still a bad idea.

But she wasn't going to hang around any longer. Lina decided to get her real clothes back, and make her way out of the city to where the *Dawnhawk* had gone to anchorage. It shouldn't be that hard to find.

If the fat bastard in front of her wouldn't leave her alone, she would *make* him.

"No," she replied. "Just *go.* Go away."

Gregory frowned petulantly. "Hey. I'm a paying customer. You *have* to give me service." His hands wrapped into flabby fists. "I take care of Mother, and she finally took her laudanum and went to sleep, and I've been looking forward to this for months and saving my allowance and I even took a bath. Now you *have* to give me service."

He panted, glaring at her with piggy, selfish eyes. Lina only stared at him, stunned by his petulance, struck by an awareness that there'd been a time when he would have been right. *Goddess, I'm so glad to be a pirate now.* At least piracy only got you hanged, in the end.

She shook her head with a weary smile. "Sod off, you silly bastard. You're not getting anything from me. And you never will." Lina pushed past as Gregory sputtered and fumed. She crossed the street to the alley she'd spent all day occupying. The narrow passage enclosed her like a maw made out of shadow. Lina ignored the gloom and marched ahead. From behind came the sound of Gregory's rustling waddle. She had just reached the pile of old boxes and crates, when his hand fell upon her shoulder.

That was it, the last straw. Lina whirled, dropping her weight and balling her hands up into fists. Runt sensed her tension and rumbled in warning.

"You can't talk to me like that," said Gregory. His double chin wobbled in anger. "You're just a—"

Lina slugged him hard in the gut. It was like hitting a cloth sack full of pudding. Gregory yelped, more in surprise than pain. Lina hit him again, a left jab followed by a right cross against his chin. The fat man fell back with another cry. Lina lifted her shoulder and pointed at him. "Runt!" she growled. "Kill!"

The scryn reared up from her shoulders and spread himself wide. A lurid red glow bathed Gregory, illuminating the alley. Her pet hissed, poisonous spittle spattering to the ground.

Something snarled from the shadows at all three of them. Runt squawked in surprise and took flight. Gregory flinched, throwing up his hands with a cry. Lina whirled to face the threat, darting out of the way as a reptilian creature leapt suddenly from out behind a crate, both arms raised and long talons gleaming. It landed before Gregory and hissed. The monster was surprisingly short.

That didn't matter to Gregory. The fat man screamed as he ran out the alley. "Help!" he cried. "Monsters! Monsters and dangerous whores!"

Lina glared after him flatly.

Rastalak snickered as Gregory careened away. He stood up straighter and shot her a look. "Are you all right?" he hissed.

Lina gave a weary sigh. *Finally, you show up.* She had worked *so* hard to avoid trouble. "I was taking care of it myself, but yes, thanks. Where've you been? I've been waiting all day for someone to come meet me." *And why did they send you?* Rastalak was a great friend, but the pygmy Draykin could hardly blend in with the locals.

He made a small shrug. "Apologies. Committee-Member Lucian directed me to meet you at the park with the big statue, earlier. I could not tell the buildings apart, but found the park. Eventually I realized that our target, this Breachtown Counting House, was not there. I heard again from Committee-Member Lucian and came to find you." He reached back into the shadows and pulled out what looked like the carcass of a fat bird, hastily plucked and roasted.

Lina blinked. "And what, you picked up a chicken along the way?" *Figures that he'd hear from Lucian and the others. They couldn't be bothered to find* me.

Rastalak appeared pleased. "The people here are polite. A human woman gave it to me."

"Really?"

Her crewmate shrugged. "She screamed, then threw it at me. I have decided that she wanted me to have it. It is impolite, not to accept a gift."

Lina sighed. *And then you stopped somewhere to cook it.* "Look, let's just get going. That fat bastard is sure to call the Bluecoaties with his bleating. We'd better get moving."

The little Draykin nodded agreement. Lina retrieved her gear from under a pile of boards and led Rastalak deeper along the alley to where it met with another back lane. When they'd moved several buildings away, Lina paused to change behind a large rain barrel. Rastalak put his back to her and kept an eye out, noisily devouring his prize.

Lina shucked off the hated dress as if it were on fire. She stripped away the stockings, pulling her old shirt and trousers back on. Then went the high-heeled shoes, replaced with her good, solid boots. She donned her ratty shirt, swearing at Runt, who didn't want to move. Lastly, she pulled on her belt, the heavy daggers a comfortable weight against her hips. Lina gave a sigh of relief. It felt good to be wearing real clothing again. The horrible dress she'd worn all day went into the rain barrel, along with the rest of the outfit. She rejoined Rastalak, now licking grease from his claws. Runt weaved from her shoulders, begging for scraps.

"Runt, you've already eaten. Now Rastalak, I've been watching the counting house all day. Noticed quite a few useful things about the place, for our purpose. Let's get back to the *Dawnhawk* so I can give my report. We'll have go carefully to get out of town; the sun's going and there's a curfew in effect, I've heard."

The little Draykin gave her an odd look. "We need not go so far."

Lina raised an eyebrow. "What?"

Rastalak fell silent a moment. He shifted his weight back and forth then shook his head. "I do not understand the sense of it myself. But...you'll see. Come."

Her crewmate skulked off into the gloom. Lina frowned and followed after.

Twilight gave over to nightfall as they made their way through the city. The tightly spaced buildings provided plenty of alleyways and backstreet lanes to move between, complementary to the more major thoroughfares. A few seemed damaged from the recent fighting, either wrecked or burned-out shells. Most were simply quiet and unlit. Here and there they passed beneath a covered window, thick draperies occluding all but the faintest slivers of the light and life that moved behind it.

The streets themselves were full of activity. Squads of Perinese Bluecoats deployed from the navy marched in lockstep, the echoes of their tromping boots resounding down the alleyways to reach Lina and her friend. Her day had been blessedly free of them so far, but now they were out on patrol, eyeing the locals and enforcing the curfew.

A forest of bobbing lights appeared past the rooftops ahead. They were lanterns, hanging from the rigging of the warships in the harbor. Lina realized that Rastalak was taking them west, toward the waterfront. *Wait, where are we going?* The *Dawnhawk* had been anchored somewhere past the Stormwall, in the Yulan Interior to the east. *What is going on?*

The two of them came to a major street at the end of their current alley. A richly built carriage rolled past, pulled by a pair of fine horses. Lina didn't see the crest on the door, but a large group of fifteen Bluecoats trailed it. She knelt down in the shadows of her alley, yanking her crewmate along with her.

"Rastalak," she whispered. "Where are you taking me? We can't keep running through the city. Look at all these patrols! Where is the *Dawnhawk*?"

Her friend didn't answer her immediately. She glanced away from the parade of soldiers in the street to see him looking at the ground, rocking back and forth on his heels, worried. He glanced up at her and gave a confused shrug. "The airship is still beyond the city. Mr. Henry Smalls will pilot it in at midnight, I am told."

Lina looked at him. "And?"

"When the committee-member sent me to find you, he mentioned there was a change in plans."

"Find me?" Lina stared at him. "What, he's here on the ground? I just thought you meant that the ship had sent you a message! What's he doing in the city? And what do you mean, a change in the plan? I didn't think he even had a plan yet!"

Lina realized her voice was carrying out into the street. She froze. But all the marines were gone, having marched past after the carriage. Lina leaned out the alley mouth and spied them dimly down at the far end of the road.

She glanced back to Rastalak, who just shook his head. "Come. I had best show you."

Before she could say anything, he darted out from the alley, through the street, and into an alley on the other side. Lina cursed and ran after him. She followed as he ran around a back-alley corner, then stumbled as she ran into his back.

The dim alley before them was far from quiet, or even empty. It appeared to be the backside of a tavern, and the majority of the crew from the *Dawnhawk* lounged about, drinking foamy mugs of ale from a broached keg in the middle of the alley. Lucian stood with Sarah Lome and Reaver Jane in the back door of the tavern chatting amiably with the publican, who was busily pocketing a satchel of coins.

"It is not just Committee-Member Lucian," said Rastalak. "Almost everyone came down. They discussed things, and all wanted to drink before the raid." He looked up at her. "I do not understand why the committee has allowed this. It seems counterproductive to our desire for stealth."

Lina worked her jaw for something to say. The words wouldn't come. Suddenly, acutely, Lina wished very much that Captain Fengel were here.

She'd even take Natasha.

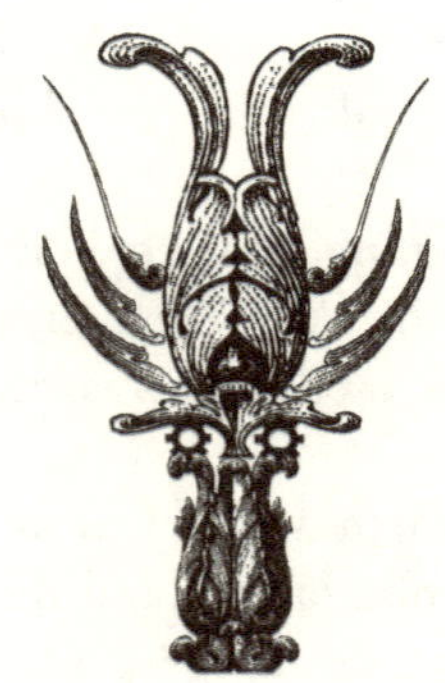

CHAPTER FIFTEEN

Natasha peered into the tunnel. It led deeper into the mountain where a pinprick of red light glimmered up ahead. At her back waited the Salomcani, their angry voices mixing with the rush of the stream into an echoing cacophony. She ignored them, focused instead on her quarry.

Her father would have warned caution. *What is that light? Some trick?* A trick was certainly possible. It's what she would have relied on, if she'd been forced to flee.

Natasha glanced back at her crew. Though wounded and tired, the fight outside the tunnel had galvanized them. Hounded by the Perinese for days now, the chance at revenge was proving sweet. They'd been ready and willing when she'd come across the men of the *Goliath* in that stream, and she'd orchestrated the fight as well as any in recent memory, hitting the oblivious sailors hard. Her new crew had even managed to divert Fengel when she'd called for it, keeping him busy long enough that even his peerless swordsmanship couldn't turn the tables. Now her raiders stood ready to finish their foes, hefting weapons and muttering curses as they waited for their Kalyon to lead them on again.

Not everyone appeared so eager, however. Both Etarin and Jahmal, her two makeshift officers, exchanged worried glances. Tall Farouk seemed oblivious, staring around at the tunnel in curiosity, and tentatively touching the deep bruise across his cheek that Fengel had left him.

Natasha snorted. *Realms Below with it. Best get this lot moving again.*

"All right," she growled. "They're limping and bloodied. Let's finish them off."

"My fingers!" wailed a crewman whose name Natasha hadn't bothered to learn. The man was short and wiry, and clutched a bloody rag around one hand. "That one with the monocle took two of my *fingers!*"

Natasha sighed. It was true. Not only had Fengel been in the gully, he hadn't been bound as a prisoner. He'd been armed, and shouting orders. Her incompetent, infuriating, lackwit husband had somehow finagled his way into leading the Perinese.

Just like he'd said he would.

I'll show him. She'd put his dupes to the sword and prove once and for all just which one of them was more capable, which one of them was the better captain.

"Walk it off," she snarled at the injured sailor. "And remember, golden sovereigns for the one who brings me Captain Fengel alive!"

Jahmal looked uneasily at her. "Kalyon...."

"What?"

"Shouldn't we be making for the *Goliath*?"

Natasha paused. What was left of the Perinese had been with Fengel, for some reason. Now they were all stuck up a tunnel leading who-knew-where, leaving their steamship behind them, lightly defended if at all.

Chasing down and thrashing her husband would be satisfying. But she'd risen to control over the crew of the *Salmalin* by more than personal force. She'd also promised a solution to their troubles. The wise move would be to retreat, take the *Goliath,* and then strand Fengel by sailing away.

But that wasn't good enough.

"Dog!" she shouted, slapping the man with her free hand. He flinched and gave a yelp. Natasha gestured down the tunnel with her sword. "The Perinese are backed into a corner here. We crush them, and *then* we'll take their ship. Now, forward!"

Etarin wiped more blood from his face and shared another look with Jahmal. Natasha ignored it, deciding to deal with them later. She raised her scimitar and led the way down the tunnel. The crew roared and followed after, sloshing through the stream deeper into the heart of the mountain.

Tiny rivulets and waterfalls appeared along the sides of the tunnel, combining together to form the stream flowing back outside. That was strange, but Natasha ignored the feature to focus instead on the sanguine light that grew with every step she took. It resolved into an opening, where the tunnel widened. Natasha steeled herself and plunged through, ready again for the fray.

The tunnel opened into a massive chamber formed of smoothly polished brass. Four walls of the same material rose up and outward, like the inside of an inverted pyramid. Natasha found herself standing in the middle of a platform dais raised several feet above a perfectly flat, square floor. A low, waist-high wall rose from the lip of the platform, smooth and unbroken but for a pair of wide stairs. One was directly ahead, leading down to the floor. Another ascended on her right, up to a causeway. That causeway spanned the length of the room to a similar stair and platform against the far opposite wall. Below it an arched opening led deeper into the mountain.

Illumination came in the form of a lurid red glow. It filled the space, emanating from ten tall, fat, transparent cylinders. Glass or translucent crystal, Natasha didn't know. But within flowed something viscous that resembled nothing so much as red-hot magma, rising up from below the floor to disappear past the half-seen gearworks that covered the ceiling. Chains dangled down at regular intervals, suspending heavy metal blocks above the floor. These were taller than a man, perfectly square and formed of the same material as the rest of the room, with odd transparent panels adorning their surfaces. One of the blocks did not dangle, resting instead on the causeway to the right; the chain connecting it ran slack to the far end of the room.

Farouk and Etarin ran into her, followed by the rest of the Salomcani. Bloodthirsty yells quieted as Natasha's crew stared about in confusion.

"By the Goddess," muttered Etarin, wiping away more blood from the cut on his forehead. "Where are we?"

"Voornish ruin," said Natasha with a smile. She'd been surprised at first, but it wasn't that hard to figure out. Her father had seen enough of them, and she wasn't unfamiliar with the places either. "Ha. We'll loot this place down to the bone once we take care of business. There's more than a few nobles back on Edrus who'll pay their eyeteeth for Voorn leftovers, and I know just the fences to reach them." She raised her scimitar. "Congratulations, me hearties. We're all richer than pig shit!" Her new crew gave a ragged cheer, not entirely seeming to understand.

Jahmal grabbed at her arm. Natasha opened her mouth to snarl at the man, then stopped. With his other hand, the thin sailor pointed down the platform stair at the center of the room. "Kalyon," he said. "Look."

Natasha jerked her arm away, then peered through the gloom. A figure stood there, wavering slightly. Human-shaped, though it reflected the light of the magma as if it were wearing armor.

"Hara hailo!" it called out, in a tinny voice that just reached up to her on the platform.

She didn't recognize the language. Natasha exchanged a look with Jahmal, then faced the rest of the crew. "Forward, all of you. And have your weapons at the ready. Fengel, I mean, the Perinese, are in here somewhere."

Cautiously, she led the way down to the floor of the great room. No one jumped out at her. No one triggered any clever traps.

When Natasha reached the figure, she stopped. It was a metallic armature, almost a skeleton, formed out of the same Voornish brass as everything else here. The torso, head, and forearms were like a child's suit of armor, covered in alien scrollwork. Two great glass eyes peered at her. It tottered on skeletal feet, its arms bound around its midsection by coils of well-tied rope.

"*Hara hailo?*" it asked. "*Korstachi?* Or this one? Can you understand this dialect?"

The last had come in clear, though weirdly accented, Perinese. Natasha frowned.

"This one is reasonably certain that this dialect is correct," continued the machine. "Earlier speech samples indicate a 95 percent chance of success, with only a 5 percent chance of failure." It struggled unsuccessfully against the ropes that bound it. Whoever had tied it up had done a thorough job. It wiggled back and forth, threatening to tip over entirely.

"What is it, Kalyon?" asked Farouk. He peered past Natasha, worry and fascination playing out on his face, the swollen bruise twisting it ghastly in the reddish glow. The other crewmen stared at the thing as well, keeping well at her back.

"It's an automaton," muttered Natasha in Perinese. "An actual Voornish automaton."

"Ah!" exclaimed the machine. "The calculations were correct. Please, you must not be here. Take yourselves from this facility, all of you! It is very dangerous, and recent external activity has damaged the cooling pumps—"

Jahmal raised his long knife and took a half-step back. "It's some trap. The thing speaks Perinese!"

"Shut up," replied Natasha in irritation. "I think it speaks many languages. I've heard of these. It's a working Voornish machine. Probably priceless. But who tied it up? It's Fengel. It had to be Fengel...but why?" She straightened, peering around at the cavernous room.

"Do you know the other humans?" asked the machine. "Oh, please. You must ask them to leave. They did not listen to this one, though this one is certain that the appropriate dialect was used, especially in light of recent evidence. But! The machineries here are very delicate, especially after an unknown violent event on the exterior of the facility—"

Natasha looked back at the rambling automaton. "Where did these others go?"

"Oh," said the automaton. "They never left."

A screeching cacophony echoed from up above. Natasha glanced up to see the block resting upon the causeway up above slide over and fall off. The chains anchoring it to the machineries in the ceiling went taut, and the thing swung down at the gathered Salomcani.

The raiders yelled and scrabbled to get out of the way. Natasha's instincts kicked in and she dropped, throwing herself flat. Farouk landed beside her, covering her head and torso protectively. She opened her mouth to yell at him, but then the block swung overhead with just inches to spare. It connected with the Voornish automaton, and both went flying past.

Natasha glanced back up. The block continued on, the attached chains guiding it in a long arc toward the translucent tubes on the far left wall. As it reached the apex of its swing, the chains suspending it from the ceiling snapped, letting the thing fly through the air. It slammed violently into the tubes with a resounding clang. The metal block and the Voornish automaton fell away, the latter with a distressed wail. Natasha spied several long, glowing cracks that the impact had left in the glass. She winced as the block slammed into the ground, clattering out of sight.

"Hayes!" called a familiar voice. "You idiot!"

Natasha would know Fengel's holler anywhere. She looked up to see him standing on the far platform, where he'd risen from hiding behind the low wall there. He shook his saber at the causeway, where a panting, disheveled figure stood. Natasha recognized the sub-lieutenant of the *Goliath*, looking a little worse for wear.

"You've missed them all completely!" continued her husband. "And that automaton was a priceless artifact, probably."

Natasha glanced around. It was true. Her new crew lay all wherever they had thrown themselves. By some miracle the trap had managed to miss them all.

Now I've got you. Natasha grinned and climbed to her feet. Or tried to. Farouk still had her clasped protectively tight. "Off," she hissed at him. "Get off, fool!" She slapped with her free hand until he let go and then scrabbled upwards. She raised her scimitar, resting the blade against one shoulder. "There you are," she said. "I figured that you'd have tried to set an ambush, but I didn't expect it would be anything worth worrying over. Looks like I was right."

Fengel rapped the pommel of his saber against the metal wall. "Well, you would have, if *that idiot up on the causeway* could follow orders!" The last he obviously shouted so that Hayes would hear.

The Salomcani climbed to their feet behind her, muttering curses and angry threats. Fengel blinked down at them. Then he gave a whistle. The rest of the men of the *Goliath* rose up from behind the wall where they'd been likewise hiding.

Natasha cheered. She hadn't stopped to check casualties after the fight in the gully outside, but there were fewer Perinese than she remembered. "I seem to recall someone saying that the crew was only as good as the captain," she sneered.

Fengel's eyes widened in outrage, his eyepiece falling away to dangle from its chain. He started in alarm and carefully replaced it, wiping the monocle against his jacket first. When he looked back to her, it was focused through the crazed glass of a cracked lens.

A warm, fuzzy feeling grew in Natasha's belly. *Finally*. He'd finally failed to beat her in wordplay. Oh, she was sure he'd had a clever response, but it was ruined by his ridiculous affectation.

"You make a very good point," said Fengel.

Natasha blinked. "I do?"

"Yes. I take full responsibility for this trap's failure to crush you. Even if the hands that set it in motion belonged to my moderately treacherous, and *increasingly incompetent* sub-lieutenant," Fengel projected his voice toward the causeway. "I was still the one who placed him in charge, and thus it's my fault."

Fengel examined the nails of his free hand. The room was momentarily silent, save for the clanking whirr of the machineries overhead.

"What?" exclaimed Natasha. "No. You don't get to do that!"

Her husband raised an eyebrow. Somehow, the monocle stayed in place. "I'm sorry?"

"You don't get to win by giving in. I got you that time. Admit it!"

"I haven't the faintest idea what you are talking about. I've already said that you had a point—"

"There!" Natasha pointed her scimitar at him. "That! You're doing it again."

Fengel sighed. "As always, you're being irrational. Not to mention childish. Not that I expect anything else of you."

Natasha realized that he'd turned the conversation around on her. Again.

"You. Ass." She gritted her teeth. "You smug, condescending pig. How you conned your way atop that sad sack of low-tide leavings beside you is mystifying."

"There was a need," replied Fengel. "I filled it." He swept his arms wide to encompass the Perinese sailors to either side. "You see, a *real* leader doesn't just command. He lifts his people up and shows them the way to victory. He listens. Which I'm guessing isn't something you've ever done. How much bullying did you have to do in order to get that pack of feral animals to follow you?"

"Feral animals?" Rage and pride filled her voice. Natasha stood up straighter and slashed out with the tip of her blade. "My men are Salomcani! The people of the Sheikdom are fiercer fighters and better sailors by far than those sheep-loving peacocks you've got following you."

Fengel slammed his free hand against the brass wall before him. "Fierce fighters? Hardly. Any intensity they show is only to make up for their lack of skill. And the Perinese consistently sail circles around them on the open water. The *Salmalin* was running from the *Goliath,* I seem to recall."

"The only reason your sots can even sail is because they can't wait to escape the Kingdom!"

"How dare you, you pox-ridden harlot. The people of the Kingdom are men of breeding and—"

"Breeding with sheep!" snarled Natasha. "With the odd nag of a horse thrown in for variety."

"Perinese horses are the finest in the world," growled Fengel. "I recall that the Salomcani used to have some decent lines, until they all got *eaten!*"

"You bastard!"

"Bitch!"

Natasha pointed her sword at Fengel. "I'm going to wipe that smirk off your face with the bottom of my boot!"

"You and what army?" asked Fengel

A figure appeared at Natasha's side. "Kalyon," cried Etarin. "Enough prattle! Let us end these filthy mongrels."

She looked back at the rest of her crew. Bloodlust twisted their faces into ugly masks. Not all of them understood Fengel's insults. But no one could mistake his intent.

Natasha faced her husband. "With this one," she said, smiling wickedly.

A loud crack echoed throughout the room. Natasha glanced up, along with everyone else, at the massive crystal pipes along the west wall. The fracture left by Fengel's mis-aimed trap was stretching. She watched as several spiderweb fissures crawled madly across the glass.

"Oh?" said Fengel. He smiled smugly back at the men of the *Goliath*. "That pipe is going to break open any moment," said Fengel, "dumping hundreds of gallons of lava, or whatever is in there, all over the floor. We will be perfectly safe up here on the platform. We don't *need* to come down and meet you, if we just keep you at bay on these stairs. And there isn't a single thing you can say to change that."

Natasha shifted her gaze to the assembled crew of the *Goliath*. They glared at her and her men, muttering their own threats and curses. "Fengel's first name," she said loudly and clearly, "is Ashley."

Fengel howled in anger. He charged down the stair with his saber raised above his head. The men of the *Goliath* looked to each other in surprise before following with a wordless cry. Her own crewmen roared their response. Both sides rushed forward, crashing into each other like a pair of opposing waves. The battle was on.

Natasha itched to meet her husband. She'd ambushed him, driven him off, and then provoked him again into a fight. But if she crossed blades with him now she knew she would lose. Fengel was better with a blade by far, and while facing him down directly would be satisfying, it wouldn't work. No. She couldn't let herself be beaten again. Just like outside, she had to orchestrate this just right if she wanted to win.

Her father always said to cheat, if you couldn't win a fair fight. She retreated, letting the crew of the *Salmalin* flow past her to face her enraged husband. While Fengel was a skilled swordsman, he had other weaknesses. And she'd hit those where they *hurt*.

She picked several faces out of the melee, those of the hated Perinese. Natasha grinned and reached out as both Farouk and Jahmal went past. "With me!" she cried. "This way!"

The two sailors looked at her in confusion, but followed as she pulled them alongside the fight out toward its edges. There she found a small cluster of Bluecoat marines led by her former gaolers, Sergeant Cumbers and Private Simon. *Good.* She'd made a note of who stood closest to Fengel during his tirade on the platform; they were sure to be his followers, the ones he used to keep everyone in line. Fengel wasn't strong enough to rule his crew directly by force. He loved to delegate. Removing the sergeant would deal him, and the Perinese, a serious blow.

But she had to be quick about it. Natasha threw herself at the smaller, less-experienced Simon, aiming a punch with the hilt of her scimitar at his freckled face. The blow connected with a thud. Simon cried out and fell back, spitting teeth and flailing his gangly limbs in a blue blur. Cumbers yelled in alarm, just as Farouk bulled forward with a two-handed chop, breaking through the blade of the marine and biting into the man's shoulder. The sergeant fell back into the knot of Bluecoats. Farouk kept up the assault as the Perinese defense along this side of the battle folded.

A resounding crack reached Natasha through the noise. She glanced up to see another spiderweb crack flaring out up high on the crystal pipe.

Time was running out, but she could still win this. Next was the aetherite, Dawkins. As an aetherite, he was a potent tool for Fengel. As Natasha moved back through the melee, she spied Fengel. He was fending off three of her Salomcani, keeping them at bay with a skillful blur of parries and ripostes. Though close to being overwhelmed, he still lashed out at any opportunities that presented themselves.

Natasha saw Dawkins on the other flank. Fortunately the man was drained of any real Workings; that much she'd learned while in captivity. However, he still had a few tricks left, it seemed. Any blade directed at him jerked away, almost as if alive. Though the aetherite was unarmed, his hands were wreathed in a cool glowing nimbus. Whenever he touched one of her men, they would shriek in pain and collapse to the floor.

Most folk knew very little about Worked aetherite magic. Fortunately, she'd had Konrad on retainer for years now, and knew how to tell the various spells apart. Dawkins's Bladeward Working was useful, but it had limits. Natasha sheathed her scimitar and cracked the knuckles of both hands. Then she threw herself at him.

The aetherite saw her out of the corner of his eye. He spun about to meet her and raised both hands, smiling grimly in recognition. Natasha didn't bother returning the gesture. As he swung out with aether-charged hands, Natasha ducked low, coming up past and along his side, almost as if she'd tried to tackle him and decided against it at the last second. Her fist found his sternum just beneath the breastbone, knocking the air out of the magician in a loud gasp. His concentration faltered, and along with it, the spell he held. Natasha grabbed him by the coat and held on as she landed blow upon blow against the side of his head. Feebly, he tried to fend her off. Only when he wasn't moving anymore did she relent.

As her men moved forward, Natasha released the aetherite, and another loud crack sounded from the great tube on the western wall. Its surface was a fine spiderweb now, ready to give way at any moment. Below, the Perinese were folding. Without Cumbers and Dawkins to hold the flanks and reissue Fengel's orders, her men were driving them back. They'd almost won.

Time to drive this home. Natasha pressed back into the melee, drawing her scimitar as she went.

Fengel still stood at the center of the fight. He was almost surrounded now. Still, though, he refused to give up. By himself now, he held the line of battle for his men, but he was at his limits. Sweat poured down his features and he bled from a number of minor cuts.

Natasha grinned and threw herself at his blind side, right where he wore that idiotic monocle. Her blade licked out, but his saber appeared to block it. He glared at her just long enough to make his point before dodging a dagger-thrust by Jahmal.

"I may not have your skill," purred Natasha, "but there's only so much you can handle, and we both know it."

"I'll hold...my own...as long as I have to," muttered Fengel. He tried a cut at her thighs.

Natasha danced away with a laugh. "That'll be a long wait, then. I've taken care of both your sergeant and your aetherite. Your people are failing. No one's coming to help you."

Fengel rammed the pommel of his saber into Jahmal's forehead, dropping the man. He cut at the throat of a Salomcani sailor beside him, forcing him back with a yelp. Then, quicker than she would have thought possible, his blade was there, singing down for her face.

Natasha threw up her scimitar, catching the saber at the last second. She foiled his blow, but the blade bit down across the back of her hand. Natasha grunted and fell back, blood running in rivulets down her arm.

His eyes were cold. "It seems that you learned something from Mordecai, after all."

Her mouth twisted into an ugly snarl. She made to reply, but the pipe on the far wall chose that exact moment to burst. Boiling magma shot out into the room in an incandescent stream. The air heated, becoming instantly almost unbreathable. The liquid splashed only a dozen feet from the edge of the fight, spattering and scatting molten rock all about.

Those nearest the splash yelled in alarm. Salomcani and Perinese sailors both flung themselves back from the overwhelming heat, all thoughts of conflict forgotten. One unlucky Bluecoat caught fire. He ran back for the platform, screaming.

The crack in the crystal pipe widened to unleash even more pressurized magma. Natasha cursed and ducked out of the way. The rest of her crewmen followed suit, scrambling for safety. She kicked and fought to get away from the melee, until the smooth metal floor was empty around her and she could clamber back up the steps of the platform where she'd entered the room.

Natasha took a breath and looked back. Her crew ascended to safety beside her, having moved almost as fast. On the opposite side of the room,

Fengel and the Perinese had done the same. Remarkably few of her own people had fallen in the fight. Fengel wouldn't be able to say the same. Natasha watched the spreading magma ignite Perinese clothing and flesh.

A flash of light caught at the corner of her eye. Natasha looked up to see Fengel standing on the steps to the far platform, watching her, the flames from the corpses of his men reflecting in the cracked glass of his monocle. Behind him, the Perinese nursed their wounds, looking demoralized.

Natasha smiled at her husband. She blew him a wide and extravagant kiss. Her crewmen threw jeers and catcalls along with it.

Fengel said nothing. Wordlessly he herded his crew through the archway leading deeper into the mountain. Natasha drew her scimitar and pointed at the stair up to the causeway that would lead them in pursuit.

I'm not done yet. This day will be mine.

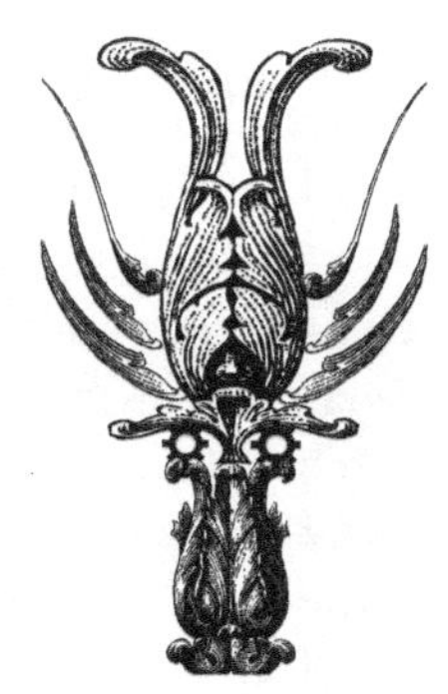

CHAPTER SIXTEEN

THE ARCH LED INTO A LOW TUNNEL OF SMOOTH VOORNISH BRASS. Though dim, it was a reprieve from the infernal heat of the magma pumping into the room behind them. Fengel led his new crew with saber in hand, questing forward through the gloom. Behind him came the men of the *Goliath*, groaning in pain, shock, and fear.

Someone tugged at Fengel's sleeve. He turned to see Midshipman Paine, breathless and bloodied by a slew of scratches above one ear. "Sir!" he cried. "Sergeant Cumbers is hurt."

"Can he still walk?" Fengel asked.

"Yes. He's bringing up the rear. Private Simon is helpin' him because Cumbers won't rest. But his shoulder is all messed up, an' bleedin bad. You need to come help!"

The idea was ridiculous. There were far more important considerations at the moment. Natasha was *winning*. "If he can still walk, then he isn't dead yet. His wounds can wait."

Paine was taken aback. "But, sir—"

"No buts," snapped Fengel. "If you're so concerned, get back there and prop the sergeant up until he can find a better place to die. I am busy at the moment."

Fengel turned away, feeling Paine's eyes upon his back. He ignored them, moving farther ahead from the rest of the crew. Hopefully he could find something defensible soon. *This is just...repositioning, tactical repositioning. Yes. That's it.*

It still felt like running away. Which was galling. A small part of Fengel had to admit it was true. Natasha had surprised him in the ravine, forced his retreat into this mountain. Worse, the hasty ambush he'd set up had failed. To top it all off, Natasha had routed him, crushing his lieutenants and forcing him again to flee.

But I can still do this. She is not clever, and she is not skilled. I can still beat her. I just have to arrange the pieces correctly. Somehow.

The tunnel ended in an arch up ahead. Fengel passed through and found himself in another massive chamber, even larger than the one behind them. Polished brass made up the floor, with two rows of glowing crystal orbs illuminating a path that led deeper into the room. They failed to fully dispel the gloom, leaving the boundaries of the chamber shrouded and dark. Encompassing the orbs and the path were long, low platforms made of the same burnished material as the floor, covered with tables and racks full of strange machineries.

A rumbling susurrus of clockwork mechanisms echoed down from the darkness above. They clicked and whirred much like the room before, but held a discordant note, as if their machineries were distressed.

Is this whole damned mountain hollow? It certainly seemed like it. Fengel could only guess at the purpose of this strange enclave. Was it a gigantic workshop? An alien factory? That was certainly plausible; the few Voornish ruins he had come across always showed signs of great engineering and advanced technologies.

Enough woolgathering. Fengel looked to his crew as they emerged from the tunnel. They came in twos and threes, eyes panicked and wild. Not a one of them was hale, with injuries running from assorted light cuts to heavily bandaged gashes and contusions. A quick count confirmed that these were the lucky ones, however. All told, there were less than ten surviving members of the crew of the *Goliath*.

Still, they would serve. *He* certainly wasn't ready to give up quite yet. When young Paine emerged out of the tunnel, helping Private Simon to support Sergeant Cumbers, Fengel clapped his hands for their attention.

"All right, lads!" he called. "That didn't go so well, admittedly, but we're not out of the game yet."

Deckhand Riley Gordon helped a Bluecoat marine carry the unconscious Mr. Dawkins. He let go of the aetherite and then collapsed. "It's over!" he cried. "That madwoman is right behind us. She'll be the end of us all!"

"Ridiculous," replied Fengel. "We just need to be clever about things."

Sub-Lieutenant Hayes glared at Fengel sullenly. "Is that the same kind of clever you had in the last room?"

Goddess, I am sick of this man. Fengel smiled. "Of course, Mr. Hayes. After all, my plan was excellent. It was only your incompetent execution that earned us such a miserable failure."

There. Insulting Hayes always earned him a bit of good-feeling among the crew. But a quick glance revealed that not a single man of the *Goliath* was smiling. Even young Paine and the milksop Private Simon were glaring at him. *Wait. What's this?*

"Anyway," continued Fengel. He gestured about them at the cavernous room. "Look at this place. Obviously a factory of some sort. There's got to be something that we can use here. Something we can use to get the advantage again over that horrible witch."

The nearest platform caught his eye. A rack of the machineries atop it had fallen over, spilling long, strangely-shaped metal rods all over the floor. Fengel sheathed his sword and walked over to pick one up. The Voorn artifact was cool in his hands, like glass or ceramic. He tossed it back at the sub-lieutenant. "Here. Figure out some use for this."

The rest of the crew weren't even watching him anymore. Instead they glanced around the chamber, looking for places to hide and talking with their fellows quietly, as if they didn't want him to overhear.

Fengel frowned. This wasn't good. He needed everyone together, or they were beaten before Natasha even came through the tunnel. And he'd be damned to the Realms Below before he let that happen.

"Come now, lads," he called. Fengel pointed at another platform a little farther down the path. Racks full of the odd metal rods were stacked atop it in rows. "High ground, up there. Perfectly good place for another ambush, and we've no time. Let's hop to it."

Riley Gordon and a few of the others moved immediately, just glad to follow orders. They clambered up atop the platform and moved to take cover. The rest of the crew milled about, eyeing Fengel and other avenues of escape.

Something moved abruptly in the corner of his eye. Fengel wheeled, drawing his saber as he went. From out behind the nearest platforms stalked the Voornish automaton. It tottered awkwardly, but seemed no worse from the blow it had suffered in the previous room.

"You must not be here!" it cried, voice mechanical and tinny. "And this one is 90 percent certain that you are capable of understanding this dialect. Further ignorance of this communication is inexcusable." It stopped to glare at the assembled sailors. "Also, further mistreatment of this unit. That is inexcusable as well."

Everyone stared at the machine. Fengel lowered his sword and grappled for something to say. He coughed, and it whirled to peer at him through the great glass eyes in its faceplate. "Look...fellow," he said. "I'm sorry about what happened back there. But we're in a spot of trouble. So if you could just point us at some method of crushing that raving bitch who's after us, it would be greatly appreciated."

A rumbling shook the room. Distant machineries groaned. The sailors glanced around in alarm, as did Fengel and the automaton. It raised its hands.

"This one is pleading now! You must not be here! Your presence has already destabilized many important systems. There is great danger! The geothermal tap has been damaged, and now you stand in the Foundry of Garaam. Many and varied are the weapons stored here. You must not awaken them, or the other engines of destruction built in this place."

The automaton fell silent. It wrung its hands together in a too-human gesture of worry.

Fengel blinked at the thing, then he yelled at the crew of the *Goliath*. "All right, you lot! You heard the thing—there are weapons stored here; find them!"

Salomcani curses and howls of bloodlust echoed out of the tunnel. Midshipman Paine raced back from where he'd been peering into it. "They're coming!"

"No!" cried the automaton. "This one is asking, pleading, please to all of you for leaving this facility. Do not be travelling deeper—"

A bright flash of viridian lightning struck the automaton full in the chest. It flew up across the path and crashed into a pile of machinery atop a distant platform. Fengel looked to Hayes, along with everyone else. The sub-lieutenant gripped his rod awkwardly, still pointing, apparently by accident, to where the Voornish machine had stood only a minute ago.

"Ah," said Fengel. "Some sort of lightning-muskets. Well done Hayes, for once. Lads, arm yourselves. I think the tables just turned in our favor."

The crew of the *Goliath* ran for the fallen rack of Voornish weapons. Riley Gordon was first, followed by old Harvey the shipwright. Private Simon emerged after them a moment later bearing a lightning-musket with one arm and supporting the still-incoherent Sergeant Cumbers with the other. Midshipman Paine had grabbed up two of the things, and glared angrily at the tunnel opening. The look he gave Fengel wasn't much kinder.

I may have misstepped here. Fengel glanced over at Cumbers. The sergeant's face was covered in blood, and he stumbled like a drunken sailor, dagger clutched in one hand. Private Simon, ever loyal, kept pointing him toward the entrance to the chamber. *Damnation.* Still, there wasn't any time for that now.

Hot for blood, the sailors of the *Salmalin* emerged into the Foundry of Garaam. Natasha was in the lead, flanked by two familiar-looking sailors. One was tall and dark-haired, with a scimitar and a nasty bruise on his face. The other was short and older, and had a nasty gash across his forehead. Behind them came the rest of her crew, blades brandished high in the air.

The crew of the *Dawnhawk* fired their pilfered lightning-muskets. Or tried to, at least. Some shook the things violently and received no response. Others frantically hunted for a trigger along the inhuman handgrips. Private Simon threw his away and drew his cutlass as the enemy closed the distance to within a few dozen feet.

It was young Paine who figured out the trick of it. He pressed a large stud at the rear of each weapon, sending viridian lightning crackling forth. One shot went high, impacting the near wall of the foundry and exploding in a half-second sunburst of light. The other shot just past Natasha and took the big sailor behind her in the chest. As with the automaton, there was a burst of light and the man went flying.

The Salomcani faltered in their charge. Natasha herself stared in sudden shock and surprise at the crew of the *Goliath.* Then a few more of the Perinese managed to fire their lightning-muskets. None of the shots hit, but the look on the face of his wife brought warmth to Fengel's heart.

"Take cover!" Natasha cried in Salomcani. She dove off the path between a pair of platforms, and her crew scrambled to get out of the way as well.

Fengel raised his saber. "Fire at will!"

The rest of his crew found the firing studs and unleashed more alien energy at their Salomcani enemies. Not all of them did so successfully. Some held the things backward, sending stray shots out among the men of the *Goliath.* Fengel danced away from a blast while the Bluecoat beside him clutched at the blackened, bleeding stump where his hand had been.

"Grab the rods!" said Natasha in high, clear Salomcani. He saw her point at the platform she was currently hiding behind. "Just like the bastard Perinese have got! They're all over the place!"

Damn, damn, damn! Things were falling apart. Fengel glanced at his crew; some were still firing away, others still frantically tried to master their new weapons. A few lay still and scorched.

"Fall back!" Fengel cried, for what seemed the thousandth time today. "We need better cover!"

He reached out and grabbed at the nearest crewman, repeating his call and shoving whoever was closest down the path. In moments he'd gotten them all up, if not moving. That changed when the first volley of Salomcani lightning spit in their direction.

Fengel goaded the crew of the *Goliath* into retreat. Two stood with him as he withdrew, covering the rear. One was Midshipman Paine, who yelled wordlessly and fired viridian blasts from a lightning-musket in each arm. The other was a Bluecoat who caught a return shot in the face and fell down dead with his skin blackened and burned. The rest fled deeper down the path into the Foundry of Garaam.

The platforms and their machineries became stranger and stranger as they ran. Fengel spied blazing lights glimmering from glass spheres and great cables dangling down from the ceiling, attached to equipment that chugged and whirred. Shapes half-seen in the gloom hinted at more ominous and malevolent things.

A forest of large mechanical legs occluded the path up ahead. They were long, heavy things that dangled down from a complicated chain conveyor, canted backward like those of a lizard. Each of the vicious claws was longer than Fengel was tall.

A viridian blast flashed past Fengel's head, exploding against one of the legs with a flash of light. "There!" Fengel pointed with his saber. "Through there!"

The men of the *Goliath* didn't need to hear him, if they still paid him any heed at all. They charged past him, disappearing behind the dangling mechanical limbs. Fengel followed, racking his brains for something, anything that he could do to regain the advantage over his wife.

Fengel ducked behind a gigantic foot just as a trio of viridian blasts scorched the ground he'd been standing on. The cover was only momentary. Any moment, Natasha and her minions would overtake him. Fengel took in his new surroundings.

A dozen yards away hung another row of limbs. Tails this time, all in a row, with tall, sail-like plates running down their length. Past these were another row of dangling arms. And beyond those hung huge armored necks. The globe-lamps still shone from their places along the floor, but their light was hidden and occluded within the inverted forest of Voornish machinery. The whole place was dim and close-in.

The crew of the *Goliath* were scattering. Some ran beyond where he could see. Others hid down behind a metal leg, sobbing and tending to their wounds. A few still fought back, having mastered the lightning-muskets. Young Paine was among the most competent, it seemed. And the angriest.

Damnation! His men were broken. Worse, he would never regain control of them all before Natasha reached their position. Fengel glanced about for something he could do to even the odds. He spied Simon and Cumbers, dodging with two other men through the shadows as they made their escape. A viridian blast shot after them, stopped by a mammoth mechanical tail.

His men may have been broken, but he was not. Clashing out in the open had gone consistently poorly. Fengel always thought Natasha's old first mate, Mordecai, had been behind her successes in battle. Maybe it really had been her, though. But here, in the dark and behind cover? Fengel drew his sword. "Keep falling back!" he yelled, hoping the crew would heed him. Then, stealthily, he moved behind a clawed leg and clambered up onto it from behind.

He had just reached a shadowed space below the knee when Natasha ran past, yelling at the top of her lungs. The big Salomcani followed her, despite his scorched chest, along with several others. They spread out in pairs to hunt the disparate Perinese. Fengel gritted his teeth as viridian blasts and the cries of battle echoed amongst the limbs. When the stream of Salomcani had faded to a trickle, he dropped down, saber at the ready.

A trio of enemy sailors saw him. They checked their charge and came for him instead. One had wide mustachios and a pair of long daggers. Another bore a scimitar and an ugly gash across his lips. The third had a cudgel. All three glared at Fengel with murder in their eyes.

Fengel took a crude hack at the nearest man. As the fellow raised his scimitar to parry, Fengel dropped his sword down under the man's guard in a thrust that took him high in the chest. He withdrew and made a low parry just in time to block the daggers aimed for his gut. Fengel replied by ramming his pommel into his assailant's face, feeling the momentary resistance of breaking teeth. The man fell back into the darkness, screaming, just in time for the third sailor with the cudgel to step in. Fengel blocked two solid blows aimed for his head, sending wood chips flying out into the dark. He answered with a cut at the knuckles that bit home, sending the sailor down to join his fellow, yelling as his fingers fell to the Factory floor along with the cudgel. Fengel laid him out with a left cross to the head.

Fengel slipped like a shadow through the forest of hanging machine-parts. From the sounds echoing back to him, most of his new crew were nearby, their Salomcani foes engaging them in outnumbered skirmishes. Fengel did what he could, taking care never to engage enough of them that he'd be pinned down again, the way he had in the first chamber of the hollow mountain.

He found Private Simon standing with his back to a massive metal torso, cut free from its suspending chains by a stray energy blast. Cumbers lay behind him at his feet, groaning incoherently. Five Salomcani sailors faced him in a semicircle. The private held one of the lightning-muskets by the wrong end, ready to swing it like a club.

"This thing may be out of fire," he cried with more conviction than Fengel had ever heard from him, "but I'm not! Come forward, men of the Sheik! I'll see you to your graves!"

They made to rush in, and Fengel stepped in to block their progress. A few parries, cuts, a thrust, and all five were bleeding or crying out on the ground.

Fengel raised an eyebrow. "Admirable spirit," he said. "But I consider it a great virtue, Simon, to avoid getting boxed-in so."

The young soldier swallowed. "I didn't have a choice, sir. The sergeant, he collapsed, and I couldn't get him moving."

Fengel nodded. "Well, all right. Still, let's get you two up. We'll get him somewhere safe for the moment, maybe back near the platforms. Then I could use your help."

Simon nodded. He bent to pick up his comrade, and Fengel reached down with his off-hand to assist.

A bolt of viridian lightning brushed against his left side. Pain bloomed, crawling its way down through his innards to shake his arms and legs. Fengel cried out and fell to his knees, managing just barely to keep his hand clenched around his saber.

Natasha stepped out around from behind the mechanical torso. In one hand she held her scimitar, the other a lightning-musket. The tip of the thing glowed green and tiny sparks crackled around it. Private Simon raised his bludgeon, readying to fling himself at her. She pointed the artifact at him and he froze.

"Now, now," she said with a smile. "I'd like to think that you wouldn't underestimate me." She glanced down at Fengel. "How are you doing down there, you supercilious prig?"

Fengel glared up at his wife. "You shot me!" he gasped.

"Oh, please. Grazed you, barely." She raised the lightning-musket. "These are amazing. And there's hundreds of them here! I'm going to loot this place from teeth to toes—no one'll be able to stand against me. Especially not that collection of treasonous bastards that have my ship. Oh, they'll rue the day they crossed me. I'll make certain of it. I've gotten ever-so-many bright ideas—"

"You. Shot. Me!" Fengel threw himself at her, enraged. Natasha blinked in surprise and parried his overhead chop with the lightning-musket. The blow jarred his arm and sent the alien weapon flying. She cursed, cutting at his head with the scimitar in her off-hand. Fengel blocked the blow and countered with one of his own, driving her backward.

Natasha laughed. "Being angry isn't going to do it, lover-mine. Though maybe if you'd been paying attention, then I wouldn't have tagged you in the first place?" She feigned a cut at his chest, looping the blade around when he parried the blow.

Fengel ducked away at the last second. He hissed, every breath making his ribs feel as if they were on fire. Natasha pressed her advantage with a flurry of blows. Fengel fell back against the onslaught, ducking behind another of the hanging torsos and then behind a long clawed arm. He came around the opposite side with a lunge that almost caught his wife between the shoulders. She spun at the last moment, crying out as the tip of his blade drew blood. Natasha whirled then, knocking his blade aside with a squeal of metal and a shower of sparks.

"I am *far* from helpless," said Fengel. He glared at her through the cracked lens of his monocle, making her answering snarl seem broken and crazed.

"That is a matter of opinion," she replied.

"Shooting a man in the back, though? How basely done."

"I needed the advantage," she replied. "I'm not stupid."

"That," he replied nastily, "is a matter of opinion."

Natasha growled and shoved forward. Fengel fell back. He rebounded and threw himself at her again. They met, each of them with a curse on their lips, their blades clattering and clanging together. Fengel withdrew, lunged, pirouetted. Natasha did the same, and they danced through the forest of mechanical limbs, the cold steel in their hands flickering against the burnished Voorn brass all around them.

Fengel's aching side sapped at his strength. Any other time, he'd have handily finished Natasha. But every bit of swordplay he tried sent an aching flare through his burned ribs, wrecking his finesse.

The ground gave another tremor beneath them. It rumbled and shook, setting the forest of dangling machinery to swaying. Fengel ignored it, focusing on his footwork. He tried a new tactic, shifting to defense and seeing if he could draw Natasha into the path of one of the limbs.

She redoubled her assault, chasing after as he'd expected. Fengel spun, ducking behind a mechanical leg as Natasha followed, stepping past a long clawed toe hidden by shadows near the floor. She tripped on it and he exulted, darting back in with saber upraised. Natasha swore and desperately parried a blow for her head.

No finesse now. Fengel hacked and stabbed, seeking to overpower his wife where she half-crouched in distress. She beat back each blow, barely, failing to recover a little more each time. Her snarl was marred now, frozen with uncertainty. He had her now.

A green flash from the corner of his eye warned him just in time. Fengel fell away with a curse as an errant blast of Voorn lightning flashed between them, blinding him for a half-second as it burst against the mechanical leg. He raised his saber just in time to parry the cut Natasha had aimed at his head. The moment was lost—she'd recovered and pressed her attack as he regained his footing. Fengel admitted a grudging kernel of admiration; his wife was a tenacious woman.

Abruptly, they broke free of the dangling chain conveyors. The chamber opened up again into a wide space floored in Voornish brass. At its center rose something improbable; a mechanical dragon over eighty feet in height. The thing squatted on powerful mechanical legs, its reptilian form hunched forward and still. The long segmented tail curled lightly on the floor, rising up to meet the torso, which had wickedly sharp spines rising from the top. The torso itself was thick and armored, with heavy plates protecting the more delicate cables, clockwork, and flywheel mechanisms he could see half-buried within it. Two forearms hunched in tight to the chest, long and strong, though not as heavyset as the legs. Up above the body continued a long reptilian neck rising to support the massive and fearsome head, crowned with wicked horns that swept down to a long maw filled with jagged teeth.

The thing did not move. Its eyes were shuttered and still. Great cables descended from the dim ceiling to varying positions along the construct. Whether for fuel or restraint or some other arcane purpose, Fengel did not know. Scaffolding and ramp-work enclosed the machine, rising up from the foundry floor in a series of thin metal walkways all the way to the head of the thing itself. Just past the beast was wall of rock and stone, incongruous in comparison to the rest of the foundry. It spanned around to the front of the dragon where a giant pair of double doors stood half-opened, filled with earth and stone that spilled down to form a slope all the way to the ground.

Small fights raged across the floor of the foundry. The crews of the *Salmalin* and the *Goliath* warred, continuing the struggle they'd fought since before Fengel had even come to the island. The Perinese were outnumbered now two to one, fighting half a dozen separate duels. An occasional flare of viridian lightning arced across the great space. Yet most of the battles were up close and personal with blade, fist, and truncheon.

"Your men don't seem to be doing so well," laughed Natasha.

"They'll do just fine until I can rally them," replied Fengel. "They're Perinese, after all."

Their duel brought them across the floor, ducking, weaving, and circling. Natasha laughed again. "What's this? Nationalism? Pride? A bit late for that, you traitor. You *mutinied* against them, remember? Do the scrubs you've conned here even know that?"

Fengel found himself at the base of the scaffold and the mechanical dragon, the ramp leading upward at his back. A tremor shook the chamber again. Natasha fell back into a guard position, and he took the opportunity to climb up the ramp; higher ground was a great advantage.

"I wouldn't expect you to understand," he replied. "The people of the Sheikdom are an unwashed rabble, and you don't even have *that* much to cling to. You're one of the Copper Islanders, a bunch of castaways that weren't even important enough to keep fighting for."

Natasha's eyes widened. Her lips drew back in a feral snarl. She bulled forward with over-handed chops that Fengel parried with ease. "So is that it, then?" she asked. "Is that what you've really thought, all these years? For King and Country? If they'd have given you what you wanted, you'd have never left."

Fengel backed into one of the thick cables that jutted out from the side of the dragon and rose to the ceiling somewhere above. Natasha tried to take advantage, and he hurriedly dodged around behind it. Her blade punctured the rubbery hose, letting loose a cloud of heated steam that obscured and stung them both. As she cursed, Fengel climbed farther upward. He ducked a cluster of smaller cables, then moved to where the ramp met the slope of the dragon's back, rising up toward the head and neck.

He paused to catch his breath and consider. Had he really meant what he'd said? The Kingdom of Perinault and its institutions were arrogant, cruel, and elitist. He'd always thought himself noble for rebelling. But was Natasha right?

His wife emerged from the steam. He shoved these thoughts aside. It was no matter. He'd meant his own words to injure, and they obviously had. It was enough.

They met again, blades flashing. Fengel glowered. Didn't she get tired? His own stamina was flagging; the wound in his side flared with every step he took, scalding. He ducked behind more cables, using them for cover and half-second breaks to catch his breath. Natasha didn't care. She cut away the ones she could, releasing sprays of strange liquids and yet more hissing steam.

A quick glance told him he was running out of room. The ramp ran up to the hunched shoulder of the dragon and abruptly stopped. A small forest of thin, tangled cables rose there from between the armored plates.

An idea came to him then; Natasha's intemperance would be her undoing. He gave more ground, falling back until he was just behind the bundle. Natasha narrowed her eyes and raised her scimitar. She swung, aiming to cut through to him, just as he'd suspected. Fengel ducked out of the way and grabbed the cables. When her scimitar sheared through, he twisted them, pointing the severed ends directly at her. Something like hot oil sprayed free. Natasha gave a cry of pain and scrabbled away, back up onto the shoulders of the dragon.

Fengel pursued, the tables now turned. Natasha cursed inventively, trying to ward him off and clear stinging oil from her eyes and face at the same time. She staggered over the line of blades rising from the spine of the dragon. Fengel pressed forward, saber raised.

The chamber shook. Fengel cursed and fought for balance. This one was the worst yet, setting the dragon they stood upon to shifting and quaking. Shouts of surprise and alarm echoed up to him from the battles down below. The whole chamber heaved, and Fengel grabbed at one of the spines, letting out a surprised hiss as it cut his palm.

He looked up to see Natasha kneeling as well, just opposite him. She glared, the skin around her eyes swollen and puffy, and as one they raised their blades to renew their conflict.

A shadow fell over them both. Natasha looked away, and Fengel exulted; she'd finally made her last mistake. Fengel prepared to strike, then paused. She wasn't even paying attention to him anymore. In fact, she seemed to be staring at something just off to their right. Fengel tried to focus, tried to resist glancing away. This was a trick, had to be.

A rumbling shiver vibrated the metal chassis beneath him. *Maybe a quick peek won't hurt.*

Fengel glanced to his right and froze. The dragon sat still no longer. Its armored metal neck was upraised, the massive head sweeping back and forth. The eyelid shutters had opened to reveal great red lenses, like burning embers caught behind glass.

It stood upright, scattering the fragile scaffold that enclosed it. The pieces rained down to clatter on the foundry floor.

Fengel caught Natasha's eyes. "Look what you've done!" he cried.

She stared at him in surprise. "Me? You did this!"

"I wasn't the one cutting all those cables!"

"No, you were the one who kept ducking behind them!"

The dragon cocked its head, then peered back around at the two people on its back. Fengel took one look at the metal maw and bolted upright. He rushed past Natasha and leapt for a ledge along the rocky wall past the spine of the dragon. There was a brief, sickening moment where only air lay beneath his feet, and then he landed. The ledge he found himself on was wide, leading into a shallow niche that led to a small double door of Voornish brass was set into the wall only a short distance within. Fengel glanced about for somewhere else to go.

Natasha landed on the ledge with a wild cry. She hadn't quite cleared the gap, however, and clung to it, half on, half off.

The dragon rose to its full height. It wheeled about, with a rumble of hidden gears and shifting mechanisms, to peer at the two pirates before it.

A tiny voice cut through the yells of the sailors on the floor. *"Hastra Hailo!"* it cried. "What have you done? This Dray Engine was never to be activated! How could you have even done so?"

Fengel peered down over the ledge, past the Dray Engine, to the foundry floor below. The Voornish automaton stood there, gesticulating wildly up at them.

The Dray Engine turned as well. It peered down at the automaton and snorted in something like irritation, unleashing a great cloud of steam. Then, as the automaton spun in worried circles, it lifted one heavy foot and stamped down, hard. The tinny, buzzing voice of the automaton fell silent.

Then the dragon raised its head to the unseen ceiling and roared. Fengel dropped his sword and fell to his knees as the cacophony shook the chamber. Dirt and rocks fell from the ledge. Something brushed past him, and he opened his eyes again, to see Natasha running for the double doors at his back.

The Dray Engine closed its jaws and peered down at them. It raised one arm and reached for Fengel. He rolled aside as the armored limb slammed down only inches from where he now lay, carving dirt and rock alike aside in a crushing grip that punched through the metal doors. It pulled back, revealing both daylight and open air through the opening beyond the ledge; the door had been burst wide open to reveal the exterior of the volcano.

Natasha had likewise ducked aside, barely missed. As the dragon reached out to claw at them again, she leapt through the opening into the space beyond. Fengel took one look at the massive claw descending and threw himself through it as well.

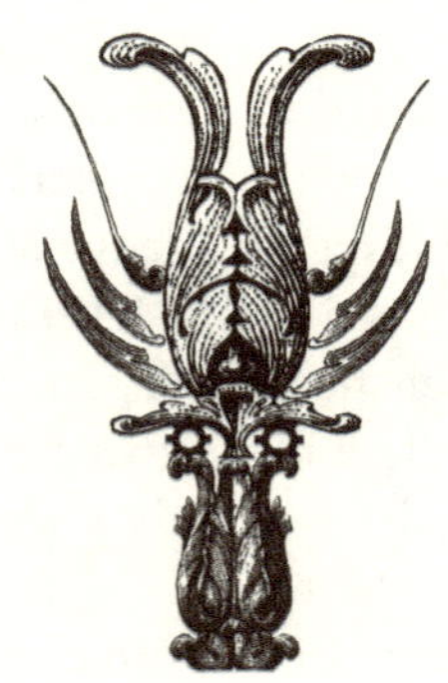

CHAPTER SEVENTEEN

The pirates slipped through Breachtown in a conga-line mockery of stealth. They stumbled from one shadow to the next, whispering exaggerated warnings to their friends and snickering as they went. More than a few were singing.

"This is ridiculous!" hissed Lina. She ran ahead of the committee as they led the crew toward the Breachtown Counting House in an attempt to face them down. "We don't need *nearly* this many people down here on the ground."

"Now, Lina," said Lucian as he strode past, "extra hands are prudent. Especially for an undertaking such as this." The committee-member held a wineskin in one hand, gesturing with it at the alley around them. "We could be ambushed at any moment."

This struck her as especially likely. The crew of the *Dawnhawk* were taking a discreet route back to the counting house, almost the same path she'd taken earlier with Rastalak. But where she had skulked through the colony, some thirty of her crewmates were now stumbling along beneath the rising moon without a care in the world. *It's only sheer luck that some damned patrol hasn't spotted us by now.*

Lucian took a swig and tossed his wineskin behind him. It sailed past Reaver Jane to bounce off of Sarah Lome. She stopped in surprise, causing Allen the Mechanist to run into her. The committee-member glowered back at him through the ink stains that covered her face like tribal tattoos.

"And that's another thing!" hissed Lina as they all walked past. "Everyone's drunk! Who thought that was a good idea? How could this have *ever* been a good idea?"

Reaver Jane shook a hand lazily back her way. "Yer worryin' too much, Stone." She paused to hiccup. "The lads just needed something to take the edge off. S'not like we don't deserve it. Besides, I know that tavern-keep. He'll keep his quiet." She frowned. "I think."

Lucian reached the alley mouth and paused to look around. "Ah! Here we are." He glanced back to Lina and the rest. "No worries, right?"

Lina ran up beside him. The alley they stood in sat directly across the street from the Breachtown Counting House. Its windows were darkened in accordance with the curfew, and the front of the building sat shaded but for two gas lanterns on each side of a pair of great wooden double doors. Two bored guards framed the entrance, leaning against the wall and chatting amiably.

"Right," continued Lucian. He clapped his hands together and looked to the rest of the crew. "Everyone ready?"

Both Sarah Lome and Reaver Jane drew cutlasses, eyeing each other. Rastalak merely appeared confused. Nate Wiley abruptly whirled, throwing up cheap ale all over the wall to his right and startling Allen, who fell back against Tricia, who shoved him in irritation. Behind her, Jonas Wiley loudly asked why they'd stopped. So it went down the line, with most of the pirates failing to respond at all.

"Wait," said Lina. "'Everyone ready' for what?"

Lucian gave her an annoyed look. "We're going to raid the counting house."

*We're going to raid....*Lina all but yelled at him. "What? Head on? That's your great plan? That's what you've been setting up all this time? Why you had me come down here and play the floozy all day, fending off all the lonely punters, *including* the hideous Gregory? Which I'm sure gave you a good laugh, yes, ha-ha, but *I* was the one stuck here all by myself and the directions you gave Rastalak weren't even clear and *why* would you even send him down, he's a *lizard-man,* for Her sake?"

She fell silent, panting. Lucian shared a surprised look with Sarah Lome and Reaver Jane. "Well...yes." He gestured across the street. "Look, the counting house is right there. In the end I wasn't coming up with anything especially clever like Captain Fengel always does. So I decided we'd just do what came naturally. We're pirates, after all."

Lina threw up her hands. "There's guards! They've got muskets! The second those go off, *more guards* are going to be called. And those will only bring others! Have you completely forgotten what we're about, here?"

"Watch your tone," said Lucian sharply. Then he glanced back at the alley of complaining crewmen and grimaced. "But perhaps you have a point." He looked to the other members of the committee. "Thoughts?"

Sarah Lome peered out across the street. "Well, there's that building next door. We could break in and use it to reach the rooftop."

The committee-member had a point, but Lina thought back to Omari and Mr. Gravelin and winced. "Let's...not," she said. "There's something seriously wrong in Gravelin's Apothecarium."

Lucian rolled his eyes. "All right, then. What else?"

"Well, the guards are the problem," said Sarah Lome. "We take care of them quietly, and we can walk right in."

"There's still the door," replied Lucian. "But go on."

"We need something to distract those two, pull them away for a moment."

"How about Miss Stone?" suggested Reaver Jane. "Didn't she used to be a harlot?"

Lina ground her teeth. *Oh for the love of....*

"Oh, yes," replied Lucian. "In fact, she's already got the clothes. I scrounged them up myself yesterday."

"Perfect," said Jane. "She really needs more of a bust to pull it off decently, though."

"That's...true," added Sarah Lome. "It kind of goes without saying."

"Well, we could get some old stockings—"

Runt gave an uncomfortable chirrup. Lina realized she was crushing his wormy length in a white-knuckled grip. She didn't care. Her mouth worked furiously.

Allen joined in before she could say anything. "I think she looks just gorgeous as she is," he said, voice dreamy. "Like one of the Servants from on high, come down to show us true grace and beauty."

Even Runt blinked at him.

"Enough!" shouted Lina. "Enough of this!" She pointed a finger at Lucian. "You! Enough of your slipshod leadership and obsession with prostitutes! I'm never dressing up like that again!" She wheeled on Allen. "And you! I've had enough of this stupid, puppy-dog infatuation of yours! The poetry, and the saccharine compliments. Knock them off, they make you sound like an utter tit!"

The young Mechanist shrank bank. But Lucian only raised an eyebrow at her. "Weren't you going on a moment ago about the need to do things quietly?"

Lina glared death at him. Then she spun about and stalked into the empty street toward the counting house. Her vision was hazy, and she faintly felt the low growl filling her throat. Dimly, she was aware she had Runt coiled up in a ball under one arm. The little scryn squirmed and chirped uncomfortably as it tried to get away from her.

Both the guards were chatting amiably as she approached. They were Royal Marines, with blue coats and black tricorn caps. One leaned on his musket; the other had his against the wall of the counting house. Neither noticed her until she was almost upon them.

"Ho, what's this?" said one. "Hello, miss, but there's a curfew on. You'll need to be heading home now."

The Bluecoatie was only a year or two older than she was herself. He was thin, with dark hair and a kind smile. Lina threw Runt in his face. The man let out a cry of surprise as the scryn fell on him, and Runt, for his part, seemed just as surprised. The two of them went down in a writhing, yelling ball.

His partner was a broad man, who cursed and went for the musket propped up at his side. Lina drew her dagger and leapt forward, sinking it deeply into his thigh. He collapsed with a yell and she fell with him, withdrawing the blade and straddling him. She beat him about the head with the pommel, and in short order the guard fell into unconsciousness.

Lucian ran up from across the street, somewhat breathless, with the other pirates trailing behind. "Well, now," he said. "I thought you said we needed a plan." He gestured, and Sarah Lome moved to the doors of the building.

Lina glowered at him. "Henry'll be here in a few minutes." She found that she felt a *little* better after beating the guardsman unconscious. But that didn't change the fact that there should have been a plan.

"That he will. All right, get these two tied up and gagged. Miss Stone, if you could...retrieve your pet?"

Lina looked over to where Runt was savaging at the soldier and whistled. Her pet flew back to her and the man curled up in a whimpering ball. Reaver Jane and two others moved to tie them up.

"Committee-Member?" said Sarah Lome. Lina glanced back to see her standing before the opened front doors to the counting house. "Doors 're open."

Lucian smiled. "That was quick, Sarah."

The huge gunnery mistress shrugged. "They weren't locked."

Lucian frowned, then shook his head. "Someone screwed up. Oh well, their loss. Our gain. Everyone inside!"

The pirates gave a ragged cheer and surged into the counting house. Lina held back, watching the still-empty street in trepidation. Why wasn't the door locked? Something felt wrong.

But no Bluecoat patrols appeared to help their fellows. No musket shots fired, and no alarm rang out. Lina shrugged, then helped Reaver Jane haul the now-bound guardsmen inside before shutting the doors.

The counting house interior was a workmanlike space that gave the occasional nod to opulence. It was a great open square, paneled in expensive oiled wood along the walls and floored with marble tiles. Two wide stairs at either side of the entryway led up to a balcony that circled the space, allowing a manager to keep a bird's-eye view on the accountants working below. Heavy desks were arranged for such workers, split by a path running from the entrance back to a low wooden rail before a wide, empty space. Beyond the space, at the rear of the room, was a wide cage formed by heavy iron bars set into the floor. Chests and boxes filled that cell—the promise of secured wealth.

The pirates swarmed through the place like ants at a picnic. "That's it, boyos,'" crowed Lucian. "Loot the place from stem to stern! Get it all out into the middle of the floor, by that railing. The *Dawnhawk* will be arriving shortly, and we want to make this quick! Sarah, get that cell door open. Jane, keep an eye on this rabble. Allen, get over there and help with the door. You, Wiley brothers, clear a space below the dome. Come on now, move it, move it!"

Most of the crew ignored him, heading straight for the cell at the back of the room. Reaver Jane corralled Jonas Wiley, Tricia, Charlie Green, and Jeremiah Frey with a combination of voice and fists, driving them back through the desks and less obvious hiding places in a flurry of violent looting.

Lina held off on joining in, fun though it appeared. *Something's still off here.* She moved to where Jane had left the two Bluecoats about a quarter of the way into the counting house. Hopefully these two could assuage her fears. Both were bound and gagged, and while the bigger one was just groaning his way back to consciousness, the one she'd thrown Runt at watched her with wary eyes.

She knelt down before the latter. The Bluecoat was fairly handsome, actually, which she hadn't noticed in her earlier rage. His eyes were bright blue and both his hair and beard were short and dark. His features were lean and angular, with pale Perinese skin only mostly marred by scryn bites and the red inflammations of Runt's spittle. The marks made him look rather vulnerable, and Lina felt the sudden urge to reach out and touch his face.

Instead, she held up her dagger. "You see this?" she asked.

The soldier nodded slowly.

"I'm going to lower that gag of yours, and then we're going to converse. Civilly. You shout or scream for help, or make me regret this in any way, and I'm going to bury this in your throat. Understand?"

"Muh-huh." The soldier nodded slowly.

"You're not going to scream?"

The soldier shook his head.

"All right, then."

Lina leaned forward and tugged the gag down around the soldier's chin. His beard was soft against her fingers. She kept the dagger up, just in case.

The soldier worked his jaw, then spat off to one side. He glanced around at Reaver Jane and the others as they upended desks nearby, tearing out drawers in their hunt for plunder. Looking back to Lina, he held her eyes a moment before speaking. "Thank you," he said in a soft Perinese voice. "That tasted terrible."

Lina nodded. Lucian called out, and those near the rear cell door gave a mighty grunt, which was followed by the squeal of iron bars being wrenched out of shape. "Yeah," she said. "That's about right. Reaver Jane is cheap. So she just reuses the same gags whenever we have to take prisoners. Never gets around to washing them, I don't think."

"Oh," said the soldier. He shut his mouth and looked paler than before.

Lina grinned. *He's adorable.* She caught herself and sobered. *Wait. I thought I was done with this kind of thing?*

The soldier abruptly met her eyes again. "My name's Michael," he said. "Michael Hockton."

"Stone," replied Lina. "Lina Stone, of the airship *Dawnhawk*." She frowned as the soldier visibly relaxed. "What? Did I...did I say something?"

Michael shook his head. "Yes. I mean, no. I just wasn't sure if I was going to get your name."

A storm of butterflies took flight in her belly. "You wanted to know who I am?"

Michael nodded. "Yeah. I've found that it's harder to kill someone when they've got your name. Just a little thing I've figured out over the years."

Her elation changed to dismay. "You think I'm going to kill you?"

The soldier raised an eyebrow at her. "Well, you *did* just threaten to cut my throat."

Lina glanced at the dagger in her hand. A wave of embarrassment washed over her, and she smiled suddenly at him. She sheathed her blade. "Right! Right. I did. Say that, I mean. Ha. Well, just don't shout out and you'll be fine. All right?" A distant part of her realized that she was getting worse with every passing second. But she couldn't help it. He was just *gorgeous*. Her heart felt like it was going to climb out of her throat.

"All right."

Silence stretched between the two of them. Off to one side, Tricia was loudly hacking open the stuck drawer of a desk with an axe, though Lina didn't know where she'd gotten it. The wood of the desk splintered and the drawer fell open to disgorge a spray of documents. Tricia swore loudly and moved down to the next desk, pausing to pick up a golden sovereign that someone else had missed.

"So...." said Michael after a moment.

"Yes?" said Lina, a little too quickly. "That's a neat trick, though. About the names. I'll have to remember it. Makes a kind of sense, I guess. You get taken prisoner here often?"

Michael sighed and looked away. "No. Not here, usually. But often enough that I've learned the ins and outs. Which is to say, too often. Last deployment into the Interior we got jumped by a bunch of lizard-pygmies, which was—"

Lina laughed, overloud. Michael only watched her. Jeremiah Frey ran past them toward the back of the room, one arm clutching a pry bar, the other holding a large bag of pennies that spilled in a jingling rain as he went.

"So...." continued Michael after the pirate had passed. "I can't help but notice that you're not sacking the place like the rest of your friends. Was there some reason you wanted to talk?"

Lina started, slapping herself mentally. She was acting like an idiot. *But he's just* so *very cute.* And his voice was soft, with just the right hint of Perinese accent. *It just makes him sound so cultured.*

"Ah. Aha. Yes. Questions. I had a question for you." She smiled winningly. "If, that is, you're willing to answer it."

"Well," said Michael. "I'm not in an ideal position to refuse."

Lina felt abruptly ashamed. "Oh, I'm sorry. I didn't think about that, about how you'd feel. Want me to cut your boots free?" She drew the dagger again and leaned down over him. "I can do that, if you'd like."

Michael peered down at her. "Uh, all right?"

She slashed the ropes around his boots. They were a Royal Marine's, black and shiny. Like the rest of his uniform, trim and proper. She'd never really paid too much attention to the Bluecoaties before. But now she couldn't help but think of how he looked in the blue coat. "There," she said, instead. "You're a captive, sure, but I'd hate to have you be uncomfortable."

Michael blinked. "You threw a scryn at me."

"What, Runt?"

The scryn in question had been coiled around her shoulders, peering quietly at the chaos around them and avoiding her attention. But at mention of his name, Runt eeled up to peer at them both. Upon seeing Michael, he spread his wings and hissed, spraying venomous spittle that conjured wisps of smoke where they hit the floor. The soldier scrabbled backward reflexively.

"See?" said Lina. "He likes you! You've got a rapport."

Michael just stared at her. Lucian called out again and the pirates gave groan of effort. Something made of metal snapped with a ringing noise, and Lina's crewmates all cheered.

Idiot. Focus! "Anyway," Lina continued. "We can chat about that some more later. What I really wanted to know, though, was why the doors to this place were left unlocked. I mean, that can't be normal, can it?"

Michael shook his head. "No. You're not the first to hit this place up. I mean, so much money flows through here. During the recent uprising, the locals tried to sack it. So now there's a guard. But we had to clean up earlier, and make sure things were ready for the...." He quieted, peering at the door. A shadow passed across his face as he looked back at her, as if he was waging two now-unpleasant options. "For the inspection."

Lina frowned. "Inspection?"

He looked awkward for a moment, then glanced at the front doors again. "Yes. The Governor and his people were supposed to pass through this evening."

Her heart sank down into her belly like a stone. Lina shot to her feet and cupped her hands to her mouth. "Bluecoats! We're about to be joined by the Royal Marines!"

The pirates froze in their looting, turning to face her as if they hadn't heard her the first time. Those rummaging through the cell at the back slowly came to a halt.

"What's that?" called Lucian Thorne. "What did you say, Stone?"

"I said that there are Bluecoats coming, you stupid b—"

The front doors of the counting house burst open. Royal Marines marched in, led by an imperious-looking man with a powdered wig, tricorn hat, and a rich officer's coat. Beside him walked a lean, raw-boned fellow in slightly less ostentatious clothing, though still of expensive fabric and a rich cut.

"Those men have abandoned their post, Acting Governor," said the man in the officer's coat. "I'll have them shot, then hanged."

"Really, Admiral," replied the other. "I'm sure that there is a very... good...reason...."

Both men and their detachment came to a halt as they spied the pirates and took in the ransacked counting house. They stared, with the crew of the *Dawnhawk* staring back in surprise. For a long moment there was a perfect silence.

Then everything exploded into chaos.

The Admiral drew the saber at his side and barked out a terse set of orders. Two of his Bluecoats grabbed the Acting Governor and hauled him away, while more marched out in front of their commander to form ranks, one kneeling before the other.

Reaver Jane appeared beside Lina. She grabbed up the other, still-unconscious guard to act as a shield, then retreated back to the railing and the other pirates at the back of the room. Ryan Gae lifted Michael Hockton and did the same, Lina falling back with him. The others who had been pillaging around them fled as well, forming a cluster around the rail. Fistfuls of coins joined uncut gems from the Yulan in pockets while knives, swords, and pistols all were drawn.

"Oh no," said Hockton. "Oh no."

"Don't fret," said Lina cheerfully. "There's a chance we can work all this out." She patted him on the arm and glanced up at the glass windows of the dome above them. *Any minute now....*

"No," said Hockton in a worried voice. "You don't understand. This is Admiral Wintermourn. He wasn't supposed to come here tonight! That was *me* he was talking about having executed. Me and Andrews here."

The pirates shuffled around until they had all clambered over to stand behind the railing. Lucian shoved through to the front of the group, with Sarah Lome and Reaver Jane beside him. He gestured for Ryan and Lina to bring Michael over next to the other prisoner. Then faced down the Bluecoats.

"Ahoy there," he said, hooking both thumbs into his belt. "Don't mind us; we'll be out of here in a jiffy. I do apologize about the mess though, and if you give us just a little bit longer, we will be certain to clean up on our way out."

Admiral Wintermourn raised an eyebrow at Lucian. He was older, stately and middle-aged, with a commanding presence that Fengel would envy. "I do not quite believe what I am seeing," he said slowly. "Are you honest-to-the-Goddess *pirates*? Here? In the middle of Breachtown?" He shook his head. "Will wonders never cease."

Lucian grinned. "We're wondrous folk, us pirates."

"Mayhap," harrumphed the Admiral. "But I'm afraid your little lark has come to an end. Surrender now, and, we'll give you a trial before we hang you."

The committee-member gestured at their captives. "I'm afraid we can't be doing that, sir. And I don't think you should try and force the issue. We've a pair of your men here, see?"

At his signal both Reaver Jane and Ryan Gae lifted blades to the necks of their captives. The man Andrews, wide awake now, stared at the cutlass before him, pop-eyed. Michael Hockton only gave a measured swallow.

"Ah," said Admiral Wintermourn. "I was just thinking about those two." He looked to the ranks of soldiers kneeling before him. "Sergeant Lanters!"

One of the Bluecoats stood to attention. "Sir!"

"Prepare the men to fire."

The sergeant nodded. He barked a command, and the marines unshouldered their muskets to line up shots at the pirates.

"Wait," said Lucian. "We've got your men here—"

"Indeed," said Admiral Wintermourn. "And they are guilty of leaving their post. The penalty for such an infraction is death, to be carried out on the spot." Wintermourn gave a careless flourish with the tip of his saber that nicked the ear of a soldier kneeling before him, who flinched away with a low cry.

Andrews jerked forward against the knife at his throat. "Wait!" he cried. "Sir, please, we were captured!"

Reaver Jane nodded furiously. "Yes! Captured! Right here!"

"Two birds, as they say," remarked Wintermourn. "Men? Fire."

The gun line obeyed and an instant stormcloud burst into life as plumes of gunsmoke erupted out toward the pirates. The staccato thunder of the volley followed an eyeblink after, echoing around the interior of the counting house.

A hail of musket balls fell upon the crewmen of the *Dawnhawk*. Andersen, the captive Bluecoat, jerked violently as one found his head, exiting out the back and splattering Reaver Jane in gore. She cried in shock and pain at the glancing blow, dropping the corpse to the ground and ducking for cover as she went. The railing before them splintered, showering Lucian Thorne and Sarah Lome with a rain of jagged slivers. Rastalak let out a hiss as a ball grazed his shoulder, twisting him away. Ryan Gae crumpled, grabbing for support at the railing and those beside him.

Lina fell to the ground, half tripping, half diving for cover. Bodies toppled beside her, some howling in pain, some already lifeless. Michael Hockton flailed where he'd landed beside her, tearing at the ropes around his wrists with his teeth. Her eyes met his while Runt panicked, hissing and spitting and, trying to take flight.

"We have to get out of here!" he cried. "Wintermourn's an evil bastard who solves every problem with an execution. He doesn't *care* about prisoners!"

"You think?" Lina shouted back, hating the note of hysteria that colored her voice.

"Look, I'm a dead man anyway. I just want to get away! Help me, and I can get us out of this."

"How?"

"There's a side door." Hockton jerked his head off to the right. "It's locked from this side, but there's a key in my right pocket."

Lina risked lifting her head up past the groaning bulk of a pirate. The ex-Bluecoat was correct; along the wall off to their right stood a heavy door, hidden from view earlier by a row of wooden filing cabinets.

No time like the present. She grabbed Runt with one hand and scrabbled atop Hockton. At the front of the room, she heard the sharp commands of the Perinese sergeant as he ordered the second rank to take aim, and for the first to affix bayonets.

Her fingers skittered over the unfamiliar cut of Hockton's coat. He twisted, trying to help her as he climbed to his feet. Finding his pocket, Lina pulled forth a half-eaten orange and a small brass skeleton key.

"It was a snack," said Hockton. "Now, come on!"

The Perinese captive sprinted for the side of the room, stepping over the groaning, startled pirates. Lina hurled the orange at the Bluecoats and ran after him, one hand to Runt, who hugged her shoulders and hissed protectively. Out the corner of her eye, she spied Lucian clambering up from where he lay as he called out a garbled question.

"Side door!" cried Lina as she ran. "There's a way out—"

The rest of her directions were lost in the second volley from the Bluecoats. Again, thunder boomed within the confines of the counting house, followed by the whip-hiss of hot lead sent hunting. Fortunately, most of her crewmates had already fallen, either injured or diving for cover. The musket fire flew past them to ricochet against the backdrop of the barred cell at the rear of the room.

Lina felt a musket ball pass within a hair's breadth of her face. She cursed and threw herself forward to slam against the wooden panel beside the side door. Michael Hockton was already there, ducking behind one of the filing cabinets and frantically rubbing the rope around his wrists against its edge.

She fumbled at the door, hunting for the lock. It was heavy, made of some dark wood reinforced by iron. The handle was black iron, and in the shadows she couldn't make out the keyhole.

More of her crewmates appeared beside her. Sarah Lome held Ryan Gae up in one arm, while he fired a pistol over Hockton's head back at the Bluecoats. Reaver Jane appeared, along with Allen the Mechanist, his face covered in blood. A glance told Lina that the men and women of the *Dawnhawk* were in full flight, waiting only for her to continue their escape.

From the front of the building came a roar as Admiral Wintermourn barked a command and the Bluecoats charged. They came with bayonet-tipped muskets raised like spears. The last few pirates scrabbled to get out of the way, using what feeble cover the shattered rail provided. Heartbreakingly, Lina spied Tricia, Jonas Wiley, and Lucian Thorne, all lying injured or too slow to get away from the coming assault.

Glass shattered overhead. It fell in a sharp-edged rain that shimmered in the feeble lantern light. The Bluecoat charge faltered as a heavy crate slammed into the floor before them, throwing soldiers every which way as it exploded to reveal a collection of burned rugs.

A shape moved in the sky beyond the counting house dome. It was the *Dawnhawk*, the smooth pumpkin-seed hull clear to Lina even half-occluded as it was by the roof. Thin figures that had to be Henry Smalls and the others who'd stayed aboard moved frantically alongside the port gunwales, dropping another bit of their plundered cargo as a makeshift grenado. It tumbled through the opening in the dome, falling and further driving the Perinese marines into disarray. Lucian and the others made good use of the interruption to clamber to their feet and run for the crowd surrounding Lina, though they left far too many friends unconscious or dead upon the counting house floor.

Come on, come on. Lina felt the head of the key skitter along the lock plate. She ignored the desperate cries, orders, and suggestions that the others shouted her way. Admiral Wintermourn's strident commands reached her, though, and as soon as the head of the key slid inside the door, she twisted it, along with the handle, yanking the portal open. The press of the pirates pushed her outward, and she left the Breachtown Counting House for the alley outside.

Cold night air washed over her, almost shocking after the gunpowder stink and violence of the building at her back. Lina now stood in an alleyway between the counting house and Gravelin's Apothecarium. Up above floated the prow of the *Dawnhawk*. To the right ended the alley at a high brick wall. At her left the alley mouth opened onto the main thoroughfare before the counting house. It was no longer empty and quiet, though. Bluecoats clutched their muskets and peered about, curious at the noise caused by their compatriots inside. Directly ahead of her, another servants' door led into the Apothecarium, a simple wooden entryway recessed slightly and set above a stoop.

Michael Hockton leapt across the alley and rammed the servants' door with his shoulder. He bounced away with a curse, then looked back at Lina. "Come on!" he cried.

She joined him, running full tilt at the closed doorway. Lina bent her shoulder and gritted her teeth; still, the impact jarred her, bouncing her back into the alleyway, slightly dazed.

A cry came from the mouth of the alley, followed by a gunshot that puffed up a small cloud of brick dust from the wall of the Apothecarium. The ball ricocheted back and forth, raining grit on the pirates. Lina clambered to her feet. Distantly, she realized that Runt still hissed and spat, casting lurid red light from his belly at the door before them. Michael Hockton tried to ram open the door again, and failed. Lina joined him as Perinese shouts echoed closer, both from the mouth of the alley and the interior of the counting house.

Then a boot appeared between them both, attached to the tree-trunk leg of Sarah Lome. The gunnery mistress kicked the servants' door open with one blow, sending it all but flying inward. Hockton went first, and Lina followed him through the now-open portal.

The room beyond was cozy and clean. It stank of medicinal herbs that hung drying from the rafters and fumes that rose from boiling alembics along the back wall. A curtained doorway on the left led to the front of the building, while a wide ladder ascended past the rafters to a room above. Mr. Gravelin, the undead apothecary, worked at the table with its alchemical devices. Off to the right, in a cozy chair beside a burning fireplace, sat Omari with a book in one hand.

The dark-skinned woman stared at them in surprised outrage. "Who are you people?" She cried. "What are you doing here?" She put the book down and stood. "How dare you just barge in and—"

Sarah Lome stalked over to confront the woman. "Which way to the roof?"

Omari folded her arms. "What? I'm not telling you a thing. Now, get out!"

The gunnery mistress gestured, and three of the pirates moved forward. Tricia and a heavily bleeding Jonas Wiley restrained Omari, who fought and cursed at them. Elly Minel grabbed Gravelin, yanking him from the table where he sat.

"Um," said Lina. "I don't think that's a good—"

A cry from behind interrupted her. Lina turned to see that most of the pirates had moved inside the back room of the Apothecarium now. Lucian, Reaver Jane, and three others covered the rear, trying to shut the door. Bluecoats appeared in the alley, charging for the opening with sabers and muskets raised.

They clashed in the doorway. Lucian parried a hacking blow, only to find the barrel of a pistol in his face. He ducked, and grizzled Jeremiah Frey took the ball meant for him in the neck. Reaver Jane snarled and fell on the shooter with her cutlass, cleaving through the Bluecoat's collarbone down into his chest. The man died screaming, and Jane fell with him, trying to recover her sword. Someone leapt over her—Lanters, the Bluecoat sergeant who'd led the charge back in the counting house. He bowled into Charlie Green, knocking the man back with his fist, then gave a thrust with his saber that spit the pirate like a kebab. Sarah Lome appeared above the two, and picked up the sergeant with one hand. She proceeded to batter the fellow with her fists like he was a side of beef, and his cries of pain joined the cacophony of the struggle.

"Oh no," said Omari. "No! You can't fight here! Not while I'm in here!"

She jerked against the pirates who restrained her. Gravelin fought his captor as well, groaning and growling in such an inhuman tone that Elly Minel let him go. The Revenant tottered right back to his alembics and sat down to putter with a mortar and pestle, completely ignoring the chaos at his back.

Omari spied Lina in the crowd. "You! You're the harlot from earlier. You've got to get these people out of here!"

Lina resented the accusation. She opened her mouth to reply, when Michael Hockton finally freed himself from the bindings around his wrists. He threw them away with a yell of relief, and then looked about for a weapon. At that point a mouse fell from above, landed on his shoulder, and fell into the breast pocket of his coat. Perturbed, he fished it out, revealing a tiny disemboweled mouse-corpse. It still moved, even without its guts and belly; the legs, tail and head twitched back and forth.

The Bluecoat deserter stared at the thing in horror, when an orange ball of fur and teeth fell from the rafters and landed squarely on Hockton's face. He screamed, and it yowled, and the both of them fell off to the side.

As the Bluecoats pressed inside, Lina's crewmates let go of Omari and drew their blades. One stared at the undead mouse where it crawled on the floor. The other threw himself into the fray. Lina tore her gaze from the scene to look at Omari. "Why?" she asked, throwing up her hands. "What are you *doing* here? Why are there so many dead things in here?"

Omari looked pained. Behind them, Sarah Lome yelled and a man let out a scream.

"It's not my fault! Except that it somewhat is." Omari shook her head. "Look, you can't fight here, you'll ruin everything I've built! The dead come back when I am around. I don't know why, but they just...come back. You've got to stop fighting!"

Oh no. Lina looked back at the struggle in the doorway. The fighting had calmed, for the moment, with both sides withdrawing to rally and rearm. All three members of the committee held the interior of the portal, supported by her wounded crewmates. Outside stood Admiral Wintermourn with the now-battered sergeant, and three ranks of Royal Marines. In the doorway between them rose a waist-high pile of the dying and the dead. The door itself had been half-carved off its hinges, and would never close again.

"Well done, you rogues," said Wintermourn, voice light and airy. "You've had a good run. Short, but good. I commend you on your ferocity. However inept it is proving, in the end."

Lucian waved his saber at the man. The tip of it dipped slightly, and he supported the arm that held it with his other hand. Blood streamed down his face from half a dozen wounds. "Just come on in here and take us," he said. "You can join your fellows in growing cold upon the stoop."

"That we will," replied Wintermourn. "The alarm is out. I'll have another eighty men here within moments." The admiral paused to tap his chin. "However, it occurs to me that I should at least make the attempt to accept your surrender. You'll still hang, of course. But one must observe tradition." He folded his hands behind his back as the sergeant barked out a command. The two back rows of soldiers removed the bayonets from their muskets and began to reload.

"It's like talkin' to that bloody mad captain of yours," hissed Reaver Jane.

Lucian shared a look with Sarah Lome. "Well," he replied. "More like what Fengel always wanted to be." He threw a glance at Lina, looking pointedly up the ladder toward the roof, before turning his attention back to the alley outside. "You can take your tradition and jam it up your backside," he crowed. "We're the men and women of the *Dawnhawk*, and surrender isn't any kind of thing we know."

Lina rolled her eyes, even as she moved for the ladder.

"Good," said the Admiral. "I do so hate dealing with prisoners, even in the interim on their way to the gallows. Sergeant? If you please."

The sergeant nodded. He bellowed another order and the Bluecoats took aim.

Then the corpses began to move. They lurched and groaned and shifted where they lay in the doorway, every last one of them suddenly crawling and trying to stand upright. The noises they made caused the hairs on the back of Lina's neck to stand up straight.

One of the Bluecoats panicked. His musket erupted with the sound of a thunderclap. The rest opened fire, and lead balls ripped through the mass of Revenants. Undead flesh stopped most of the shots, but a few flew past. Lina watched in horror as one took Elly Minel in the chest.

Elly tottered backward with a cry of pain. She landed against Gravelin's table, knocking a whole array of bubbling glassware onto the floor. It shattered with a sound like a bomb, and Gravelin himself rose up, groaning angrily. The Revenant fell on the dying Jeremiah Frey, who gurgled and fought weakly back. In the doorway, several of the undead pirates tottered for the Bluecoats outside, while the undead soldiers in the same pile came for the crewmen of the *Dawnhawk*.

The room descended into screaming anarchy. Runt launched himself from Lina's shoulder and circled the room up near the rafters, spitting and hissing in distress. Someone knocked over a flask of some oil, which fell before the hearth, igniting instantly and spreading flames as it went.

Lina shook herself and grabbed Omari by the shoulders. "The roof!" she cried. "The roof, damn it to the Realms Below! We just need to get to your roof!"

Omari focused on her. She nodded twice and gestured at the ladder. "There's a hatchway and another ladder in my room above!" A pistol went off by her head and she cursed. Lina glanced over to see Reaver Jane gun down an already-dead Bluecoat. Horribly, the corpse had merely been knocked down momentarily, even with a hole in its throat the size of a peach pit.

Lina screamed to the room at large. "The ladder! Up the ladder to the rooftop!" Then she followed her own advice, pulling Omari up behind. *To the Realms Below with this nightmare.* It was well past time to leave.

She ascended quickly through to another room. A soft-looking bed was set in one corner, piled high with pillows. Beside it stood a lady's vanity. The wall opposite looked out onto the street before the shop. Next to the window was another ladder leading up to a small closed hatch set against the slanted interior of the roof.

No sooner was she up than the others appeared as well. A panicked Reaver Jane and Lucian Thorne climbed up, only some of the blood covering them their own. Ryan Gae climbed up, grey-faced and clutching his chest, half-supported by Sarah Lome. More of her friends and crewmates ascended in an attempt to escape the chaos below.

They didn't even need prompting. Everyone rushed for the other ladder, Reaver Jane winning out and nimbly making her way up to and through the hatch onto the roof. Allen the Mechanist came next, wild-eyed and clutching a bloodied knife like it was a lifeline. Then the others followed, fighting to escape. Lina held Omari back from the press by reflex. There wasn't any way either of them were getting through right now.

Others climbed up from below now. Lina saw a pair of hands that belonged to Elly Minel. Jeremiah Frey's face appeared, half stove-in and his throat slit. Flickering reflections gave a hellish cast to the visage. The Revenants were climbing after them.

It was Omari who acted first. She pushed past Lina, ran to the vanity, and retrieved a chair. Thrusting it down the opening, she knocked free the first undead corpse, which fell back down into the burning room below. Lina joined her with a broom she'd found in the corner, gorge rising in her throat.

They defended the top of the ladder until the rest of the still-living crew had climbed onto the rooftop. Then Lina threw her broom down and went to make her own escape. Omari joined her, angry tears running down her cheeks.

Lina ascended through the hatch into cool night air. The roof of the Apothecarium was flat, with a decorative crenellation that ran around the edge. Lantern lights illuminated the street, along with soldiers whistling and shouting commands. Above, the *Dawnhawk* floated, its edges lit by the light of the moon. Ropes and rope ladders dangled from every side, and the surviving crew were already making their escape back aboard the airship.

She made to urge Omari onward, and spied four blue-coated figures rising up into the room below. Lina recognized the sergeant and Admiral Wintermourn among them. The Admiral shouted at the others, who frantically tried to fight off the Revenants climbing up after them. Just as Omari cleared the hatch onto the roof, he glanced up, looking directly at Lina.

"Up there!" he cried, his arrogant features twisted into an ugly snarl. "Get me their heads if you want to keep yours! Neither flames nor these abominations are going to stop me from bringing righteous—"

A fat orange tabby cat flew out from the hatch to land on the admiral's face. It hissed and spat and fought, and Wintermourn let out a yell as it clawed at him. The sergeant turned back just as Michael Hockton rose up from the ladder from the room below, swinging Runt about him like a flail.

The scryn snarled angrily, flapping its manta-ray wings and spitting furiously. Caustic, poisonous spittle caught one soldier full in the face, and then Runt smacked into the sergeant, sending them both crumpling to the floor.

Hockton clambered past, running straight for the other ladder and the rooftop hatch. He grabbed up Runt and threw the dazed scryn around his neck like scarf. As he passed the admiral he snatched Cubbins the tabby cat by the scruff of its neck. Then, one-handed, he clambered up to the rooftop hatch, quicker than Lina would have thought possible.

"Must be going," said Hockton. The renegade Bluecoat's face was covered in scryn-bite welts and cat-claw scratches. "I really hope you've got a good escape planned up here, because—"

He fell silent as he looked past Lina's shoulder to the *Dawnhawk* above. Out of the corner of her eye, Lina spied Omari already climbing the ladder.

"Yeah," she said, butterflies in her stomach. "The raid was a damned shambles, but we've a pretty good escape plan." She glanced at Runt, worried. The scryn hung limply, chirping to himself, as if addled. "What did you do to my pet?"

Michael Hockton blinked. "What? Him? Nothing. We've a rapport, like you said."

The hatchway frame exploded between them, sending splinters and grit flying up. Admiral Wintermourn was at the foot of the ladder, cursing and calling for a fresh pistol from his sergeant.

"Time to go," said Lina.

Hockton leapt nimbly out onto the roof, then kicked the hatch shut. He adjusted his grip on the snarling, squirming Cubbins, then drew a dagger with his free hand. This he jammed through the outside handle of the latch, preventing it from opening.

The *Dawnhawk* was just starting to drift away. Lina scrabbled up the nearest rope ladder, Hockton jumping up just below. The propellers on the airship whirred to life, and steam-cloud contrails belched out between them.

Lina listened to the groans of pain from those still climbing above her toward the gunwales. The sounds only grew louder as the adrenaline in her body faded, bringing to mind all that had been lost on this foolish, wasteful exercise. She thought of all the friends she'd lost tonight, merely the edge of a horrible abyss that fell farther than the drop below her feet.

A low whistle shook her from her introspection. Michael Hockton dangled just beneath her, watching the colony of Breachtown drift past, the hordes of Royal Marines in its streets like an angry colony of ants. He grinned up at her, absent-mindedly fighting with the now-terrified tabby cat in his free hand.

"It's quite the view that you get from up here," he said.

Lina thought of the failed raid, her dead crewmates, and the long, ugly day that had preceded it all. *I guess it's not a complete loss, though.*

"That we do," she replied. "Want to come up and see it proper?"

Michael Hockton grinned. Then he let out a yell as both Runt and Cubbins bit him sharply at the same time.

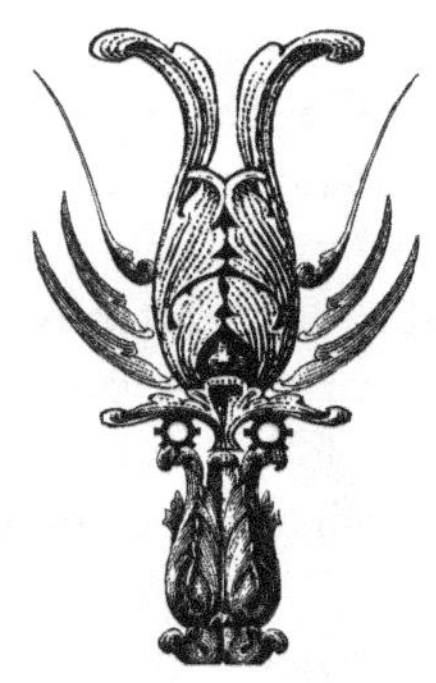

CHAPTER EIGHTEEN

Natasha tumbled through the moonlit night.

The opening back into the volcano behind her collapsed in a shower of earth and rock. That scree slid beneath her down the slope of the mountain, tumbling and pouring and collecting strength as it went. Vines and bushes disappeared beneath the detritus until the crumbled dirt stilled and found new stasis high above the dark jungles below.

Then Natasha landed upon it. Hard. She sank in the earth and slid, scrabbling desperately for purchase to slow herself. Her fingers brushed a vine and she wrapped both hands around it, digging in with knees and elbows until the scree ceased sliding. Faintly, she felt the bellows-vibrations of the Dray Engine, buried in the ancient Voornish ruins beneath the mountain.

Fengel landed beside her with a curse. He bounced, slid, and grabbed at the slope beneath them both. His grasping hands dug through the dirt and found her vine, stopping him only a few feet below her.

I'll be damned if I'm sharing this. Natasha gave a growl and kicked down at him. "This is mine," she hissed. "Get. Off!"

"Ow! I go where I like, wench. Ow! To the Realms Below with both you and your goliath feet!" He grabbed for a rock and then threw it, missing her forehead by only an inch.

Natasha snarled. She lifted her leg for a kick that would take off Fengel's head. Then the vine snapped, sending the two of them tumbling down again.

The world churned as she rolled end over end. Fine volcanic grit fell through her fingers as she desperately tried to stop. Rocks, roots, and low brush battered her head and stuck in her hair. Then the boots she'd taken from the *Salmalin* were skidding, sliding over hard rock, before flying out into nothingness. Natasha almost followed her feet as a cracked, irregular stone passed beneath her. She turned and grabbed at it with manic desperation as her legs slid over a ledge toward unseen oblivion.

Natasha realized that she was clutching one of the many strange monoliths dotting the flanks of the volcano that dominated the island. Triangular and oddly metallic, it lay half-buried in the volcano's silt, yet toppled over to form a small ledge that dropped ten feet to the rest of the slope below.

A loud grunt sounded above her, and a pair of boots landed painfully on her forearms. Fengel scrabbled to keep from falling any farther, causing the whole monolith to shift. He froze, just as she did, until the rain of earth that carried them along gradually stilled.

Natasha didn't dare move. She didn't even dare turn her head, and could only stare at the shredded top of Fengel's boot. *All right. If I don't move, I should be fine. Just…don't move. There's got to be a way out of this. Don't move. Things can't really get any worse.*

Fengel shifted, and Natasha found herself staring at his crotch.

Natasha blinked. *Oh, you Servants and Daemons of the Realms Above. You mock me, but I'll show you. I'll—*

Her husband's face appeared just within her line of vision. "Well," he said, as he slowly and carefully wedged the cracked, hateful monocle back into place from where it had dangled on its chain. "That was quite a ride." Then he glared down at her. "But I don't think you're quite finished with yours yet." He gripped both sides of the strange rock and raised his boot. "Please remember not to write." Then he kicked out.

Natasha grunted in pain at the blow. As Fengel raised his boot to strike again, she pushed down with both arms against the monolith, lifting herself up just enough to grab his leg around the ankle before slamming back down. The whole thing shifted, and more dirt and rock slid down around them. Fengel cried out in fear and pain as she dangled, his ankle caught on a sharp edge of the stone with all her weight atop it.

"How clever!" she yelled, throwing her weight against his leg. "Remember not to write? You're *such* a funny man!"

"*Agh!* Let go, you madwoman!" Fengel bent at the waist, tried to grab at her fingers. The monolith shifted again.

"Madwoman? That's so *original*. Do you see how I'm laughing?" She shouted the last and jerked at the monolith, tugging, doing everything she could to hurt him, to pull him down.

The weird stone broke free of its moorings. Natasha fell ten feet to land hard on her side, and started sliding down the slope again. She'd gone only inches when the monolith landed behind her with Fengel atop it, crying out in pain and shock at the impact. It tumbled past both of them, flinging him aside as it generated another cascade of dirt, rocks, and grit that carried them both away.

Natasha tumbled freely, unable to restrain her fall. Rocks battered her, and the gravel of the mountain tore at her clothing. Fengel was just behind her, easy to find, due to the steady stream of creative invective that he spewed. She kept her own mouth shut; fewer things flew into it that way.

The triangular monolith disappeared up ahead. Natasha prepared herself for another sheer drop. It came suddenly, and she found herself tumbling from a series of stair-step terraces down a stony cliff. Each was thick with greenery that softened her fall but did little to stop it. The monolith was carving a path before them, channeling both her and Fengel down through the trail of destruction and preventing any kind of stop.

Then she was in the air, falling. The final lip of the terraces gave way to a sheer cliff. Natasha had a half-second's glimpse of the jungle canopy below, and a deep, wide pool of water reflecting the moonlight. Then she slammed hard into a narrow rock ledge with an impact that punched the air from her chest and left her seeing stars.

Natasha dimly felt something land beside her. She ignored it, too stunned to do anything but lie there. Gradually, the stars faded and her lungs drew raspy breath. Sense returned, along with the pain of a thousand scrapes and cuts, and a whole-body ache that ran from the burned, battered skin on her head all the way down to her toes.

Dirt rained lightly down on her face. So did the occasional pebble. Natasha tried to raise her arm to block the debris, and only succeeded in waving at it. She turned her head, trying to take in her surroundings.

The ledge was barely wide enough for a body, but three times that in length. Thick, flowery bushes dotted its surface, clinging to the only flat space around for a hundred feet. It jutted out from a wide cliff that dropped maybe another hundred and fifty feet to the jungle canopy of the island, near a wide pool of water that hugged the base of the volcano. Above, the next terrace was about twenty feet up smooth volcanic rock. Past that she could just spy the plume of the volcano itself, belching thick black smoke into the moonlit sky. What she'd thought to be a ringing in her ears was actually a waterfall, tumbling out of a crevice in the cliff face a dozen yards away to spill into the pool below.

Someone groaned nearby.

Natasha glanced up to see Fengel lying a body's length away on the far side of the ledge. He lay as she did, head toward hers, feet out over the opposite lip of the ledge. Her husband groaned and twitched, but did not otherwise move.

Now's my chance! Her father would have agreed. She made to draw the sword at her side, and realized she'd lost it. She went for the dagger she kept at her hip and realized that was missing too. *Oh, for the love of….*But wait. There was the pistol in her boot and the dagger down her bodice, all taken from the *Salmalin.* Either one would do.

She grinned and went for the dagger. Natasha rolled up onto one arm and raised the other to fish out the weapon. The brush she lay upon shifted alarmingly. The branches beneath the foliage gave way with a loud snap, and the rock of the ledge beneath her ankles started to crumble. Natasha froze.

Fengel started at the noise. His eyes popped open behind his cracked and broken monocle, which had ironically fallen into place when he landed, and he looked directly at her. Fengel reacted the same way she had, attempting to roll over and bring himself to a fighting position. But the bush under him sagged, and more rock fell away from the ledge beneath his legs. He glanced around, clearly alarmed, then swallowed and stilled.

Great. Just great. He's right here, and I can't do a damned thing about it without dooming myself in the process. Natasha pondered. Would it be worth it, just so long as the snooty bastard went first?

Something like the sound of breaking stone and twisting steel erupted over the island. Natasha froze, then grabbed for dear life at the bush beneath her. *Of course. This would be the perfect time for an earthquake.* She eyed the distance to the pistol in her boot. She would *not* die without taking him with her.

But the ledge did not shake, nor the cliff to which it was attached. The sound continued, a consistent wrenching noise. Movement in the night caught her eye, around the lip of the cliff off to the south and another part of the island. It was a massive shape that flew haphazardly through the air; a huge boulder, jagged and covered in earth. Another object came after it: a massive, twisted door of Voornish brass. Both of them crashed down through into the jungle. The ruckus stilled, and for a moment Natasha thought the odd sight over.

Then it came; a mechanical roar that seemed to shake the very sky. It sounded like angry thunder trapped in a bottle, holding only the promise of ruin for the world.

The Voornish Dray Engine appeared, head just cresting over a distant cliff, maybe half a mile away. It raised its great maw toward the sky and roared again, then bent low and disappeared out of sight. The rustle and snap of trees breaking like matchsticks echoed over the island.

"Well, that's just great," Natasha croaked. Trapped on a crumbling ledge with her asshole husband, no crew to help her, and a horrible Voornish war-machine lose on the island. She closed her eyes and sighed. At least *now* things couldn't possibly get any worse.

A fluttering, flapping noise reached her. Natasha opened her eyes to see a hideous, brightly colored bird with a short, round body and a great butter-yellow beak land on a sapling sprouting from the cliff face a dozen feet above her. It twisted its head to peer down with one malevolent eye. Then it opened its beak and screamed. The sound seemed to pierce her eardrums and go straight to her brain.

Natasha started to curse the world with the vilest insults she could think of.

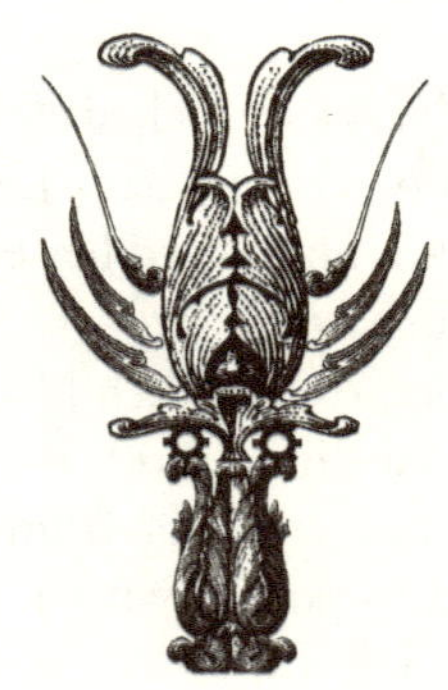

CHAPTER NINETEEN

FENGEL WATCHED THE SUN COME UP.

There wasn't much else to do, really. The mass of springy bushes supporting him were only lightly rooted to the narrow ledge he lay upon. All of the things that he really wanted to do, such as escape, or violently murder his harpy wife where she lay a few feet away, would pitch him into a plummet that he could not survive. The only things left to do were converse with said harpy wife, or watch the sun come up. Fengel chose the latter.

It rose out over the ocean to the east, a burning orb of molten gold that seemed to set the few sparse clouds above it on fire. The waters of the Atalian Sea lightened as it blazed, from dark purple to shifting shades of cerulean blue while gulls pinwheeled above the waves. The seabirds were illuminated and brilliant, falling like winged stars to hook the fish that danced below them.

Yet Isle Almhazlik resisted the dawn. From Fengel's vantage, the golden sand of the beaches remained hidden, and the thick green canopy refused to reveal its secrets. The curtain of the cliff at his side occluded any further view of the island, save for the peak of the volcano angrily belching ash high above.

Almhazlik was hardly peaceful, however. Fengel's evening had been interrupted not only by the constant sleep-shredding sensation of sliding off the ledge, but by the riotous noise that the place never seemed to do without. Parrots squawked and gibbons hooted in the jungles below. The volcano at the center of the isle rumbled ominously. The Voornish Dray Engine tore its way through the jungle, cracking trees and periodically pausing to roar a mechanical call that reverberated across the isle. A waterfall nearby thundered into a pool down below, while on a branch above his head, a ridiculous, raucous parrot squawked that Fengel could have sworn he'd seen before. Worst of all was Natasha, who kept up a steady stream of colorful invective, cursing the Goddess, her father, the island, her crew, the parrot, Fengel himself, and really, just anyone she'd ever met. Her voice was quite hoarse now, but she showed no signs of slowing down or granting him anything like peace.

I'd ask what I've done to deserve this, but it's a question I'm beginning to grow weary of. Fengel frowned up at the rising sun, then blinked in surprise as it started to dance.

No, not dance. Sway. And it was he that was rocking, shifting back and forth upon his bed of precariously placed foliage. The whole ledge, the jungle below and the cliff itself, were shaking.

Great. Fengel grabbed with both hands at the bushes near the base of the ledge. There really wasn't anything else to do. The earthquake continued to rise in ferocity. It added a rumbling roar that rose to drown out all the other sounds of the jungle.

He closed his eyes against the dirt and rocks that rained down on him from above, hoping that none would be too large. An image of the odd monolith that he'd half-ridden down the slope came to mind, and Fengel shuddered.

A crack sounded on the ledge, and suddenly Fengel felt his boots dangling even farther. The ledge was giving away beneath his feet. He cursed and scrabbled through the brush, but the tiny branches were springy and he made little to no progress at all.

Then the earthquake stopped just as abruptly as it had started. An explosion sounded somewhere nearby with such force that for a second Fengel thought it a cannon shot. The peak of the volcano erupted, belching black smoke and hot ash into the sky. He watched as molten lava spewed from it, falling like liquid meteors to land in the ocean and around the isle. A stream of the stuff oozed out over the lip of the volcano top, and he watched as it trailed away toward the far side of the island from where he lay.

After a few minutes, the eruption spent itself, and the volcano fell back into restless quiescence, with the whole of the island laying still. Even the ocean surf seemed unnaturally loud in the quiet.

"This is all your fault," hissed a raspy voice.

Fengel opened his eyes and blinked away the grit. He peered ahead from where he crouched almost fetally, to see Natasha glaring at him through puffy eyes and a mask of dirt and blood. "I beg your pardon?" he said acidly.

"If you hadn't run up the damned dragon, it wouldn't have woken up. We wouldn't have fallen out that hole, down half the mountain, and gotten stuck *here*."

Fengel stared at her, outraged. "We were fleeing! You were killing my men left and right. Good, honest souls who didn't deserve that butchery!"

"Honest souls? They're Perinese soldiers! They were going to hang the both of us only days ago!"

"Regardless, you might have noticed we were doing poorly. So we fled." Fengel looked pointedly away. "It is not *my* fault that an ancient alien race left their wind-up doom machines lying around for anyone to trod upon."

She glared at him. "You *could* have surrendered."

Fengel returned her glare. "Like that's gotten us anywhere before," he snarled. "The last time someone tried that with you, it almost killed them all."

Natasha started. She looked away, momentarily uncomfortable. "That wasn't my fault," she said quietly. Then she rallied. "And besides, you and your good, honest soldiers were already halfway across the isle when we found you. Coming straight for the *Salmalin*." Natasha pointed an accusing finger. "You were already looking for a fight! And I damn well wasn't going to back down."

"We were not," replied Fengel. He tried to push aside the memory of the crew of the *Goliath*, their swords raised and shouting after he'd worked them into blood lust. "I'll have you know that we were only interested in the *Salmalin* itself."

"Horseshit," said Natasha. "You already had the *Goliath*. A little work and you'd have had it off that sand bar. The *Salmalin* is a shattered wreck."

What? Fengel decided to cover his confusion with aggression. "So that's what you were doing in the jungle! You were coming over to steal *our* ship!" He pointed a finger at her, shifted dangerously, and grabbed the brush again to steady himself. "I'd expect nothing less, you horrible rogue."

Natasha stared at him. "You just admitted to wanting to steal the *Salmalin*. You hypocrite!"

"How dare you, you ravenous, man-eating harpy!"

"Bastard!"

"Horse-faced trollop!"

"Pompous arse!"

"Fool!"

"Incompetent!"

Fengel drew back. "Incompetent?" he said in mock surprise. "I'm the incompetent one? But you've done so well for yourself, *Mrs. Blackheart*. You suckered a crew of desperate sailors into following after you somehow, only to lose them inside of a volcano when you were on the verge of winning. I'm sure that your father would be very—"

A thunderbolt explosion interrupted his words. Rock chips rained down onto his head from where the cliff beside it had exploded. The ridiculous parrot flew away, squawking indignation. He peeked past his upraised arms to see Natasha holding a small pistol with one hand, its barrel smoking.

Fengel threw up his hands. "Damn you, woman! This! This is the problem with you!" He rocked precariously and grabbed for the bushes beneath him. "You're barmy, mad and insane! You're a hair's breadth away from killing a man at the slightest provocation! You're unpredictable, and you think that's the best way to deal with the world! You are *horrible*."

The emptied pistol flew past his head and impacted with the cliff wall. "You just keep talking, you—"

"I'll say what I like!" shouted Fengel. "You had your chance to take my head off, and you missed! By the Goddess, you are a terrible shot. But you daren't do anything more for fear that you'll pitch over this ledge to your doom, just like me. So you're going to sit there and listen to me tell you that you are your own worst problem! And you'll listen, because you know I'm right!"

"You're a terrible pirate," growled Natasha. "You should have been a priest."

"Shut up!" roared Fengel in response. "Shut! Up! I've my own Goddess-damned flaws, but you are just the worst! Nobody *likes* you Natasha. And they're never going to! You treat people like tools, toys and treats, then throw a damned tantrum when they want to be something more. And for some mad reason, you just expect them to fall back in line because of it!"

"I'm a pirate!" she yelled back at him. "That's how you maintain control! To the Realms Below with 'like.' Fear and violence are how you get things done." Natasha pointed a shaking finger at him. "Not that I'd ever expect your great soft heart to understand that."

Fengel lowered his voice abruptly. "I understand far better than you do. The carrot and the stick, they're both just two ways toward respect. Everyone but you seems to have that figured out. When that snake Mordecai was around, you could sit at a distance, and have him keep things in line. That was the closest you ever got, and that was because none of your old crew really knew you the way I do." He narrowed his eyes. "Look how quickly the *Dawnhawk* crew got rid of us. Oh, yes, it was my fault too. I'll own up to that. But only because I hid! Because I couldn't stand dealing with you on a day-by-Goddess-damned-day basis. *No one* can stand to be around you, and we've seen the results of that firsthand. How long? Eh? How long before that Salomcani rabble would have ditched you? You grabbed ahold of them, certainly. But how long would it have lasted if my Perinese sailors weren't around to hate?" Fengel shook his head. "I don't know why I agreed to it, that day over Yrinium. Damn it, I still…" He faltered as he realized what he was about to say, but the words were already slipping over his tongue. "I still *love* you, you witch. For some unfathomable reason. But I'm done now. I'm done! Partnering with you was a mistake!"

Silence followed his words. The wind whistled past the ledge the two of them lay upon. The waterfall splashed down into its pool below. She glared hatefully at him with beautiful golden eyes.

Then a tear welled up and started down her cheek.

"You *love* me?" she growled, voice taut with anger and emotion. "You say that now, you ass, of all possible times? After all that's happened? Like it's some secret word that you can use to get your way, like it's going to change a damned thing between us?" She looked away, then glared back at him, pointing an accusing finger with a hand half-wrapped around a thorny vine. "To the Realms Below with that! I remember, you bastard. You already *gave* that to me. It's mine! You swore to love me years ago. You swore to love me through everything, even if I tried to kill you!"

Fengel looked away to cover his surprise. The rock wall of the cliff was dark, even in the morning sun. "I told you I have my flaws," he said after a moment, voice calmer than he felt by far. "I'm weaker than you think. I can only take so much." He glanced out at the ocean. *Though I always keep coming back to you, for some damnable reason.*

The tears were streaming down Natasha's cheeks now. They cut channels through the volcanic dirt caked onto her skin, dripping to feed the plants on ledge below them. "Well, to the Realms Below with your flaws," she said, voice strained. "*I* still love *you*. And I hate that. I hate how soft it makes me. How I never get around to finishing the job, when I do get the upper hand. I can never bring myself to kill you. I haven't been even able to do it now! Instead, I do foolish things, like try to have you taken alive, or intentionally miss my shots, or leave you dangling off the prow of a derelict airship. Because I need to be hard. I need to be strong. You don't know what it's like. Shut up! You don't know what it's like to be a *woman*. How Goddess-damned hard that makes it. I've got to prove myself every second of every damned day. And if not to my crew, or the scurvy-ridden lice that make up Haventown, then I've got to prove it to my father."

Natasha closed her eyes and looked away. "Who is the *worst*. Because he's supportive. He's taught me my whole damned life. I can't help but think on what he'd say or what he'd do. He's proud of me. Because, in the end, he wants me to be just like he is; hard and strong and cruel. And damn him, I'm a little more like him every day, because that's what it takes to be truly great. Every little lesson he taught I usually follow, because it *works*. I'm never going to be my own person, because the only choices before me are spineless tramp or the nastiest, ugliest cutthroat I can be."

Natasha shifted to keep from sliding over her end of the ledge. "I don't know how you do it," she admitted. "I hate how *easy* you have it, compared to me. I hate how effortlessly you made yourself successful. And I haven't the faintest idea why the way you do things works. I try and I try, and in the end it just isn't enough. The bastards always find a way to toss me off the ship." She shifted again.

Fengel stared at his wife. The waterfall and the seagulls in the ocean breeze were the only sounds for long minutes. He opened his mouth, closed it, opened it again. He thought long and hard. Then Fengel shook his head. *I just know I'm going to regret this.* He held out one hand toward Natasha. "Take my hand," he said.

She glared at him. "What?"

"We're both going to slide off if we don't share the ledge a bit more, and the fall will kill us. We also can't do anything to each other, assuming you haven't another pistol, or we'll slide off the ledge and the fall will kill us. Now, give me your hand."

Natasha eyed him warily. "I've still got a knife."

"I know," replied Fengel. "It's in the sheath down your bodice. It's where you always put it. Remember the one I gave you that one year, as a birthday gift?"

His wife cracked a small, grudging smile. She grabbed his hand with her own, violently. Fengel pulled, and so did she, and the two of them slid to the center of the ledge, face to face.

Fengel shifted until his back was up against the cliff face. "I'm going to tell you something I've never told a living soul," he began. "And I'm only going to say it once, so shut up and listen. You know where I came up, right?"

"Darrenway, in the Kingdom. You're the son of a back-alley horse doctor."

He shook his head. "Not really. Da was called an 'animal physician' by the aristocrats, but he was a quack. No, his real line of work was prad-rolling."

Natasha blinked. "What?"

Fengel shrugged. "It's street slang for 'horse thief.' You see, the nobility in Perinault can get very, very bored. So they like to steal things from each other. Butlers and other servants are popular. But horses are good too. Except that you can't talk a horse into leaving for a few more sovereigns a month, so they hire specialists like Da to steal them. S'not good for the little folk, when they get caught. But the aristos don't care."

"Fascinating," said Natasha, voice dripping with sarcasm.

"Anyway, I came up in Darrenway, on Coal Street. Dad had a little back-alley shop where he peddled his tonics, and hid from the law. I was a skinny thing back then. Weak, too. Which meant, of course, that all the little shits in the neighborhood made my life horrible. There was one particular horse-apple that took a special pleasure in tormenting me. He was the leader of the local gang, who went by the name of Jacob Lanters. Would always corner me, no matter how hard I ran, and beat seven kinds of blue out of my hide. The only thing he loved torturing more than me were all the stray cats infesting Darrenway back then.

"Now, I wasn't going to take that lying down. Or, bleeding in an alley, rather. But I knew that I couldn't match Lanters with my fists. So I cheated. The local precinct of the Guard had a training field. One wall had a loose brick, so I was able to pry it out and watch them. And watch them I did. I learned to parry and riposte, and how to cut. Just the basics, mind, but it was enough. I managed to nick an old arming sword, so that when Lanters and I next met I'd have the advantage.

"I'll say this for the bastard, though. He saw me with a sword and kept right on coming, sneering all the while. In fact, he didn't stop until he was almost atop me, and that alley cat dropped onto his head from a window ledge above." Fengel shook his head. "I'll never know if it recognized Lanters, or it was just a particularly mean old tom. Either way, it fought like a daemon. My tormentor screamed and flailed, trying to get the thing off. He tripped and slammed his head against a rubbish bin, then toppled like a felled tree. The cat ran away, and there I stood. When the rest of the Coal Street Boys found us, they thought I'd flattened Jacob Lanters all on my own. That was my first crew, really. And they were mine until the day I joined the navy."

Fengel held his wife's gaze. "I learned something important that day. If you can't make it on your own, then pretend. Never let them see you stumble. And in the end? There isn't any difference between that and being the hardest, meanest bastard on the Atalian Sea."

He fell silent and looked away. The breeze from off the ocean was warm, and salt-tinged. It carried with it a faint whiff of the volcanic ash falling down like black snow.

"It's more than that," continued Natasha, after a moment. "Fraud or not, you inspire something real in Henry and the others."

Fengel turned to look at her again. The set of her jaw was soft, her lips missing their customary sneer. Her eyes were golden, and very large. "Faking is good enough for them." He chuckled, and it hurt. "It's a funny thing. People want someone who can lead them, show them the way. But I've found those that follow you are the ones you deserve, all the same."

He watched Natasha frown at the thought and look away. *Food for thought, my wife. After all, Mordecai was no accident. Henry Smalls, Sarah Lome, Lucian, and even young Miss Stone are the crew that I deserve, and in turn, they deserve me.* Fengel started. *Goddess. How could I let this mess with Natasha get between me and them?*

Ash rained down in periodic silence, punctuated only by the mechanical roaring of the Dray Engine on some distant part of the isle. Fengel rolled the epiphany around in his head, only noting Natasha's continued silence after the sun had climbed a hand's width above the horizon.

"Why do we fight?" asked Natasha.

Fengel looked to her. His wife was observing the seabirds as they flew out over the ocean. He watched one of the filthy birds dart down to snap up a fish from the cresting waves. It made for the beach, but then another attacked it. The two squabbled over the meal. Seen from so far away, their fight seemed small, set against the backdrop of the sky and the sea.

"Because we enjoy it," said Fengel.

Natasha made a grunt of agreement. "And because we both like to win."

Fengel nodded. There was a choice before him, he realized. He turned his head slightly, catching Natasha's gaze out of the corner of her eye. "You know," he said, "I see something too, in the faces of those that follow you."

She arched an eyebrow at him. "Oh?"

"Fear."

Natasha blushed. She looked away and toyed with the flower bud growing from the bushes being slowly crushed beneath them. "You're just saying that."

"No, it's true—"

The rest of his words were lost as Natasha grabbed the back of his head and crushed her lips to his. Fengel froze, then gave in. He returned her kiss tentatively at first, then with increasing passion. The ledge shook and the ground rumbled again. Distantly, he heard another explosion from the volcano at the center of the isle. Fengel realized that he didn't care.

Natasha broke away suddenly. Ash rained down between them and her face was now a picture of concern. "Wait," she said. "I shot you with that weird Voorn musket. Why aren't you dying?"

He'd been ignoring the pain, but her words brought it back to the fore. "It hurts…" Fengel rolled over to reveal the injured side. His jacket was torn, and scorched where the beam had hit. Amazingly, though, his shirt underneath was barely burned through to the skin. "Huh. Something stopped the blast."

He gingerly fished around in the pocket on that side of his jacket. Something round and hard fell into his fingers and he pulled it out. The object was an eyepiece, bound in brass with a gold chain. The lens was brightly reflective on one side, though. And the brass ring was smoothed, half-melted almost in the shape of an eyepatch, now.

"Oh," said Fengel. "My spare monocle. The blast did something to it."

Natasha was nonplussed. "You keep a spare monocle?"

Fengel gave her a confused look. "Of course."

"But you're still wearing that cracked, messed-up thing."

"Well, yes. Then I wouldn't have a spare."

Natasha made a snort of disgust. She snatched both eyepieces, the one he was wearing, with its now-broken chain, and the one in his hand. His wife shook her head, then threw away the old and planted the spare squarely on his face. A pang of loss shot through Fengel. He tried not to look out over the ledge after his lost monocle. Natasha climbed up onto his chest and took his head with both hands. "Shouldn't we think about getting down, somehow?" he asked.

His wife only grinned crookedly. "We'll figure something out. If we have to, I'll just scream at you like the harpy you say I am, and you can fake it as we go."

Fengel smiled. "Oh. That's all right, then."

She bent her lips to his as the island rumbled, the dragon roared, and volcanic ash fluttered down around them.

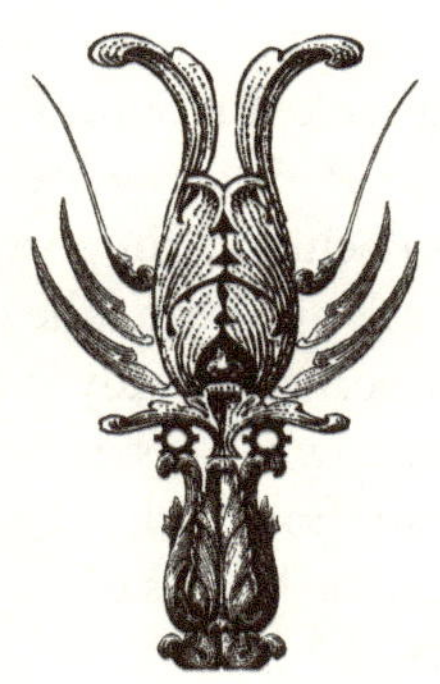

CHAPTER TWENTY

It was Jonas Wiley, the unburned twin. He lay in the hammock below, between her and the deck, his eyes wide and staring. The pool of blood below him was mostly dry. He had likely died sometime during her nap.

Jonas had been obnoxious, but that was small in the face of his death. Lina breathed a heartfelt sigh and sat up. Her back creaked and her muscles were sore. A glance at the rest of the quarterdeck revealed that it was all but empty; only those injured in the raid still rested uneasily in their hammocks. Having been awake as the *Dawnhawk*'s scout, she'd evidently slept longer than any of the others who'd partaken in the raid. It had been an uncomfortable, dreamless sleep, yet for all that, she'd been completely oblivious to the man dying slowly beneath her.

Blue skies and daylight showed through the portholes, accompanied by the dulled crack of muskets and the distant thump of cannon. *We're still being chased, then.* Sleep wouldn't come again any time soon. Lina hardened her heart and decided to go check up on things. *Besides, I'm going to need someone to help with the body.*

Lina gingerly tried to avoid the pool of blood as she hopped down from her hammock. Jonas's death was an unpleasant surprise, though not entirely unexpected; she'd lost many friends last night during the escape from Breachtown. In fact, this entire trip had been one catastrophe after another. *How did things get this bad?*

There was one bright spot, at least. Lina cheered as she thought of Michael Hockton, and the way he had smiled at her. His screams, too. There had been a lot of screaming and yelling last night, really.

Lina stretched again and looked around for Runt. "All right, you little monster," she said. "Where are you? Let's go see what the day has in store."

She glanced up to see him behind a support strut stretching between the mess hall bulkhead and the deck up above. The scryn was curled into a tight, anxious coil, glaring down at her with beady eyes.

"There you are. Come on down. Let's go find everyone."

Runt poked his head out from behind the strut and hissed at her. Caustic spittle spattered across the boards of the deck, smoking. Lina cursed and took a step back.

"What in the Realms Below was that for? Get down here this instant, you horrible thing!" There was a bottle of Corsair's Cure-all in her stowed gear, but if her pet was going to be cranky he could damned well stay up there.

Runt pulled his head back into the coil and rumbled to himself. Lina made fists with her hands and was about to turn away when a low groan sounded behind her. The hairs on the back of her neck stood up. She looked back over her shoulder, already knowing what she'd find.

The corpse of Jonas Wiley was staring right at her. There wasn't any doubt that he was dead — his usually tanned skin was waxy and his chest did not rise with breath.

"Oh," said Lina in a small voice. "Oh no."

The Revenant gave a low groan that sent a cold shiver running down her spine. Runt hissed violently and squirmed deeper into its recess behind the strut. Ryan Gae and the other injured pirates shifted fitfully in their sleep.

"Okay," said Lina. "I'm, I'm going to just go...find someone. Runt! Keep an eye on Jonas here, okay?"

And then she fled.

The quarterdeck moved by in a blur. She raced up the stairwell past storage, past the captain's cabin, and up out onto the cool wind of the main deck.

The *Dawnhawk* in daytime was a welcome sight, even if the great airship was somewhat unkempt at the moment. Coils of rope lay across the deck, intermixed with toolboxes, winches, and great bolts of spare canvas patching. Almost the whole crew was currently present, barring those who had been lost in the raid and those sleeping below. The majority milled about, peering over the gunwales at their pursuers or crouched in some out-of-the-way place, focused on their own internal miseries. The remaining minority saw to the running of the ship itself, and were busy calling reports back to the helm or hauling gear aloft to the gasbag.

Lina paused, half out of the stairway hatch. Where were they going? What was the point of going on? The colony raid had been a failure. A good number of her friends were dead and they had less than nothing to show for it. The Ship's Committee had proven worthless. They'd already mutinied, and the captains were gone.

What were they all going to do?

A distant thump of cannon fire sounded, followed by the scream of a ball flying past the stern of the airship. Lina shook herself. *Foolish.* There was always something more to lose. And right now, not only did the Perinese want them dead, but there were Revenants in the quarterdeck.

She peered around for someone to bring that fact up with. Nate Wiley certainly wasn't it; Lina didn't relish being around when the Jonas's twin found out. Henry Smalls stood at the helm with Konrad and Maxim. Her friend Andrea hung from the port-side gas-bag rigging. Tricia and a few others were on the deck, hoisting a light-air gas canister up to her via winch and pulley. The older Mechanist oversaw this, while Committee-Member Lome argued with Reaver Jane about something near the starboard skysails. Lucian Thorne sat on the exhaust pipe rising from the deck nearby with Lina's stolen bottle of Cure-all in hand, looking out into the sky. She frowned at that, but kept looking, hoping for a glimpse of Michael Hockton. The renegade Bluecoat wasn't anywhere to be seen, though she did spy Omari's blonde dreadlocks up near the bow.

Perfect. If she told anyone on the crew they'd overreact, and the committee, well, was a failure. Omari had the most experience dealing with Revenants, she suspected. *She made the damned things, after all.*

Lina rose from the hatch and stalked up to the front of the airship. The ex-apothecary's assistant stood at the very front rail, looking out at the horizon where the sea met the sky. The air was clear but for a few puffy clouds, and the sun hung at midmorning. White-capped waves rolled several hundred feet below, unblemished by any sight of land.

A cannonball flew below, before disappearing into the ocean.

"I can pretend we're not being chased up here," said Omari. "At least, until something like that happens." She looked at Lina. "Why don't we fly higher?"

Lina listened to the whirr of the propellers before answering. "We're at full steam already," she said. "That takes coal and light-air gas, which we probably don't have a lot of to spare at the moment. Also, we hit a bunch of merchant ships on the way over to Breachtown, so we're running a little heavy. I wouldn't worry about getting shot down, though. It's pretty much impossible to hit something in the sky with a cannon, and musket shot won't do near enough damage, even if they can manage it."

Omari only grunted and went back to watching the waves.

"So...." continued Lina. "We've got a problem in the quarterdeck that I think you should handle."

The Yulan woman wheeled on her. "What? You wreck my home, my business, kidnap me, and now you want to put me to work?" She shook her head. "The gall of you Perinese."

"Hey!" said Lina, affronted. "I'm from Triskelion, the machine-city. Don't lump me in with these dogs chasing after us." She lowered her voice. "Besides. This is one of *your* problems."

She caught Omari's gaze and held it. After a moment the other woman sagged. "Oh," she said. "You pirates are dropping like mayflies. But I don't know what you want me to do about it."

"Well, stop raising them for starters," she said heatedly. "Jonas being dead is bad enough, but no one's going to be able to handle watching him walk around. Especially after last night."

Omari threw her hands wide. "What, do you think this is a game I play? That I enjoy? I have no control over who comes back, or how. He's not some conjured daemon, to come at my beck and call." She shook her head. "Just put them out of the way somewhere. They're not usually violent unless you get in their way a lot." She paused to think. "Or unless they were really violent people in life."

"Well, you'd better think fast on what you *can* control," said Lina. "Or—"

"Take cover!" came a cry from back near the helm.

Lina heard the rudder-assemblies at the rear of the ship give a loud *clack*. Then the airship pitched abruptly to its port side. Omari yelled and grabbed the gunwale railing, echoing the surprise of the rest of the crew.

A black blur flew overhead. It thrust past the gunwales amidships and up at the gasbag frame above them, pressing the semirigid canvas skin until it was concave. Lina had a half-second's horror as the canvas split and the cannonball punched up out of sight through the interior of the 'bag.

"Puncture!" called the Mechanist from the middle of the deck. "Clear amidships for gas leak!"

Everyone knew the danger present. Light-air gas was not only intensely flammable, but extremely poisonous as well. The Brothers of the Cog tended toward gas-mask respirators for a reason.

"I thought you said we were safe!" yelled Omari. "I thought you said that they couldn't hit us! Now we're going to sink and drown in the ocean."

She hugged up against the gunwales and said prayers in Perinese before switching to some other, native tongue.

"That was a one-in-a-million shot!" exclaimed Lina, somewhat stunned herself. "And the 'bag is made of individual cells. We'll be fine! Probably!"

Those nearest the breach rose to their feet to obey the Mechanist. Though the gas was mostly invisible, it left a blur in the air when it passed in enough concentration. The gas billowed down at the deck in a hazy column, and the pirates scrambled to get away from it. Tricia wasn't so lucky, and Lina's heart sank as the woman dropped abruptly to the deck beneath the breach in the gas bag where the haze was thickest.

The sound of a thousand hammers pounding against the hull added to the chaos. Splinters flew from the gunwales as fat iron marbles skipped up over the side with lethal force. Lina watched Fat Thomlin jerk violently as he was struck, and a dozen others fell to the deck as they were hailed with spars of broken wood.

"Grapeshot?" gasped Lina. "They're able to hit us with grapeshot?"

The airship heaved beneath her feet as it twisted back onto its course. Distantly, she spied Henry and tall, gaunt Maxim fighting with the helm. Konrad was closer, raising his thick-fingered hands at gas bag and deck. A wind kicked up, too strong and sudden to be anything natural. The heat-haze poison of the light-air gas dissipated before it, and Lina caught only the faintest whiff of the stuff. It smelled sour, like milk gone bad.

Once the airship had righted, the Mechanist marched down the deck, calling out commands in his harsh voice. A few of those crew uninjured by the attack and not crippled by wounds suffered last evening rushed to obey. In such a situation, he was in charge, and they all knew it. Her friend Andrea led the race to the equipment lockers running down the deck, breaching them to pass out gas masks and coils of rope. The Mechanist then led them up the rigging to repair the damage above.

Lina's gaze went to those still on the deck. Gunney Lome and the others of the committee were helping where they could, but most of the emergency supplies had been used during their escape from Breachtown. She couldn't tell how serious the grapeshot volley had been, but there would be at least two on the crew who wouldn't rise again.

A horrible thought occurred to Lina. *Or will they?*

She wheeled around on Omari. "Stop! Don't do it!"

The other woman stared at her with frightened, angry eyes. She shrugged after a moment, helplessly.

Lina cursed and ran away, down the deck to where she'd seen Fat Thomlin and Tricia fall. Pirates screamed and yelled for help as she passed them. *What am I going to do? I can't just toss the bodies off the ship!* Couldn't she? The others would never understand....

A dozen paces away, she saw she was already, horribly, too late. Fat Thomlin twitched. He raised one mangled arm, then another. Groaning, he sat up and stared at Lina with dead eyes.

"Thomlin!"

Reaver Jane appeared at Lina's side. Belatedly, she remembered that the committee-member was close friends with the recently returned corpse; both had been on Natasha's original crew.

Fat Thomlin the Revenant gave a guttural groan and faced Jane. Blood soaked his torso, and still dribbled from where the grapeshot ball had destroyed his right arm and torn out his throat.

The committee-member gasped in horror and drew her cutlass.

"Wait!" cried Lina. "Wait, they shouldn't be violent."

Reaver Jane turned a horrified, incredulous look on Lina. "They?"

Lina closed her eyes as Tricia groaned as well, and the young piratess lurched and gurgled and crawled to her knees, tongue lolling and skin blackening from light-air gas overexposure.

Omari appeared beside Lina, along with several others. The Yulan woman grabbed her by the arm and pulled her back. "What mad horror is this?" she cried, casting a meaningful look at Lina, wanting her to play along.

"Oh by the Goddess," breathed Sarah Lome, wide-eyed.

"Revenants!" cried Nate Wiley.

"Just like back in Breachtown," moaned Reaver Jane.

The Revenants twitched and groaned, but did little else. Thomlin tried to stand again and failed. Tricia let out a horrible wet gurgle, emptying hemorrhaged lungs onto the deck. More of the crew clustered to see the cause of the commotion, only to fall back and draw their weapons.

"We've got to destroy them!" called a pirate.

"How do you kill them?" asked another. "They're already dead."

"Cut off the head," replied the first. "A priest once told me that works."

"You can't cut off his head! And why are they even coming back?"

"It's her fault," said Lina. Everyone looked at her. She jerked a thumb back at Omari, who glared daggers. "She's cursed, or an aetherite, or some damned thing. Says dead things just come back around her."

The crew exploded. Rough hands grabbed Omari.

"Why? Why would you do this?"

"And after we take you onto our ship?"

"Toss her over the side!"

"End your magics, damn you!"

"It's not my fault!" howled Omari. "It just happens when I'm around! They're harmless if you leave them alone! Mostly!"

Lucian Thorne stepped forward. "As if everything else going on wasn't bad enough, now we've got to contend with this." He shook his head. "I'm sorry, miss, but there's *really* no place for you aboard. We'll give you a float, and maybe the Perinese can pick you up."

"Wait!" growled Reaver Jane. "Aren't we a committee? There should be a vote. And my suggestion is to just gut her here and now. Why give her anything?"

"But what do we do about the Revenants?" asked Sarah Lome.

"No one is doing a damned thing," growled Henry Smalls.

The steward shoved his way violently into the crowd. At his back came Andrea Holt, both Allen and the older Mechanist, and the aetherites, Maxim and Konrad. Behind them stood the small knot of crew who had remained onboard during the Breachtown excursion. All held gas-mask respirators, tools, and swathes of canvas and rope.

Lina felt a moment's panic. If they were up here, who was piloting the *Dawnhawk?* The thump of cannon fire had grown faint. She realized that they had gained a lead again on their pursuers.

Henry stared at them all in turn. The pleasant, older fellow who had always politely suffered through inconvenience was gone now, replaced by a grizzled bulldog of a man who wore the threat of violence like an old pair of boots. Lina was shocked at the change.

"I don't like it any more than you," replied Lucian, "but the committee—"

"To the Realms Below with your committee," snarled Henry Smalls. "It's been a miserable failure ever since it started. You argue and you bluster and in the end, you just throw up your hands and take whatever path is easiest, with no thought to who gets hurt. And look at you now! We're being chased by the damned Perinese, we're trying to keep this ship in the air, and you're arguing about a couple of probably harmless corpses!"

He shook his head and quieted. No one said anything in response. Lucian, Sarah Lome, and Reaver Jane all stared at him, as if a loyal hound had suddenly transformed into a dragon. Even the Revenants watched the proceedings with their dead-alive eyes.

Henry pointed a finger at Omari. "You say they're not violent?"

She shrugged. "Mostly! They tend to get agitated if there's violence around them, or if they are kept from doing what they loved most in life. Or, uh, if they were really violent to begin with. But I'm sure they're fine!"

The steward watched her a moment longer. Then he shook his head. "This woman stays aboard. What happens to her isn't our call to make."

Lucian threw up his hands. "She's making Revenants, Henry! We've got to do something about that."

The steward glared at Lucian. "No, we don't. In fact, we're not changing a thing. Everything is as-is until we get to where we're going and fix this mess." Those behind him all muttered an affirmation.

"But where are we going?" asked Lucian. "How are we going to fix this?

"We're going to get the captains back."

Henry Smalls spun about and stalked back to the helm. The rest of the crowd dissipated, slinking off to tend to the damage the ship had just taken. Lina and the rest of the committee were left with the groaning Revenants.

"But what about the Revenants?" asked Lucian, shouting back at the helm while gesturing to the corpses writhing beside him.

Lina shook her head and turned away to find Omari standing before her, glaring furiously.

"Why did you do that?" she demanded. "They would have killed me!"

Lina's emotions shifted from hard and unyielding to feeling like a bag of broken glass, but the other woman's fury stoked her own. "Because you're *raising the dead!* These people were my friends! I've gamed and laughed and drank with them. They're the closest thing to a family I've got left!"

"I told you that it's not my fault," growled the other woman. "I don't do this intentionally! What—"

A panicked cry from above cut her short. Lina glanced up just as a bright flash exploded out from the bottom breach in the bag, and a jet of fire shot down toward them. Omari threw herself aside with catlike reflexes, and then Lina was flying back, through no fault of her own.

She hit the deck beside Michael Hockton, who'd appeared from nowhere to knock her out of the way. Heat washed over her half-bared face, almost scalding. The air filled with the stink of Hockton's sweat, burning hair, and light-air gas.

The ex-marine held her a moment longer. "Are you all right?" he asked.

Oh no. Echoes reverberated through the deck below them as pirates pounded past, rushing to extinguish the flames. She looked up at the gas bag above.

The opening in the belly of the frame was a smoky hole, blackened around the edges. Just beneath it hung the corpse of another pirate, one who'd been suspended from the gas bag to stitch canvas, squarely catching the blast. The Mechanist stood directly below, yelling commands at the crew as they scurried to maintain the ship. She spied Allen disappearing around the corner of the gas bag, reaching it through the primary hatch.

"If another cell lights off, we're all dead," said Lina.

Michael swallowed at that and looked past her to the airship gasbag. Lina let herself be held, and watched with him. Seconds ticked down, and she held her breath.

A yell came from inside the hole, and a round, red-black object fell to the deck like a stone. It was the cannonball that had struck the *Dawnhawk* earlier, still hot, scorching the deck where it lay. Allen poked his head out of the smoking hole, peering through his gas mask at the pirates below. He held up a hand with his thumb upraised, before disappearing back inside.

The crew clapped and gave a ragged cheer. Lina sighed in deep relief and extricated herself from Hockton's grasp. She spied Omari out of the corner of her eye, climbing wearily to her feet.

Andrea Holt stalked past with a gas mask around her neck and a bolt of canvas over one shoulder. She took five steps and stopped suddenly, whipping around to stare at Lina. No, not at Lina, at Hockton behind her.

"What?" she said. "What is *he* doing *here*?"

Michael Hockton gave a lazy smile. "Hello. I don't think we've been acquainted. I've, ah, been hiding in the forward stairwell the last few hours. Seemed a nice, out-of-the-way place. Michael Hockton, pleased to meet you. I'd like to sign aboard, if I could—"

Andrea dropped the bolt of fabric and darted forward, lashing out with a right cross that jerked the ex-marine's head around like a top. He fell back against the deck, and before he could recover, she was there, with both hands on the lapels of his battered blue jacket, hauling him up to the gunwales as if to throw him over.

"Scum," growled Andrea. "Worm. Good friends of mine are dead because of you and yours. Even in just the last half an hourglass!"

Lina started. "Wait! He's with us!"

Andrea glanced back over her shoulder. "Realms Below he is." She bent Hockton back just as Lucian Thorne and Sarah Lome came over to see the commotion.

Lina looked to Lucian and back to her friend. "No! Really, he's with us! He came over, left the marines, helped us get out of the counting house last night."

"A Bluecoat?" said Lucian. He held a length of rope in his hands, while Sarah Lome held a long gaff-hook on a pole. "Ridiculous. Toss him over the side."

"No!" cried Hockton. "No, really! I mean it, I'm on your side now." He hunted from face to face for an ally. "I gave you all the key to the side door. I'm done with the navy, and the Kingdom. They were going to kill me!"

"Quiet you," said Lucian. "Over the side, Miss Holt, if you please."

Sarah Lome stepped forward. Her face was colored with ink, stained blue from too many long hours attempting to work out the mathematics of supply. The huge gunnery mistress put out a hand to Andrea's shoulder. "No," she said.

Lucian raised an eyebrow. "Sarah?"

"Ship's injured. We've got work to do."

Andrea's shoulders sagged. "You're right." She shook her head and released the ex-marine. Hockton slumped down the gunwales to the deck. "Henry's right. We're not doing anything. But if Ryan dies because some Bluecoat bastard shot him...and, and comes back as a *thing* because of her"—she jerked a thumb at Omari—"then I...." She fell silent, shaking her head again. "Just stay out of my way."

She pushed past Lina. The rest of the committee watched her go. Hockton gave a relieved sigh. Lucian looked at him sharply.

"Don't think you're getting off free, just because we're not throwing you overboard. The question now is, what do we do with you?"

"Really, sir," said Hockton. "I promise to stay out of the way. I'll be quiet as a mouse."

"What you'll be," growled Sarah Lome, "is useful." She hauled the man up to his feet. "Doing something that will keep you out of sight. Stitching canvas in the hold should suit."

Lina winced. Stitching together old canvas for the frame was a miserable, thankless job that took forever. If Lome buried him down in the hold doing *that*, she'd never see him. Worse, it wasn't that important. What he needed was a task that would keep him at least mildly protected because no one else wanted to do it.

It came to her then. "He can wrangle the Revenants!" she exclaimed, bringing up the first thing that came to mind.

Everyone looked at her. Then they looked to where Fat Thomlin and Tricia sat groaning. Hockton gave her an incredulous look and she winced, holding her hands out in apology.

"Someone's got to," mused Lucian. "And if they eat your face, I surely won't weep. All right, Bluecoatie, take up that pole and some rope."

Fear and revulsion shot across Hockton's features. He pointed at Omari. "Wait! What about her? They're her fault. She can take care of the things!"

Omari made a flippant gesture and turned to walk away. "What made you think that *I* like them? I need to go find my cat, anyway."

As Sarah and Lucian escorted Michael to his new duties, he looked back at Lina, somewhat betrayed. She started and called after them as she abruptly remembered. "There's one down in the quarterdeck too!"

After they had left, Lina sighed and joined in the work. She grabbed a mask and climbed aloft to the gas-bag interior, where the Mechanist put her to work replacing torn and scorched gas cells. It took hours, and it wasn't until after noon that she was back down on the deck again, running cord and canvas to make a patch, then inspecting the gear-train linkages that went from the skysails to the propellers at the stern of the ship.

She was passing beneath the port-side linkage when she spied the cannonball. It was the same one that had punctured the gas bag earlier. Apparently, it had rolled back here, and everyone had been too busy to dispose of the thing.

Lina knelt and picked the thing up. It was heavy, and it took her three tries before she was able to lift it up over the gunwales to fall into blue ocean below. The dull thump of a cannon sounded as she let go, startling her.

She peered out and down at the ships that chased the *Dawnhawk*. Not just one or two vessels plied the waves in their wake, but dozens. Hundreds, maybe. The entire Perinese Royal Navy was after them, and for over half a day now, they hadn't given up. Those in the lead fired chase guns, hurriedly elevated at the sky. But the airship was too high, and now too far ahead, to be clearly reached. Now and again someone tried a musket shot, but those never had the power, let alone the accuracy, to reach them.

Allen joined her at the stern. The young Mechanist was filthy and frazzled. His hair stuck up like an old paintbrush, caked with sweat and grease and the stinking of light-air gas. His gas mask hung around his neck, revealing the ugly gash across his face that he'd earned the other night, slathered in some healing ointment. His greatcoat was stained and scorched. Surprisingly, there was a metal hip flask in his hand.

"Look at this," said Lina. Still puzzled by it all, she gestured vaguely at the crew on the deck, then down at the assembled Perinese navy. "How did things come to this? How did they all get so screwed up?"

Allen gave her a quizzical look. "How in the Realms Below should I know? Though, I suppose it's all your fault, really." He took a swig from the flask.

Lina started back in surprise. "What? What do you mean?"

"You were the one who came up with all this. With the mutiny. With getting rid of Fengel and Natasha. You were the one who held the meeting, and brought it up to everyone."

Lina blinked. *What's gotten into him?* It might have been exhaustion, or the drink, but something was seriously amiss; Allen was never short with her. "Of course I brought it up!" she exclaimed. "We were headed for a catastrophe! They would have gotten us all killed!"

Allen ignored her a moment. He took another swig and then chucked the flask off the back of the airship, clearly as hard as he could, watching it fall like a shooting star before looking back at her. "And we've done so much better now ourselves, haven't we?"

He walked away. Lina watched him go, troubled. She glanced back at their pursuers: the entirety of the Perinese Royal Navy, hunting for their blood.

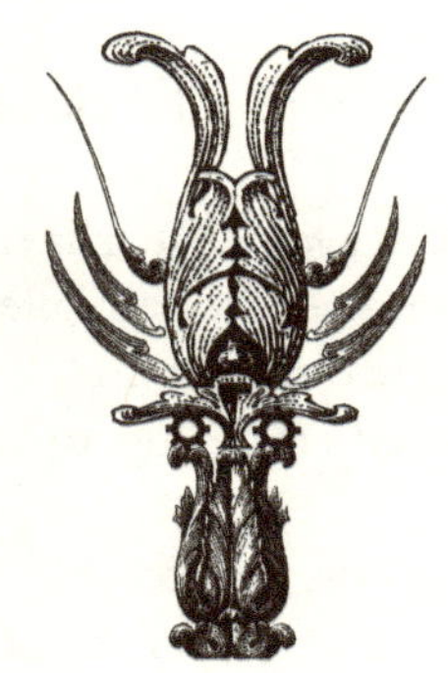

CHAPTER TWENTY-ONE

THE DROP WAS ABOUT TEN FEET. Natasha let go of the rock face and fell, landing feetfirst on the soil below with a grunt.

The base of the cliff that she'd spent the last day and a half stuck upon wasn't much different when viewed from up close. A thin sliver of loamy earth dotted with ferns sloped down to a wide pool, caught between thick jungle and a sheer face of volcanic rock. The waterfall thundered down into the pool, shedding a mist that shimmered with rainbow hues in the late morning sun. At her side stood the triangular monolith that had been dislodged during their fall down the flanks of the volcano. It pierced the ground, inverted, its wide base at head level.

Natasha ran a hand across the monolith. It was smooth and unblemished by the fall. She paused to smell the jungle, the scents of rich earth and falling water.

A rain of pebbles spilled down the cliff wall behind her. Natasha glanced back up to see her husband, hugging the stone face for dear life. She smiled. Fengel was a nimble and competent climber, but there was something about this stretch that had troubled him, making her the first one down.

"Come on," she said. "It's only a dozen feet at most."

Fengel half-turned his head to glance back down at her. Sweat plastered his hair to his forehead. "I am *resting*," he said, voice overloud and somewhat hoarse from exertion. "This climb has been ruinous, regretful, and altogether repugnant."

Natasha rolled her eyes. "You've spent *years* climbing about, both on sail ships and flying vessels. What's the difference here?"

"It never took me two hours of solid clambering to get about one of those!"

He slowly began his descent again. Natasha shook her head. She retrieved Fengel's battered tricorn from where it had fallen sometime last night, and moved to meet him as he reached the ground.

"Ridiculous," he continued, tottering to his feet again. "Ridiculous, riotous, re—"

She shut him up with a kiss. Mostly. He continued to murmur, but returned her affections in between. When she plunked his hat back atop his head and broke away, he finally quieted, leaning after her with puckered lips.

"Enough of that," she said with a chuckle. "We've been on that damned rock for too long. I'm parched and starving."

"Hmm," agreed Fengel. He eyed the waterfall. "That should suit. All the water on the island I've found so far has been fresh."

They staggered to the pool's edge. Natasha fell to her knees and tried an experimental sip from a cupped hand. It proved potable, and then she was drinking, gulping down as much as she could with both hands. The water was clear and clean and cold. When finished, she fell back and lay on the earth, listening to Fengel. They'd spent close to a day and a half stuck on the cliff without any food or water. Natasha could remember worse privations, and there had certainly been distractions, but that hadn't made it any less comfortable.

Fengel stripped off his jacket, shirt, and hat before wading into the pool to wash. She eyed his figure appreciatively, and counted the scars on his arms and torso. There were dozens of them, some large and others small. Some he'd gained in battle and some by accident. A decent number, more than half, had been acquired in her honor, either directly at her hand or by someone she'd upset, just to goad him into protecting her. It made her smile.

Her husband took a breath, submerged, and rose again with a shout. He floated backward into deeper water and smiled back at her. "This was needed," he said with boyish enthusiasm.

Natasha rolled over onto her belly and rested her chin on her hands. "I can think of something else I need," she replied.

He smiled and paddled towards the shore. She growled and crawled to her feet, just enough to launch herself at him. He grabbed her out of the air as they collided, falling back into the pool. The cold water was a shock and she rose up with a yelp, then he had her again in his arms.

I almost regret everything I've ever done to him. She met Fengel's smile with one of her own. His eyes were very green.

Something garish flew past. It landed on a tree branch as a speck of white dung fell past her head into the pool, just barely missing her. It was the parrot, butter-yellow beak and all. The thing cocked its head to glared at her with malicious enthusiasm. Fengel gave a faint grunt of surprise.

Her father would have killed the thing. Instead, Natasha let out a laugh. She shook her head and ignored the parrot, turning back to kiss her husband. Out of the corner of her eye, she thought she saw the bird rear back in surprise. It let out a great raucous shriek at her, and Fengel made a noise of irritation, but she continued to pay it no mind. After a moment the bird just stared at them, hunkering low over the branch, seeming somewhat crestfallen.

"We should find something to eat," murmured Natasha.

"More than that," said Fengel. "We should really find a way off—"

A mechanical bellow cut him off, echoing down past the canopy and off the cliff face. It was deafening, silencing even the waterfall, for a moment. The parrot flapped off in alarm as the thin shapes of gibbons swung away deeper within the jungle.

"Ah," said Fengel. "I'd forgotten about that monster."

"Yes," replied Natasha. "Kind of ruins the mood. Think it'll let us be?"

"In a word: no. I'm rather certain that the Voorn didn't build it to care for orphans. Still. I think we should take a holiday sometime soon. Just you and I."

Natasha smiled. "That sounds fine."

"Good. In the meantime, shall we work together to find a way off this rock?"

"Yes. Let's."

She held out her hand as if she were a highborn Perinese lady, and Fengel bent over it, giving it a kiss and leading her back up out of the pool ceremoniously. They laughed as he dressed again, and they moved off into the jungle.

A little bit of scouting seemed in order. She followed Fengel as he led the way through the green shade of the foliage, pushing for the beach. Neither of them were certain what side of the island they were even on. From the cliff, she had seen the sun rise, but neither the *Salmalin* nor the *Goliath* were visible. It likely meant that they were on the eastern half, which they had not, until now, untraveled.

A question occurred to Natasha. "Fengel?" she asked as she pushed a branch out of her way.

"Yes?"

"How *are* we going to get off this rock?"

He was silent a moment. They traversed between the trunks of an old mangrove, disturbing a large snake, which Natasha killed using a branch.

"It's not going to be easy," said Fengel as he pushed through a fern. "Or pleasant. Unfortunately, the best thing I can think of is to grab a longboat from the *Goliath*, and set ourselves adrift. If we're lucky, we'll get caught up in one of the shipping lanes. Or maybe just blown back to Yulan."

Natasha grunted. "That's not exactly appealing."

He shrugged. "I've none better, alas."

She sighed and nodded. He was always more creative than she was. If that was the best he could come up with…."You're right," she said. "It won't be easy. But there's a whole huge stash of supplies on the *Salmalin*, left by Kalyon Mahmoud. We can pillage what we need there, and haul it around the isle to take with us when we steal a boat."

"Capital!" he smiled. "See? Better already. Let's find out exactly where we are first, though."

They pressed on and found the beach. The unblemished white sand stretched down from the tree line to where cerulean waves smoothed it like cloth across a child's chalkboard. Natasha looked out upon the horizon, and keenly felt the isolation of Almhazlik. Her crew was gone, and the *Dawnhawk* with them.

Natasha snorted to herself. *Assholes.* Her rage at mutiny and abandonment hadn't cooled, really. But it was what it was, and there was little she could do about it.

For now.

Fengel waded out into the surf and spun around to examine the island. The ground suddenly rumbled, and he fell with a splash. Natasha fought to remain standing, as always, refusing to be beaten by the place. The tremor stilled, and her husband picked himself up. She threw him a cocky smile, and he just shook his head.

"Look there," said Fengel, pointing.

She followed his gesture to a rocky bluff toward the west. It bisected the isle all the way from the volcano down to the shore.

"Oh," said Natasha. She glanced around at the beach. "Is this where we were originally abandoned?"

Fengel shook his head. "I don't think so. I think that's the next space over. If we followed the beach counter-clockwise, we'd hit the *Salmalin*, I'm guessing. Come on. Let's climb up there and take a look."

He led the way down the sand until they reached the black cliff. It was made of volcanic rock, just like the one they'd climbed when they first came to the isle. The slope of it rose up from the waves like a black wall running all the way to the flanks of the volcano itself. Maybe fifty paces from the shoreline, the crag descended enough to be climbed. Fengel discarded his jacket and hat, but not the monocle, and swam the distance to the rock. Natasha shook her head and followed, taking his hand when she reached him and clambering up to the top of the bluff.

The ridge they stood upon bordered a wedge of jungle stretching from the volcano to the ocean. On the opposite end sloped a similar wall of rock with a familiar carved stone effigy of a dragon's head upon the volcano. A large hole had been burned in the middle of the jungle canopy, leaving bare, ashen earth around the base of an ancient baobab. Barely visible beyond this stretch of jungle, and the cliff beyond, were the mast tips of a modern sail ship, poking up like ghostly finger bones.

Natasha let out a sigh. This was definitely the part of the island where they'd been abandoned.

"Well," said Fengel with a grin. "At least we know where we are now." He peered at the damage her campfire had caused a few days ago. "You really left your mark, you know."

Natasha narrowed her eyes and elbowed him roughly in the ribs. *Like you could have done any better.* "So there's the Perinese ship. Should we—"

The rapid-fire snapping of underbrush echoed out across the jungle. Trees shook and swayed, and up from the unintentional clearing rose the Dray Engine. It stretched to its full length and roared at the sky.

"Get down!" hissed Fengel, grabbing her arm. She yanked it free and dropped to a crouch as he moved to follow his own advice.

"So there's the thing," she said.

The Voornish machine pivoted about with the squeal of grinding metal. Flywheels twisted under the armored plates of its body while teethed gears churned furiously. It swung about, lashing its tail back and forth, crushing several trees and widening the clearing.

"What is it doing?" wondered Fengel.

"Haven't the faintest," she muttered.

"It's like it's trampling the dirt, getting rid of the mess you made. Is that your lean-to?"

Natasha glanced back in time to see the thing bend over and swipe with one arm. The ragged collection of branches and cloth that she'd tried to assemble into a shelter went flying out over the jungle.

"My tent," Natasha muttered.

Fengel gestured, and they clambered back down the slope before wading back to the beach. "All right," he said. "That thing is penned in there. We run for the *Salmalin*, gather what supplies we can, and make our way back around the far side of the island to the other ship for a longboat."

Natasha spread her hands. "Sounds good to me."

She led the way as they jogged back around the beach. The sand made it hard going, but at least this way they could avoid the jungle and the sheer cliffs that the volcano presented to the ocean along this face. By the time they passed the cliff they'd been trapped upon, it was well past noon.

The ground became swampy and bog-like. Natasha half swam and half walked between the branching trunks of baobab trees, climbing up on them whenever she needed a rest. Fengel held his own behind her, and before too long they found themselves on firm earth and white sands again.

An object came into view around the curve of the island up ahead. It was long and squarish, with long spars of wood hanging from its side like broken sticks; the wreck of the *Salmalin*.

Natasha stopped for a moment, bending over to place her hands on her knees and rest. "There it is," she said, pointing. "Tidal wave from that bad earthquake the other day. Sucked her out to sea and then hammered her flat. Total loss, but Kalyon Mahmoud hoarded all the food for himself."

"Lucky for us, then," said Fengel. He looked away, pensive.

"What's that look for?" asked Natasha.

Fengel shook his head. "I don't know. I just…." He met her gaze. "Shouldn't we look for some of the others? Some survivors, mayhap?"

Oh, for the Goddess's sake. Her husband was such a bleeding heart, sometimes.

Natasha shook her head. "Fengel, they were only tools. Face it, you were using them just as much as I was. And it only worked because they were both doing their damndest to kill each other in the first place."

He nodded sadly. "You're right." Then he let out a sigh and raised an eyebrow at her. "But still…maybe we can tell them where to find the supplies, if we spot any?"

Natasha rolled her eyes. "All right. But only after we raid them for ourselves."

"Well, of course."

They strolled until the stretch of beach that the Salomcani warship lay upon came fully into view. Natasha had to admit that the island had not been kind to it. She'd only been gone two days, and the vessel seemed worse than ever, set against the stark backdrop of the low bluff leading deeper back into the island. The sails of the ship were torn and tattered, its glass windows in the stern were all shattered, the hull was warped, and the keel was bent like a crippled old man.

Fortunately, though, they seemed to be the only ones there.

She started forward, but stopped abruptly as Fengel put a hand on her shoulder. Natasha glared back at him, but Fengel only held a finger up to his mouth for quiet. He peered around, warily, as if he'd noticed something that troubled him.

"What?" she asked.

"Do you hear that?"

Natasha listened. There were the waves, and the seagulls, and the sound of the wind rustling the branches of the nearby jungle. A brightly colored crab climbed the bluff behind the ship, only to slip and topple back down to the sand of the beach. "I don't...." No, there. A rumbling. Natasha shook her head. "It's just another tremor," she said.

The Dray Engine burst up from beyond the low bluff behind the *Salmalin* with a roar. It stomped toward the shore, lowered its shoulder, and slammed into the broken warship. The *Salmalin* rocked with the blow. It rolled over until it was fully upside down, the masts snapping like matchwood and the boards of the hull splitting in a hundred places.

"Oh *horseshit*!" screamed Natasha. "That damned thing would have had to come straight here. This is ridiculous!"

The great brazen head rose. Two eyes like malevolent red suns fell upon them as the Dray Engine looked their way.

"Ah," said Fengel. "Maybe you should quiet down, a bit?"

"No, I will not!" howled Natasha. "I'm sick of this island and all the ridiculous obstacles that keep throwing themselves in my way. You hear me, you great wind-up lizard? I have had enough!"

The Dray Engine raised one foot up upon the hull of the *Salmalin* as it faced them fully. It rose to its full height, its head hovering a hundred feet above the sand. Then it shifted to glare down at them, eyes forming narrow slits.

"That's right," continued Natasha. "Go on, get out of here, you outdated piece of junk! I will *break* you!"

A deep rumble came from the Dray Engine. It pressed down with its foot, crushing the hull of the *Salmalin* underneath.

"Natasha?" said Fengel. "Dearest?"

She wheeled about and snarled at him, "What?"

"Run."

The Dray Engine gave a thundering roar. Fengel fled back up the beach. *Ah*. Her outrage cooled as Natasha realized just what she'd been doing.

She turned and ran. The sand proved treacherous, shifting and sagging under her feet. Sudden fear gave her strength, though, and she pulled up alongside her husband, already halfway to the jungle.

Another thundering roar echoed behind them, punctuated by an earth-tremor footfall. Then another, nearer. Natasha didn't look over her shoulder; she just ran.

The wall of greenery grew closer. Twenty feet, fifteen, ten. Then she dodged between Fengel and a mango tree and into the shade of the jungle undergrowth.

Got to hide. Got to find somewhere to hole up. The Dray Engine wasn't going to be stopped by a tree or two, that was obvious. She needed something really solid. Even though this was the only sane solution, it still galled her. Natasha wanted to strike back at the thing. She wanted to *fight*.

She pushed through a fern just as the mechanical monstrosity slammed into the tree line. The tree line gave first. Snapping trunks and cracking limbs accompanied the thundering call of the beast. Fengel swore aloud behind her, his voice hoarse with exertion.

A hedge of ferns rose up before her. Natasha plowed through them. Beyond lay an open clearing maybe a hundred feet across. A large stone dominated the space, thrown here who knew how long ago, covered in moss and lichen. She didn't stop to examine it, only plowed along ahead.

The lichen proved slick, shifting and sliding beneath her feet. A coating of fine volcanic ash covered the stone where it was otherwise bare, making it even more treacherous. Natasha fought for balance, calling upon the same resolve that had helped her escape the Perinese and dominate the Salomcani.

They were halfway across when the Dray Engine plowed into the clearing. It roared again, lowering its head to snap at Fengel just behind her. The jaws closed with a metallic echo, and she heard her husband swear loudly and fervently in every language he knew. He pulled equal with her, white-faced and sweating.

Natasha focused on putting one foot after another. The ground shook with the tremor of the massive Voornish automaton. She could almost feel the hiss of steam upon her back as the vapors poured from joints and baffles. To trip here would be death.

The beast snapped at her head and missed. She felt the wind of its jaws, the vibration of brazen teeth slamming shut. Then she was through the trees and into the greenery again.

Ha! Natasha looked back over her shoulder. "Missed me, you clockwork joke!" Then she looked back, just in time to see a garish ball of feathers land on a branch just up ahead, its butter-yellow beak wide open to shriek at her maliciously.

There wasn't enough time to stop. The parrot's malevolent glare changed to shock as Natasha ran face-first into the ugly thing. It squawked and flapped, and Natasha swore and got a mouthful of feathers for her trouble. She was trying to pry the thing away from her when, suddenly, the ground disappeared from beneath her feet.

Natasha tumbled down a sandy slope, her curses punctuated by outraged squawks from the parrot. The two of them slammed hard into a shallow stream at the base, momentarily stunned.

Then Fengel was there, grabbing her and hauling her forward. The sunlight faded into darkness, and she realized he had dragged her into a low cave on the other side of the embankment.

The Dray Engine roared just outside and at the top of the slope. The shadow of its massive bulk swung back and forth, casting the stream and cave mouth into darkness. They seemed to have lost it.

Natasha held silent. So did Fengel. Even the ridiculous parrot—clutched in Natasha's hands, scratched bloody from their escape—quieted. The thump and tremor of the machine pacing back and forth was like the workings of a massive clock, poorly timed. Rocks, sand, and dirt slid down into the stream as it went. The parrot made to squawk as a particularly large stone fell with a splash. Natasha grabbed its beak with one hand, silencing the thing. Still it fought her, jerking around and trying to bite and claw her.

Presently, the Dray Engine moved off a little way, though not so distant that they could leave. Fengel sighed and stood. "That was nerve-racking," he said. "Fortunately, this burrow was here. I swear, this whole island seems riddled with tiny caverns. Probably some Voornish coffeehouse down this—"

He fell silent and Natasha glanced back. Then she froze.

A small crowd of sailors, Salomcani and Perinese both, clustered at the back of the cave behind them. They glared with outraged eyes at both Fengel and her.

Then they drew their weapons.

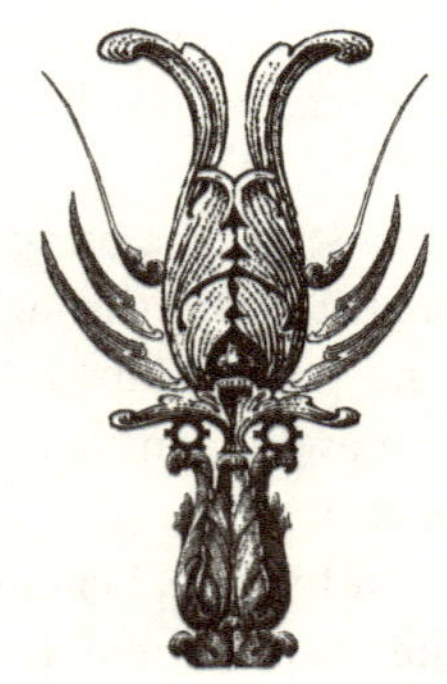

CHAPTER TWENTY-TWO

F ENGEL EYED THE MIXED CROWD OF S ALOMCANI AND P ERINESE survivors at the back of the cave. They flinched with every passing of the Dray Engine, yet never shifted their gaze away from his direction. Their weapons were notched and battered but still quite serviceable. By the glares they sent his way, this was something they intended to show firsthand.

Never let them see you stumble.

"Well, gents," said Fengel. "It's about time I found you. Now, I have to ask; what are you doing hiding in a cave? There's work to be done."

Dead silence reigned.

"We're not following you anymore!" cried Paine, the young midshipman. His voice carried overloud in the cave, and others reached out to shush him. They all froze then, listening to the pace of the Voornish war machine outside.

Sergeant Cumbers pushed forward. The ugly wound across his scalp was barely bandaged, but his eyes were clear again. "You tricked us," he said accusingly. "You wormed yer way into our confidence while we were weak, and the second you could, you abandoned us. The few of us here barely made it out of that place alive!"

"So much for loyalty." Natasha smirked before glaring at the three Salomcani.

One of them Fengel did not know, though the other pair were more familiar. The first of these was a tall man with a huge bruise above his mustaches and a chest wrapped with an impromptu bandage. The second was a short, stout fellow with a bloody, dried gash over his eyes.

"But you know better, right, Etarin?" she said.

The stout one stepped forward and gestured sharply at Natasha with his scimitar. "No! Your words are poison and your actions serve only yourself!" He gestured to his tall fellow with a bruised face and bandaged chest, and then to the thin one. "Neither I, Farouk, or Jahmal will follow your madness any longer." He looked to the Perinese as Natasha blinked in surprise. "She slew our Kalyon and then took advantage, only to use us in her petty conflict with this captain of yours."

"He's not our captain," hissed Sub-Lieutenant Hayes. "He's just a damned pirate."

"Oh?" said the thin man, Jahmal. "It certainly *seemed* like you were following him when we found you in the ravine."

The crewmen fell to bickering among one another. Fengel glanced back over his shoulder and caught Natasha's eye. She nodded sharply, glaring still at her ex-crewmen.

Fengel clapped his hands at them. "Gentleman," he said. "Gentleman, there's no need for argument. I'm certain we can all come to an accord, especially with the assistance of a third party."

The Perinese all fell silent and stared at him.

"No!" said Hayes. "No, we're not listening to any more of your damned wordplay." He turned to the others at the back of his cave. "Kill him!" he said. "Just kill these two pirates and get it over with!"

The sailors began nodding and muttering agreement. They brandished their weapons again. Even young Paine joined in, raising a dagger in clearly frustrated bloodlust.

Fengel snapped his fingers.

At the signal, Natasha let go the beak of the horrible parrot. It immediately uttered a piercing shriek that almost deafened everyone in the cave, and certainly echoed outside. Hayes and Jahmal both dropped their weapons in surprise, the latter covering his ears.

The Dray Engine ceased to pace. It froze from where it had been stomping some short distance away, then tromped back up toward the cave. Dirt and sand fell from the ceiling. The water of the thin stream outside jumped like raindrops bouncing off a hot skillet. Then a massive clawed foot slammed down to occlude the entrance.

Everyone froze. Hayes's features shifted comically from righteous indignation to utter horror. Sergeant Cumbers opened his mouth to cry out, and Private Simon clapped his hand over it. The Salomcani pressed together back into the cave against a stack of crates that Fengel hadn't noticed before. Natasha grabbed the parrot's beak and tried to look unphased. Fengel made sure to meet the eyes of every person in the space, holding them a moment before moving on.

Gears whirled and pistons churned as the beast bent about. It gave a great bellows-snort, pushing steam down the ravine and into the cave, a hot, wet vapor that wafted up past Fengel's legs.

Silence held for a long moment. Then the creature shifted again. It took one tremor-inducing step, then another, and moved slowly away from the ravine.

Fengel counted to one hundred, then folded his hands behind his back and met the eyes of the still-frozen crewmen. "As I said, there's no reason to argue. That's the mark of rash, desperate men. And we wouldn't want to do anything *rash,* now, would we?"

He winked back at Natasha. She gave him an amused smile.

Farouk stepped forward. "We are at an impasse, then. We cannot kill you without you bringing that mechanical beast down upon us."

"You've an acute grasp of the situation," said Fengel. He eyed the crates behind the men. "Let us move on to more pleasant matters. However did you all come to be in this hole?"

The varying crewmen exchanged awkward looks.

"We needed supplies," said Simon after a moment. "We stripped the *Goliath* when we left like you said to, but as we fled the inside of the volcano, the Dray Engine out there was killing everyone, and most of it was lost."

"It crushed Dawkins," said Paine, his face white and his eyes wide. "Just stepped on him like it did that Voornish automaton. Flat like a bug! It grabbed up Riley Gordon too, when he tried to run, and ripped him in half." He choked back a sob. "Harvey the carpenter and I had almost got away, when he cried out and fell over, clutching at his chest." The midshipman closed his eyes. "That monster still came over and stepped on him, just to be sure."

Simon put a hand on the youth's shoulder. Then he glanced back up at Fengel. "We're all that's left. When we got away, we thought we'd go to the *Salmalin* and see what they had. We found these rats"—he gestured to Etarin—"already tearing things apart."

"Then they attacked us!" said the man. He glared at the Perinese private. "That monster killed all our fellows as well, and still you attacked us, stealing from the less fortunate like the dogs that you are."

"You stole those supplies from honest Perinese merchantmen!" cried Cumbers.

"Honest Perinese?" snorted Jahmal. "Don't make me laugh."

"Gentleman," said Fengel. He held his hands out until everyone looked his way, then pointed significantly at the ravine outside. Faintly, they could all hear the Dray Engine, still pacing about, looking for its prey.

The group quieted. "Anyway," said Hayes after a moment. "They fled—"

"No, you fled!"

"You both fled," interrupted Fengel. "The Dray Engine, right? You heard the Dray Engine coming out from the interior of the island, hid down here, and were just about to leave when we came in, yes?"

Everyone nodded.

"Well, why not just *say so*?" Fengel shook his head. Now that they'd all been talked down, it was time to try the next step.

He eyed the stack of crates behind the sailors. There were only a few, stamped with both Kingdom and Sheikdom insignia. It was easy enough to make out the contents.

"Let's see...some dried fish, hardtack, of course, a satchel of onions, and some goat meat jerky." He raised an eyebrow. "This is what you've been fighting over?

"We're going to need it," said Hayes. "At least until we can find a way to avoid that beast outside. Once next season comes, we should have it all figured out, and then the mango trees will be fruiting."

Fengel gave them a piteous look. "Oh, lads," he said. "You're thinking of *staying* here?"

"Well, what else are we going to do?" asked Paine. "We can't sail away. Both the ships are ruined."

"I mean to do exactly that," said Fengel. "And I'll even take you along, though the way be perilous hard." He almost felt Natasha's glare at the back of his head; there wasn't nearly enough food for two people in the cave, let alone ten.

Hayes leaned forward. "S'not going to work," he said snidely. "We all know what you're both really like."

Sergeant Cumbers held up a hand. "Hold on, now. How are you going to leave the island?"

The sub-lieutenant rounded on Cumbers in surprise. "What? No!"

Etarin stepped forward from the Salomcani side of the cave. "I would hear this as well."

"It's not going to be easy," said Fengel, cutting in before Hayes could speak up. "But there's enough material on the *Goliath*. We can build a raft of longboats, and head back to the open ocean. It'll take all we've got, and more than a few of us won't survive, but it's the best chance we have." He met each pair of eyes. "We'll have to work together on this, no Salomcani, no Perinese. Just us."

The cave grew silent. Hayes worked his jaw, obviously fighting to find the words to express his outrage. Farouk stepped forward, looking past Fengel to Natasha. "Kalyon," he said. "Does he mean this? Can you both do this?"

Natasha gave a bitter shrug. "I guess," she said, rolling her eyes at Fengel.

"I don't want to die here," said Paine. The youth lowered the dagger he held. "I want to go back to the Kingdom."

And just like that, they were his. *Capital.* There still wasn't enough food...but they'd figure something out. "Excellent. Now—"

"No. No! *No!*" Hayes pushed violently past Cumbers and the Salomcani, past Fengel and Natasha and out the cave mouth into the stream beyond. "I won't follow you!" he screamed back at them all. "I won't be party to this *again!*"

Then he ran off.

The Dray Engine gave a thundering roar. It pounded through the jungle, growing closer and closer until the great brazen claws passed by, leaving a cloud of steam in its wake. Hayes screamed somewhere outside, the sound falling fainter as he ran farther away. The Dray Engine gave chase.

Fengel looked sharply back at the rest of his crew. "Hayes has inadvertently given us a chance. Grab the crates and follow me. We make for the *Goliath.* Go!"

Natasha was already outside, the ridiculous parrot still clutched in her hands. She scrabbled up the embankment they'd been hidden beneath. Fengel climbed after her, but only halfway up before turning back to watch as the others appeared. They followed him up the slope and into the jungle beyond.

They ran. The jungle seemed to fight Fengel as never before. Fern bushes tangled his feet and green vines snaked around his head. The darkness of the jungle canopy occluded vision, causing missteps and collisions with hidden palm trees. Even when they broke free into a clearing things were dark; the sun hid its face behind the volcanic cloud streaming up from the mountaintop.

The Dray Engine remained hidden, but it could still be heard. Thunderous footfalls shook the ground they ran upon and set the trees to shaking. Once or twice he spied its reptilian form distantly through the undergrowth. To his surprise he still caught the echo of faint screams; Sub-Lieutenant Hayes still lived.

His wife drew close as they neared the southern shore of the island. She appeared battered, but defiant, filled with tenacity as usual. The gaudy parrot she had held was gone, at the moment.

"Where's your bird?" he asked.

She made a disgusted sound. "That thing. *Pfagh*. Threw it away."

"Oh?"

"I shoved it down a burrow of some sort. Looked like a badger's den, or something."

"Ah."

They focused on moving through the underbrush for a moment. The rest of the crew still trailed along behind them. As he stopped to get his bearings, Natasha reached out and grabbed his arm, forcing him face her.

"Fengel. How in the Realms Below are we going to survive with these worms dragging us down?"

He smiled sheepishly. Both of them knew that this was his doing, what he really wanted rather than what she did. "Well. I'm sure that something will come up." He shrugged. "Besides. It's very, very likely that most of us are going to be dead before we can even leave the island. That'll balance the equation a little."

She sighed and looked away before giving him a wry smile. "Whatever. I have to admit I'm impressed, though. I'd have just started killing them until I got my way."

Fengel blinked. Neither of them had any weapons anymore. "What, with that bird?"

"Just so."

They both broke out into laughter at the same time. He patted her shoulder and they moved on again.

The sun had set when the jungle parted to reveal the southern beach. Fengel gave a sigh of relief and gathered the others around. Miraculously, they hadn't lost anyone. There were a few close calls, but the Dray Engine remained elsewhere on the island. Equally miraculously, Fengel was sure he'd heard the sound of Hayes's screams whenever they caught sight of the Voornish monster. It had been hours since there'd been any hint of either of them, though.

Paine gave a shout and pointed. Fengel followed his finger along with everyone else, and breathed a sigh of relief as he spied the tall, thin masts of the *Goliath* rising beyond a spit of jungle to the east. He smiled at the assembled crew and led them down to the beach.

A ridge of rock stretched out from the jungle into the sand. Fengel recognized it as the same one from earlier, where the Salomcani had launched their raid upon the Perinese. *And now I'm helping what's left of them to take the Goliath. Ironic.*

He led the way, focusing on the immediate future. Natasha was right; there wasn't any way he could keep ten people alive. Fengel was going to have enough trouble with just the two of them. *Am I? Stranger things have happened. And if we can hit a shipping lane somehow. Still, it's going to be obvious to them too—*

He ascended the top of the rock and cursed, throwing himself down flat.

The Dray Engine lay on the beach before the *Goliath* a hundred feet away. It was prostrate, belly down and arrow-straight from the tip of the tail all the way up to the jaws, the moonlight shining from its brazen hide. The great fire-lamp eyes were shuttered, and its foreclaws were folded neatly beneath the chest. Fengel could see that it wasn't dead, though. Brass flywheels spun beneath the armored carapace and clockwork gears twitched along. For all the world though, the machine appeared to be sleeping.

Fengel held his hands out at the sailors and made shushing noises as the tall Salomcani, Farouk, climbed the ridge, followed by Natasha, and then Sergeant Cumbers. They paused a moment to stare in surprise and horror. Then Natasha swore.

"You overbuilt piece of trash!" she cried. "You wind-up joke! No! No! I refuse to believe that you can just show up wherever I—"

Fengel and the others moved as one. He leapt up to clap hands over her mouth, while Cumbers and Farouk tackled her to the rock. The three of them carried her back down behind the ridge, where the rest of the crew stared up at them in surprise.

Natasha kicked, fought, and bit, but Fengel and the others held her still. He gestured with his head back up the rock, and Farouk moved to obey. Only when the big sailor nodded back down at them did Fengel relax his grip. His wife fought her way free, furious. Fengel only held a bite-mark-covered finger to his lips for silence.

"I would really rather not wake the thing up, if you don't mind," he whispered.

Natasha only glared at him. Farouk slid back down the slope and leaned in close. "It shifted," he said in thick Perinese. "But it hasn't woken up."

Fengel sighed. "How can such a monstrosity move so quickly? How did we not hear it on this side of the island?"

Paine went white. "Here? Is that machine-dragon here?"

"Yes, now sit down and be quiet while I think on this."

Fengel rubbed his beard while he ran through ideas. The monster was obviously quite formidable, but if it hadn't heard Natasha's squalling, then they might slip past it. Fortunately, he had caught a glimpse of one of the *Goliath's* longboats beached past it upon the shore.

The rest of the crew, Natasha included, were watching him somberly, waiting to see what he would come up with. Fengel gave them a smile. "All right. Best bet is still to reach the ship. there's another boat or two along the starboard side that never got used. We can use those for our escape. Might still be a provision or two aboard as well. The Dray Engine is asleep or... something. We can slip past it, I think, then quietly, *quietly* use the longboat on the shore to row out to the *Goliath*."

Natasha slammed a fist down into the sand. "I've had enough of that thing. I want to kill it."

"Well," continued Fengel. "It occurs to me that taking more time to prepare for the open ocean would be very possible, if we could kill the beast. But I don't think it's worth the risk. It'd take cannon fire, at the very least, and there isn't very much powder left aboard the ship."

The Perinese sailors all exchanged looks. "But you said the *Goliath* was all out," replied Sergeant Cumbers. "There was barely enough for half the men to take muskets!"

"So did you!" said Etarin with a pointed look at Natasha.

"Oh," replied Fengel, waving them off. "I lied, of course. There was some left in the magazine that I hid back in the captain's cabin. You people were just never going to attack the *Salmalin* if you could have kept holding up aboard the ship."

The surviving Perinese stared at him, incredulous. Then they all set an uproar.

"You bastard!" said Paine.

"We could have had more musket and pistol shot!" said Cumbers

"But, but," stammered Simon.

"Oh, well done," murmured Natasha, smiling viciously.

Fengel held up a finger. "Ah!" he said. "Quiet now. Sleeping mechanical dragon, remember?"

The crew quieted, though they were clearly still furious. Thin Jahmal said something quietly to his fellows, and they all shook their heads sadly.

"I still want to kill the thing," sulked Natasha.

Fengel patted her hand. "Sorry, love. I'm going to have to say no for the moment. It's just not worth it. Let's get aboard, gather what we can, and prepare the longboats. Come along now."

He stood without waiting for a response, then crept along to the edge of the rock, hiding for the moment in the long, soft shadow cast by the moon as he peered around at the beach. The Dray Engine was still sleeping, right atop the patch of burned and broken sand Natasha had originally obliterated. The tip of its tail twitched, carving furrows.

Fengel closed his eyes and took a breath. *Never let them see you stumble.* Then he took a step out onto the beach past the rock.

A hundred yards away lay the longboat, wedged into the sand where the surf met the shore. Wreckage floated on the waves behind it, the leftover legacy of what had once been the Perinese encampment. Dominating the beach was the slumbering Dray Engine. There wasn't a lot of room left to skirt the machine, and to reach the boat they would have to pass within twenty paces of it.

Fengel crept across the shadowed sand. It gave under his feet, making each step precarious and shorter than it should have been. Fragments of burned wood and the occasional cannonball found themselves beneath his feet, all colored into stark black-and-white by the light of the moon.

He paused to take in the remnants upon the beach and the great metal war machine upon it. *It seems as if all this island has ever known is woe.* The Voornish facility within the volcano certainly hadn't been for baking cakes, and from what he'd heard, that ancient race had predated the rise of mankind.

A hissing noise made him glance back. It was the rest of the survivors, Natasha at the lead. They'd slipped out onto the beach after him, a conga line of would-be sneaks. All stood still in their tracks now, though, wondering why he'd stopped. His wife glared at him, gesturing violently at the longboat in between nervous glances at the Dray Engine.

Fengel smiled and gestured flippantly. Then he made his way back down to the shore. The longboat seen up close was filthy, coated with ash from the volcanic explosion yesterday. Half a foot of water sloshed along the bottom, muddy and dark. But it appeared otherwise sound. Even the oars were properly shipped within.

The rest of the combined crew reached him, huddling up to the boat and glancing back at the Dray Engine. Fengel caught their attention and gestured at the rim of the longboat.

"Everyone grab a spot," he stage-whispered. "We're going to slide her into the water and hop aboard. All right?" He waited for everyone to spread out. "On the count of three, now. One. Two. Thr—"

A clatter and the groan of shifting metal froze them all. Fengel's heart leapt into his throat. Slowly, he glanced back over his shoulder.

The Dray Engine had one eye open. It wasn't watching them directly, but they still stood in the corner of its vision. The thing shifted, raising one foreleg up before slamming it down on a lone Perinese tent that Fengel hadn't seen, standing on the far side of the monster. It ground the canvas into the sand, then the great brazen shutters fell back over its eye-lamps and it stilled again.

Fengel reached a count of fifty, then gestured frantically to the others still frozen beside him. "Go!" he whispered. "Go!"

They slid the longboat into the waves and a little farther beyond. Fengel hopped in with the ease of long practice, followed by Natasha and then all the rest of the surviving crewmen. For all their failings and injuries, both sets of men were professional sailors, and knew their business. They were all aboard and pointed at the *Goliath* with scant trouble, Sergeant Cumbers and big Farouk at the oars and pushing them toward the warship.

Fengel sat in the bow and kept watch on the mechanical titan behind them. Natasha joined him, glaring at it.

"Careful," he said quietly, playfully. "Your face might stick like that."

"It did years ago," she growled. "What I can't understand is how the damned thing seems to know where we want to go every single damned time. I want to kill it. I want *blood*, Fengel."

Fengel rubbed his chin. "I know you do," he replied. "But I don't think it does. Know where we are, I mean."

Natasha raised an eyebrow at him.

"Consider," he continued. "It destroyed your lean-to—"

"Tent."

"Lean-to. Out of all the things on that side of the island, it hunted that down. Then it ran straight for the *Salmalin*. I don't think it's after us specifically. I think it's wiping out anything non-Voornish on the island."

"That doesn't make sense," she replied. "Remember how it stepped on that automaton."

"Well," conceded Fengel. "It also seems enormously ill-tempered."

The longboat made it to the hull of the *Goliath*, which had shifted only a little from how he'd left it last. Under cover of dark, they began their ascent up the rope ladder that had been left in place, Fengel holding it still for Natasha.

A scream cut through the night.

Everyone glanced back at the island. The moon gave clear view of the beach and the jungle behind it. Balls of superheated magma shot up from the volcano at the center of the isle, coloring the view like a great holiday firework. A man had run out of the jungle, wearing the tattered jacket of a low-ranking Perinese officer. It was Sub-Lieutenant Hayes.

"Don't go!" he yelled. "Don't leave me behind!"

Hayes ran down the beach, right for the shore. To Fengel's growing horror, he didn't seem to notice the sleeping Dray Engine, or was just too desperate to care. Hayes ran over the snout of the thing, his boots ringing the maw like a bell before he tripped back down to the sand. He tore off his jacket as he reached the shore and threw it away before diving into the surf.

The Dray Engine shifted.

Oh, by the Goddess's hairy teats. Fengel cursed under his breath and shouted to the others. "Up!" he cried. "Up now, all of you!"

The mixed crew of survivors moved like he'd cracked a whip. Natasha went first, then Cumbers, Paine and then rest. Fengel went last, and didn't bother to keep an eye out for Hayes.

The great red lantern-glass eyes snapped open. They peered about, the Voorn machine lifting its head to look at the figures scurrying over the hull of the *Goliath*. It rumbled—a hollow, echoing noise from somewhere deep within its chassis.

Fengel gave orders as soon as he cleared the deck. "Cumbers, go over to the captain's cabin and take an inventory. I locked it, but the door fits the frame badly. There should be enough powder for the deck guns, at least. Paine! Check out the mess and see if anything's worth saving. Simon, you're on boat-duty." Fengel eyed the Salomcani, who shifted between watching him carefully and eyeing the rising Dray Engine. "Etarin, Farouk, Jahmal, split up and help the others."

They didn't immediately move to obey. Instead they looked to Natasha, who jerked her head and cursed them in their native tongue. Only then did they leap into action.

Fengel walked to the gunwales, watching the island and the Dray Engine. Hayes was barely visible below, a dark speck that coughed and shouted as he swam their way.

"I still want to run," said Fengel. "But I'm very much afraid that we're going to have to fight."

The Dray Engine rose to its feet. It raised its great brazen head and roared in defiance at the sky. As if in response, the island shook, and the volcano vomited a great blast of ash and magma.

Natasha leaned into his arm. "You always say the sweetest things."

Fengel patted her hand, then reached up to adjust his monocle. He very much wished he had a spare, at that moment. Things were about to get ugly.

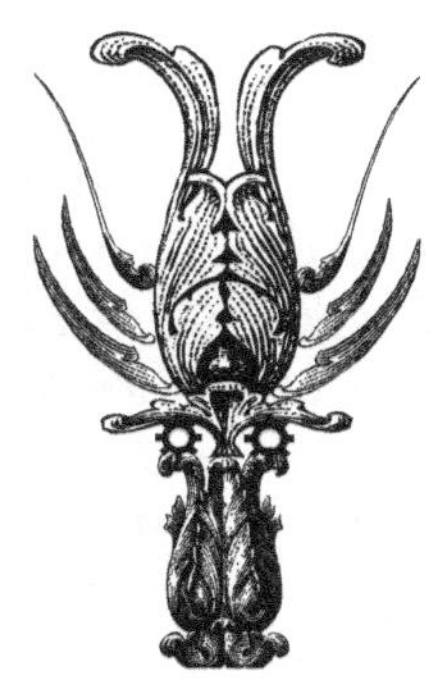

CHAPTER TWENTY-THREE

Lina forced the needle through thick canvas. It poked back out from the surface of the gasbag, a piece of sharp spiral steel as long as her hand. The cord it pulled was thin, but of a heavy gauge that she had yet to snap, no matter how she yanked at it. *I'll say this for the Mechanists: they make good tools.*

That didn't make her any less tired, or the labor of patching the airship any less irksome. She put her feet up against the torn canvas skin of the gas bag and leaned back in the rope harness suspending her alongside it. The ocean breeze played with her hair and chilled her hands, its usual salt scent tinged by coalsmoke from the Perinese Royal Navy at their backs.

She looked down past the gas bag and the hull of the *Dawnhawk* at the navy warships chasing them. Most were mere specks upon the horizon; Henry Smalls had managed to lose them with a goodly bit of distance. One in particular was proving quite tenacious. It was a massive vessel, modern, with both sails and hull-mounted paddlewheels to port and starboard. The *H.M.S. Colossus* had kept pace with them through wind and rain, both night and day. It fired on them regularly, managing glancing blows on their hull and gas bag twice more. In clear weather they'd spotted an imperious figure stalking the poop deck. Lina didn't know how, but she was certain it was the villainous Admiral Wintermourn.

Lina bent back to her task. The light-air cells pushed out against her as she sewed the patch, but it wasn't too much effort to stuff them back inside the gas bag as she worked. Then she finished the final knot, stowed the tools in her harness, and grabbed the rope at her chest. Kicking her way over to the rigging, she waved at Rastalak, up above, where the little Draykin watched over her and the others as they worked.

She descended back to the deck and found the Mechanist. The taciturn old man directed repairs and adjustments to the airship like a conductor overseeing his orchestra. Pirates moved about the deck, the gas bag, and even alongside the hull with a frenetic energy. After several days of constant pursuit by the most powerful navy in the world, there were quite a few things to fix.

"Starboard patch applied," Lina said when he turned her way.

The Brother of the Cog pulled a scarred pocketwatch from a pocket of his greatcoat. He nodded once, sharply. "Exactly within the allotted time period. Very well. I require no further assistance from you at the moment, Miss Stone." He made to move away, then paused. "Miss Stone?"

"Yes, Mechanist?"

"Your work is almost always perfectly satisfactory. Which is more than I can say for most of the drunkards and villains aboard this vessel."

"Thank you, Mechanist. I think."

"In fact, you might have made a fine Mechanist, aspiring even to second or third-class Aspirant, if only you were born male. Though never fourth or fifth."

"Uh. Thank you. Mechanist."

"I mention this, because it would be a shame to see you consistently squander what little potential you do have by making such colossal mistakes as this…committee…of yours."

He walked, away and Lina glared at him as he went. Then she sighed, frustrated, before moving across the deck toward her customary spot alongside the exhaust-pipe.

Lina forgot about the mechanist and chided herself. *Coward.* What she should be doing was visiting the injured below. Ryan Gae still hadn't recovered from the wounds he'd taken in Breachtown. There wasn't a real physician aboard, but both Henry and the aetherites had some skill at anatomy. All said that her friend could go either way, at this point.

Andrea, her only other close friend, had been devastated. The piratess was angry, furious at first, but more and more she had withdrawn, until now she spent almost all her time with Ryan.

Lina couldn't face either of them at the moment. Andrea hadn't said anything, but along with most of the rest of the crew, she had grown cold toward Lina. They all blamed her for their current state of affairs, even Nate Wiley, who was disconsolate after the death of his twin brother. To be fair, she *had* made the original suggestion to mutiny. But even Runt wasn't around much of late. He haunted the top of the gas bag to avoid the smell of the Revenants being kept in the hold down below.

The only ones not actively avoiding her were the old members of the committee, who were even more miserable than she was. Lucian, Reaver Jane, and Sarah Lome were being obeyed by the crew, but only when acting with the approval of Henry Smalls. When it came to any further socializing, they were outcasts.

But what could we have done? Natasha and Fengel had been destroying them. Would the Breachtown raid have gone any better if they hadn't mutinied? Would they have succeeded, despite the odds?

"Gnrrhh."

The low groan shook her from her thoughts. Tricia the Revenant stood a short distance away, up against the corner of the exhaust pipe. She was not doing well in her new, undead state. The gas leak that killed her had left her physically whole enough, though puffy-skinned and stinking. She seemed even less focused than her fellows, bumping repeatedly against the pipe beside Lina, reaching for an skysail whose chains were cut free from the rest of the assembly.

A wide noose attached to a long pole slipped over the undead abomination. Michael Hockton appeared from where he'd been sneaking up along the gunwales.

"Ha!" he cried as he wrangled the Revenant with his catch-pole. "Gotcha." His eyes met Lina's and he blushed abruptly. "Oh. Hello, Lina. Tricia here keeps coming up on the deck, for some reason."

"Hi," she replied. Lina looked down at his boots, and found herself wringing her hands. Cursing quietly, she put them behind her back.

"How are you—"

"How are you—"

Lina coughed and looked away to the Revenant he'd caught. Tricia was groaning in irritation now, but didn't seem to have the fine motor skills necessary to raise the noose over her waist.

"They're not so bad," said Hockton suddenly. "I mean, I don't really want to do this. At all. And that Nate Wiley fellow keeps getting in the way when he visits his brother, but if it keeps the others from throwing me overboard, then I'll do it."

Lina realized that this was as close as she was getting to being forgiven. "You're all right with this, then?" she asked, looking up at him.

Hockton gave her a wry smile. "For now. I'll wrangle corpses if I have to." He looked back at Tricia. "They seem to remember some of the skills they used to have," he continued, "and don't get violent unless you really get in their way. This one can even see that sail there is all busted up. The stink's a shame, though."

"Oh," said Lina. "That's—"

A series of stuttering grunts interrupted them. Lina glanced up to see the white ape hanging from the rigging above by one hairy arm. With the other it pointed at something off the bow.

Lina cupped her hands. "Lookout sees something dead ahead!" she shouted at the deck.

Crewmen dropped what they were doing and ran forward. Lina waved for Hockton to join her and made her way up as well. She pushed through the still-forming crowd until she was up against the gunwales, looking out at the moonlit night.

Almhazlik Isle lay directly ahead. But the once-quiet peak at its center now shot hot ash and flaming magma to rain down on the island below. The jungle shook as if in an earthquake, and Lina thought she could see the tall masts of a sail ship past a small spit of palm-tree-covered land jutting out into the ocean. There was something else too...a large moving figure made of bright metal.

Henry Smalls appeared beside her. He took in the scene, then pulled a spyglass from the folds of his jacket. Extending it, he peered through, and the crew all quieted to hear what he would say.

"Huh," said the steward, after a moment. He lowered the spyglass and stared ahead, looking puzzled.

The crew were still, then they all fought for the glass. Lina was small and quick and got it first, jamming it to her eye and leaning forward to keep it from the others. She stared, and then uttered an exclamation of surprise.

There was indeed a ship moored up near the beach of the isle. It was a warship, in fact, Perinese. And on the beach beside it raged a massive reptilian creature, armored somehow. The thing stood on its hind legs, forearms stretched out to reveal wicked claws. It roared at the moon, and even at this distance, Lina could hear the echo of its thunderclap call.

Someone snagged the spyglass away. One by one the crew took their turns peering through it. When they were done, Lucian retrieved the tool and handed it back to Henry.

"Only Captain Fengel," said Lucian, "when left on a deserted island, could manage to find a Perinese warship, a live volcano, and what appears to be an ancient Voornish war-dragon."

The entire crew muttered assent. Lina had to admit that a small part of her was completely unsurprised.

Cannon fire sounded from somewhere past the stern. The rippling whistle of a cannonball echoed down the deck, and everyone reflexively ducked.

Lucian shook his fist at their unseen pursuer. "Damn him to the Realms Below!" snarled the first mate. "Doesn't that fool know when to give up?"

"There were figures moving on the deck of that ship ahead," said Henry Smalls. "One of them had a monocle, I'm sure of it."

"Then we'll have to swing by and pick them up," said Sarah Lome. "But how do we deal with *that*," she asked, gesturing at the towering armored monster that grew larger with every passing moment.

"We can't fend that off," said Reaver Jane. "It'd take cannon of our own, at least. And we haven't any. Almost no airship does. Only Euron Blackheart himself was ever mad enough to really try and pack on a full broadside."

Henry turned to Konrad and Maxim. "Can either of you do anything to that monster? Even just long enough to distract it?"

Konrad made a gesture that Lina couldn't interpret. "We have not had chance to recover Workings, of late. None of you understand. They must be bartered, but then the preparations for fine control utilize significant—"

"Yes or no would have worked," said Henry in irritation. "I don't need to know—"

The *Colossus* loosed another volley of cannon fire. Grapeshot whipped past in a cloud off the starboard side of the airship. One passed so close that it played with Tricia the Revenant's hair.

An idea came to Lina.

That's it. She grabbed Henry Smalls by one arm, turning the short steward to face her. "Henry," she said, licking her lips nervously. "I've got a plan."

The crew fell dead silent. Every last one of them glared at her. Even undead Tricia at the back of the crowd turned to stare her way. But Henry only looked past her shoulder at the island.

Quickly, before they could throw her overboard, Lina told them what they should do.

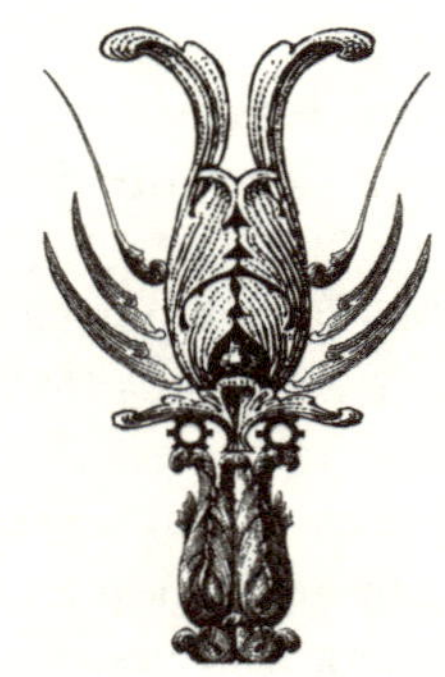

CHAPTER TWENTY-FOUR

Natasha was getting her wish.

The Dray Engine turned to face the *Goliath*. It lowered its head and stalked down from the sandy beach of Almhazlik into the crashing ocean surf. Both arms were spread wide, the claws ready to grasp and tear. Seawater churned as the thing came, crashing into its ankles only to fall back in a scintillating spray.

"Fire!" shouted her husband.

Natasha yanked the lanyard of the cannon guncock. The weapon leapt back with an ear-splitting eruption, belching a half-second blast of fire and fury. It slammed against the chains holding it in place near the bow, even as Sergeant Cumbers and Farouk leaned in to brace it again, looking away.

The cannonball was a silver-black blur in the moonlight. She could barely see it. But it struck the Dray Engine across the side of the head before spinning off to throw up a spray of sand where it landed upon the beach.

The Voornish monster halted its charge. It shook its head as if confused, then lowered itself to the attack again.

Damn. Natasha wanted to snarl. *Only a glancing blow.* She could see that they wouldn't have time to aim another shot, even with other cannons they'd loaded on the deck.

Fengel glanced back over his shoulder at the rest of the makeshift crew on the far starboard side of the vessel. They stood in a longboat stacked with the meager supplies, ready to drop into the water at a moment's notice.

"Launch the boat!" he cried. "We'll swim to you, now launch!" Fengel faced her. "We can try one more, but—"

Too late. The Dray Engine rose up before the *Goliath*. It slammed into the port hull with an impact that cracked wood and tore iron chain. Natasha slipped and fell along with the others, starting to slide backward as the deck tilted up. The row of port-side cannons fell back faster, either broken from their mooring chains or insecurely fastened in the first place. She wrapped her hands around her head, hoping she was clear. Being crushed by loose cannon was a common death, as such things went.

Hard wood slammed into her side. It was the capstan. Natasha wrapped an arm around it and reached out to Fengel as he slid past. Her husband saw in time and grabbed for her hand. Their fingers clasped, and he held on for dear life in the cacophony that thundered around them.

The deck fell abruptly, shifting down again to something like level. Above them, the Dray Engine roared at the sky before turning its gaze back downward. The machine stood chest-high with the deck, both arms resting where they'd crushed the gunwales.

Something flew past over head. It was large and dark and blocked out the moon. The Dray Engine looked up at the shadow, only to be struck by a number of falling metal canisters lit by the firefly glow of burning fuses.

Most fell off into the sea. The rest sundered on the Dray Engine's armor. A familiar stink washed over the deck of the *Goliath* as light-air gas exploded about the head of the ancient Voornish weapon.

It was the *Dawnhawk*.

Natasha only stared a moment, too stunned to react. Rage, pride, and relief all warred within her as she spied the heads and faces of her mutinous crew, peering over the side. Rage mostly won out.

Her husband was more practical, however. As usual.

"Starboard side!" he yelled. "Pick us up in the water! On the starboard side!"

Fengel clambered to his feet and pointed furiously out toward the ocean. The longboat had already dropped, either torn or let free from the ropes used to lower it. Farouk and Cumbers were already fleeing, jumping over the starboard side of the ship.

Natasha scrabbled upward. The *Dawnhawk* flew past, banking for the island, now illuminated by the light of the moon and the burning cinders of Almhazlik's volcano. The once-beautiful airship was a wreck. The stern cabin windows were broken and boarded over. The great canvas gasbag was a mess of crazy patching. Her skysails were shredded and torn, the controlling mechanisms dangling out from their armatures.

What had those treacherous pirates done to her ship?

The Dray Engine spun to follow the airship, unharmed by the bombardment. One paw still grasped the deck of the *Goliath*, and the vessel shook as the machine-beast roared its defiance.

Fengel turned to face her. His face was twisted with worry. "We can't let that thing chase after the *Dawnhawk*. It'll never be able to pick us all up if the Dray Engine is hounding it. I'll stay behind to draw its attention."

"That's stupid," she said to him. "You'll never be able to get away in time."

He looked aggrieved. "It's doubtful. I know you don't care about them, but I think we've done these folk wrong enough. I've got to try and save them if I can."

Natasha didn't say anything to that. She only looked up at him as the Dray Engine raged at her airship, and she rose up to kiss him. He lowered his head to meet her.

Then she sucker punched him in the stomach.

Fengel bent low with a gasp and she grabbed him by the jacket. Natasha ran him at the starboard side of the deck, picking up speed as she went. Her husband stumbled along beside her, fighting to keep his balance and recover his breath. When she reached the broken gunwales where an errant cannon had punched through, she threw him off of it. Fengel made a nice cannonball splash in the water below.

"I don't care about them," she yelled at him as he resurfaced. "But I do care about you. Now get your arse up on that airship, and get them out of here!" She made to turn away, paused, then glanced back over her shoulder. "Oh. And make sure you have good, *long* chat with our mutinous crew."

Then Natasha faced the Dray Engine. The monster still watched the airship, with one paw crushing the deck up near the bow. She drew a pistol that Sergeant Cumbers had found below and went to meet the thing. Fengel would have set a trap, or dreamed up some clever plan to distract the monster. But that wasn't her.

She tried to stalk vengefully up the deck and mostly failed. It was a mess, littered with fallen rope, canvas sail and long spars torn from the masts up above. The cannons lay every which way, most of them still loaded.

An idea came to Natasha. *Wait,* the voice of her father seemed to say. *You can use this.*

She vaulted up to the forecastle deck near the great brazen claws of the beast. One cannon was still shipped in place, but its mount had shattered, leaving it to point askew. Natasha knelt down beside it and glanced along its length. Then she nodded and set the guncock before rising with its lanyard in her off hand, her other raising the pistol at the monster.

"Hey!" Natasha cried. "Hey beast!" Then she fired.

Compared to cannon fire, exploding light-air gas canisters, and the constant noise of the Voornish Dray Engine, her pistol was almost silent. But it did the trick. The ball ricochet away from the monster's neck. The Dray Engine shifted in surprise, peering back down at her and moving just into the cannon's line of fire.

Natasha yanked the guncock lanyard. The blast and the noise deafened her. Yet the ball struck true, slamming into the lower shoulder of the Dray Engine. It held together, not even scratched, really, but the beast rocked back with its eyelid shutters opening wide in surprise. The thing let out a bellow, as if it could feel pain. Behind it, the *Dawnhawk* wheeled around to make a run for the ocean.

Not quite enough. But you felt that. Oh yes, you did. Natasha rose to run. And just as she went to flee, something landed on the shattered rails beside her.

It was the parrot with the butter-yellow beak. The thing appeared bedraggled, covered in dirt and blood and missing some feathers, as if it had escaped in haste from the claws of some burrowing creature. It peered at her with beady eyes, twisting its head back and forth. Then it opened its mouth to unleash a raucous and defiant squawk her way.

The bird paused. It seemed to realize that it wasn't alone, peering up in almost-human surprise at the clanking monster that towered above the deck. Then it threw its stubby wings wide as the brazen paw of the Dray Engine lowered at them both.

Natasha felt a half-second's satisfaction. *Where do you think you're going?* She dropped her pistol and grabbed the bird as she ran. The crunch and impact of the Dray Engine crushing the gun station behind her travelled up the deck, felt and heard as one. She reached another cannon, pointed at the island, still, but near the opposite side of the ship along the bow. Natasha slid down alongside it with the parrot squawking madly in one hand. She triggered the guncock with her free hand and the weapon leapt back, throwing itself into the water. But the blast struck true, hammering the machine in its chest with the sound of a ringing gong.

The Dray Engine howled again. Then it pressed down with both arms against the deck. Polished wood snapped and buckled. Natasha's eyes widened in surprise as she realized that she certainly had the monster's attention now; the thing was trying to climb up onto the warship to come after her.

It reached out and grabbed the foremast in one hand for support. The spar gave easily, cracking and tumbling below. Natasha cursed and climbed to her feet, running for the next gun she could reach. The parrot in her hand was too dazed by fear or by the cannon to utter its usual obnoxious squawk.

Near the forward hatch, she reached another gun. One wheel on the mount was cracked, pointing the nose of the weapon far too low. Natasha grabbed up the lanyard and yanked hard; she didn't care whether it hit at this point, so long as it fired.

The cannon erupted, flinging its shot to skip across the deck and strike the thing in the one ankle it had upraised. Natasha didn't watch to see the reaction. Instead she was moving, looking around for another cannon and saw one amidships, pointed forward. She reached it and managed to hit the monster in the arm.

Again and again she repeated the trick, each time skipping away before the Dray Engine could bring ruin down upon her. The thing was big, but slow upon the confines of the *Goliath*. She reached the last of the loaded deck cannon where it had come to rest against the stern castle and port-side ladder leading up to the poop deck. A thick tangle of rigging had fallen into a pile beside it. Natasha made to leap over it to the cannon and tripped on a hidden pulley in the pile.

The fall knocked the wind out of her. She lay stunned, one hand still clutching the parrot, the other pinned against the rough wooden wheel of the cannon-mount.

The parrot gave out a massive, raucous squawk. It pierced her daze just quickly enough for her to notice the moon-cast shadow of a brazen paw about to fall on her.

Natasha didn't even try to get up. She rolled away from the cannon toward the center of the ship. The claw of the Dray Engine slammed down where she'd been lying, flattening the gun, the ladder and even that portion of the deck itself.

She stared up at the machine. It towered above her, awful and inhuman. *What kind of people could make such a thing?*

A quick glance told her that the *Dawnhawk* was past the *Goliath,* descending down to the ocean. Her mutinous crew would rescue Fengel. It was enough.

A thunderous eruption sounded somewhere past the ship. Natasha caught a glimpse of many bright tongues of flame somewhere off the starboard bow, and then the air was filled with the whistling echo of falling cannon balls. They tore sails, rigging, and masts. They hammered the Dray Engine with the sound of a blacksmith beating upon an anvil. Splinters rained down upon Natasha. By some great fortune she managed to avoid all of the iron shot. The creature roared in defiance. It shifted its massive bulk away from the *Goliath,* and Natasha glanced up for a better look.

Down past the bow and the southwestern curve of the island came a warship. In the light of the moon it was huge, even bigger than the *Goliath,* with a fuller complement of guns, all aimed straight at the Dray Engine.

She was Perinese, that much Natasha could tell at a glance. *Does she think she's coming to assist?*

It didn't matter. Natasha glanced again out the starboard side, over the ocean. The *Dawnhawk* now floated over the longboat. Three figures swam for the rope ladders dangled from the airship.

In her hands the parrot gave a half-stunned, miserable squawk. Natasha glanced down at the thing, which huddled, looking ludicrous. She laughed and climbed to her feet. "Oh no," she said. "I'm not done with you yet, bird."

Natasha ran for the port-side railing as the other Perinese warship unleashed another broadside. At its edge she leapt, landing in the waters with a cannonball splash. She rose, sputtering for air, the parrot flapping feebly.

The Dray Engine roared again as cannon fire fell upon it. It shook away the blows of those that had hit and charged down the coastline at the new vessel.

Her father would have applauded her escape.

Natasha shrugged, then swam with one arm toward the waiting *Dawnhawk.*

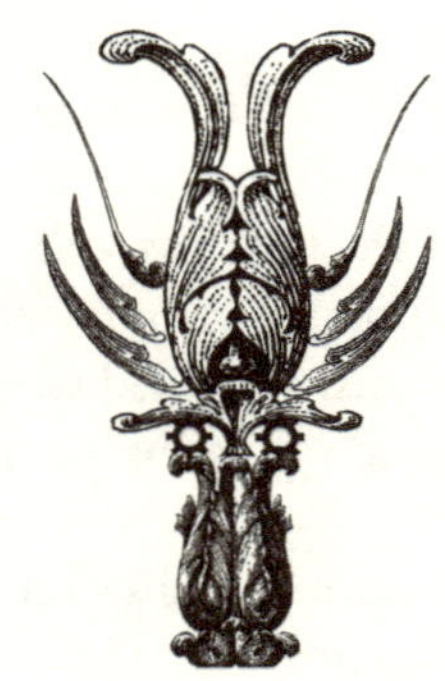

CHAPTER TWENTY-FIVE

FENGEL EYED HIS MONOCLE.

It was weird. The glass was still perfectly see-through, but the exterior lens was reflective now, and the brass rim had stretched and flattened, almost taking the shape of an eyepatch. He had to admit that it appeared ludicrous, but with his other one broken and lost, it was the only eyepiece he had left. With a sigh, he fit it into place. Then he adjusted his battered hat and left the captain's cabin.

The stairwell beyond was cool and dark. It stank, which was usual, being placed so close to the crew on the quarterdeck. But the air was tinged with the sickly, cloying scent of blood, illness and strong alcohol. Many people had died aboard recently, as he understood it.

He knew he should see to those injured. But later, later. Instead he climbed the stairway past a fat orange tomcat to the hatch above, emerging onto the deck of the *Dawnhawk*.

His airship flew over the sea beneath a midafternoon sun on a warm, clear day. Their skysails were extended, stretched taut to catch the stream of immaterial aether pushing them north by northwest, headed toward home. All about the deck moved the crew, quite busy. There was much work to be done, after this most recent misadventure.

"Your tea, sir."

Henry Smalls appeared at his elbow with a silver tea service in both hands. Fengel nodded and took up his cup. He sipped, savoring the taste of it. After being abandoned on a somewhat-deserted isle for a week, this little civility almost brought a tear to his eye.

But no. He couldn't be that soft. Not yet.

"Not quite enough sugar, Mr. Smalls."

The steward looked away. "Sorry, sir," he apologized. "Won't happen again, sir."

Fengel gave a grunt. "See that it doesn't, Mr. Smalls."

He finished the tea and gave the cup back to Henry, who disappeared belowdecks. Fengel strolled over to the helm, where two people were arguing in thickly accented Perinese, and a third was trying very hard to not exist.

"Havelthrum's Quotient makes perfect sense," said Maxim in a lofty voice. Fengel noted that the aetherite's usual slovenly appearance was somewhat cleaner at the moment. "Aether naturally sinks, congeals, even, so theoretically it could be found to be so dense that it should be minable—"

"Utter hogwash," rasped Konrad. The big aetherite had apparently decided to wax his mustache. "If that were true, miners would have found such stuff centuries ago."

"Hogwash? Your linens may be hog—"

"I'll wring your neck with my linens, you rail-boned—"

"I do not *care!*" exclaimed the woman between them, her face held in her hands. Both aetherites appeared not to notice her distress.

Fengel eyed Omari. The woman was a Yulan native, which was rare enough. But she was well-spoken, and unlike everyone else aboard the ship, was mostly innocent in the recent affairs. He'd been appraised of her strange ability after coming aboard last night, though he wasn't quite sure what to think of it yet. Or ready to deal with the results.

"Good afternoon," he said to the three.

Maxim and Konrad both shut up. They looked away, refusing to meet his eyes. Omari peered at him appraisingly.

"Good afternoon, sir," coughed Maxim.

"Ah. Yes," said Konrad. "Good afternoon."

"The helm is responding all right?" asked Fengel.

"Yes," they both said at once.

Fengel nodded. "Omari, is it? Walk with me a moment."

Both aetherites looked suddenly crestfallen. The young woman moved to join him, gratefully. They walked up the deck a way in silence, before she faced him.

"So," she said. "You are the captain of this ship of fools?"

"Nominally," replied Fengel.

"Well, I want off. I don't care where, so long as they speak Perinese."

"We are returning to our home port in the Copper Isles," he replied. "It's where we'll drop off Cumbers and Etarin and the others recovering below. Not exactly perfect, but the best we can do, I'm afraid. Will that suffice?"

The woman grimaced. "Homeless in yet another strange city. Such appears to be my lot in life." She looked back up at him. "That will suit then, Captain. It will have to."

She made to leave, and Fengel gave a cough. "Ah, Omari?"

She looked back his way. "Yes?"

"I would appreciate it if you could refrain from utilizing your aetherite magics until we reach port." He gestured up the deck toward a group of armless, neckless, and skinless Revenants.

Omari frowned fiercely. She stomped her foot. "But it's not my *fault!*" she said.

Fengel only shrugged. He walked up the deck to where the main hatch had been opened. Lucian and Sarah Lome were there, supervising Rastalak and a sulking Reaver Jane as they performed some work down in the hold.

"What's this, then?" he asked.

Lucian whirled in surprise. He smiled a brittle smile, opened his mouth, closed it, and opened it again. Sarah Lome gave the sharpest military salute Fengel had ever seen, which amused him, as he knew that the huge piratess had never been in the navy before.

"Sir!" cried Lucian. "Just taking inventory. Mechanist asked us to check on the light-air reserves. And let me just say sir, we're all so glad to have you back."

Fengel nodded absent-mindedly. Then he peered down into the hold. "Good, good. I think this is a two-person job, though, don't you? Go on down and tend to it yourselves, if you please. The other two are relieved." He paused as he went to leave. "Gunney Lome?"

"Yes, sir?"

"What's that on your face?"

"Ink, sir."

"You got a tattoo?"

"No, sir."

"Ah. Sums, then. Oh well, carry on."

Fengel continued to walk up the deck, smiling as he went. Before long he reached the clutch of Revenants, all tied together in a crowd up against the deck. They were repulsive, and Fengel found that he couldn't hide his dismay at their presence aboard the *Dawnhawk*. *How in the Realms Below did anyone let this come to pass?*

Their herder, for lack of a better term, stood nearby. Michael Hockton was of average height and build, but appeared quick-witted and agile. He leaned back against the gunwales with a catch-pole, idly watching over the walking dead that were in his care. A clothespin was pinched over the bridge of his nose. On occasion, one of the corpses would try to lift the rope that restrained it, and he would carefully bat the arm aside.

"And you look ridiculous!"

Fengel glanced over to see Allen, the younger Mechanist, hanging off the side of the ship from a rope and harness. He appeared to be working on the skysails there, but from what Fengel could tell, seemed to have most of his attention focused on Hockton.

"Well," replied Hockton nasally. "It's the only coat I've got. So I'll suppose I'll have to wear it. At least until I can get a proper pirate's jacket."

"But it makes you stink of Revenant!" cried Allen.

"No," said Hockton. "That's the Revenants. If you want to take over for me, I'll be glad to give those thingamabobs you're working on a try."

Fengel stepped a little closer. "I believe you've been assigned a task, Mr. Hockton. You would do well to stick to it."

Allen looked up in surprise, then dropped out of view. Hockton went to salute him, then stopped, uncertain what to do.

Fengel peered at the young man carefully. Hockton was a *very* familiar name. For someone that he had downright hated, upon a time. *He's got the right build, but the face is wrong. Hmm.* "So," he said. "I understand that you're a recent addition to the crew?"

"Sir, yes, sir," he said. "I've no love for the service any longer, if that's what worries you, sir."

"You needn't salute," said Fengel. "We're all brothers here, more or less." He made to walk away, and paused. "Tell me. Do you happen to know an Elijah Hockton, at all?"

Michael Hockton looked embarrassed. "Ah. Can't say that I do, sir."

Fengel nodded. "Very well. Carry on."

A short distance away he found Lina Stone. The waif was swabbing the deck angrily, her horrible pet scryn draped around her shoulders. By unanimous assent, it had been decided that she wasn't to speak any further for a period of one week. Naturally, a gag had gone with the plan.

"Hello, Miss Stone! And how are you this fine day?"

Lina dropped her mop. She glanced up, tried to smile, and failed due to the gag.

"Never mind, never mind," said Fengel with mock cheerfulness. "You've quite a number of tasks to see to. *Much* work to be done. I'll have to bring it up to Gunney Lome if I can think of any others of course, naturally."

Lina winced again, then she picked up her mop. "Yeff, fur."

"Good, good." He let a note of seriousness creep into his voice. "So, Miss Stone. Have you had enough yet?"

Lina pondered a moment. "Woulgn't trave if for zhe vurld, fur."

Fengel nodded, and walked away.

He found Natasha up at the bow. She stood facing the deck, and gave him a crooked smile as he approached.

"This monocle makes me look ridiculous," he said.

"Aye. So throw it away."

"But it's the only one I've got."

His wife shrugged.

Fengel rested his arms on the bow rails and looked past her out over the ocean. "So how are you handling it?" she asked him after a moment.

"Mostly by pretending it didn't happen. They seem regretful enough. But...I think I'll let them stew a little while longer. You?"

A raucous squawk exploded behind them. Fengel winced, then turned in time to see the gaudy parrot perched on the edge of the hold. Rastalak and Reaver Jane had just climbed up from the hatch, and he watched as both almost slipped and fell back into the hold out of surprise, only just catching themselves by the lip of the opening.

"Most of them act like I'm going to explode and gut someone at any moment," she said. "But I've thought a lot about what you said." She leaned into his arm. "I'm not as kind as you. Don't have the temperament for it. So I'm still going to take my revenge. I demoted Reaver Jane...but by and large I've decided to try something else."

They watched as the parrot sidled over and started pecking maliciously at Reaver Jane's fingers.

"I thought you were going to cook and eat that thing," said Fengel.

"Remembered I can't cook," she replied. "And it's making itself...useful, for now. You see, I'm going to try *subtlety* for my revenge."

Fengel smiled. He rolled around to put the rail at his back and lifted an arm over her shoulders. Natasha leaned in close.

"I love you," she said.

"I love you, too," he replied.

"Conditionally?"

"Of course. There're always conditions."

"That there are. Real partners this time?"

"I'm willing, if you are," he said.

They watched the penitent crew slowly repair their airship. Eventually Fengel shifted and they looked out upon the horizon, wondering what they'd find beyond.

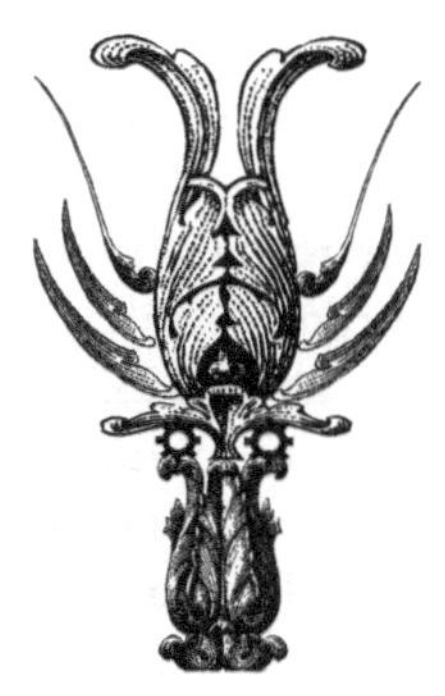

EPILOGUE

Admiral Wintermourn examined the chart on his desk. It showed a crude depiction of the Atalian Sea, the few landmasses upon it drawn to wildly inaccurate scale. Still, it filled in a blank on the more professional charts he referenced to one side, and that alone made it valuable.

Out on the deck, he could hear the sounds of the crew going about their business. A warship was a machine, and this one was still ticking along, though not as perfectly as he would have liked.

The *Colossus* had taken quite a bit of damage two days ago. That Voornish machine-dragon had proven ridiculously resilient, and it was only once they'd steamed back to deeper waters that they'd been able to dislodge the thing. Even then, it had wrecked their starboard paddlewheel, staved in the port side deck, destroyed a mast, and killed over forty people. Even with support fire from the *Behemoth* and the *Titan*, they hadn't even managed to scratch its armored skin.

But so it went. He'd seen the missing *Goliath* under attack, and had acted. While any surviving crew on the island deserved a flogging for being caught up in such a ridiculous affair, they were still Perinese, and an attack upon one of His Majesty's warships was a slight upon the Kingdom itself, even when committed by the ancient derelict of a highly advanced pre-human race.

Wintermourn shook his head. *I was greedy.* He'd hoped—in vain, as it turned out—to kill two birds with one stone. If the Voornish weapon had been hurriedly enough dispatched, then the *Goliath's* guns would have had the perfect shot on the *Dawnhawk* foundering nearby.

I'll have to have a chat with the fleet about that. Of all the ships ordered to give chase after the sky pirates, only his flagship had been able to consistently catch up. He'd almost thought to have downed it once or twice as well, though that hadn't been the purpose, entirely.

Range, height, speed. It was all valuable information, the kind that the Kingdom lacked when dealing directly with any of the damnable sky pirates. The standing bounty for capture had gone unclaimed for *decades*. But now he had another piece to solving that puzzle, and the clever gents back at port would get right to work when he returned. With the Salomcani War in its final stages, and the pacification of Breachtown Colony complete, there came the opportunity for new targets to be eliminated.

A knock sounded on his door. "Come," he said.

The portal swung wide to reveal a rat-faced man in an ill-fitting seaman's uniform. He came inside and struck a sloppy salute.

"You wanted to see me sir?" said Oscar Pleasant.

"Yes," replied Wintermourn. "And you will smarten up that salute, or I will have you flogged. The only reason I didn't have you hanged when we found you was that you are quite valuable. In your own way."

The ex-pirate paled. "But I still am, right, sir? Valuable? I get a pardon and a berth in the navy?"

"Of course. Now, this map you've drawn is atrocious. But it does appear to have some legitimacy. You are certain that it shows the inner passages of the Copper Isles?"

"Yes, sir. I'd stake my life on it."

Admiral Wintermourn raised his eyes and held the gaze of the other man. "I do believe you are doing so, at that." He looked back down, retrieved a pencil, and began scratching notations on the map. "That will be all. Oh, and if you would, go down and have the quartermaster bring up Able Seaman Hayes from the bilge. His back should have recovered from the lash by now, and I intend to debrief him."

Oscar Pleasant left as quietly as he could. The Admiral put him out of mind and focused on the map. It was part of a plan that hinged upon a great many things indeed. But pursuit of that plan was his duty, for King and Kingdom. And Admiral Horatio Wintermourn had never failed in his duty yet. He swore before the Goddess Herself that he never would.

END BOOK TWO

ACKNOWLEDGEMENTS

I've heard it said that writing is a lonely task. In some ways that's true. In others it is decidedly not. There are people who stand behind and beside me, goading me on and pushing me forward. Thanks go always to my wife, Shawna. I'd like to give a shout out to my first readers Erik Hansen, Willy Traub, Rori Bumgarner, Rachelle Helmkamp, and Tyler Netzel, whose input helped make this novel readable. Jennifer Lerud and the rest of the Screaming Sandcrabs at farlandswritersgroups.com also deserve special mention for their exceptional critiques; you're a great writing group, guys. Thanks must go again to Susan Defreitas of Indigo Editing for her hard work, along with Ksenia Mamaeva for an exceptional job with the art. Vladimir Verano did excellent work turning that art into a novel cover. And Susan Morman deserves special mention for helping with the character of Omari.

Last (and again, not least!) thanks go out to all my Kickstarter backers spread around the globe. You guys are the best, and I couldn't have done this without you. I hope you enjoy the novel, and that it is what you were hoping to support.

ABOUT THE AUTHOR

I haunt the Pacific Northwest.

Find out more at WWW.JONATHONBURGESS.COM.

www.ingramcontent.com/pod-product-compliance
Lightning Source LLC
Chambersburg PA
CBHW021001120726
47905CB00009B/2803